D1736051

BOOKS BY DORIEN KELLY

The Ballymuir Series:
The Last Bride in Ballymuir
The Boldest Man in Ballymuir
The Brightest Flame in Ballymuir
The Wedding Party (a Ballymuir novella)

The Sandy Bend Series:
The Girl Least Likely To...
The Girl Most Likely To...
Tempting Trouble

Romantic Comedy:
Designs on Jake
Do-Over
In Like Flynn

Women's Fiction:
Off the Map
All Good Things...

With Janet Evanovich:
Love in a Nutshell
The Husband List

With The Indie Voice:
Summer on Seeker's Island
The Naked Truth About Self-Publishing (non-fiction)

THE
BRIGHTEST FLAME
IN BALLYMUIR

By Dorien Kelly

Copyright 2012 Dorien Kelly

This book is a work of fiction. Names, places, characters, or incidents are products of the author's imagination or used fictitiously. Any resemblance to actual events or locales or persons, living or dead, is entirely coincidental.

Publishing History:
Published in paperback as Hot Whispers of an Irishman by Pocket Books, 2005
Revised, preferred edition e-book published in 2012
Print edition published in 2013

ISBN-13: 978-1490533322

CHAPTER ONE

May you retain your eyes, and your inheritance from your grandmother.
—IRISH PROVERB

Vi Kilbride considered herself a skilled collector of many things: stones and seashells, homely dogs and fine looking men. It seemed, though, that she had nothing on her grandmother. Except potentially in the man department, as Nan had been dead these past ten years, which could prove a handicap, indeed.

Vi looked about Nan's tumbledown cottage, shaking her head at the sheer volume of Nan-things left stacked in great piles. She didn't recall seeing so much a decade ago, when she'd last journeyed to this western edge of County Kilkenny.

"Well, then, time for a bit of wishcraft," Vi said, though there was no one inside but Roger, her stumpy and well-loved terrier, to hear her. At least, no one living.

She settled her palm atop a box on which she recognized Nan's plain writing. It was madness, what Vi was about to do. But she rather enjoyed madness.

"Come on, Nan, send it back," Vi said. Then she closed her eyes and tried to will into being the second sight that Nan had urged her to treasure and hone. The second sight that had always been a frustratingly imperfect gift and lately had gone bat-bloody-blind. After months of hoping and reading and meditation, she was down to this—using this clean-up-and-sell visit to see if her sight had flitted back home to where Nan once was.

All Vi knew was that deep inside, a jagged, ash gray landscape had settled where once ancient voices had whispered and lush secrets had flowered and let her create her art and dream her dreams. This awful silence was slowly diminishing her, and she was growing terrified of disappearing altogether. Nan would tell her that there was a purpose to the silence, a lesson to be learned. But Vi was so very tired and often sad, and had no desire left to learn.

Tightening her muscles, she concentrated until she literally ached. If she were a goose, she'd have laid a twenty-four-karat-filled nest by now.

Please, she thought. *I've already had damn well enough taken from me, haven't I?*

Suddenly her skin tingled and toes curled as a wave of anticipation rolled from the soles of her feet to the top of her soul.

Yes! Come to me...

And coming it was, on a nearly palpable wave of excitement. An instant later, Vi's eyes flew open at a rattling of boxes and the scrabbling of claws on the cottage floor. Roger burst into the front room, something clenched between his teeth. And that something possessed a twitching and suspiciously rodent-like tail.

She'd lost her vision to a miserable mouse! Or worse, perhaps it had been Roger's excitement that she'd been sensing all along.... She narrowed her gaze at Rog's captive. At moments such as this, it was taxing to be a vegetarian.

"Drop!" Vi shouted.

Roger froze.

"Now!"

She watched as a fierce battle between instinct and the demands of civility took place behind her hound's chocolaty brown eyes. If the mouse's life weren't in the balance, she'd empathize, for she felt the same pull herself, daily.

"Don't make me take that from you," she threatened.

Roger curled back his lips, opened his lower jaw, and dropped one stunned and wet mouse to the floor.

"Fine job of hunting, *a ghra,*" she said to Rog as she wrapped her fingers round his collar. "Now, sit."

Half surprised that he continued to obey, she quickly reached toward the mouse, whose sides rose and fell in panicked breaths.

"I ask for a vision and I get you, eh?" she said to it. Nan must be having a fine laugh up among the stars.

Before Vi could get a grip on the creature, it tucked its feet beneath itself and began to stagger away. Roger jumped to attention and wriggled from her grasp.

"Stay!" she commanded both dog and mouse.

Neither listened.

As dog shot for mouse and mouse sought shelter, Vi opened the cottage door, then scooped a yellowed newspaper from a teetering stack and began waving it along the floorboards.

"Out with you!"

Three circuits of the front room later, dog, mouse, and woman were outside in the dour late autumn rain. Once the mouse made it to the underbrush clogging Nan's garden, Rog gave up the chase and retreated inside. Vi stood in the rain a moment more, frowning at her da, who still sat in her car, reading a much less mildewed paper than the one Vi clutched.

Wise man for declining to come inside, but his holiday was over. If she couldn't have her damned sight back this morning, at the very least she could begin to make sense of Nan's cottage. No one would buy it as it was.

She waved him in, and the car door opened with the same slow unwillingness as had Roger's jaws.

"Tell you what," she said to Da once they were out of the wet. "Help me in here, and then this afternoon we'll pop over to the pub for a pint."

"I'd rather be in this," he said, gesturing about, "than in the middle of a pack of Raffertys."

Vi could understand. The village of Duncarraig was hardly a vast place, but what it lacked in size, it made up for in sheer numbers of Raffertys. In the years since she'd last been here, it seemed that the family had taken over with a particularly Irish glee.

While driving through town she'd seen the pub, plus a dry cleaner's and a market all emblazoned with the Rafferty name. She sorrowed for their originality as well as the size of the familial ego, naming all things the same. Of course, it had been some years since she'd thought anything but pig's-trotters-low of the Rafferty clan.

"We could hire out the cleaning," Da said, looking as overwhelmed by the chaos as Vi felt.

Tempting, but she had never been well-stocked in money and soon would have even less. "I'd rather pay myself. Can you imagine what those Raffertys might extort?"

"True enough," muttered her da.

"This can't all have been Nan's," Vi said.

Her da shifted uncomfortably, fussing with the cuffs of his crisp, white, and bloody impractical shirt.

"Well," he said, "I did tell a friend that it would be fine if he kept a wee thing or two here. He must have forgotten it when he moved to Dublin to live with his daughter."

Forgotten, indeed. This was dumping, pure and simple.

"A generous offer, Da." Vi rued the day she'd turned oversight of the property back to her father, who lived only thirty miles off in Kilkenny City, instead of her hours-long drive away, in the County Kerry village of Ballymuir.

Da looked at his shoes, then back to Vi. "I'm sorry it's come to this. It's not right, you selling the land my mother left you, and I've only myself to blame."

"Da, don't be so hard—"

"No," he said with a vehement shake of his head. "I've let it all come to rest on your doorstep for far too long. I looked the other way when you took in your brother Michael with him straight out of prison, thinking he needed your love and your shoe to his behind, too. When Danny and Pat left home and moved in with you, I told myself it was a fine thing, all four of my children under the same roof. But what I was really thinking was how easy you'd made it for me. All my troubles had come down to one. Your mam's not so very simple to live with."

Vi laughed. "And you've a fine way with understatement, but don't be mistaking me for a saint. I've had the best of the bargain." She arched a brow at him before adding, "But if you send me Mam, I'll ship her back."

Da managed a wan smile, and then even that faded. "Ah, but you and Nan, what you had was special. It's wrong that you're losing this." He gave one helpless look around and amended, "Well, not *this,* exactly."

"It's time I let go. I don't need the land or the house to have Nan. She lives here," Vi said, settling a hand over her heart. It was a fib, but not one in which her father could catch her.

"I should have been better prepared," he said. "I should have saved more. Bastards, pushing me out before my time."

She knew it stung Da's pride to have been declared redundant at the insurance company where he'd worked so many years. Here it was six months later and still Michael Kilbride Senior dressed daily in a suit and tie for a job no longer his.

And so, as Da had said, it had come down to her again. Money was needed for Danny's years at university, and given the bad spot he'd had at sixteen, he was no scholarship candidate. Da was unemployed. Michael had moved out and his fine carpentry business was growing, but he and his wife Kylie had a child on the way. For a while at least Kylie would not be teaching and money would be tight.

Vi was the Kilbride family's last, best hope. And she would do anything for them, even clean this bloody mess.

"It will all come right," she said, though her own faith had worn thin.

With her father trailing behind, she walked from the front room to the kitchen. This space was little better than the front, except the items clogging it were things Vi knew—a mad jumble of furniture that ten years ago she'd had no house to hold.

Vi turned a tap at the kitchen sink and received a grudging dribble of rust-colored water in return.

"Bleak," she said. The thrill of the mouse-chase had faded, and her weariness of soul had seeped back in.

"True enough," Da said from behind her.

Vi closed the tap. "The supplies I brought will do us little good. Tomorrow, I'll talk to someone about getting a rubbish tip brought to the house."

Her father eyed her glumly. "Then with nothing to be done here, it's back home for us?"

At her sound of agreement, Da sighed. "The pub's sounding none too bad, just now."

"Too early," Vi pointed out, and though she was equally unready to see Mam, she whistled for Rog.

"Home," she said when he arrived to nudge her shin with his nose.

"Home," her da echoed.

At least Roger danced at the word, but he was likely thinking doggie thoughts of Ballymuir, not the land of torture-by-Maeve. *Two weeks,* Vi told herself, *I can survive two weeks of nearly anything.*

If it was possible to die from a surfeit of family, Liam Rafferty was well on the way. From his early afternoon vantage point at the back of Rafferty's Pub, it would appear that the nonpaying Rafferty clientele was outnumbering the guests. This was no way to run a business. Neither was it any way for him to get work done, but if he went back to the house he kept here in town, they'd just troop to his doorstep.

He'd left Duncarraig for America fifteen years before, and though he always dropped in for a stay when his tight business schedule would permit, never had he lasted three bloody weeks. Make that three bloody weeks with no end to the visit in sight, he reminded himself while contemplating the photocopies of historical documents in front of him.

"You've heard who's here, have you not?"

Liam looked up from his paperwork and gave his brother Cullen a terse "no."

"It's a shocker, all right," Cullen added.

Liam ignored him.

Cullen lingered in that silent yet somehow plaintive way that younger siblings perfect early on. Liam held fast to his determination to ignore him as long as he could. Cullen was the worst gossipmonger among Liam's six brothers and sisters, which was a lofty status to achieve, what with all the competition. There was no good to be gained from encouraging him. And very little accurate information, either.

"You don't want to know? That's near unnatural," Cullen said after a few moments.

"For you, maybe." Liam closed the folder. "If I let you tell me, will you leave me to my work?"

Cullen looked ready to burst with glee. "Violet Kilbride and her da are staying out to the old Kilbride house."

Buffeted by an adrenaline-charged rush, Liam lost all words. Then reason set in. Right. Vi would be living there when cows let whiskey instead of milk. He'd been walking the Kilbride land these past three weeks and could guarantee there wasn't a mongrel in town desperate enough to live in Nan's uninhabitable house, let alone two humans.

"Tell me another one," he said in bored reply. No point in letting his brother know that he'd struck a very raw nerve.

"But it's true," Cullen insisted. "Brenda Teevey saw her getting out of a car with all sorts of bags and cases. She said that Vi's the same as she was years ago. Of course Brenda thinks she is too, though her arse is grown so big, it's taken additional land in County Tipperary."

Using his water glass, Liam raised a toast to his brother. "There's a reason you're not married."

His brother laughed. "And this coming from you, the first Rafferty ever to be..." He gave a dramatic look around the room and finished with a stage whispered, *"divorced."*

"Better I just rob a petrol station like Cousin Manus."

"Hell, yes. When Manus comes back, he'll be forgiven. You, my brother, will be forever married in Mam's eyes. 'Unless I hear it from His Holiness himself, Beth is Liam's wife,'" Cullen finished in an uncanny imitation of their mother.

Beth, however, had seen fit to make Liam's marital status otherwise. As an American—and a holidays-only Catholic—she was a wee bit less worried about the pope's opinion of divorce. In any case, Liam didn't blame her. He'd be the first to say that he'd been a balls-out awful example of a husband. His work in marine salvage pulled him from the North Sea to Tahiti, with few stops home.

Had it been just Beth, who was busy enough as a mechanical engineer, he suspected that she would have put up with his absences. But they had their daughter Meghan to consider. Beth had felt that Meghan didn't need to readjust her life every time her father showed up. She needed constancy, and that was something Liam was incapable of providing.

The irony of it was that he'd just gotten Meghan full time for the next six months, as Beth had taken an assignment in a volatile part of the Middle East. He knew she'd had little choice. It had been take the job or become unemployed. Still, the aggravated part of his soul could only grumble, *"So bloody much for constancy."*

Cullen nudged the edge of Liam's table, which like everything in Rafferty's pub wasn't quite level. Liam watched as the water in his glass sloshed from side to side.

"So are you not the least bit curious to see if it's Violet?" Cullen asked.

"No," Liam said, thinking that if she were here and heard her hated full name of Violet being bandied about, blood would be spilled. God knew he had his share of scars from that sin.

Cullen's cat-shaped brown eyes—a consistent Rafferty trait— grew wider. "I don't feckin' believe it. It's been—what—thirteen years and still you're battling her memory, aren't you?" He snorted. "Here I am, five years younger than you and I'm the mature one."

"It's been fifteen years and you'd best leave alone what you don't understand." Hell, Liam didn't fully understand it. He tapped the research file in front of him. "Now, if you don't mind ..."

"But—"

"And even if you do. Go to the market and share your gossip with Nora," he said, referring to their sister closest in age to Vi. "She'll make a better audience."

"I can remember when you used to be fun," Cullen said before wandering back to his mates by the front door.

"Fun," Liam muttered. Christ, at this point he'd settle for being passably civil. His business was in one bollocks of a mess, thanks to Alex, his partner. Alex had begun thieving cargoes under the company flag. And in crossing this line from salvor to pirate, he had dragged Liam with him. As business dwindled, Liam was slowly drowning in debt. Knowing that he had only his own ego and ambition to blame for not catching on to Alex sooner did nothing to help his attitude.

And then there was Meghan. Liam was coming to the conclusion that he made a fine absentee da, showering Meghan with trinkets from his travels around the world when he did show up. As an everyday enforcer, he was useless. Who'd have thought that females became so vicious and moody when not even yet thirteen? Had he missed the easy years? Liam could nearly understand why work in a near war zone seemed an acceptable option to Beth. Twelve-year-old girls were walking strife and conflict.

So here he was, home with Mam, seeking any bit of help she'd give. After all, she'd thus far managed to raise six children to productive adulthood. And even Annie, the last of the brood, who at sixteen was nearly twenty years younger than Liam, seemed to be a normal, presentable teen, once you got past the neon lipstick and fat slashes of eyeliner.

Liam took a swallow of his water and watched as the next Rafferty approached to sling some grief his way

"So your old sweetheart's in town," said Jamie, Liam's second-youngest brother, and owner of this pub along with Mam and Da.

Liam hooked a thumb in the direction of the bar. "Don't you need to go pull a pint?"

"I remember Vi Kilbride," Jamie said with a broad smile.

"Not much, you don't. You were eleven the last summer she was here."

"Ah, but I do. I followed her just the way Mam said she used to follow you. God, but she was the sun in my summertimes."

Liam snorted. "Publican and half-assed poet. Not a one of us has seen Vi Kilbride in a decade, nor will we."

"Dabbling in denial?" Jamie asked.

"Feck it." Liam stood, the legs of his chair squealing in protest against the wooden floor. He bundled his papers back into their folder. "I'm going for a drive."

Jamie shook his head. "It'll have to be a walk. I gave Catherine the spare keys to your car this morning. Her Maura had a doctor's appointment in Kilkenny and Tadgh had their car."

"Grand of you to mention it to me."

Jamie shrugged. "I just did."

Liam pushed on.

"Where are you going?" his mam asked, looking up from the table she'd commandeered to sort some of the fancy yarn—llama and god-knows-what—that his sister Catherine spun and sold.

"Change of scenery," he said.

"Fine then, but be back before Meghan's home from school. I've plans for tonight and won't be watching her."

"Mind the rain," called his da from behind the bar. Liam didn't pause to think how bad it must be if a sixty-six-year-old Kilkennyman was issuing the warning.

Once out the pub's heavy green door, it hit him—a downpour like he'd last experienced in the tropics, yet with none of the warmth. He muttered an obscenity, but didn't retreat. At the very least, he'd walk home. Behind him, the door opened. Liam turned back, and Cullen flung a bundle his way. He unwadded it and saw that it was a waxed jacket, perhaps some protection against the wet, but not one hell of a lot.

Liam wrenched on the jacket, then rolled the documents he'd been reading into a cylinder and tucked them in the jacket's inside pocket. By the time he'd walked the four blocks to his house, the rain had seen fit to let up. And thank God it had. For a man who'd spent probably a quarter of his adult life underwater for one reason or another, he hated the stuff when it fell from the sky. A sad state of affairs for an Irishman.

Feeling energized by the lack of rain, Liam decided to walk on. He'd already missed his morning run. Breakfast had been extended by a row with Meghan over why twelve-year-old girls—or even the older girls—did not wear black fishnet stockings to the parish school. He was sure the boys would be sorry to hear that he'd banned the stockings, but she was his daughter and no matter how old she looked for her age, she remained a child. As this morning's tantrum and tears had proved.

As he walked, he thought of another girl from summers long ago... one who had been overtall and gangly, could run and fight and hungered to be one of the boys. He'd been a vastly superior three years her elder and had scarcely tolerated her tagging behind him and his cousins.

But then Vi had turned sixteen, and then seventeen. There had been no ignoring her as a female.

"Leave it," Liam muttered to himself, then swiped his hand through his hair, sluicing off what was left of the rain. But he couldn't lose thoughts of Vi Kilbride with such ease.

Of course he'd always thought of her, but never so much as when he was on Irish soil. The wet green of the countryside, the sight of hedgerows and the smell of newly mown fields, all of it made her seem closer. She lingered with him, taunting him, making him hard late at night, leaving him empty with regret.

Liam walked until the town's sidewalks gave way to fields with signs touting "new commuter developments" with "finest amenities," all evidence of the growth slowly coming to the area. He detoured round the deepest of puddles, and waved to passing motorists, mostly out of the hope that if he appeared friendly they might not aim their tire spray at him.

After a distance, even the developers' signs dwindled.

Liam automatically turned down a narrow track marked by a sole standing stone that had once been painted purple, red, and green, with knots and spirals and beasts consuming their own tails. Nan Kilbride's work had fallen victim to the wet and the years, but it still shone in Liam's memory and in a small watercolor she'd bequeathed to him.

He had known that he was coming here, seeking proof with his eyes, though to admit it even to himself seemed a weakness. And one had best not be weak, even when facing the memories of Vi Kilbride. She'd come to Duncarraig each summer, living with her nan and running through his life like a wild thing. And after each summer had passed, much as he'd loudly claimed otherwise, Liam had counted the days until she'd return again.

A thin sheet of water stood in the farmyard, and the fence that once held Nan's cow and few sheep stood gap-mawed, its gate no doubt "borrowed" by a neighbor. Liam had covered these lands in measured steps no less than six times in the past three weeks, and nothing had changed from the last time he'd visited.

He walked to the house, seeing no footprints, not that he would with the rain that had fallen. He cut between two overgrown rose bushes that were cowed and beaten from the earlier deluge. Using the side of one hand, he rubbed away enough grime to peer in the front window of the house, and saw only the same clutter he had vaguely noticed the last time.

And seeing this, he felt... empty.

"Fool," he told himself.

Had he wanted her there?

No, for she'd only complicate his life when he'd finally found a purity of task. What he sought—and he was sure it existed outside family tales told fireside— was likely on Kilbride land, and he'd liked having that land empty.

Truly, had he wanted her there?

Liam kicked at a rock on the edge of the rutted ribbon of road. Yes, he wanted her there, for while his fury at her had banked with time to anger, his hunger for her hadn't diminished.

And then the rain began again.

"Fool, indeed."

Liam turned up his collar and aimed for town.

CHAPTER TWO

Three things that make for happiness: hedges, shelter, and early rising.
—IRISH TRIAD

Maeve Kilbride's house smelled of furniture polish and resentment. That, Vi had concluded sometime late the prior night, was no atmosphere in which to have a good sleep. It was not yet eight and already she was on the road from Kilkenny to Duncarraig. And this from a woman who'd prefer to work late and rise even later.

To Vi's left, Rog had his nose pressed to the window, growling at sheep in the field as though he'd never before seen them.

"You're brave enough at this speed, aren't you?" she teased.

He gave her a look as though to say he'd be braver yet on the ground. Much as she loved a good wander, Vi wasn't of the mind to oblige him. Today she meant to come up with a plan, to make some sense of the disaster occupying Nan's house. She longed to have the place perfect, not sterile like Mam's by any means, but the warm home she recalled from her youth. Of course with Nan gone, and Vi's frustrating lack of focus as of late, that was asking much. Still, far less mess would be required before she could permit a real estate agent in.

As Vi arrived in Duncarraig, she slowed beneath what the law would require. Yesterday, she'd allowed herself a cool inventory of shops and buildings, but had looked no deeper. And the time before that—ten years ago when she'd been here for Nan's funeral—her sight had been none too clear. It had been dulled by grief and blinkered by the fear that Liam Rafferty would somehow return from America. He hadn't, of course. She doubted that it had been out of concern for her feelings. He'd operated more on a grand scale of disregard.

"Prosperous," she said, taking in all the new brick-fronted buildings built to emulate the older architecture of the town. Rafferty's Market's window signs boasted catering, imported specialty foods, and organic produce. Vi smiled. Jenna, her best friend back in Ballymuir, was a chef and would dearly love to have something this sophisticated nearby her restaurant

Vi tapped the brakes and then came to a halt when she saw the name painted on the door in gold leaf: Nora Rafferty, Proprietor.

"Ah, Nora. You've done well for yourself, girl."

Nora and she had once been friends. Then again, she'd once felt as though this town were hers to rule. No more, though. She was about to pull away when she saw a lone figure running down the walk. The light was dim yet, with the pale autumn sun taking its time in rising. Still, Vi could see that the person was male and tall, moving with athletic ease.

As he drew closer, her heart sped and her skin grew chill. Were it not for yesterday's mouse incident, she'd believe that the second sight was on her. This morning she was more inclined to think that indigestion might be setting in.

The man was a block away now. Roger began to growl. The sensation filling Vi grew stronger, and she gave in to the inevitable. She let her eyes slip closed, waiting... Waiting...

For nothing.

The feeling passed, and she opened her eyes. She gripped her steering wheel tighter, murmuring a heartfelt curse in the Irish that Nan had taught her.

"Indigestion for certain," she said to Rog, who was now baring his upper teeth at the approaching jogger. "And have you an excuse?"

He barked, and Vi looked more closely at the stranger.

Her breath left her in a wordless gasp, for toward her ran the ghost of Liam Rafferty.

It could be Cullen, she told herself, or perhaps Jamie or one of the countless dark-haired Rafferty cousins. They'd be running on this fine morning, not a man whom she knew had moved thousands of miles away. Aye, it could be Jamie Rafferty all grown up, but the rapid drumming of Vi's heart told her otherwise. It was Liam, God help her.

Vi wanted to look, to take in the changes time had brought this man, but she didn't dare. It would simply be too much. She had faced more than one battle in her life head-on, but for this she was woefully unprepared. Sliding low in the car's seat so that the steering wheel provided some camouflage, she pulled away from the curb and sped from town.

Mere minutes later, as she neared the cluttered sanctuary of Nan's, Vi began to laugh. Fleeing as though she'd just looted the Bank of Ireland? Insanity, it was, and a rather ugly repetition of her past.

"I'll not be judging your bravery again," she said to Roger, who was looking as superior as a short-legged creature in a fast-moving vehicle could.

When they arrived at Nan's, Vi remained too unsettled to work. With Rog at her side, she walked to the standing stone that her Nan had painted. It was no relic, just Nan's twentieth-century nod to the past. Vi traced the remnants of one boldly painted green concentric spiral, the rock cool, damp, and rough beneath her fingertip.

"Well, Nan, what shall I do?"

There was no answer other than the twittering of a linnet in the field nearby. Then again, Vi hadn't expected one.

Nan had always said that only fools fought the seasons. Much to Vi's regret, in this instance as in many others, Nan had been right. One could dodge the inevitable for only so long. Matters had remained incomplete with Liam for nearly half of Vi's life. Now fate had presented her the opportunity to close a circle. Yet here she was, feeling so bloody graceless and stubborn about the matter, as though just beneath the skin she remained a rash and impassioned seventeen. Perhaps, she admitted to herself, that's because when it came to Liam Rafferty, she was.

Beside her, Rog fixed his attention on a far sight and stilled. A shiver rippled its way across his coat. Vi knew this sign. He had scented prey.

"Rog, no," she warned. "Not again."

Without so much as an apologetic glance her way, the beast bolted down the drive and across the road. A hare briefly broke from the hedgerow, then wriggled back through it. Roger, a terrier's terrier, followed after.

Vi pursued the hunter and the hunted, but kept to the road. Her fine green cloak wouldn't meet well with the knot of chill-nipped wild roses, stunted saplings, and greens that made the hedge. Knowing Rog's determination, she was glad she'd worn her sensible boots, black, round-toed affairs that had held up to Ballymuir's most mountainous paths.

"Give it up, dog," she called, but Rog was having none of it, even though he was outmatched. "Ah, well," she murmured, then broke into a run. At least the weather had turned fair. All in all, it was a fine day for a chase.

Liam had seen Vi. At least he was fairly certain that the woman tucked low in the passing car had been Violet Kilbride. He bolted in the front door of his house, fighting for balance as his running shoes wet with dew slipped on the tile floor.

"Meghan, are you up and about? I have to be leaving."

"I'm in here."

After wiping his feet on a fussy flowered mat that one or another of his relatives had left as a welcome gift, Liam strode to the kitchen, where he found his daughter eating breakfast. And drinking his coffee, too. Arguments about the suitability of coffee for a child would have to wait, for he had a redhead to hunt. Liam took the mug from Meghan. He swallowed a gulp, then nearly sent it back up.

"What have you put in here?" he asked once he was sure the vile drink was down for good.

"I tried mixing in some Nutella. Didn't you like it?" She had a grand talent for widening those toffee-brown eyes to a full innocent look.

"Stay out of my coffee." He dumped it into the sink, ignoring her howl of protest. "You're dressed, I see," he added as he poured himself what dribbles of caffeine she'd left in the bottom of the pot. "And in proper uniform, too. Well done. Would you like a lift to school?"

"I can walk," she said.

"Grand, then," he replied, and then drank his thimbleful of coffee while double-checking out the kitchen window to be sure his car was where he'd last seen it this morning, parked by the old carriage house. Thankfully, the vehicle hadn't yet been appropriated. "I'll be seeing you this afternoon."

Liam ignored his daughter's response of "whatever" and made his way out the back door. He pulled the little Nissan out of the courtyard and onto the road out of town before he had time to think too hard about what he was doing. Instinct was the way to go when it came to dealing with Vi Kilbride. Instinct and a fair dose of madness.

Heedless of civilities such as speed limits, on he drove. Within minutes he was nearing Nan's. As he rounded a bend in the road, an absurd wee dog—part terrier, part possibly warthog—appeared to his right, coming out of a gap in the hedgerow. He was in no danger of hitting it, but out of instinct he checked the rearview mirror once he passed. The dog was gone and standing in its stead was a tall redheaded woman with a flowing green cape of some sort.

Vi!

The bend had ended, but with his attention fixed elsewhere, Liam was curving on. His car bounced and shuddered as it skidded into the shallow ditch that marked the border between road and hedge. The vehicle spun in a quarter-circle, ground against something really quite solid, then stalled out.

Liam smacked the steering wheel with open palms. "Holy slice of shite on burnt toast!"

He wrenched open his door, stepped out and landed ankle deep in cold, wet mud. It soaked through his running shoe and formerly white athletic sock before he could even react. When he did, the shoe made a squelching sound as he pulled his foot from the mud. For Liam, swearing was an art form, not worth doing unless done with flair. As the mud seemed to have leached all flair from him, he kept silent.

First, he looked for the objects that had distracted him. Neither woman nor dog was visible, probably still back around the bend. Next, he picked his way through the mud, circling his car to see what he had hit. An initial look showed nothing, but then he found a stray boulder beneath the vehicle.

Liam squatted down and ran his hand along the trim below the car's front grille. He'd been as lucky as one could be under the circumstances. A lower portion of the Nissan's bumper appeared to have taken the worst of the blow. And he'd live with it cracked before he'd pay the rates his cousin Sean charged for auto repairs.

"Hello? You're all right, then?" called a woman's voice. One he hadn't heard in fifteen years. At least, not while awake. Liam slowly stood. He took a perverse sort of satisfaction that Vi was shocked to see just who had run off the road.

"Liam," she said, the perpetual note of good cheer in her voice muted near to silence.

"Vi," he offered in return, walking from the shallow ditch to join her on the side of the road. As he did, he marveled that instantaneous hunger and sharp bitterness could coexist in the simple male mind she'd once accused him of having.

Vi was as beautiful as ever. Tall—perhaps too formidably so for some men, but never for him. Strong-boned—she was no anorectic model. And angry, likely still over his past bad acts—perceived and real—since he'd hardly had time to add anything new. That he knew would change in a matter of days unless she had grown less perceptive. And while he was a lucky man, he wasn't that lucky.

"It's been a long time," he said, yet just now it felt as if the years had compressed to nothing at all. Aye, he was twenty, hungry, and at a loss for what to do with the woman in front of him.

Vi drew a deep breath, seeking inner calm. God, she could remember that last moment when she'd walked from him. She could feel the knife-slice of pain as though it were *now,* here again to eat her soul. She had loved this man beyond time, beyond reason. And that never-to-be-repeated love had almost killed her.

"It could have been longer," she replied. And if fate weren't set on running headlong at her, it would have been.

"You look the same," he said, then tipped his head to assess her more carefully. "Taller, maybe."

She wondered if that was meant as a dig. When she was seventeen, she'd hated her height. But now she was working her way to twice-seventeen and had come to terms with who she was.

"All the better to look you in the eye." she said.

"And tell me what?"

She gave him a smile, hoping it would distract. "Why, hello again, of course." She offered her hand in greeting.

Liam hesitated. "That simple, is it?"

"It's as simple as we make it," she replied, knowing that the words were far easier to speak than to live.

When he took her hand, she made sure the contact was fast and impersonal. Anything more would be dangerous, just now. He was still watching her too carefully for her comfort.

"Will your car start?" she asked, drawing his attention elsewhere.

He glanced back at it and frowned. "I don't know. Let me give it a check."

Liam folded his tall frame into the vehicle, and Vi moved just enough to keep him in her view. The lines creasing his forehead eased away when the car's engine caught and purred. He turned it off and stepped out, stretching his long legs to avoid mud at his door.

"That's half the trouble," he said. "Now for the rock she's hung up on."

"Bad bit of luck," she said aloud. Another thought she kept to herself, that this was exactly the anchoring in spot that he deserved.

Liam's preoccupation gave her a chance to watch him unobserved. He'd aged well, but she would have expected no less. At twenty, he'd had a tall, raw-boned strength. In the intervening years he had filled out, not in a running-to-fat sort of way, but with bulk and muscle that made her think his days weren't spent behind a desk. He remained as potently attractive to her as he'd been all those years ago. More so, perhaps, she thought as he came toward her.

Their gazes locked. Ah, definitely more so, Vi concluded. She had always loved Liam's eyes. They were tilted in a most un-Irish way, making him look as though he were savoring a secret. The small lines that now fanned from his eyes' outer corners only improved his looks. Were she the sort to be jealous over appearances, she might be annoyed. Instead, she'd simply appreciate his beauty, if not what he'd once done to her heart.

She wondered if at this moment he was remembering the same parts of their past as she. How hungry they'd been for each other...

nearly obsessed. That last summer they would sneak off to make love as many times a day as they could. She looked at his broad hands, and recalling how they'd played hot and sure across her skin, she shivered. Mouth tightening to a thin line, Liam turned away. Vi smiled. So he was remembering, too.

Many thanks to Nan, Vi had never been afraid of or embarrassed by her innate sensuality. She had been born to feel deeply and to experience all. So long as she brought no harm to others, there was no sin to living the life for which she'd been formed. As for the other half of the equation—what happened when harm was brought to her—it was far stickier. And the reason that she'd been really quite sparing with her passion. None of which she'd allow Liam Rafferty to know, for he had power enough already.

Liam stood, bracing both hands on his car's roof. "Looks like the only way out is back over it."

Indeed.

"I'll leave you to it, then," Vi said. "And you," she said to Roger, who was engaged in a round of tire-sniffing, "away from the car."

Liam hesitated. "Would you like a lift?"

She wanted quiet to sort her thoughts. "Thank you, but no. I'm best off exhausting Roger, here, so he'll let me get my work done."

"Work?"

"I'm sorting through my nan's house."

"Ah." He looked at the ground, then back to her. "I want to see you again. In fact, I think it's bordering on a need," he added with the self-deprecating smile she recalled so well.

Only fools fight the seasons. And she'd be an even greater fool to deny that she wanted to see him again, too, if only to tidy up her past.

"Stop out to Nan's today," she heard herself saying. "You remember where it is, don't you?"

His expression was so serious that it made her heart jolt. "I remember everything, Vi. Everything."

And so did she, which was why she and her dog turned away and began the walk to safety. Rog was forced to a full run to keep his short legs alongside her longer ones. Within heartbeats, Vi heard Liam's car start, then the dreadful grind of rock against metal as he freed it.

Wincing, Vi drew her cloak tighter about her. Aye, back over the way one had come could be a painful route, but if the journey were taken, one just might come out whole.

Liam pulled off his right shoe outside his back door and then peeled off the muddy sock, too. Of all the ways he'd imagined having Violet Kilbride see him again, being found ankle-deep in mud was not on the bloody list. Half-shod, he entered his house, intent on a fast shower followed by a longer stay at Nan Kilbride's.

"You seem to be short a shoe," his mother said from her seat at his pine kitchen table.

Unaccustomed as he was to sharing his house with whoever saw fit to drop in, Liam started at her voice.

"Grand to see you, Mam. Did I know you were coming for a visit?"

"Mothers needn't ask."

"Mothers, especially, should ask."

"I called your cell," she said in self-defense.

Which he'd left upstairs on the bureau in his hurry to get to Vi.

"So, do you know what else you're missing this morning?" his mam asked before taking a sip of the tea she'd apparently made herself.

Missing? Breakfast. Sanity. Uninterrupted time to research the family legend of lost gold—the list was long.

"No, I don't," he said.

"Have you seen your daughter this morning?"

"Of course I have. She was drinking my coffee not an hour ago. I offered her a lift to school but she said she'd rather walk."

His mother's brows rose and she tapped one manicured finger on the edge of her teacup. "Did she, really? I've not seen her voluntarily walk in the three weeks you've been here. I'm thinking in America she must drive from room to room."

"It's not all that bad," he protested.

The look she gave him said "a lot you know." Liam sat opposite his mother and pulled off his other shoe and sock. That done, he stood, thinking Mam or no Mam in the kitchen, it was time to go upstairs and shower.

"You might want to know that St. Brigid's is short a Rafferty this morning," she said.

Liam froze. He didn't much like the amused glint in her eyes. "Meghan?"

"Of course, Meghan. Why else would I be sitting here drinking your tea, old as it is? You need to come home more, Liam."

Mam could work a lecture into nearly anything. "Have you looked for her?"

"Your child. Your chase. But I did see a wee face in an upstairs window of the carriage house," she added.

Liam pulled aside the lace panel over the window above the kitchen sink. The carriage house. Grand. Every time they argued, Meghan went there, which meant it was well on its way to becoming her residence.

"Oh, and you've had a delivery down to the market this morning. You'd best pick up your package before you offend Nora's sense of order."

"I will." Liam knew it was the ground-penetrating radar rig he'd ordered, though just now the excitement at having a new tool to help with his research was dampened by his daughter's troubles.

"Well," said Mam, "round the girl up and get her to school."

"It's more the keeping her there I'm worried about. I'm too damn big to be fitting in one of those desks beside her. Any words of wisdom?"

She smiled, looking far younger than her fifty-odd years. "You've got two choices, son. You can either muddle through or fail miserably."

The third option, that of having Mam bail him out for the next six months, was growing more remote by the day.

"Don't forget. Supper tonight back home," she said on her way out.

"Might I bring a guest?" Liam asked impulsively.

Mam stopped in the doorway. "Vi Kilbride?"

He nodded. "How did you know?"

"It was no great challenge. In fact, you lasted nearly twelve hours longer than I thought you would once you heard she was about."

"So I may bring her?"

His mam gave a resigned shake of her head. "If you must."

"That's invitation enough for me," Liam said.

"As would have been a flat no," she replied before leaving Liam to play a game of seek-the-truant.

Liam hurried through his shower and a change of clothes, even though he knew Meghan was wily enough that she'd not be leaving her lair. As he'd expected, he spied Meghan perched on the window seat in the carriage house's upper bedroom, looking out at the November remains of the courtyard herb garden that his sister Nora had started. He didn't mind Nora using the place. In fact, he'd had it converted from web-ridden, antiquated garage to guest quarters with the hope that eventually he'd persuade one sibling or another to manage the property during tourist season.

Duncarraig didn't get the seasonal buses bulging with souls, but still enough individual travelers made their way through town on the way to Jerpoint Abbey or Kilkenny Castle that it made some sense to have spent the money for the improvements. And soon a more local site, Castle Duneen, would be reopened after nearly a decade of renovations. Last he'd visited, it had lacked a roof among other niceties. His sister Catherine's husband, Tadgh, had worked there as a stonemason. Mam was in a holy terror that they'd move away once the job was done. She still hadn't quite forgiven Liam for having moved away fifteen years before. Liam had seen no option. As there was none right now.

Steeling himself, he crossed the cobblestone courtyard to the red-painted door of the carriage house.

"Meghan?" he called as the door swung open.

"She's not here," answered a hostile voice from above.

"Ah, then you must be the ghost of a young American tourist. Have you a tragic tale to tell?" Liam climbed the steep oak stairs to the second floor, and then entered the bedroom.

Meghan's resemblance to her mother ran deeper than the dark blond hair and hazel eyes, for when he stepped inside, his daughter gave him the same thoroughly irked look that Beth had specialized in.

"Once upon a time, a father dragged his daughter to a town

where everyone treated her like she was some kind of freak. How's that?" she asked.

Ah, another schoolyard set-to, no doubt. "You're not the standard fare in Duncarraig, love. Be patient and they'll come 'round."

"Right. Like I care."

She did, and it made his heart ache to see her hurt. "You can't just stay in your tower, Meghan. You have to give them a chance."

"I've given them a chance. I'm not going back."

Liam made a mental note to get in contact with Beth. It was a fine line he'd be walking, trying to see if his child's mother had ever had a like problem without admitting to his own ineptitude. It wasn't so much that he cared about his image with Beth. When it came to the mechanics of being a parent, she knew him all too well. He was more concerned about not upsetting her. She had enough on her plate at present.

"I'm afraid you have to go back," he said. "Your mother would have me cooked alive if I didn't get you to school."

"How much longer do we have to be here?"

Liam had no answer, so he volleyed a question instead. "Do you have your school bag?"

"Over there," she said, swinging her foot in the general direction of the bed.

"Well, let's get it and be on our way. No point in falling farther behind in your studies."

He was lucky that she fought no more, for other than dragging the girl down the stairs and out the door, he was without ideas.

Five minutes later he had Meghan in the school office, where Mrs. McCormack, the principal, was waiting. Once Meghan was shuttled off to class, she said, "We're trying to accommodate you, Mr. Rafferty, but there's nothing we can do if she refuses to work."

Liam nodded. "I know, and I thank you for your efforts. I'll talk to her. Things will improve. I promise." And then he left before the principal's frown brought rain to this uncharacteristically bright day.

As he drove to Nan Kilbride's, he considered his promise regarding Meghan. A vow of improvement was easy to make, for matters could not get much worse. Meghan was far too old to spank, even if he'd been that sort of da, which he wasn't. He could hardly deprive her of a privilege, for she'd already been removed from friends, sports, and the shopping malls that seemed to be a point of worship in her pre-teen life. But now that he'd pulled her from her school in Atlanta and made the commitment to Ireland, he could hardly change his mind. Not that he was of a mind to, anyway.

For the first time in the weeks since he'd realized that the company he'd spent his adult life building was about to implode, he felt something near to a sense of promise in Duncarraig's crisp air. And the something grew stronger the closer he got to Kilbride land. *Promise* and *Duncarraig* were two words that had never in Liam's life played in the same thought, and he enjoyed the irony of them doing so now. But, he thought as he pulled up to Nan's house, there were things in life even finer than irony...say, perhaps like indulging in Violet Kilbride.

Vi sifted through the papers in one of Nan's boxes, paying half-attention to the contents. A car door slammed, and she set aside the scraps of notes she'd been reading. She didn't need a look out the window to tell her that Liam had arrived. Roger's growl was warning enough.

"I'll take your opinion under advisement," she told her dog as she brushed her hands off on her worn blue jeans.

Rog was generally a fine judge of character. That he'd been less than charmed with Liam was a matter for worry. Of course, she was feeling a bit cautious on the topic of the man, too.

She opened the front door and gave him a greeting in Irish.

He responded in kind with a *Dia s'Muire duit,* but then added, "Don't go much beyond the weather or you'll have me sounding a fool."

She felt a fool already as she had no idea how to make up the lag of fifteen years. *Chat,* she thought. *Chat, damn it.*

"No Irish speakers where you live?" she managed to pull from some musty corner of her mind.

"Boston might have its share, but I've not run across them."

"Pity. So, you're living in Boston?"

"When I'm not on the road, which is nearly never."

"What do you do?" *By Brid and the gods, wasn't that a horrible bit of cocktail party talk?*

"I'm a partner in a marine salvage company," he was kind enough to reply. "We recover cargoes and right damaged ships."

Vi laughed. The man would never cease to surprise her. "And this from a man who grew up landlocked."

"Ah, but I had the King's River," he said.

"True enough." And he'd been one of the few who always swam its chilly currents when early summer water ran deep.

"What brings you here, Vi? You said you were sorting?"

"Loose ends, mostly," she said. "I'll be selling this place."

"Selling it? Why?"

She felt uncomfortable giving him the details of her life. Her need and her worries were her own—two of the few things that were. "I'm never here, and it would serve me better as cash."

He nodded.

"I've been trying to find a company to deliver a rubbish tip," she said. "You'd think the bloody things were made of gold, for what they're charging."

An odd expression passed across Liam's face before he said, "Let me call my cousin Brian. He's been developing one of those new housing schemes outside town and might have a less costly way to deal with your rubbish."

"Thank you," she said. "It's odd to think of Brian as a grown man, you know?"

He nodded. "This whole thing is a bit off, isn't it?" He paused, then added, "My mother was asking after you. She was wondering if perhaps you'd like to join us for a family supper at her house tonight?"

"All of you?"

"Well, Stephen's off to university in Australia, so he won't be there. And Mam usually has early supper for the children, then sends them all to Catherine's, so we'll be a mere eight. Nothing too terrifying," he teased.

The other Raffertys she could handle. It was Rafferty singular—Liam—who left her scattered and scarcely able to sort a stormy past from an unexpected present.

"What time?" she asked.

"Seven."

Vi hedged. "We'll see what time I finish up here."

He smiled. "Not quite a yes, then?"

"We'll see."

He came round to her side of the box. She worried that he was going to touch her and feel how quickly her heart was dancing.

"Have you thought of me, Vi?"

"Now and again," she said, all casual. "After all, you were my first lover." She didn't bother to add that he was also her best, as she was sure his ego couldn't survive the added inflation without coming apart like a child's balloon.

Each step he neared, her blood rushed faster.

"I've thought of you," he said. "All the time. Even when I tried not to do it. You remember what it was like, don't you? That last summer, I don't think we slept at all."

"I remember."

"Are you married?" he asked.

"No."

"Involved?"

"No, again. Any reason you're asking?"

"Many, but mostly because I'd like to kiss you."

Because she wanted to see if she could still feel the joy of teasing him, she added a little bluster to their brew of emotions. "If you kiss me, you might find your nose back in place."

Liam laughed at the shared memory.

She'd been thirteen and he sixteen when she'd spied on him from a balcony in the nearby ruin of Castle Duneen. He'd been with his cousin Brian, looking at a magazine with pictures of naked women. The boys were deep in a discussion regarding American women's breasts when she'd scuffed her foot on the crumbled rock and shards of slate that coated much of the abandoned castle's upper floor. They had stilled at the noise, but only Liam had looked up and seen her. As she'd backed from her hiding place, she'd heard Liam convincing Brian that she was the spirit of poor Lady Sarah Dunhill, foully murdered by her husband centuries before.

Once Brian had fled, Vi had tried to do the same. Instead, she'd flown around a corner and smacked straight on into Liam. Whether it was because he'd tried to cushion her fall to the floor, or just out of sheer adolescent clumsiness, he'd ended up with a broken nose. To this day it was located a wee bit left of center.

Vi couldn't help herself. She traced her index finger down the ridge of his nose. When he reached out and pulled her closer, her breath left on a surprised gasp. She braced one hand on his chest, thinking if she were sane she'd push him away.

Ah, but sanity was a highly overrated state.

She curled her hand around to the back of his neck, inviting him closer. He brushed his mouth against hers once, so briefly that she thought she might have imagined it.

"It's a risk my nose is willing to take," he said, then returned for a deeper taste.

In a perfect world, this would have been a shattering kiss—hot, practiced, and easy. But Vi's world was regrettably far from perfect, a fact for which at this unusual moment, she was grateful.

Their mouths met at an odd angle, and when they moved to readjust, their noses clashed.

"One last try," she said, "and then we'll give it up for lost."

She had forgotten that Liam Rafferty was a most determined man. He framed her face between his hands.

"I never lose," he said before bringing his mouth to hers again.

This time it was a kiss for the bloody ages, with his tongue tangling with hers and his taste tart and male and perfect. A rush of sexual excitement shot through her, leaving her flushed with fire and ready to burn.

When Liam drew away, a hungry sound escaped her throat. His eyes grew dark, and she thought he'd come to her again. Instead his muttered words proved that he remembered how to curse in Irish well enough. The fact that his tone carried more awe than anger pleased her.

She said nothing, just wrapped her arms about her middle, trying to hold herself together.

"Supper at seven," he said, then left.

Vi was thinking more of dessert.

CHAPTER THREE

A short visit is best, and that not too often.
—IRISH PROVERB

Time, Liam recalled, was a matter of small consequence to Vi Kilbride. His family was as relaxed as the next about such things, unless a meal was involved. Food seemed to kick in some sort of survival imperative, making his relatives act as though they'd been starved for centuries. Which was true enough in its own way, considering their ancestors.

The twenty-first century Raffertys were gathered in the comfortable if overstuffed front room of the senior Raffertys' home, listening to the loud ticking of Mam's antique mantel clock. Catherine, quite pregnant with children numbers four and five, sat next to her husband Tadgh on the sofa. Da had taken his spot in the chair he'd not let his wife reupholster, though it had sadly needed it since 1980. Jamie, always Da's shadow, stood behind him. Mam was by the windows practicing her authoritarian glare, no doubt in preparation for Vi's arrival. She'd never been especially fond of Vi, who though respectful had seemed to view Una Rafferty as an equal, even when Vi had been a child.

"Seven-fifteen," Cullen said from the desk chair he'd pulled by the fireplace.

"Seven-eighteen," corrected Nora, always a stickler for detail.

Liam's da stood. "What do you say, Una?" he asked his wife. "Is it time to start without her?"

"Assuming she's coming at all," Mam said. "The girl was never much for proprieties."

"The girl's a grown woman," Liam said, privately relishing the memory of the way that woman had felt in his arms. It had been a sudden pleasure, and one he intended to repeat.

"Bell," Annie announced over her family's grumbling. How she'd heard it with the music blasting from her perpetually-in-place headphones was beyond Liam. He went to the front entry, knowing the rest of the group would be making a mad dash to the dining room.

Liam swung open the door and gave Vi his hello. When she stepped inside, it was as though his vision had grown more acute. The rich green of her eyes was startling, and the lush set of her mouth enough to make him want to pull her back outside and be done with civilized behavior. But he had a starving family waiting, so he made a conscious effort to slow his heart and ignore regions farther south making themselves known.

"Sorry I'm late," Vi said, holding out a bottle of wine. "I found a box of Nan's journals that I must have missed before. I got to reading, and time escaped." She smiled. "But I suppose you've heard that from me before."

She'd clearly been in a rush once she'd recaptured time, as the side of her face was smudged with dirt and her hair flowing wild over her shoulders and down her back. Liam could imagine it spread across the white of his bed. Ah, well, perhaps not his bed in Duncarraig, with Meghan in the next room. But some bed, and damn soon, too.

Vi tipped her head to a quizzical angle. "Is something wrong with the wine? The girl at your sister's market promised me that Una bought this very Bordeaux all the time."

Taking the wine, Liam shook off thoughts of creamy skin and hot passion. "It's fine, though you might be wanting a stop in front of a mirror. It looks as though you've brought part of Nan's house with you."

"Ah." She took a quick check in the mirror above the old telephone stand and wiped away the smudge. "It wouldn't do to be that 'wild Kilbride girl' in front of Una with all these years passed."

"She'll be thrilled to see you, dust or none," Liam lied.

"Right, she will" said Vi.

"Well, not thrilled, but tolerant, maybe."

Vi laughed. "Now, that has the ring of truth," she said, unwrapping her green cloak and handing it to him. "Shall we get this over with? I've some grand plans for dessert."

Humor and a frank sexual hunger lit her eyes. There was no mistaking her intent, and Liam planned to make this the fastest meal on Rafferty record. He tossed her cloak onto the living room couch and then took her by the hand to the dining room. The small intimacy had been a mistake. Touching her only made him want her more. It also made his mam look as though someone had dropped a shovelful of manure onto her Aubusson rug.

"Everyone, you remember Vi," Liam said as he put the wine she'd brought onto the sideboard. "And Vi, you probably recall everyone but Catherine's husband, Tadgh."

"It's a pleasure to meet you," she said to Tadgh.

"Oh, and Annie's grown a full head of hair since you last saw her," Liam added.

Annie rolled her eyes, and Vi laughed.

"You were not yet quite one, I'm thinking, Annie," Vi said. "And you were lovely bald."

"Maybe I'll try it again," Annie said, shooting a sly look her mam's way.

"Not on my account," Vi cautioned, then sat at the empty place to Liam's left.

Grace was quickly said and the Raffertys staked their claim on the roasted chicken and vegetables with a ferocity that had to rattle an outsider. There was nothing but a wing on the meat platter by the time it made its way to Vi.

She handed it off to Liam, murmuring, "I'm still a vegetarian."

"Then don't ask what Mam roasted the vegetables in," he whispered in reply.

"Pass down the chicken, Liam," Mam ordered from her end of the table. "I've more in the oven, though it might be a bit dry by now."

A lesser woman would have winced at the barb, but hardly a ripple passed across Vi's face.

"The chicken will be fine as always, Una," Liam's da—always the peacemaker—pronounced.

She made a *humph-ing* sound and left to refill the platter. Liam watched as Vi took advantage of the hostess's absence by strategically arranging vegetables on her plate so that a lack of meat might not be noted. By the time Mam had returned, both Jamie and Cullen's plates were nothing but a scattering of bones. Mam set the platter in front of them, and the savagery began again.

"So has Liam told you about his wife?" Mam asked Vi.

"Christ, Mam, we've been divorced nearly four years," Liam said over his brothers' sniggering. At least the girls looked more sympathetic to his situation.

"Watch your language," his mam directed. "And you'll be married until—"

Cullen's laughter drowned out Mam's standard line.

"My mother has a doctrinal issue with divorce," Liam said by way of explanation to Vi, who was looking as though she might have figured out as much on her own.

Mam pressed on. "Beth is a mechanical engineer. Very well respected, she is."

"That's grand," Vi said, then took a forkful of cooked carrot.

"And you, Violet, what have you been doing? Any children?" Mam asked while Vi chewed.

Liam saw a spark in Vi's eyes at Mam's use of her hated full name, but he also had faith that she'd not crawl across the table and choke his mam, much as she must want to, the way the meal was going.

"No children and no husband, just a very spoilt dog who's no doubt baying at the moon from my nan's house."

Mam nodded. "Catherine, here, will be having her fourth and fifth this winter."

"Dogs?" Annie asked from her perch at the far corner of the table. Liam hid his smile in his napkin. Only a youngest child would have license for such lip with Una the Enforcer.

"Children," Mam corrected, shooting an out-of-sorts glare Annie's way.

"I had twins the first time out, too," Catherine said to Vi. "I think God's pushed this efficiency thing a bit too far with me."

Vi smiled. "I have twin brothers, Pat and Danny. They're just nineteen now and didn't visit our nan as often, but you might have seen them about as children."

"Redheads, right?" asked Catherine.

"Red as my own," Vi agreed.

"And still so?" asked Liam's mother.

"They've darkened a little, but there's no mistaking the color for other than red."

"Pity," opined Mam. "Redheaded men never look quite right."

Vi's smile grew to a dangerous curve. Beneath Mam's linen tablecloth, Liam settled a hand on Vi's leg and gave it a brief squeeze. He doubted that it calmed her any, but he liked the feel of her long and slender thigh beneath his palm.

"Plenty of girls in Ballymuir think the boys look better than right," she said to Una.

Nora stepped into the breach. "So you're an artist, are you not, Vi?"

"On good days," Vi said. "On bad, I'm merely an ill-tempered dabbler."

"A dabbler? Hardly. I've one of your pieces over my mantel," Nora said. "I picked it up at the Design Centre in Kilkenny."

Liam felt as though he'd been hit with a mallet. "The abstract of Castle Duneen? That's yours?" he asked Vi.

She took a sip of her wine, then nodded. "I'd suppose it is."

He wasn't the artsy sort, except perhaps as it pertained to the beauty of ancient treasure. Paintings didn't "speak" to him any more than did his mother's cat. But he'd been drawn to that particular work since he'd first seen it in Nora's house three years ago.

"You didn't tell me that was Vi's," he said to his sister.

Nora shrugged. "You've eyes enough. Her name's right on it."

"Not very neatly, I'm afraid," Vi added, giving him some grounds for self-defense.

"An artist," Mam mused. "Liam, doesn't your Meghan have an interest in painting? Perhaps you can have her chat with Violet. If you wouldn't mind too much?" she added with a nod to Vi, in what Liam had to say was one of the finest devious acts dressed in party manners that he'd ever witnessed.

"I— Of course," Vi said, looking confused.

He'd fully intended to tell her about Meghan, but not yet, and surely not force-fed the way that Mam had just done it. They had history enough to deal with.

Liam pushed his plate an inch forward, done with his mother's chicken. He'd underestimated the fierceness of her maternal instincts, and while he loved the woman with all his heart, doing so was easier from a distance. Tonight, it seemed, the greater, the better.

He looked at Vi. "I've a daughter, Meghan, who's with me in Duncarraig just now."

"I see." She took another swallow of wine and then asked, "How old is she?"

"Twelve last month, though she feels there's been a severe misdelivery of fate and she's actually twenty," Liam said.

Vi's smile would have fooled most anyone at the table, but not Liam. Beneath it waited a storm of emotions that he knew he'd soon face.

"A daughter. I'd be pleased to talk with her," Vi said.

"Grand," Mam replied, looking content with her evening's mischief. She stood and took her plate, then reached for Annie's.

"Let me help you clear the table, Una," Vi said.

When others rose, too, Vi gave them a firm "sit." To a soul, they complied. If Liam weren't so worried over the bloodbath about to take place in the Rafferty kitchen, he'd have been impressed with Vi's powers of command.

Una pushed through the dining room door, and Vi followed. Jamie rose and put his ear to the door, but Cullen hauled him away.

"You'd be marked for life, lad, hearing what's being said in there," Cullen told his younger brother.

Da pushed away from the table. "I'm thinking a walk to the pub might be good."

He wasn't alone in his thoughts of escape, for soon Liam was the only one left in the dining room. He heard two female voices in the kitchen, so took comfort that one had not yet killed the other. Realizing he was in for a wait, he refilled his wine glass and settled in.

Dishes rattled, silverware clinked, and voices grew marginally louder. Liam filled his glass again. He was half through it when Mam pushed her way into the dining room.

"She hasn't changed a bit," she said, then stalked upstairs.

Liam expected that she hadn't meant the words as praise.

Vi joined him.

"Are you all right?" he asked.

"Fine, of course."

She looked weary to Liam, with her milky skin nearly sallow, but he'd do neither of them good by pointing it out.

"Your mother and I needed to reach an understanding," Vi said.

"And that would be?"

"That I'm no adversary."

At least not one to be taken lightly, he thought.

"Would you mind walking with me a bit?" she asked. "I'd like to feel the night on my skin."

He was discovering that he still had a great many things he'd like to do with her. Walking was a start. Liam gathered her cloak and draped it over her shoulders. She neatly fixed it in place with a large silver pin.

"Nice piece," he said, touching the pin simply so he could touch her.

She glanced down. "It's the work of a silversmith friend. I took a fancy to it, so we traded for one of my paintings."

It seemed a bargain to the smith's benefit, but Liam wisely kept his mouth shut. He opened the front door. Once they'd cleared the threshold, he said, "Let's just call tonight the Last Supper."

She laughed, but the sound lacked its usual rich depth. "You mother would be boxing your ears for sacrilege."

"Una did it often enough when I was little, which might explain the way I flinch during Mass." All right, maybe he was exaggerating matters a bit, but the cause was a noble one.

"I have my doubts you even go to Mass, Liam Rafferty."

"You caught me there," he replied.

Without plan or talk, they walked west out of town, toward the King's River and Castle Duneen. It was a walk they'd taken many nights before. Those nights had been warmer, and he had passed them trying to meet Vi's challenge of giving her a kiss for every star in the sky. He took a glance upward, noting it had grown cloudy. A bad omen for kisses, that. He knew the time had come to talk about the unspoken subject that was darker than the clouds blotting out the moon.

They had reached the park on the river, a refined place with streetlights and benches. He stopped and took both her hands, warming them between his. She didn't pull away, for which he was grateful.

"Vi, it's not as though I was trying to hold my marriage from you, or Meghan's existence, either. It's just I wasn't sure where to fit the words. I've never been in a situation like this, and I'm making a mess of it."

"I know you meant no harm, and you've given none," she said after a moment's pause. "It's just all so much to take in. I feel..." She shook her head. "There's the thing, Liam, I feel *something,* which believe it or not is a great change as of late. I just don't know what it is riding me. I'm angry when I have no right to be, and I'm sad, too."

"I've had a life, and you have, too," he said. "We're neither of us the same person we were fifteen years before." He thought of his marriage, doomed to fail from the start, and of his business, now in tatters, too. He thought, and he knew some of Vi's anger. "Life's so damn complicated. Can we not just take a grab at some happiness while we're here in the same place?"

She led him to a bench, and they sat. Liam liked the feel of her body next to his, liked that she had substance to her. He moved closer and tried to relax.

"Where's your daughter tonight?" she asked, and he hoped the question was a sort of tacit acceptance of his past.

"At Catherine's house watching her three little ones." Liam sat in silence before adding, "Meghan's not happy in Duncarraig. She's so American. I know it sounds bloody absurd to say this, but it never occurred to me that we'd have these troubles. She's my child, after all..."

Vi flicked a lock of hair over her shoulder and gave him an arch smile. "So she was bred to assimilate?"

"I know. Stupid, isn't it? I'm afraid I don't make much of a da."

"I'm sure you make a fine one. Where's her mother?"

"Working in the Middle East for the next six months. Beth's

parents are too far along in years to handle Meghan for that long."

"Not that the responsibility should have rested with them."

"True enough," he said, thinking, *but not easy enough.*

"Why did you not stay in Boston with her?"

Liam gave the simple answer, the one without lying business partners and the specters of bankruptcy and federal grand juries in front of which his testimony would soon be compelled. "She'd been living in Atlanta, so I had no familiarity to offer. And my home is a one-bedroom town house that sits empty most of the year, as I stay where projects arise. I brought her where I thought we'd have the most support."

"Wise choice, so long as you're on Una's good side."

He smiled at Vi's bone-dry proviso. "I've never understood why she has such a dislike for you."

Vi shrugged. "We've different views. I think she found my nan a bit too earthy, and now me, too, if you know what I'm meaning."

"And then there's the issue of the gold," Liam added. "Mam's a true believer."

Family legend held that a trove of Rafferty gold had ended in the hands of Vi's great-many-times-over-grandmam. Liam's grandda had told the tale with a *seanachie's* skill so great that Una had begun to believe it. Though a Rafferty by marriage only, she took the claim fully and vocally to heart. Liam had put little stock in the lore. Until lately...

"But that's a tale, nothing more," Vi said. "Do you think that my nan would have been living in the same four-room house as her nan before her if she'd been sitting on a mountain of Rafferty family gold?"

"I learned a long time ago that your nan did whatever suited her. Including blister my ears with a lecture or two."

Vi laughed. "She wasn't a woman to cross."

"But she was always a woman to respect."

Months after her death, Liam had been forwarded a package by his da, who'd been passing friendly with Nan. The package had contained a watercolor Nan had done of the opened gate to her property and her painted rock just the other side. Also enclosed was a letter telling him that he was a fine young man and how sorry she was that matters hadn't worked out better with Vi, for the families needed to resolve their differences. He still had both the small picture and the letter in a personal file back in Boston.

Liam glanced skyward, thinking of Nan. The clouds had cleared, and the moon had pulled higher.

"I'd best be getting back," Vi said. "I'm sure Roger is more than ready for his supper and a break outside before we head back to Kilkenny."

"You could stay in my carriage house," Liam said, as surprised as she appeared at the offer he'd voiced. "It's been refitted as guest quarters."

"I can't. My parents will be expecting me, and I've left all my clothes there, too."

"Then walk with me around the river bend, at least. I've something I want you to see."

Castle Duneen hadn't ever precisely been a castle, at least not one of those multiple-turreted fantasies that romantics sighed over. It was foursquare and utilitarian, with high stone walls that had held it in good stead until the 1920s, when the local Republicans had heard a rumor that British troops were to be garrisoned there. They'd executed a preemptive burning, which history proved was unnecessary, too. The British had no intention of using the place. Liam knew that tonight the view of the castle would be impressive, as its current owners seemed to care little about electricity bills.

"Let me cover your eyes," he said before they came to the turn that would bring the castle into view.

She laughed and fussed, but let him have his way, and he led her to a vantage point.

"There, now," Liam said as he took his hands down.

"There are lights on the castle! And in it, too," she cried.

Liam nodded. "An American couple bought it and have been renovating for several years. It's nearly done from what Tadgh tells me. He's been fixing the stonework."

"I'd like to tour it one day," she said.

As would he, for not only had he broken his nose inside those stout walls, it was also there that he'd first made love to Vi Kilbride.

"How long are you in Duncarraig?" he asked.

"As long as it takes."

"To empty your nan's house?"

She nodded.

"You know I'll not be able to stay away," he said, taking her into the circle of his arms.

"Ah, but I was the one who always followed you."

"Not this time." He kissed her once because he had to, then again for another of her stars in the sky. And after that he let her be. Tonight had made even clearer what he already knew: He could not have her in his bed and then tell her later about his search for Rafferty's gold. She deserved better from him this time, for he'd failed her horribly in the forthrightness department their last.

"Shall we go back?" he asked, tilting his head in the direction of the path they'd taken.

"We will," she answered, and for the first time that night, Liam knew peace.

It was nearly ten-thirty by the time Vi was on the road to Kilkenny. She knew her parents would be worried and she regretted that she'd not called them from Duncarraig before leaving. Jenna and her Ballymuir family were right—soon she'd have to leave the dark ages and get herself a cell phone. The thought chafed.

"I'd rather walk around wearing your leash," she said to Roger.

And after washing up the Raffertys' dishes this evening, she'd pay a fat stack of euros to see Una in a muzzle. Liam's mother had actually had the nerve to warn her off Liam, as though she, Vi Kilbride, were the round-heeled town tart out to sully the Rafferty name.

Vi shook her head at the absurdity of Una's claims. So she'd broken Liam's heart? His mother had the wrong end of that particular beast. If there had been a broken heart fifteen years ago, it had been Vi's. It had healed, but not with the speed of Liam's, assuming he'd even suffered as his mother had claimed.

A daughter of twelve meant he'd loved another woman two years after they'd parted. Brave man. Vi had been living in a tourist caravan on Inch beach, hoping for the money to eat and the courage to paint. Men had been anathema.

"Broken heart, indeed," she said.

Roger, who had fallen asleep on the seat next to her, snorted a wee bit.

Kilkenny appeared soon enough. She turned off onto her parents' road and found a parking space a mere block from her former home. Mam and Da's attached house was identical to every other house in the row. Tiny patch of grass, over-pruned shrubs, four steps to the stoop, and drab tan brick. In the dark, it was a neat trick indeed to find the proper front door.

Years ago, when she'd been a teen and her elder brother Michael implicated in the Troubles in the north, she'd filched a bottle of her mam's horrible Chablis and tried to drink herself numb behind the butcher's shop. Numbness had never arrived. All she'd succeeded in doing was staggering into the wrong damn house.

Luckily, she had Roger to sniff his way home tonight. She stopped to let him have a pee or ten before going into the house. He was male through and through, marking what was his every time he walked by. God forbid if a stray cat or cheeky neighbor dog had eradicated his scent.

A bluish light glowed from her parents' front room, letting her know that Da was still awake and at his sentinel post by the television. As Roger finished his business, the porch light switched on.

"Do you have any idea of the hour?" her mother hissed from the entry.

"It's not yet tomorrow, I'd wager."

"You should have let us know you'd be this late. Your da's been worried."

"Sorry, Mam. I meant to call."

"Then next time, you'd best do it."

Vi apologized one more time. All she needed was the bellyful of Chablis and she'd be that muddled teen again, a stage in her life she could do well without. Vi shooed Rog inside and edged past Mam, wishing her a restful sleep.

"At this hour, it will be more of a nap," Maeve said before going upstairs.

Vi shook her head. Liam's offer of a place in Duncarraig was developing a fine appeal.

She went into the front room and gave her father a kiss on the cheek. He absently patted her hand where it rested on the arm of his chair.

"Danny called while you were out. He wants you to give him a ring," Da said without once turning his eyes from the golf tournament he was watching.

"It's getting late. I'd best do it in the morning."

"He said he'd be waiting up for you."

"Well, then..." Vi went to the kitchen phone and dialed her number back in Ballymuir. Danny picked up almost immediately.

"I've missed your voice," she said, feeling some of the night's tension leave her.

"Well, you also missed Pat cutting his finger at work."

So much for finding peace. "Was it bad? He wasn't using that horrible band saw again, was he? After the last cut, Michael promised me he'd keep him from it."

"He was, but it's not bad at all. I wasn't even going to tell you, except I knew you'd give me hell when you got home and saw him."

"Which I might do yet," Vi said.

"You're acting a bigger baby than Pat did. He was stitched, given some antibiotic cream, and sent home. Jenna stopped by, and Kylie's here now, asleep in front of the fire. The reason I'm calling is because her students want to do something special for her before the baby's here and were hoping you'd give a hand."

Lord, more cooing and ahh-ing when she'd already reached her limit.

"So long as they can wait 'til I'm back," she said aloud, for sharing bitterness was something she'd never do.

"And when will that be? Not that we're missing you, but we like having Rog about."

She laughed at that male evasion of love. "Soon. A fortnight more at the most."

"Then I'll pass along word that you're in."

"Fine, then. Now you're not hiding the truth from me about Pat?"

"You'll know if you come home to a spare finger under your pillow, won't you?" With that, her bloodthirsty brother hung up.

Vi pulled out a chair from the kitchen table and sat.

Upon first meeting Kylie over two years ago, Vi had become the official arts ambassador to Gaelscoil Pearse, where Kylie taught. Once Vi was to school, she loved working with the children, but of late it had grown harder and harder to get herself there. Everyone around her was rolling in fertility the way Roger would in rabbit droppings. She was tired of hearing about birth and offspring and annoyed with herself for feeling so cross. Kylie pregnant, Catherine twice so, and Liam with a child. The last was the coldest cut of all. Tired beyond thought, Vi pushed away from the table and checked in the fridge for a bedtime snack but found its shelves empty of quick edibles.

"Barren, eh?" she said to Nan and the other spirits watching over her. "Sharp. Grand joke, indeed."

No doubt about it, the dead had nasty senses of humor.

CHAPTER FOUR

The ambitions man is seldom at peace.
—IRISH PROVERB

Vi staggered downstairs at nearly ten the next morning, her crimson silk robe wrapped haphazardly about her, and her hair still in sleep tangles. She'd been restless past three o'clock with thoughts of Liam—a circuit of "what ifs" that had led her back to where she'd started: the past was unchangeable and the future not a matter of relevance. At five-thirty, Mam had begun to stir, with tea kettle shrilly whistling and television chattering away. Vi should have surrendered to the inevitable and started her day then. The additional doze she'd instead allowed herself had set her behind.

After a quick bit of snooping, she found Roger and Da in the kitchen, Da all suited up for his day with no work and Roger beneath the table, gnawing on a joint bone of some poor beast or another.

"Morning," she said to her father.

He returned the greeting over a sip of orange juice. She noted that he was reading a brochure about employment opportunities in sales. He must be desperate, for her da was among the quietest men she knew. Both he and his namesake son, Michael, would happily go hours without talking if others didn't shake words loose.

At floor-level, Roger drew her attention, growling and worrying at his bone as though it might escape.

"Give it back," she said to her hound, not quite sure she wanted to touch it if he were willing. Rog backed until he was safely between her da's feet.

"What, no meat for him, either?" Da asked. "Are you making over your dog in your own image?"

With Rog's carnivore's fondness for mice and hares, she stood no chance.

"Just avoiding another scolding from Mam. If she sees him acting a savage in her kitchen, he'll be sleeping on the stoop."

Da smiled. "I've already taken the scolding in Roger's name. Your mother had planned the bone for her ham and bean soup, dreadful stuff that it is."

"Which is exactly why you gave the bone to Rog, no doubt."

"A wise man learns to avert disaster." He set aside his glass of juice. "Speaking of which, are you off to Duncarraig again this morning?"

Unlike his mother or Vi herself, Da had never possessed a bit of the second sight, which left her wondering what disaster he might be referring to, if not Una Rafferty's chicken feast.

"I am, and far later than I planned to be," she said. "Why do you ask?"

He had the look of a man about to suffer. "Your mother's at the bakery. The flower committee from church will be here this afternoon for a meeting. They're fine women, all, for about twenty minutes. After that, my head begins to ring with their talking, and there's no place away from them."

Vi could imagine.

"You're welcome to come along," she said as she inventoried the cleaning supplies beneath the sink. Since Mam had enough to last to Armageddon, she'd not miss some liquid soap and a sponge or two. Vi emerged with her pilfered goods. "I have to say, Da, handsome as you are, you're also overdressed to help me."

He glanced briefly at the sales brochure still on the table. "I was thinking more of a visit in town today...a look-see for new opportunities. Hard to believe I grew up there, what little I've been back."

Often enough to settle a friend's jetsam on her, that much was certain.

Vi found an empty grocery sack in a drawer by the back door

and tucked her supplies inside. That done, she opened the fridge. It seemed that Mam's priorities lay with cleanliness. Nothing had appeared in the refrigerator since last night except some rashers, and she'd leave the pig-nibbling to Roger.

Like Da, she settled for a glass of juice—the bottled, watery type that he preferred. The first swallow brought a wince. The second was enough to force surrender. Vi dumped the rest of the juice into the sink.

"Twenty minutes and we'll be gone," she said.

"Time enough," her father replied.

Twenty minutes beyond that, as they headed toward Duncarraig, Da made his plans better known. "I doubt I'll be as long as you will," he said. "How about we drop you at your nan's and I take your car back into town?"

Vi glanced over at him and was pleased to see that he appeared nearly content. He wasn't a man to wear his unhappiness on the outside, and he hadn't looked well in the days that she'd been home.

"Just promise to be back for me before sundown, if you could." Candlelight was a fine thing, but not enough to clean by.

"Of course."

They drove on in her da's favored state—quiet—and soon made Duncarraig. Town was bustling under the thin sun. Mothers had babies out in prams, and in a sign of optimism, had rolled back the babies' clear plastic weather shields that were nearly perpetually in place. Unwilling to travel the baby path any farther, Vi returned her focus to the road. Town dwindled, fields took over, and the narrow and rutted *bothareen* to Nan's appeared.

As Vi neared the house, she spotted a new addition. A rusted red container almost large enough to hold her car sat beside the house. It seemed that in matters of trash, if not of the heart, Liam was better than his word. She parked in front of the house, then climbed out, leaving the motor running.

"C'mon, Rog," she said, opening the back door. He hopped out, and she gathered her cleaning supplies. Da came around to the driver's side.

"I'll be back no later than teatime," he said to Vi.

"Bring food," Vi said over her stomach's grumbling, which was noting its disapproval over both last night's sparse supper and this morning's tease of a breakfast. "Scones, and lots of them," she called as he closed the car door and drove off.

With luck, Da would know that she was serious. Otherwise she would be left to forage among those of Nan's herbs that had managed to reseed and survive encroaching weeds over the past decade. Vi bent down. Using her free hand, she pinched a leaf off a plant close to the weed-clotted stone walkway.

"Peppermint," she said to Roger after rubbing the leaf between her fingers and inhaling its fragrance. "Nan always said it helped bring love."

Roger lifted his leg, marked the plant and trotted on.

Aye, and then there was that view, too.

Vi and dog entered the house and headed back to the kitchen, where she'd made a decent dent in the chaos the day before. Nan's garden journal was sitting by the sink, just where Vi had left it in her haste to avoid being too late to supper.

"Behind as I am, a few pages more of reading will make no difference," she said to Rog.

Yesterday she'd made a nest of sorts for herself in the back bedroom—a chair that Nan had painted white and blue in a wild pattern, tucked into an old writing desk. Vi settled in and read, smiling at the knot designs her grandmother had imagined but never quite coaxed from the soil. Some of the herbal cures she'd listed had seen more success. Nan had even managed to persuade a few down Vi's stubborn throat, and Vi in turn had given them more recently to her cold-ridden friends.

It was warm and quiet in the small room, with the sun shining in the south-facing window. She felt almost as though Nan's comforting presence was with her. As the minutes passed, much needed sleep crept up on her. She closed the journal, folded her arms on the desk like a schoolchild, then cradled her head and finally, blissfully slept.

Liam wasn't the sort to think much about God, though having a preteen in-house had tempted him to take the Creator's name in vain more than once. When he'd been a child, God was the anonymous entity whom he'd involuntarily visited each Sunday in Duncarraig's church. He'd spent his time stuck mid-pew among siblings and cousins, fantasizing about a hidden talent that might separate him from the pack whispering and elbowing about him.

Now grown, Liam found God in science, another view his traditional mother would deem near heretical. Whether it was the beauty of the formulae that permitted him to know just how deep he could dive and how long to decompress, or the complex mechanics involved in righting a damaged ship, it was all glorious religion to him.

This morning's marvel was the ground-penetrating radar unit that had arrived at Nora's market yesterday. It was a fine rig, more than adequate for his purposes. As it should be, since he was out nearly forty-five hundred euros for the pleasure of owning it. This with business bills mounting would seem irresponsible to some. For Liam, it was a necessary cost. Necessary to keep his mind moving as his regular work ground to a halt and, most of all, necessary to give him hope.

"Hope," Liam said aloud, thinking what a small word it was to balance against the unpleasantness in life.

As Liam drove the slight distance from town to Nan Kilbride's house, he mentally reviewed what more he'd learned this morning in his two-hour-long phone session with the GPR technician. It was already past noon and he had yet to do what he most craved—take the unit for a stroll on Nan's potentially treasure-rich land.

Oh, he was aware that Vi owned the land now, but it was easier to nose about when he thought of himself as offending only Nan, who surely had better things to do than watch over him. Otherwise, he'd have been obliterated by a lightning bolt through the heart the day she died. Since he hadn't, she was either occupied elsewhere or didn't share Vi's beliefs regarding his behavior that last Duncarraig summer.

Nosing looked to be an easy task today. No car was in front of the house, and the massive rubbish container he'd had Cousin Brian drop early this morning still sat untouched. Liam pulled past the dwelling and as far toward the open land behind it as the ruts in the road would permit. When at the lane's end, he parked.

Using a mallet and stakes he'd also borrowed from Brian's

construction supplies, he marked the perimeter of the field in the grid pattern that the equipment's training manual had instructed. Once done, it was back to the car. He fiddled for a while, coordinating the GPR unit's wireless function with his laptop computer, all loaded with software to help him interpret what he might find.

Liam didn't give a dead rat about fashion, but even he had to admit a certain amount of unhappiness with the next step. Thankful there was no one to witness him, he strapped the unit's belt-and-brace rigging about his waist, shaking his head at the little black metal arm that now protruded in front of him. An aluminum foil cap and antennae for his head and he'd be bait for the local *Gardaí* to question. Luckily, Duncarraig had always been protective of its madmen, or half his family would be in trouble.

"Ready, then," he said to himself. Liam locked the GPR unit onto the arm. This being part man and part machine definitely felt more natural in the sea than it did on land. He switched on the unit, gave one last check of his laptop, and then settled the computer on his car's roof.

For the third time in less than a week, he walked Nan's field. This time, though, he was far less interested in its topography than in what might be hidden beneath the surface. This land had passed down woman to woman for as long as anyone knew. And while Nan's decrepit house was hardly modern, neither was it old enough to have been standing in the days of legend.

His shiny new GPR would map not only metal, but also remnants of former structures that Liam's untrained though careful eyes might not discern. Ancient foundations, cisterns, and other voids beneath the earth's surface would be revealed without so much as a needless shovelful of dirt being turned. Technology was miraculous, indeed, especially for a man with limited time to devote to a task.

If Liam found nothing, he could confess to Vi what madness he'd been up to...how he'd begun a chase based on a jeweler's notations regarding sale of gold by a Rafferty in the 1800s. Hell, for all Liam knew, that long-ago Rafferty had sold a British general's gold teeth rather than a piece of a trove long disappeared.

After Vi had cooled—for he knew she'd initially respond with fire—they would laugh it off as a grand joke. If he found something, well, that would be the more difficult conversation. Not that anything involving Vi had ever been easy. But up until the end, it had always been worth the price.

Liam walked to the northwest corner of the field and began his square grid pattern, keeping one eye on the GPR screen and one on the rough, pitted sod knotted with weeds below his feet. It was slow work, and mystifying, too. The bluish bars on the small display dipped and wavered from time to time as he tromped along. He had no idea what it meant, but his heart still jumped when the image in front of him did. After nearly an hour, he'd completed a quarter of the field.

As he made a right angle turn to cover the next quadrant in his grid, Liam stumbled. Once he'd caught his balance, he looked back to see what he might have caught his foot on, but the ground was no worse than what he'd already tread upon. Less rocky, in fact.

Odder yet was the sense that someone was watching him, even though he knew he was out of range of human eyes. As an Irishman, he was honor-bound to believe in the possibility of ghosts. As a man of science, he was equally compelled to believe that there was a concrete, rational explanation for these sensations. Either way, he didn't like it. Head down, he walked on and tripped on nothing again. This time, it seemed that the watcher was laughing at him.

"Damn obnoxious annoyance," he muttered to the thing that either existed or not, and thus could either hear or not. "Go the hell away."

Vi woke abruptly. She sat up and rubbed the side of her face, which was numb from having been pressed against the desk's wood surface. She wasn't quite sure what had snapped her from her dream—the first she'd had in months.

"Rog?" she called, thinking perhaps he'd been whining to get out. But then she spotted the little dog sleeping fat-belly-up on a bit of carpet to the room's far left.

Something had brought her from that place of lush beauty back to the everyday, and it wasn't just the ferocious growling of her stomach. Vi pushed away from the desk and surveyed the cluttered room. It was exactly as unattended as she'd left it.

As she glanced past the window, a bit of black caught her

attention. Vi moved closer. It was a car parked at the back of the property...the same black car that yesterday she'd seen hung up on a rock. In the field beyond, a figure appeared from behind the car, walking a steady line parallel to the house.

Image traveled from eyes to brain, and Vi felt so muzzy-headed that she began to doubt she'd awakened at all. If this were the old days, Liam would be a farmer out to plow his field and she would be his love. Except neither this land nor she were his, and that was no plow he wielded. It was a modern thing, a flat black rectangular box growing off him in a most absurd way. She assumed that it must have some sort of screen, the way he was down peering at it.

"You were right about the man," she said to Roger, who'd awakened and come to stand at her side. "Nothing with a Rafferty is ever as it seems, now is it?"

What, exactly, the reality was remained to be learned. Fueled by the anger that came from being trespassed against, Vi stalked out the front door, Roger on her heels. Having Liam briefly out of sight did nothing to dissipate the feeling. Vi clenched her hands, and her blunt-cut nails nipped at her palms.

She rounded to the back of the house. As she walked, her trousers' legs brushed against the lavender that bordered what was once Nan's cutting garden. The plants were spent, their stalks now more silver than green and their long and slender flower heads gone to seed. Still, their perfume wafted into the cool air as she passed. Nan would have told her that the scent was for meditative relaxing, and she would have been right to a degree. At the moment, Vi would have to roll about in a mound higher than Nan's house to relax.

Vi hurried her pace, preferring to meet Liam head-on while temper gripped her. He had seen her and was frozen like a mad bit of statuary midfield.

"I don't suppose you're divining for water, now are you?" she asked as she approached.

His mouth curved into a brief smile that she'd call embarrassed if she didn't know its owner. Nothing in life had ever embarrassed Liam Rafferty, not even when they'd been discovered naked by German tourists in Castle Duneen.

"Actually, I'm looking for Rafferty's gold."

Well now, perhaps he'd found something sufficiently ripe to match that smile. She hesitated before speaking, waiting to see if he'd say it was a joke and that he was...

She frowned at the rig he wore. God knew what else he could be doing. Perhaps God also knew how she could be finding Liam Rafferty handsome when he looked half a lunatic.

"Really, Vi, this is ground-penetrating radar. I'm treasure seeking."

It was a blessing that she'd chosen not to view this man as more than a potential source of long overdue sexual gratification. "I'll give you credit for honesty, if not a brain working full-time."

"The legend's real. I'm sure of it," he said.

She knew the legend as well as she did her own name. When young, she'd heard the story from Liam's grandda, and a rather more female-centric version of it from her nan. Either way the tale was told, it had been the sort of thing to pique a young girl's fancy. She and Liam were like history's legendary Deirdre and Naoise, star-crossed Irish lovers attached to opposing factions.

No matter that the Raffertys weren't overtly warring with her nan over treasure no one had ever actually seen. And while Vi had loved Liam with a passion that frightened her, she'd hardly have dashed her brains out on a rock for the loss of him the way woeful Deirdre had for Naoise. It had been enough to know that destiny held a hand in Vi and Liam's romance. Or so that naive, lust-addled teenager had thought.

Vi pulled herself back to a rather confusing present. "And this from a man whose mother would have done better to name him Thomas, with all the time you've doubted the tale?" she asked. "Why the change?"

"I didn't have proof before."

"And you do now?"

"Yes." He hesitated, and Vi watched as a muscle in his jaw flexed as though he were gritting his teeth. "At least it's the closest I've seen."

"Care to tell me about it?"

"I don't."

"No? You're walking my land, looking for treasure that's more mine than yours, and you don't intend to tell me what brought you into the realm of believers? I'm thinking you don't grasp our respective positions, here."

He settled his hands on his hips, a position that added little to his believability with that thing poking out before him. "I meant no, I don't care to talk proof now, in the middle of this field. And I'll tell you what I *am* grasping. I'm grasping that the gold is called Rafferty's gold for a reason."

She laughed. "Aye, so your family could feel begrudged over bloody nothing but their own bad behavior for generations."

Liam's brown eyes narrowed, not that Vi was feeling especially concerned. He switched off his radar-thing and began walking toward his car. Vi stayed even with him, stride after stride over the uneven ground, even though the effort was making her dizzy. She should have drunk more of Da's wretched juice.

"This doesn't concern you," Liam was saying. "Had you not shown up in Duncarraig, you'd know nothing of what I'm doing."

For once in her life, timing had been her friend.

"Odd how that worked out, isn't it?" she asked, giving him her pet "the spirits like me better than you" smile.

She got a scowl in return for her comment before he picked up his pace. Roger trotted along just fine, but Vi began to falter. Liam started lecturing her about something or another, and she couldn't seem to focus on the words.

Stars and tiny comets danced in front of her eyes. She blinked, and then blinked again. It was no help. Her knees grew weak, and she sat on the damp earth before she would fall.

"Vi?" she heard Liam or perhaps the rock nearest to him asking.

"Head between knees," she managed to say, then slumped forward, doing her best to make action follow words.

Bloody damn hell, she was not a woman who fainted.

Until now.

CHAPTER FIVE

The traveler has tales to tell.
—IRISH PROVERB

Never before had a woman gone unconscious at Liam's feet. He might have fantasized about it once or twice, but definitely not with the participants clothed. Neither had his fantasies included this level of alarm.

"Vi?" he asked over the slamming of his heart.

He bent down to get to her, but his newest appendage prevented him from reaching the ground. Her little dog was trotting back and forth above her head, worry on his face, to the degree a dog could look worried.

"Stinking pot of boiled sheep shite," Liam muttered as he unbuckled, unhooked, and wrenched off the GPR unit that stood between him and Vi. He knew little of where she'd been or if she'd been well these past years. It was a hard fist to the stomach to think even for a moment that she was ill. By the time he was kneeling beside her, though, she had begun to stir. Liam wasn't sure who was more relieved, himself or Vi's dog.

Because she was ever-invincible Vi, she began to scramble to her feet. Liam grasped her by the upper arms and stilled her. "Slow now or you'll be out again."

"I don't faint."

She'd spoken with such dignity that he scarcely managed to quell his smile. "Then you'd best give me a warning before you nap again."

Her exhaled breath was nearly a laugh.

Liam looked for signs of color returning beneath her skin, but she remained too pale for his comfort. He'd take her in his arms if he didn't think he'd end up with them broken for the effort. Instead, he reached out to smooth a lock of hair back from her forehead, but the obvious warning in her green eyes stopped him.

"You'd best not. I'm not through being angry," she said.

Vi and anger were things not to be trifled with, even when she was at less than her best. He dropped his hand to his side. Knowing Vi's inattention to matters mundane as food, he asked a logical question.

"So tell me, she who does not faint, when did you last eat?"

"Yesterday."

"At my parents' house?"

She nodded.

''You didn't eat. You chased a carrot round your plate."

"Close enough."

"Not when the carrot wins."

"It's grand to see the years haven't robbed you of your sense of humor," she said quite dryly. "My father will be here soon with some food."

"Define soon."

She rubbed at her temples with long-fingered hands. "By teatime."

Liam glanced at his watch. "Nowhere near good enough. I'll run you and your dog—"

"Roger," she corrected.

"Fine, then, *Roger*—into town and get some food in you."

"I can wait for Da."

A faint tinge of pink had crept under her skin, making Liam feel better, too.

"Don't be stubborn," he said, knowing he'd have a better chance in asking fire not to burn. "You can't live on less than a meal a day."

"I can and have," she replied. "But I suppose you can take me to town." She ran her hands through her hair and then began brushing off her right shoulder and hip, which had been in close contact with the ground.

"You're welcome," he replied with all the grace she was refusing to show.

He stood and held out a hand to her. She hesitated.

"For God's sake, Vi, I'm helping you up from the ground. You can shred me alive for trespassing after you've eaten."

She gripped his hand and rose. "Don't think I'll be forgetting."

Liam knew better than to even think that.

"I'll be right back," she said.

He shook his head as she marched shoulders back and head high in the direction of the house. He took a moment more to gather his gear. Vi had returned with a patchwork bag made of a mad jumble of fabric by the time he was saving the data he'd captured. She and her dog got into the car while he stowed the equipment. When he went to get in the driver's side, the dog was sitting in his seat.

"To the back," he said to Roger.

"I don't know," said Vi. "He could do no worse than you did yesterday."

A diplomat, the dog hopped in back.

"Don't be discussing driving or I'll remind you of your first time behind the wheel," Liam said once he'd climbed in and closed the door.

That settled her into silence for a few minutes. He supposed it would have done the same to him, had he ended up going the wrong way round and round and round a rotary with a *Garda* hot on his tail. It had been ugly enough sitting in the passenger's seat.

Vi wasn't daunted for long. "About being on my nan's property..."

"Yes?"

Her hand shot out, and she plucked a few hairs from his head. Liam yelped and swerved, then rubbed at his scalp once he'd put the car back on course.

"Jesus, Vi! Has no one ever taught you to leave the driver alone?"

She smiled as she tucked the hairs into a smaller velvet bag that she'd pulled from her patchwork sack. "I will. Now."

He shot her a baleful look. "What have you in mind, a voodoo doll?"

She laughed. "An Irish voodoo doll? Never! It's Nan's recipes I'm thinking of. Somewhere in her writings is one fit for curing a trespasser. Something with tar to make you stick where you should be. A bit into your food or drink when you're not looking and my problem will be gone."

Liam grimaced. "As would be my gut. I've run across her 'recipes' before."

Vi nodded. "Good, then. This one has done its job already, and you know not to wander."

A fine threat indeed from a woman who'd been in a faint not long before. Liam would have to weigh the risks of actually letting her get to full strength.

"Pull in there," she said when they were just down the street from his family's pub. "That's my car, which means Da must be near."

Liam did as asked. Once parked, he came round to her side of the car and opened the door for her, earning a surprised sounding "thank you." Her dog hopped out and waited next to her on the curb as she slung her bag—and Liam's pirated hairs—over her shoulder.

"Did your father have any plans?" Liam asked.

"Just to catch up on life in Duncarraig," Vi said.

"Then he's sure to be in the pub."

When they were all inside, including Roger, Jamie came round the bar with a speed that could make him the first Irishman to win track and field gold at the Olympics.

"Welcome to my pub, Vi," he said, placing himself squarely in front of her and subtly nudging Liam aside.

"Yours and Da's," Liam muttered while his brother kissed her on the cheek.

Vi shot him an arch look. It wasn't jealousy he was feeling, so much as what he usually did when in Duncarraig—that his place in the world was being trampled flat by others. Liam beat his brother to a table and pulled out a chair for Vi, who thanked him again. Thinking he must not have had the same manners fifteen years ago, Liam sat opposite her.

"Vi's in need of a meal," he said to his brother, who lingered at her right hand.

"We've a ginger carrot soup today," Jamie said. "Would you like to start with that?"

"Since I can catch them pureed, I will," she replied, brows raised in Liam's direction. Then she sent a sunny smile to Jamie. "After the soup, I think a toasted cheese sandwich. And have you some lettuce and tomato slices? No mayonnaise, though. Liam here was saying that I've put on weight."

He'd said no bloody such thing and was about to point that out when he saw the laughter in her eyes. Threats of being snuck one of Nan's recipes weren't to be his sole punishment.

"He's got no eye for beauty, then," Jamie said.

"I always did like you best," Vi nearly purred.

Liam was sure his brother's tongue was going to be spiked with splinters from the wood of the floor by the time he rolled it back into his mouth.

"Anything for your dog?" Jamie managed to stammer with a nod toward Roger, who had curled up in front of the fireplace.

This time, Vi's smile was enough to light the town for a week. "No, but it's fine of you to have asked. I can tell you're the sort of man who likes dogs. Unlike some," she added, with a nod toward Liam.

Grand, now he was a dog hater. Next she'd have him defrauding aged nuns. Wait... That had been great-grandda Seamus's special talent.

"I'd like a bowl of the soup, too, if you don't mind," Liam said to his brother with the thought of moving him along.

"You know where the kitchen is," Jamie replied, never taking his gaze from Vi. "So tell me, Vi, do you plan to be visiting Duncarraig more often?"

Unwilling to listen to this exercise in flirtation any longer, Liam got himself a cup of soup, and one for Vi, too, so long as he was there. He and Jamie crossed paths as Liam returned to his seat. Jamie's smug smile was a hard one to take.

Once Liam had resettled at the table, Vi spoke. "Jamie says that my father has gone with yours to visit a bit."

Liam smiled. "My father's idea of visiting a bit is like saying that it rains a bit hereabouts. He'll be gone for hours yet."

"Then I'd say we have time for a chat," Vi said. "Are you going to tell me now what proof you have of Rafferty's gold?"

Liam gave a quick look around to see who might be listening. "When we're someplace with less ears, if you don't mind." He wanted his family as far out of his business as he could have them. Granted, when in the same town, that wasn't far, but a man could always hope. "After we eat, would you come back to my house?"

"Would it be just the two of us?"

The question confused him. "Your dog can chaperone if you're worried about appearances."

She laughed. "They've never worried me overmuch."

With that, she lifted her spoon and made short work of her soup. Liam had nearly finished his when Jamie reappeared with the rest of Vi's meal. After he'd set down the food, he pulled out the chair next to Liam as though he intended to stay. Liam hooked his foot round the chair's leg and drew it flush to the table. Jamie called Liam a word that he'd not heard since childhood and walked off.

"He's grown up handsome," Vi said.

"And spoilt, too," Liam replied, then softened his admittedly ill-tempered words. "But he's always been here for our parents, so he deserves everything they've given him. Even Cullen and Nora left town for a few years, but never Jamie."

She nibbled at her sandwich before asking, "And would you ever come back to stay?"

"No," he said automatically, until he recalled that he had little other place to be. "I don't know." He paused. "It's too far from the sea, I'm thinking."

"The sea," she echoed, and her smile stirred things in him that weren't purely physical. "I love that about my home in Ballymuir. I'm never far from the water."

"You're more beautiful now than you were at seventeen," he blurted, not really intending the thought to escape.

She laughed. "Flattery works better when there's a seed of truth, Rafferty."

There was a full forest of truth in what he'd said, but she had never taken praise well. Instead of unsettling her more, he asked her if she'd gone to art school in Cork as she'd always intended. He was surprised to hear that she hadn't. They talked a bit about his college experience in America, then Liam let her finish her meal in peace. She was almost done when Jamie came skulking back over.

"Have you nothing better to do?" Liam asked.

"No, but you do. I just took a call behind the bar. Meghan's complaining of a headache, and the school needs you to come take her home."

She no more had a headache than he did a family that respected his privacy, but there was nothing to be done for it.

"I'm sorry," he said to Vi. "Would you mind coming with me to gather her up?"

"Or you could stay here," Jamie offered.

"Go 'way, Jamie," Liam directed.

His brother shrugged. "Just offering a more pleasant alternative."

Vi stepped into the discussion. "Liam and I have some catching up to do, but thank you for the offer, Jamie."

"Might I at least keep your dog for you?"

"That would be grand, actually."

Jamie puffed like an overproud bantam rooster. "My pleasure."

"Oh, and do you think you could give a ring to Liam's house when my father reappears?" Vi asked while folding her napkin and putting it in the center of a plate that otherwise now held only a few crumbs.

"On the second, as it will get you back to me all the sooner," Jamie said.

Vi laughed, and Liam worked on keeping down his soup. Wee toady of a brother.

"Well then, my family's fully tended. Shall we see to yours?" she asked Liam.

"Let's." Liam stood and waited while Vi threw some quick praise Jamie's way about the fine meal he'd provided. Liam reached into his pocket and smacked a small handful of crumpled euros on the table.

"If it's not enough, let me know," he said.

Jamie picked up the money and without counting it replied, "It should be enough, that with the five I borrowed from your jacket pocket yesterday. It's not safe leaving money lying about like that. You never know where it might end up."

"I do, now," Liam replied.

Vi's hand in his, he made for the pub door before his brother had picked him to the bones.

* * *

As Vi sat in Liam's car, she was glad for the meal she'd eaten, but not the way it was now lurching about in her stomach. Liam had gone inside the drab beige-painted parish school to collect his daughter while Vi focused on collecting herself. Earlier at the pub when she'd asked Liam whether they'd be alone, this was Vi's concern, not some antiquated notion of propriety. Absorbing the knowledge that Liam had a child was a far simpler task than seeing her. Vi had faced down much in life, but never anything that hit quite so personally.

She watched as Liam and his daughter walked down the steps from the school building. Meghan was petite, yet even in the school's blue and green plaid skirt and oversized green jumper, she was far older looking than Vi had thought of a standard twelve-year-old as being.

They were nearly to the car now. On the surface of things, Meghan looked very little like her father. She was dark blond where he was dark. Her eyes were hazel and had only a hint of his eyes' shape to them. All of this came as welcome news. Had Vi seen more of Liam, she'd have been less able to maintain the semblance of a pleasant calm.

Meghan opened the back passenger door, flung her book bag inside, then followed herself. It was an act of high drama, with sulky glares and the car door slamming loudly behind her.

"Meghan, this is Vi Kilbride, an old family friend," Liam said as he started the car.

A family friend? That would be poor news indeed to Liam's mam, Vi thought. She moved the best she could in the confines of her seat belt and held out her hand to Meghan.

"It's grand to meet you," she said, accepting Meghan's limp and unwilling shake in return.

Meghan's mumbled response could have been a politeness or a go to hell, for all Vi could interpret. She turned back about, facing the windshield, satisfied that at least she'd done her duty.

Meghan's school had sat on the outskirts of town. Vi wasn't at all sure where Liam might have a house, but in a matter of moments, they were slowing in front of a tall, three-storied home, the ground floor of which appeared to have once been a shop. Liam pulled down a short brickwork drive to the house's left and then parked in a courtyard between the back of the house and a small two-storied carriage house.

Liam scarcely had the car turned off before Meghan grabbed her bag and bolted for the carriage house. Liam flung open his door.

"No running to your tower," he called.

Meghan pulled up short. She turned and glared at her father, who had exited the car. Vi had stopped, too, curious about this particular show.

Liam motioned toward the house's back door. "That way. And no foot-dragging, either," he added when she apparently paused an instant too long for his taste. All three of them were in the kitchen when he gave his next edict to Meghan. "Two aspirin and then to bed."

"But I'm feeling a lot better," his daughter replied. Vi marveled that she'd made the words sound so much like a threat. Amazing talent, that.

"I'm sure you are. And from here on, unless you can produce verifiable symptoms like a burning fever or a missing limb, don't be asking to come home again."

Meghan left the room. Vi hid a smile as she listened to the girl pound her way upstairs, feet dramatically heavy. Liam appeared less amused.

"Sorry about that. I'm easy game, yet," he said. "I figure we'll have worked our way through her repertoire about the time her mother returns for her."

"A manufactured headache is nothing too dire," Vi said.

"Yet. She's crafty."

This time Vi did laugh. "I wonder where she might be getting that? Speaking of which, now that your daughter's settled, would you care to show me your grand treasure map? For all the good it will do you without access to the land."

"It's no map," Liam replied. "But come this way."

He led her from the crisp new kitchen to a combination dining room and living room that would be lovely, indeed, if someone introduced some color to it. The floors were pale wood, unrelieved by carpet, as was the open stairway leading to the upper floors. The sofa and chairs in the living room were square-edged and made of cold leather of a colder white.

"So you like white?" she asked as he riffled through a briefcase on the dining room table.

"I like it well enough," he said.

Vi rubbed the fingers of her left hand together as she thought how fine the room would look with a smoky crimson on one wall, and the ceiling a buttery color. She started as she realized that this was the first time in weeks she'd thought about color as though it was a living thing, something to be stroked like a sleek cat.

Her mouth quirked at the image, for she'd always thought of Liam as a cat, too—cat's eyes, agile body, and hot to her touch.

"Ah! Found it." He pulled out a sheet of paper. "Come here, Vi, and have a look. This one first."

Vi stood beside him, forcing herself to focus less on the inviting warmth she sensed coming off him and more on what he wanted her to look at.

The paper was modern, the same as what spat from her hated, eternally uncooperative computer back home. The contents of the paper, however, came from years past. Vi took a moment to adjust to the photocopy of a page from a ledger of some sort. The writing was strongly embellished, lovely in an illegible sort of way. A few things did stand out. The first was a date of 1837 and the second was a notation for a sum paid to…. She frowned, trying to make out more. It appeared to be a sum paid to an Edward Rafferty.

"It's an account page from a jeweler in Kilkenny," Liam said. "It seems that a relative of mine sold him some gold."

She could imagine how Liam might see that as relevant in a hazy sort of way. "Treasure or none, it's possible that a Rafferty might have possessed gold, you know."

"Possible, but why so much? This was an enormous sum he received—nearly enough to send a whole family to America, which it so happens that Edward Rafferty did that very same year.

"And there's more." He flipped to the second sheet. "The jeweler also kept an inventory of the pieces he melted down, and their weights. That week he melted rings and brooches and the like, all of which might have been from his era. But look at this." Liam tapped a finger over another bit of curlicued script. "He melted something he described as a neck-collar, Vi."

Now that was not so simple to discount. Gold neck-collars could hardly have been standard fare. Could the legend be truth? If so, according to her nan's version, Vi was an heiress of sorts. Or at least the closest she would ever come to being one. Her heart beat faster, but she kept a calm demeanor before Liam.

"You need more than that," she said.

"I'm sure I'll be having more. I've contacted a woman at the National Museum. She says there's much of the same type of records regarding the Mooghaun Hoard.

"Muh-who?" came a voice from the stairway.

Vi looked up to see Meghan sitting there, no longer in her uniform, but in a pair of tight pink and black plaid trousers with a silver-studded belt. Colorful, at least, but angling toward mini-tartlike, Vi concluded with a mental shrug. The girl strolled down the stairs. She moved like Liam, with the same sort of innate grace. But it would do Vi no good to slow and make these small discoveries. She should flow on like a stream through the difficult moments.

"I've asked you not to wear those pants," Liam said. "And you might be thinking about cutting back on the eavesdropping, too."

Meghan lingered at the bottom of the stairway, her arms crossed over her black T-shirted chest. "I wasn't eavesdropping. I was coming downstairs for something to eat, okay?"

"It's Mooghaun," Vi said, avoiding the intergenerational spat. "That's the name of a place in County Clare where an amazing treasure of ancient gold jewelry was once unearthed. What pieces remain are in the National Museum in Dublin. I don't think there's a schoolchild within three hours drive of the display who hasn't been there."

"Museums are boring," the girl decreed.

Vi found very little in life boring, with the exception of her accountant's dire warnings regarding her level of savings. "And this from a girl whose family claims to have lost another such treasure? I'd think you'd be showing more interest."

"What treasure?" Meghan asked her father.

Liam looked as though Vi had already slipped him one of Nan's recipes. Whatever he was thinking he kept to himself as he tucked the papers back into his briefcase.

"You've not shared the family tale?" Vi asked, really quite surprised. It had been a regular one when Liam's grandda was still alive.

"No."

"And with you stewing over it as you have?"

Liam began to speak. "She—"

Meghan issued a dramatic sigh. "*She* is over here and *she* doesn't like being talked about like she's not here, okay?"

Vi was of the opinion that surly children were to be treated with firmness. Based on the tightness about his mouth, Liam appeared to consider them a source of aneurysm and best avoided.

"Understandable," she replied to Meghan, "though you could deliver the message with more manners. Let's have a seat and see if your da is up to telling the tale."

"She'd not be interested," Liam said.

Vi gestured in the girl's direction. "Is that so, Meghan?"

She shrugged, a marginal movement of one shoulder. "I dunno."

"Well, Liam?" Vi asked. "Perhaps it will appeal to yet another generation. Shall you give her a chance to decide?"

Time had an odd way of reeling back and smacking a man. Liam could recall sitting at his grandda's feet and hearing the tale of Rafferty's gold. Peat smoke had scented the front room in Grandda's house and his words had played almost like a movie in Liam's head. But he'd been a different child in a different world. His American daughter was about sound bites and images flashing dizzyingly quick on a flat-panel television screen.

But in many ways he'd just described himself, too. He was no longer about the romance of the tale, but far more interested in its utility. His current assets of tugs, crane-barges, and high-tech diving equipment were substantially less liquid than gold. And liquidity was something he desperately needed.

"The tale, Rafferty?" Vi prompted.

"Do you want to hear it?" he asked his daughter.

Her bored shrug was more of a positive answer than he'd expected. And while he'd prefer to let the whole idea of gold go silent until he'd completed his search, there was no graceful way out of this. Refusing to tell Meghan would only prompt her to ask one of her aunts or uncles, and that would spell disaster for discretion.

"Fine, then," he said. "Let's go sit."

They settled on the sleek white furniture by the massive, wall-mounted plasma television that Liam regretted spending a fool's fortune on, and he worked his way into the tale. "My grandda told the story much better, but it went something like this."

"Years ago, this land was a different place, occupied by rich and powerful outsiders with little connection to those who had lived here for generations. The English landlords paid so poorly for crops from a man's own field that even those with good fields were starving. Your great-great...well, I'd not be knowing how many times great... grandda Eoin Rafferty was one of the lucky few, for he still had strength to hold another job.

"He'd been hired by the Dunhills of Castle Duneen to work on a road that was to run straight and true to Kilkenny so that the Ormond earls would not have so far to travel." Liam thought it best not to tell Meghan that the road was being made shorter so Ormond could avail himself more quickly of Dunhill's wife, whom he'd made a mistress.

"Eoin had himself a sweetheart back in Duncarraig, so he was in a hurry to finish the road. It was his habit to work well ahead of the others. One afternoon, while he was digging from a trench to bring fresh soil for the roadbed, he hit upon something odd with his shovel. What do you think it was?"

Meghan rolled her eyes. "A U2 greatest hits CD?"

He laughed. "They're not quite that old, love." Except to a twelve-year-old. "Actually, your many-times-great-grandda Eoin hit upon gold."

"No lie?"

"No lie," Liam affirmed, using his daughter's sharp American diction before slipping back into the cadence he'd not lost in fifteen years gone from Ireland. "It was a grand treasure of old, hammered pieces, the kind of wealth all of the Raffertys put together never had."

"That's cool," Meghan said. "So what happened to it? Something must have or we'd be rich."

"Compared to most of the world, you are," Vi pointed out.

"You need to get out more," Meghan said to Vi, who looked as though she wasn't sure whether to laugh or lecture.

"Here's what happened," he said, drawing attention his way again. "Eoin slipped away from the others in the dead of the night, eluding thieves, liars, and friends turned foe. A wealth of gold was a hard test of loyalty, after all. Knowing that life would not be easy so long as their land was occupied, Eoin hid the treasure away somewhere in Duncarraig, vowing to use the pieces only to help another Rafferty when in need."

"Noble, indeed," Vi said. "If a wee bit limited in scope."

Liam ignored the nip at the family conscience. "Through the years the treasure was passed down from firstborn son to firstborn son, and the responsibility of keeping it passed down, too," he said. "The legend holds that pieces were smuggled away and sold to help a young Rafferty escape who'd been wrongly accused of killing an English soldier. When times grew even leaner, it's said that the gold was used to aid those Raffertys ready to face the trials of emigration.

"During the great hunger, what was left fell into the hands of a Rafferty who was always tugging at Authority's tail. In fact, it got so bad that this particular Rafferty found it advisable to head west until those he'd angered found greater troubles to address."

Which, Liam supposed was much like his choice of departing America, except he'd gone against the Rafferty flow and headed east to Ireland again.

"So then what?" Meghan asked.

"This Rafferty was enchanted by a girl in the village who the story says was the boldest and most beautiful of all. I've heard said she had glorious red hair of a deeper hue than any fire. Rather like Vi's."

"We've talked of flattery already," Vi said. "On with the story."

She was a hard woman, Vi Kilbride. Liam continued. "Rafferty was to flee to Connemara, a land to the west viewed most savage and inaccessible by the English. Travel there was no easy thing, and he felt no comfort in leaving the family treasure behind. He entrusted it to his bewitching redhead, who promised to hand it back on his return. But—"

"It was a shock to all when he came back with a wife heavy with child," Vi said, most disapprovingly. "And—"

"—with a wife and a child soon to care for, too, he begged the treasure back from the redheaded woman," said Liam, wresting control of the tale back from the redhead in the room. "But this woman claimed no knowledge of it. She quickly married another man and lived out her life in Duncarraig—"

"—and with no riches, either," Vi cut in. "Tis likely your faithless ancestor squandered the gold on drink and more women, then blamed my own blood."

"'Your own blood?'" Meghan echoed. "You mean you're related to that woman?"

Vi nodded. "It's said she was a grandmother—times removed—of mine."

Meghan sat a bit straighter, the bored adolescent slouch gone. "That's cool, too."

Vi smiled. "As I felt at your age."

"So this gold's, like, missing?" Meghan asked.

"Exactly," Liam replied. "The gold might be gone, but its tale stays with the Raffertys."

He hesitated before adding more, but he knew it would do no good to hide his activities from her. He'd heard Meghan snooping about the house at night often enough. Wanting to protect his daughter from his dire financial situation and this last-gasp search effort to repair it, Liam chose his words carefully.

"And I don't want you sharing this with the rest of the family," he said, "but I've decided it would be fun to have a look for it, so long as we're here."

"And if you find it, it's ours?" she asked.

Liam nodded. "Exactly, again."

"Not quite so," said Vi.

She was smiling, but Liam didn't much like the look of it. It was beyond sharp-edged, bordering on lethal, in fact.

"And why not quite so?" he asked.

She rose from the sofa. "Step into the kitchen with me. *Now.*"

CHAPTER SIX

A red-hot ember is easily rekindled.
—IRISH PROVERB

Had the man no sense at all? Once they'd rounded the corner to the kitchen, Vi closed her eyes and briefly tried the lavender-envisioning bit, hoping for an endless calming field, flowers swaying in a gentle breeze. No bloody luck, though. The best she was getting was a plain of razor-sharp steel pikes, which was either phallic or barbaric, and a sharp sign of her current feelings toward Rafferty.

"You're not readying to nap again, are you?" Liam asked.

Vi opened her eyes and ignored his half-smile.

"For argument's sake—" she began.

"You've always liked those well enough," he said, strolling closer.

"No baiting, Rafferty. For argument's sake," she repeated, giving him a narrow-eyed glare that she hoped made obvious the risk to his life should he cut in again, "let's say you find the treasure, either on or off my land. By what right is it yours?"

"I'm the eldest son of the eldest son, and so on." He waved his hand as if brushing away the centuries like so much dust. "It would be mine to do with as I see fit."

"Really, now? Have you done 'way with your da?"

"Of course not. I asked for the treasure as my twenty-first birthday gift. Da agreed, of course, for it was cost-free."

"Optimistic of you," she said. "And there's no one else who would have a claim, you're thinking?"

"No," he replied with blunt certainty.

Perhaps it was that she felt the weight of history more than most, which was possible given the years of Nan's teachings. Or perhaps it was that Liam had decided in advance to be an eejit about this. Having witnessed his stroll with the radar-thing, Vi was leaning in favor of his eejit status.

"Not, say, the eldest daughter next in line after Nan? The descendant of one who had been gifted the treasure?" she asked helpfully.

"Now, Vi—" he began in a long-suffering tone.

She drew a breath between clenched teeth. "A word of advice to you. A sentence begun with 'now' and immediately followed by a female's name is one that'll leave you with bloody stumps below your knees."

He laughed, which did nothing to aid his cause. "Much as I like my legs, I'll have to risk them. Vi, should it be found, it's Rafferty treasure and always has been. An act that was wrong isn't made right by time."

Finally he'd said something that made sense, though they sat on opposite sides of the issue. "Exactly so. Which is why your hunt won't be taking place beneath my nose."

Liam's dark brows drew together, making him look nearly fierce. "What have you to fear if I'm on your grandmother's land?"

Fury pushed hard against her chest. "My grandmother's? It's *my* land. *My* land and *my* house and you've stolen enough from me already."

With that, Vi fell into a confused silence. That odd word— *stolen*—had come from some ill-aired corner of her brain. She prayed that Liam wouldn't note it, for she had no explanation. But Vi knew he would pick it up because for all his faults he'd never been a poor listener.

"Stolen?" he repeated.

She turned her back to him, looking out the window above the sink at the ivory-stuccoed carriage house beyond. Meghan's tower, he'd called it. Vi fancied a tower of her own, just then. Liam walked round so she couldn't lose him from her vision.

"Stolen?" he asked again.

She forced herself to draw a deep breath. She had drifted so near the fringes of her personal universe, but now she was centered again.

"My heart," she said. "I once felt as though you stole my heart." Yes, that had to be what had nudged the word loose. Of course it was.

"And you think you didn't steal mine?" he fired back and then shook his head as the anger eased from his features. "I'd forgotten how you can set me off, and with Meghan listening, too, I'm sure," he said in a lower voice.

She didn't want to think of Meghan just now. "All I'm asking is that you admit nothing's exactly so. The treasure's neither exactly yours nor mine."

He gave a humorless laugh. "So long as you bar me from your land, the treasure's exactly lost."

"What would you have me do?" she asked.

He walked three long strides to the kitchen table and swung round to face her again. "Let me look, at least. I need this, Vi. I need to move forward, to feel as though I'm making progress. I can't be idle much longer without losing my mind."

There was a note of desperation in his voice that she'd never heard before. Vi smoothed her hands over the loose-fitting bronze top she wore, trying to lose a few wrinkles from that, at least. Aye, this treasure discussion was about nothing and everything, with the unspoken crying out loudest of all.

"I'll need to think about it," she answered, buying time, which was all she could afford.

In truth, until today she'd never considered the treasure as other than long-squandered. If it did exist, what would it mean to her? To Liam? And for that matter, to Nan and those who had come before them?

Liam appeared to relax. "Fine, then. Think today, and tomorrow you'll tell me?"

She shook her head. "I'll tell you when I'm ready. Now I'll be walking back to the pub."

"I'll run you back."

"My legs still work," she replied.

New voices sounded from the front room—booming male sorts that precipitated the heavy tread of Meghan's feet upstairs. Vi quickly realized that she was hearing none other than her da, but with more enthusiasm than she was accustomed to. And with finer timing than usual, too.

"You've found me," she said as she reentered the room with Liam at her heels.

"From what I've heard said today all one ever had to do was look for Liam. Your nan never told me you were soft on a Rafferty, Violet."

Liam's father nodded. "You'd no sooner drop her with your mother each summer than she'd be at our doorstep looking for my boy," he said. "Regular as a clock, she was."

James Rafferty had the right of it, though Vi didn't much appreciate the tidbit sharing with her father. Vi had indeed viewed Liam as a special gift, straight from Nan's spirits to her. Even now, when she trusted him none, she also found herself desiring him—the very last thing she wanted to do. She looked about for a means of escape.

"Did you happen to stop by the pub, Da?"

He shook his head. "No, we were straight here. James wanted to show me the fine job Brian and his crew did on renovating Liam's house."

Vi worked up a regretful sigh for the elder Rafferty. "Ah, well, much as I'd like us to stay and visit more, I've left Roger at the pub with Jamie. We'd best be moving on. A bit of a pest, he can be."

"Roger or Jamie?" Liam asked, humor dancing in his brown eyes.

"Apparently, both," Vi replied. "Liam, I'll be out to Nan's tomorrow, getting in my first day of real work, and with no interruptions, if you please."

He frowned. "Then I'll be seeing you...?"

"When I arrive," she said simply.

Vi linked her arm through her father's. "*Slán,*" she said to the Raffertys junior and senior and gave a glance up the stairs to see the shade of Meghan slip round the corner. "*Slán* to you, too," she called, then made good on her escape.

"You needn't have rushed so," Da complained as they walked in the direction of the pub. "It was inhospitable of you."

"I had my reasons," she replied, skirting past a mother carrying a fractious toddler, his legs kicking as though he meant serious harm.

"Did Nan ever talk to you of Rafferty's gold?" she asked her da.

"She did," Da said. "Though she made it clear that as a mere male of her blood, it could never be mine." He smiled. "The sting was lessened by the knowledge that it was imaginary."

"And you're sure of that?"

"Of course I am. With my father so long dead, we were always wanting for something in that little house. If not for an inheritance, I'd never have made it out of Duncarraig and to university. If only some distant relative would up and die and do the same for Danny."

Vi slowed. "Who did Nan inherit from?"

Da tucked his hands into his suit jacket pockets and ducked his head to fight the biting wind that had begun pushing through town. "A second cousin from County Laois. I think I might have seen her once at a family Christmas."

Miraculous, Vi thought. Miraculously convenient. And how very like Nan.

Liam's da was trolling for a chat when Liam wanted none. He'd managed to avoid conversation alone with Da for three whole weeks, which was perhaps the sole advantage of being part of a large family. Da watched all and managed the Rafferty children with a quiet sort of authority. Apparently, the time had come to draw Liam back into the fold, and there was no escape. His father pulled out a chair from the dining table and motioned for Liam to do the same.

"So have you had a fine day?" his father asked once they'd sat.

"Fine enough, for we've had little rain," he replied. It seemed a decent answer to give a publican well accustomed to chat about weather and sport. Da remained unsatisfied, though.

"Grand, then," he said in a distracted way, and brushed an imaginary speck of whatever off the table's glass top. After a moment, he gave up the pretense of casual behavior and fixed Liam with a level look. "I don't want you to think that I'm not pleased to have you home, son, because I am. Still, it's time to tell me why you're here."

Liam damn well refused to let his family have a hint of his crisis. He'd been the one to break free of the Rafferty mandate of shoulder-to-shoulder life in Duncarraig. He'd been the one to work from Aberdeen to Auckland. Knowing that after all of his successes, he'd come home this time a nearly bankrupt business partner to a modern-day pirate was something he chose to keep private, and for obvious reasons.

"There's nothing wrong with a visit now and again, is there?" he asked.

"Not a thing," Da agreed. "But visits don't usually include enrolling a child in school and developing a sudden deafness when asked how long you might be staying."

"I needed a change, that's all."

"You've not spoken of your work once since you arrived. No tales of deep-diving or of oil tankers pushed up on rocks and cargoes shifted in typhoons. And in three weeks, I have yet to see you take a phone call from Alex or call your secretary in Boston. I've not missed this, Liam."

Liam shrugged. "I'm a bit burned out is all. A decade working without time to even stop and think can do that to a man."

"It can, but three weeks is a long time to be smelling the roses, and with them not even in bloom."

"Long, but needed," Liam said, thinking to himself, *and likely permanent unless I find the means to start again.*

"You're the best judge of what you need," Da replied. "Just remember to get moving before you forget how. Cullen already has the job of lazy Rafferty quite well covered."

Cullen did conserve effort better than anyone Liam had met. "His job is safe, Da."

"So you've nothing else bothering you?" Da asked. "No reason you'd be working that jaw muscle? You've always done it when vexed, you know."

Liam relaxed the best he could. "The after-effects of Vi Kilbride, I'm sure."

"She's a challenge, that one," his father agreed. "But the jaw-flexing has been going on longer than she's been in town."

Liam made a mental note to rid himself of the habit. It wouldn't do to be perpetually transparent.

"Fatherhood, then," he offered.

Da rubbed at his forehead with one hand. "No easy job," he agreed. "But I'm thinking that's not it, either. Liam, I can't make you talk, and you're far too old to be sent to your room for refusing to do so. The best I can do is tell you that my ears still work, even if my knees are going bad."

"And I thank you for that," Liam said. "But really, it's nothing more than the usual grief, and nothing I can't work my way around."

Da smiled. "Spoken like a Rafferty." He pushed back from the table and winced a bit as he stood. Liam hated to see this. He still thought of his father as he'd been fifteen years ago, not now, with his bad knees and hair a solid silver-gray where it had once been a mix of light and dark.

"Now, then," his da said. "It's back to the pub for me before your mother misses me too much. And you might go chase wee Miss Meghan from the stairway where she's been listening and tell her that there will be no more avoiding school, eh?"

Aye, the knees might be bad, but the ears just fine.

Liam saw his da off, feeling less put out by the attempted meddling than he thought he would. Perhaps he was mellowing, he thought. Or more likely, Da had hit on the proper degree of subtlety this time about.

Liam walked the stairs to Meghan's room, contemplating his best course of action. She was hurting and had to be deeply missing her mother, whom she e-mailed many times daily. And Liam hurt for her. But Meghan would be here for another five months and would have to adjust. Perhaps it was time to reward good behavior not yet arrived. Which, Liam admitted, was a convoluted way to think of a bribe. He stopped in front of his daughter's door and raised his fist to knock. He'd rather face down the legion of claimants and attorneys assembling in America than he would one unhappy girl.

He rapped on the door. "Meghan?"

No answer.

He gave one more try and with a louder call.

Still nothing.

Knowing he'd likely get his head bitten off for doing it, he swung open the door. The room was chaos—girl-style. Clothing and disemboweled CD cases lay on the floor like so many victims of adolescent angst. The creator of the mess sat on her unmade bed, headphones plugged into her ears and eyes closed as her head bounced to a tune playing loudly enough that headphones and all, he could hear it across the room.

"Meghan?" This time he'd nearly bellowed.

She opened her eyes. "You calling me?" Her voice was equally loud, competing with the music in her head.

"Take off the headphones," he said while pantomiming the same.

His daughter gave him an eye roll, but did so.

"Headache's improved, I see," Liam commented.

The momentary blankness in her expression told him that she'd forgotten her excuse of the day, but she quickly recovered. "All better. I've been listening to music ever since Grandda got here with that other man."

She was a poor liar, thank God.

"Right," he said, but spared her another eavesdropping lecture. "I was thinking just a few minutes ago that for having been to Ireland four times now, you've seen precious little, except for the drive from the airport to here."

She shrugged. "It all looks the same to me. Green and rainy and people in stupid clothes."

She was testing him well, but Liam held fast to his temper. Someone had to be an adult in this room, and it was his poor job.

"Yes, well, it's the weekend coming up, and I think we could both use some time away from Duncarraig. What do you say to a trip to Dublin the day after tomorrow? We could stop by that gold exhibit Vi was talking about—"

"Wow." Her deadpan delivery was spot-on perfect, and Liam was almost amused.

"Fine, then, so museums aren't your first choice. Would it help to know there's fast food on Grafton Street and even some shopping malls to be found?"

She jumped from the bed, limbs quivering the way a hunting dog's might when catching the scent of prey. "Malls?"

"Malls, though perhaps not as large as what you're used to," he affirmed, knowing he'd just consigned himself to shopping hell. "And all you have to do is go to school tomorrow and promise me that you'll do the same every school day while you're here."

Meghan narrowed her eyes and placed her hands on her hips.

"So, can I shop, or are you just going to let me look at stuff?"

"We'll settle on a fair budget."

"What kind of fast food?"

"I'm not so sure there's a Taco Bell," he said, naming her favorite. "But I've seen golden arches and fried chicken for certain."

"So money and shopping and American food?"

"And a museum trip."

"Cool, except the museum thing." With that, she stuck on her headphones once again.

"The museum is non-negotiable," he warned, and got a false smile and a "whatever" in response. He'd scarcely cleared her door when it slammed behind him.

Liam chose to take the encounter as a success, though a small one. He had one wee female lured and a far more complex redhead to go.

Friday morning, Vi was determined to stop drifting and actually get work done. She'd agreed to give Da a lift to Duncarraig again and earned sharp words from her mother for the effort. It seemed that Mam had grown accustomed to having Da home and didn't appreciate having her errand-runner freed for the day. As for Vi, the sooner she had Nan's belongings sorted, the sooner she could retreat to Ballymuir and reassemble her Mam-armor to the point where jabs about selfishness and such no longer hurt.

Soon after Da was dropped at James Rafferty's house, Vi nipped into the work. Box after box of trash landed in the tip until the interior of Nan's house was almost familiar again. Her painted furniture stood out bright and cheery in each room. Vi segregated random items still fine enough for charity but without any memory attached to them into the house's small second bedroom. The rest—and there was much, for she was no expert at letting go—sat in the front room.

It was a cool enough day that Vi had started a fire in the fireplace, using as fuel a collection of scrap wood that Da's friend had left behind. Bags of Nan's financial records sat near the blaze, waiting to join those Vi had already consigned to the flames. She was, though, hanging onto all check registers and correspondence, for there she might find some proof of Nan's timely inheritance...or gold-peddling.

Overheated, Vi moved from the hearth. She stripped off the worn men's flannel shirt she'd filched from her brother Pat and pulled the damp fabric of the black silk camisole beneath it away from her skin. The camisole had been a gift from one of her lovers, lasting far longer than he had. She'd just reknotted her hair, cooling the nape of her neck, when a knock sounded at the door.

Roger moved from the fireplace and stood in the entry, tail wagging and bark sounding.

"Who's there?" Vi called.

"It's Liam."

"Inconstant hound," she said to her dog. "I thought you didn't like the man."

She glanced at her discarded shirt, still draped over a chair back, but decided against shrugging it on.

Last night, she'd done much thinking. She knew that Liam would seek the gold with or without her. She'd decided that in order to protect her interests, she must at all costs do two things: keep him off-balance and in sight.

Vi pulled open the door and took pleasure in watching him mask his surprise at her skimpy dress.

"I thought I'd told you I'd come find you when I was ready," she said.

"I, ah..." He looked over her shoulder. "I see you have a fire burning. Might I come in?"

"Of course," she said, ushering him over the threshold. She closed the door and smiled at the way he shot straight to the flames, not once glancing her way. Liam off-balance was proving a pitifully easy goal to achieve.

"Speaking of welcomes," she said, "I've decided to let you walk Nan's fields, though I'm not sure what good it will do you."

"Grand," he replied, then added in a casual sort of way, "It is warm in here, is it not?"

Without saying more, he pulled off the creamy-colored turtleneck he'd been wearing, then tossed it to the chair that held her shirt. Before turning back to her, he pulled his cell phone from his back pocket and placed it atop his shirt. When he'd finished, Vi was presented a view she'd not had in years. That, she supposed, was her punishment for being smug. And a fine punishment it was.

Liam was a man grown, not the lean boy/man who lingered in her memory. He was sun-kissed, muscled, glorious...and he knew it. She hungered to set her mouth against the warm skin at the base of his throat and to let her fingertips trace the unfamiliar scar that now ran along his left bicep. And after that, she'd trail her hand across his chest and then follow the thin line of dark hair arrowing to his navel...which of course would lead her even further down to the wonderfully gripping fit of his denims.

Liam was equally occupied looking at her, and she knew the changes were marked. She was no longer a girl of seventeen, but had a woman's breasts and rich curves.

"I had two thoughts," he said quite calmly, as though they weren't busy cataloguing each other's bodies.

"Ah, a good day for you, then," she replied, at least letting her words nip at him.

He raised a brow as if inquiring about her need to spar. "The first thought was that this house isn't the original," he said, prowling closer.

She didn't back down, and never would.

He ran one index finger along the camisole's black ribbon strap, and she shivered beneath his touch.

"In fact, I'd wager the original house didn't even stand here, or someone would have reused at least part of it," he said, then followed the lace curve of the black fabric to the V between her breasts.

Fine game, indeed, she thought. It had been madness to underestimate Liam Rafferty. Her nipples were rising even before a direct caress.

"Really?" she commented, also ignoring the heat between her legs, for it was beginning to make her too aware of how long it had been since her body had accepted a man.

"I'm almost certain." He lightly pressed his fingertips against one plump curve.

"So you're looking in the field for the original house because you think the treasure might be beneath it?" she asked, knowing the question was shallow at best, as was her breathing.

He withdrew his fingers and brushed his nails against each of her raised nipples. "Aye, and if I don't find the remnants of a house beneath ground, a cistern or other hiding place would surprise me none."

Vi's limbs were growing languorous and her will wobbly, but she was not quite ready to cede victory.

"Interesting," she said, then permitted her hand to move as she'd imagined. It was a slow journey, his muscles tightening beneath her touch. His skin was hot—wonderfully so. She watched as his eyes grew darker and the set of his mouth more tense. He wore no belt, and when she reached the closure to his denims, she worked the top snap without ever letting her gaze break from his. Only his quick intake of breath gave evidence of his surprise.

"Quite interesting," he agreed, still sounding dry as a professor giving a mathematics lecture.

'I'll let you look," she said, winnowing two fingers beneath the loosened fabric. "But only if you promise to share. What you learn, that is," she added. Pulling off an innocent smile was dicey, indeed, but she managed.

"Generous," he replied, then swallowed hard as she withdrew her fingers only to trace them over the outline of what was a finely burgeoning erection. She had to stop after a moment, though, for she feared she was losing her control before he would lose his.

"You'll share, then?" she asked.

"For a bit of gold, I can be persuaded," Liam said in a voice that had grown raspy. He came closer yet and moved his hands behind her head, freeing her hair from its knot. To Vi, the sound of her hairclip hitting the tile floor was as loud as if Nan's iron pot had tumbled to the hearth. She didn't let herself jump, though.

"You're kissed with it among all this fire," he finished, drawing her hair forward over her shoulders, then weaving his fingers through it where it flowed to her breasts.

"Gold's a fine sight," she agreed. In truth she didn't care what shades he might find in her hair, so long as he kept touching her.

"Glorious," he said, his brown eyes intent with the same passion that was making her tremble. He ran his thumbs across her cheekbones, then cupped the back of her head, tilting his own as though regarding a painting. "The most beautiful ever."

He was stealing the moment from her, and she was glad he was a thief.

"I want to know all your secrets, Vi," he said low into her ear.

Her breath hitched. "My secrets?"

His smile was slow and seductive as a lazy summer day. "If you're hiding more gold, of course."

She relaxed, which was no great feat with Liam's touch to distract her. "Ah, of course. And where do you think I might be hiding it?"

"I've some ideas," he said, toying with the button at the top of her khakis.

"Any good ones?" She'd have said *decent ones,* except her own thoughts were far from pure.

"One or two," he replied, then let his hand move from the button he'd opened to trace the V of her camisole again.

Aye, he was a master at brinksmanship. Vi couldn't bear the anticipation, so she ran her hands up then down his arms...once... twice, but it wasn't enough. She moved closer—so close that her breasts were brushing against him. It was moments like this that she especially loved her height. She was not to be ignored, not to be denied. She reached around and settled her hands on the firm cheeks of his bum.

He leaned his forehead against hers, and it was damp with perspiration. "So shall I search?"

"If you must," she said, then inhaled a shaky breath and moved her arms round his neck as he returned the favor of cupping her bum and pushing against her in a slow rhythm that flayed her self-control. She'd not felt anything so incredible in ages.

She was ready to be done with the layers of clothing between them, that much was certain. But she'd not be the one to capitulate. Using one hand, he pushed her hair aside and nipped the top of her shoulder. Vi could scarcely hold in her cry.

Then, finally—when she was sure she could bear no more, he slowly worked down the zipper on her khakis and slipped his hand beneath the elastic top of her low-cut panties. He touched her once, and she gasped, realizing how very close she was to coming apart.

"Liam, I—"

He cut off her words with his own. "Let me."

Before she could explain that letting him was the least of her issues, his cell phone began to ring.

Liam hesitated.

"Leave it," she said, trying to ignore its shrill, demanding tones.

He slipped his hand away from her. "Can't," he said. "It might be business."

She would have chided him a bit, except for his grim voice. Business was evidently no source of pleasure in Liam's life. And her pleasure had begun to ease, and her common sense return. What had she been thinking, in any case? She'd made some progress removing clutter, but there wasn't a surface in the cottage that'd she actually call fit for bare skin.

While she began to refasten her khakis, Liam answered his phone, shooting her an apologetic look at the same time.

"What is it?" she heard him say to the caller.

Vi thought of reaching for the shirt she'd left on the chair, but she'd then be in his range, and the urge to touch him would grow too strong again.

"No, Meghan," Liam said "We don't have the money to be opening a Taco Bell in Dublin."

Vi didn't even bother to hide her smile. Business, indeed.

"Yes, I'm sure," he said. "But you're twelve, a child. You don't have any idea—" He walked to the fireplace, his usual smooth strides replaced by a choppier, impatient gait. "Well, I'm sorry if you didn't like the way that sounded, but.... Meghan?" He frowned in Vi's direction. "She hung up on me."

"I'd gathered," she said. "I also gather that she has a business enterprise in mind?"

"Not one I'm wanting. A Dublin Taco Bell?" He shook his head in apparent disbelief, then tucked his phone into the right back pocket of his still-open denims.

Vi tried to pull her focus away from what might have been. "Not what every city needs, eh?" she asked.

"If you're twelve and can eat endlessly, I'm thinking it might be. But I'm neither twelve nor looking for a career change." After he'd spoken, his expression darkened for an instant. Intrigued, Vi watched as he erased the frown.

He took his shirt from the chair and pulled it over his head. Once he'd pushed his arms through the sleeves, he spoke again. "Grand timing the child had."

Vi looked around the room. "It wasn't all that bad. I'm not quite sure where we'd have ended up in all this mess."

"I'd have improvised." He nearly smiled while tucking in his shirt and refastening his denims. "And you'd not have complained, either."

"Nor would have you," she replied, doing what she could to keep his mood running in a lighter direction.

"True enough," he said. "But Meghan's call also puts back in mind why I'd come here in the first place. I'm taking her for an overnight in Dublin tomorrow. I thought she might like to see the Mooghaun gold. Would you like to come?"

Vi hid a smile at his unintended double entendre. He could hardly know that all these minutes later, her body still craved his touch.

"Very much," she replied.

He prowled closer, and she could smell the slightly woodsy scent of his skin.

"We are talking about Dublin, are we not?" he asked.

"That," she said with decent authority, considering the other thoughts now elbowing their way to the front of her mind. Aye, that and more...

He grinned, and she could no more fight back her own smile than she could tame her hunger for him.

"I'm glad to see we're understanding each other," he said, before cupping the back of her head and kissing her. "I'll be to your parents' house at seven, then. Will you be ready?"

"More than you can imagine."

"I've an idea how ready," he replied, his fingers still woven beneath her hair.

She tipped back her head, relishing his touch, and he settled a kiss against her throat, where her pulse already beat as strongly as a *bodhran* in an expert drummer's hands.

Vi pulled her thoughts together, no easy thing with the kisses he still feathered downward. "So...you know where they live?"

Liam paused and brought his gaze level with hers. "Your mam and da? Your da's with mine. He'll draw me a map...unless you'd like to just now," he said before putting his mouth against hers.

"Maybe in a minute," she whispered against his lips.

Liam chuckled before kissing her hard and fast.

"I'm thinking it will prove to be an educational weekend," he said as he stepped away from her.

"Quite," Vi said, damning the man for being a wee bit of a tease, bringing her nearly back to full fire, then leaving her to burn alone.

"Seven, then," he said and was gone.

Vi walked the few paces to the front door he'd just closed, leaned against the cool wood, and laughed with joy. It seemed forever since she'd felt this vital, blood rushing from head to toes and mind whirling. "Well met, Rafferty," she murmured, still smiling. He remained her best challenge, adversary...and match. "Well met, indeed."

CHAPTER SEVEN

There's no stopping the force of a going wheel.
—IRISH PROVERB

"Meet the mother before you marry the girl" had been advice once offered up by Liam's grandda. Now, Liam had no intention of marrying Vi or anyone else, as one failed marriage was more than sufficient. Still, at a few minutes past seven on a fine Saturday morning, as Vi's da introduced his wife to Liam, Grandda's words resounded loudly. If Liam were intending to marry, he would make damn sure he didn't meet this mother too very often. Maeve Kilbride was one of those women who exuded disapproval from the very pores of her skin.

"You're from Duncarraig, then?" she asked as they waited for Vi to make her way downstairs.

Liam sat very still in the armchair offered, for the small round table next to it was crowded with fussy porcelain figurines of women in frilly dresses. He hated to think what she'd do if one were accidentally sent floor-bound.

"I am," he said.

"And what do you do there?"

He wished he could give the first smart-arsed answer that had struck him—*little as possible*—simply to see if she could look any less pleased. He knew one thing for certain, he'd done the right thing in having Meghan wait in the car.

"Actually, I live in America now," he diplomatically replied, as he'd been raised to be more polite than naturally inclined.

Maeve brightened. "Ah, grand!"

Perhaps she was one of those deluded souls who thought that all who lived in America were rich. Hell, he'd once believed it.

"And you do...?" she prompted.

"This and that," he replied in lieu of offering up his financial particulars. "I'm somewhat between projects at the moment."

"I see."

Heredity hadn't played at all true. It would take much practice, indeed, for Vi to perfect the squint-down-from-bridge-of-the-nose look that Maeve Kilbride specialized in.

Just then, Vi came downstairs, fat overnight bag in one hand and a russet-colored wool jacket of some sort in the other. She wore a long-sleeved dress made of sleek fabric. The subtle hues and pattern were unusual, making Liam think of oak leaves readying to fall—a far too poetic thought for him. Of course, the way it caressed her breasts and waist made him think of getting her out of it—an idea more within his normal realm.

Liam rose. "Your dress suits you," he said when she'd made the landing.

She smiled. "It should. I recycled some of my old painted silks to make it."

"Efficient," her da said.

Vi laughed. "Lack of money will do that to a person."

Her mother muttered something to herself and began rearranging figurines that hadn't moved.

"Ready, then?" Liam asked Vi.

"Almost," she replied before turning to her da. "Now, you'll keep an eye on Roger, right?"

He nodded. "I will."

"And no table scraps, if you please. He's too spoilt already."

"I'll do my best to keep him away from them." Her father's smile made Liam suspect that he meant otherwise.

Liam watched as Vi hugged her da with her freest arm and gave her mother a lightning-quick peck on the cheek.

"We'll be seeing you tomorrow night, then," she said.

Liam said his goodbyes and opened the door for Vi, who fairly shot through it. He knew nothing of the way she and her parents got along. In his experience, it had always been Vi and Nan, and the rest of the world be damned. When he offered to carry Vi's bag, she assured him that she was well capable. He'd had no doubt. He was merely exercising his manners and at the same time finding an excuse to at least touch her hand.

"Mam wasn't too rough on you, was she?" Vi asked once they were walking to the car, which he'd pried into a tight spot on the other side of the street.

"Not at all," he replied, knowing that Vi had faced far worse in dinner with Una. At least Maeve Kilbride carried no preconceived notions.

Vi laughed. "Liar. Anything associated with me displeases her. I'm too unconventional...making my own clothes, living as an artist, not cooking worth a damn, and now, horror of horrors, taking a night in Dublin with a man."

"You didn't mention our chaperone?" Liam asked, nodding toward Meghan who sat in the car perfecting her sulk.

"Mam would just accuse me of corrupting more youth. As it is, she's convinced I put a spell on Pat and Danny to have them move in with me."

They arrived at the car, and Liam opened the passenger door. "Adults in the front, which means you'll have to move on into the back," he said to his daughter.

Meghan glared at Vi. "I still don't know why you have *her* coming."

He hadn't imagined this would be such a beast of a problem. "I thought you might like a shopping partner."

Beside him, Vi shuddered. "We're shopping? You didn't tell me that."

Liam was beginning to sense that he'd made a series of tactical errors.

"This sucks," Meghan muttered just loudly enough for Vi to hear.

Liam drew a deep breath, preparing for a blistering parental-type lecture, but Vi set her overnight bag on the curb and grabbed hold of the tweed of his jacket.

"Time for a chat," she said, drawing him away from the car. "Did you not tell Meghan I was coming?" she asked once they were out of earshot.

"On the way here, I did."

"On the way *here?* So she's had twenty minutes to adjust?" Vi finished by muttering something in Irish that sounded to Liam as though it addressed the utility of asses' tails and stupid men. His Irish was beyond rusty, so he took comfort in the thought that he'd misheard.

"I didn't think Meghan would mind you coming along," he said in self-defense. "Anything to help her avoid speaking to me directly seems to please her well enough."

"Have you been living in a monastery since I last saw you? Have you no insight into a female's mind?"

Now was likely not the time to note his insight into a certain redheaded female's body, he decided. "Not bloody much, it seems."

She tapped him on the chest with two fingers. "She wanted this to be the two of you, just a girl and her da, you eejit."

"And when was I to grasp this? Yesterday when she jammed on her headphones and ignored me, or when she hung up on me because I won't open a bloody Taco Bell?"

"Which has nothing to do with what's really going on. She's in a land not hers, her mother's in another part of the world, and she's frightened. She's pretending she's tough enough to take what's been thrown at her, is all."

"And this requires her to behave like a shrew? Why can't females just always say what they're thinking?"

Vi smiled. "For fear of terrifying the men. We've been raised to care for the weak, after all."

"Grand joke."

"No joke at all. Now you wait here while I try to unravel this mess," Vi said before returning to the car.

"Right," Liam muttered.

When she seemed deep enough in talk with Meghan, he edged closer. If this exchange was to be a window into the female psyche, he'd not be down-curb whistling to the morning sun.

"Your da means well," Vi was saying by the time he'd gotten close enough. "He's just unpracticed."

Fat joke, there, too. God knew he'd gotten practice aplenty in the past weeks, and it wasn't as though Vi had any experience at all.

"I'll give you the choice," she said to Meghan. "You can carry on with your da and I'll stay here, or you can let me come to Dublin with you. I'll not be hurt either way, though I'd like the chance to see the city with you."

"Why?" Meaghan asked.

Vi shrugged. "Why not? I might learn something."

"From me? Yeah, right."

"Why not from you? You've lived places and seen things I never will."

"I guess."

"So, shall I go back in the house or come along?"

Meghan was silent so long that Liam itched to step in and reassert himself. A pointed look from Vi slowed him. Without another word, Meghan exited the car, opened the rear door, and climbed back in. It was a tenuous peace, but Liam recognized it as the best he'd get. He loaded Vi's bag and got behind the wheel, thankful that the weekend was short and his patience long.

As the traffic grew thicker and they neared Dublin, Vi asked herself yet again why she had felt capable to act as intermediary between the warring nations Rafferty. Having no stake in the ultimate outcome did give her a measure of objectivity, but it also had her thinking that while Liam's child dragged him through shopping malls—places lauding despicable plastic conformity, not that Vi had a firm opinion—she would retreat to a long, hot shower and a glass of wine. Surely she deserved that much.

Vi shifted ever so slightly in her seat to see if Meghan had altered her cocooned state, headphones in place and eyes closed. She had opted for frozen silence soon after her father told her they'd first be visiting the museum. If the girl didn't move soon, Vi would have to crawl in back and check for a pulse.

Beside her, Liam said, "Nearly nine-fifteen. The traffic had best get moving if I'm to make my ten o'clock appointment."

Vi turned back about. "Appointment?"

He nodded. "With the curator who's been helping me out a bit. She has something she thought I'd like to see."

"And no word of what?"

"Not a one," Liam said, sounding not especially curious.

Vi considered that another essential difference between the sexes. A woman in the same conversation wouldn't have been off the phone without the mystery solved.

They soon pulled into the city's center, which Liam navigated while Vi called off directions to the hotel from the information he'd printed off the Internet. Branley's Hotel sat on a stretch of Molesworth Street otherwise occupied by Georgian brick town houses, their self-important facades lightened by front doors painted bright shades of yellow, blue, and red. Vi smiled at the whimsy of the sight, and that of the round and quite elderly doorman in black tailcoat with shiny gold trim making his way to the car. Liam pressed a button on his keychain that made the car's boot pop open.

While the doorman and Liam shared a jocular man-moment, Vi took her bag from the car's boot and prompted Meghan to do the same. She'd not hasten the doorman's retirement with too much heavy lifting. They climbed the steep stairs to the small hotel, built of adjacent converted town houses, and waited for Liam.

In a matter of minutes they were checked in and their bags stored until their rooms were ready. Rafferty father and daughter were to share a small family suite while Vi had a room nearby. Liam apologized that another suite hadn't been available for her, but as Vi pointed out, that would be mad extravagance as there was just one of her, and she'd be needing just one bed. An *en suite* bath and a quiet bar were all she needed at that moment, both of which the hotel provided. She glanced longingly into the currently closed pub room as Liam herded them back to the door.

When they made the sidewalk again, Meghan looked one way, then the other. "Where's the car?" she asked her father.

"In a parking garage," Liam replied.

"Then a cab?"

"We're a matter of a few blocks from Kildare Street. One foot in front of the other, if you please," her father replied.

By the time they'd arrived at the museum, Vi made a mental note that when dealing with Meghan, every detail must be considered. She'd put one foot in front of the other, all right, but at a pace that would be foot-dragging even among snails. Now, headphones in place, she'd roamed off and sat on a bench at the perimeter of the room while Liam and Vi headed to the information desk.

"I'm looking for Nuala Manion," he said to the woman behind the desk. "I'm Liam Rafferty, and we have an appointment."

"I'll ring her," the woman replied, then began a chase-by-phone that didn't want to end.

Standing next to Liam, Vi waited as patiently as she knew how, which admittedly was saying little this morning. She glanced toward Meghan to see what the girl was doing. She was no longer seated and appeared to be making a nonchalant wander toward the door.

Vi touched Liam's shoulder. "I'll be right back," she said when she had his attention.

Meghan was three steps from the exit when Vi snared her. "Taking a stroll?" she asked the girl.

"This place gives me the creeps. It's like a church."

Vi looked about the grand rotunda with its marble columns and mosaic-decorated floor. It was so far removed from tiny St. Brendan's waiting for her back in Ballymuir that she had to smile.

"You must have some grand churches in Atlanta to be thinking this looks like one," she said. As for churches upsetting the girl, that was another matter an objective outsider could simply leave for a professional. "And creeps or none, you should have a look with us. This is your heritage, too."

"Whatever," Meghan said with that roll of the eyes that Vi was beginning to weary of.

"No, that specifically," Vi said. "Now it looks as though the curator your father's been waiting for is here. Let's go have a chat." She stepped behind Meghan and guided her much as a Kerry sheepdog would a stubborn lamb, except the dog would be showing sharp teeth where Vi was fighting hard not to bare hers.

They rejoined Liam at the information desk in time to be introduced to Nuala Manion without needing to give any explanations about out-of-sorts preteens. The curator was Vi's age or a bit younger, she guessed. She was slight, businesslike, and yet genial. She took Vi's handshake, met her eyes, and asked to be called Nuala. She also glossed past Meghan's bored expression with an ease Vi was beginning to wish for.

At the curator's suggestion, they were first going to have a look at the gold exhibit. Meghan was about to clamp her headphones back in place when her father held out a hand, clearly demanding that they be relinquished. She did so, and kept her level of sulk elevated. Vi was pleased, though, to see Liam set at least one boundary for the girl.

"How much do you know about Ireland's gold?" Nuala asked them as they entered the room holding the *Or* exhibit.

"Some of us know more than others," Liam said, with a nod toward Meghan. "This is my daughter's first visit to the museum."

"I see. Well then, let me feed you a bit of history," Nuala said to the girl. "I'll try to make it tasty."

"Sure," Meghan said after giving the curator a disbelieving look.

"The first pieces we'll see come from the Late Bronze Age...things that were made over twenty-seven hundred years ago."

"I'll bet my dad remembers the Late Bronze Age," Meghan said.

"Ah, yes, those were the good old days," Liam agreed. "Back then, misbehaving children were fed to the vast packs of starving lions roaming the isle. Right, Nuala?"

"I'm not so very sure about the starving lions, but we had gold aplenty," the curator said, trying not to smile. "In fact, here at the museum we have over eighteen kilos from that era, but we believe that one hundred times that amount once existed."

"So where's the rest of it?" Meghan asked, and Vi did smile at the way the girl was fighting her own innate curiosity.

"Some is in private collections...family heirlooms and the like. A great deal was melted down, and some we're sure is yet to be discovered. And we have this..."

They entered a dimly lit room with cases backlit to glow with the treasure they held. Vi smiled at Meghan's sharply indrawn breath. *Whatever,* indeed.

The curator stood beside Meghan, looking into a central case heaped with a small mountain of gold rings and other pieces. "This represents the gold found in County Clare, at Mooghaun. Not all in the display is real, as much of the hoard was melted down. We've had to fill in to give you the sense of what the original finders happened upon. Amazing all the same, isn't it?"

Meghan nodded, seeming unable to take her eyes away from the sight. When the curator began to tell the tale of how the gold was found, Vi moved along to a smaller case in which several individual artifacts from other finds sat. There was a neck-ring of gold that looked as though it had been twisted from each end into a sharp-edged spiral. Smaller flat wrist bands rested to either side of the piece, and on either side of them sat two collars, these hammered like flat crescent moons. She wasn't the diamond-and-jewels sort, but this bit of history made her blood rush faster. She could almost feel the cold weight of the central neck-ring as though it sat against her skin.

Meghan and the curator moved on to another display in the room, but Vi stayed where she was. Liam came to stand behind her, close enough that their bodies brushed.

"Coveting?" he asked in a low voice.

"Sinfully so," she replied, thinking of more than just the gold before her. If Meghan weren't there, Vi would have leaned against him, reveling in the contact. Because she was, Vi moved marginally closer to the case.

Tempted beyond restraint, she lightly touched her fingers to the case's glass wall, then increased the contact as an odd sensation drew her in. It was almost as though she could hear the pieces talking to each other...a buzz of conversation, some words angry, some bloody bored, and others lost and sad.

This was no lack of breakfast at work, for she'd risen early and eaten endless toast and jam and yogurt with her da. No, this was very real and utterly unexpected. She shivered at the pagan hum, feeling dizzy as she tried to pick one message from the next. When it became overwhelming, Vi broke contact with the case. The sound immediately stopped.

The gift she'd gotten from Nan—this way of seeing—had always seemed tied to people, not things. Lost sets of car keys could not tell her of their owners, but lost souls could be heard. Admittedly the gift would be of greater practical utility could she be a key-locator.

She touched the case again, starting slightly as the sound

returned. Fine, then...the gold was having a wee chat. Vi knew better than to question the unanswerable. She could, though, toy with it.

Touch...release...touch...release.

She smiled as the buzz cut in and out. It was more entertaining than watching Da play with the television's remote control when in the mood to irk Mam.

Liam leaned closer. "Are you feeling all right?" he asked quietly.

"Fine," Vi replied. "Grand."

She reached out to touch again, and Liam closed his hand over hers. "Nuala's looking a bit worried about fingerprints."

Vi glanced to her right and found Nuala and Meghan both watching her as though she were a madwoman. As she was without rational explanation for her activities, she gave them a bold smile instead.

Meghan muttered, "Yeah, right."

Nuala cleared her throat in the Irish way of saying "you're mad" without actually having to say it.

"Now," she said to the group, "if you don't mind, I've something I'd like to show all of you." She led them from the main display area down a floor to museum offices. There, she had a guard unlock the door to a small meeting room.

"The questions in your e-mails piqued my curiosity, so I've been having a look in the museum's database to see if we have anything that might have to do with your Kilkenny jeweler," she said to Liam. "And as it turns out, we do."

She donned a pair of white silken gloves and then opened a putty-gray box that had been sitting on the table. While Vi and the Raffertys watched, she pulled out an item and set it on a piece of dark cloth near the box. "This was left to the museum decades ago, and isn't the sort of thing we keep on exhibit, but I thought you might enjoy a look."

Nuala had brought out a pale golden sculpture of a large crescent-moon-shaped collar similar to the gold one in the exhibit upstairs, except this one had round shield-like pieces with raised concentric circles that would rest at the back of the wearer's neck.

"That's not even gold," Meghan said, sounding gravely disappointed.

"No, it's a wax cast of a gorget made by a jeweler in Kilkenny," the curator said. She smiled at Liam. "It seems that your long-ago jeweler found certain pieces curious enough that he made molds of them before melting them down. His descendants, however, found no practical use for his work. I've brought out this one because it's the most unusual of the lot. Look at the decorative bosses on each terminus of the piece."

"They're lovely," Vi said, buoyed by the first thought that had struck her: *I can use that pattern in my art.* It had been some time since art had come into her thoughts in anything other than a negative context.

Nuala nodded. "Quite, aren't they? And while we have many lunulae—meaning this style of hammered gold necklace but without the bosses—gorgets are much rarer, indeed. It would be of great value. It's a pity the jeweler chose this to melt, but I suspect it also had the greatest weight of gold, and he was a man with work to be done."

"Supposing we had a piece like this, how would the State go about acquiring it, should it be interested?" Liam asked.

The curator returned the wax model to its box and closed it. "Assuming you can trace ownership so we have no automatic claim under the National Monuments Act, and you're not in a position to give it as a gift, we'd be bidding on it at auction, same as any private collector."

"And you have a budget for this?" Vi asked.

"I'm afraid that with the downturn in the economy, not as much as we once did, and almost never enough then to compete with private bids."

A knock sounded at the door, and another woman stuck her head in the room to tell Nuala that she was soon needed elsewhere.

"Well, thank you for your time," Liam said, offering the curator his hand once she'd peeled off her gloves.

"It was my pleasure," she said. "Do let me know if you turn up anything else."

Vi noted the way Liam smiled instead of giving any specific promise. It was a ploy he'd perfected as a youth. He'd used it with great success on her while she'd yattered on about their brilliant future together, and he'd been quietly packing his bags for a move to America.

"I'll be sure he does," Vi said for him, earning a downturn of the brows from Liam. The curator escorted them back into the public area, then said a final goodbye.

"So we go shopping now, right?" Meghan asked a mere hair of a second later. At her father's silence, she added, "You promised."

Liam rubbed his forehead, showing all the signs of a man in full regret. "I did."

Vi moved quickly, before she could be snared in a mall-trap. "Why don't you two have a fine afternoon together? Shopping, perhaps some lunch...some real da-and-daughter time? I'll be fine enough on my own. I'd like to visit the rest of the museum and even pop over to the art gallery."

Without so much as a farewell, Meghan turned heel toward the exit. She'd cleared half the distance to the door when she wheeled around and gave an impatient sigh. "Can't we move it along?"

"Think carefully or you'll be going nowhere," Liam warned before focusing again on Vi. "Dinner tonight, then?" he asked. "I might make her so weary that it will be the two of us."

Vi laughed at his brash confidence. "You're underestimating the power of youth."

"And you're underestimating the incentive in front of me," he said, then leaned forward and kissed her.

"Come on," his daughter called. "Hurry up."

He kissed Vi again, softly, and she wished for more, though not in a marble rotunda with Meghan's running commentary of "gag me" and the like playing through the kiss.

"Six or so, in the lounge, then?" he asked when they parted.

"Six," she agreed, and the time could not come soon enough.

Hapless sailors had their sirens and Liam had Vi Kilbride. It was not yet five when Liam walked past the now crowded little bar in Bramley's Hotel. He knew the reason for the crowd the instant he heard it, for the same voice had lured him to a rocky fate years before. It was the sound of Vi Kilbride singing clear and true.

The summer she'd turned sixteen, he'd heard her sing *sean nos*—

unaccompanied, in the old style—for the very first time in a *sessiun* at his da's pub. She had captured the room with a voice that was old beyond her years. Liam had been nineteen, and already drawn to her adventurous spirit that matched his. When hit with her sensual confidence, he had wanted her in ways that she couldn't have begun to imagine. Though in retrospect, he thought with a smile, perhaps she could have, after all. He'd fought the inevitable for a full year, then made her his the very first day she'd returned to Duncarraig the next summer.

"Come on," Meghan said to him, tugging on his arm already weighed down with her vast purchases. "I want to go through my stuff."

Her "stuff," as she put it, had set him back nearly three hundred euros, a sum which for his own peace of mind he refused to convert into dollars. She was exhausted, filled with food she'd not had in weeks, and clearly ready to sleep. Thus in Liam's estimation, it was money very well spent.

He forced himself to move from the doorway and to the front desk, where he retrieved a key for the suite. In mere minutes, Meghan was settled in her bedroom, ripping through her bags of clothing and sorting them into piles that made no sense at all to Liam. Not that he cared, so long as she was occupied.

"I'm going to meet Vi downstairs for a drink and a meal," he said, checking his watch. "Would you like to join us?"

"Not hardly," his daughter said. "I want to see if they get the Comedy Network here."

"Fine, then. No leaving the room, and I'll check on you later."

"Uh-huh," she said. "Can I order room service if I get hungry?"

"Of course you can." The price of peace was high, but Liam was willing to pay. He stopped at the door. "Remember, no leaving the room."

"You just said that," his daughter replied, already bonding with the television set.

Liam left, then checked to be sure the door had locked behind him. Da duties accomplished, he took a deep breath and moved on. He'd worn his willpower thin this morning, first in the drive to Dublin, then at the museum. Being close to Vi but unable to touch her had been torture of the worst sort. Too impatient to wait for the lift, he jogged the winding staircase from the fourth floor to the first, slowing only when he reached the bar's doorway.

The crowd appeared to be a mix of regular patrons and hotel guests, but Liam had eyes only for the singer. Vi sat on a barstool that had been moved to the center of the room. She was singing an old folk song, this one in English. Liam very nearly wished it were in Irish, for he didn't like fully understanding the lyrics about a man who'd left his lover to cross the sea and never come back again.

He stuck to the fringes of the small crowd around her, waiting for this particular song to end. True, they were a nation of emigrants and he'd hardly been the first to leave, but this felt so bloody personal, coming to him in her voice. And it seemed personal to her, too, the way she sang with eyes closed, telling how the woman died, never to love again. When she was finished, she was met by silence, then loud applause.

She thanked her listeners, then said, "Fine tune, but stupid woman never to love again, don't you think?"

Liam joined in the laughter, not quite sure if he should be insulted or relieved. When the couple in front of him left, taking with them his anonymity, his gaze met Vi's.

Smiling, she slipped from her stool and told her admirers that she was well and truly sung out. She looped her arm through Liam's and said, "You're early, and I'm glad for it."

As was he. "Can I buy you a drink?"

"A bottled water, I think. Our bartender's been plying me with wine to get me to sing. Little did he know I'd do it for free, eh?"

They were to the bar then. Vi got her water and Liam a whiskey, neat. With her still smiling and chatting as though among old friends, they wove through the remaining crowd and found a seat on a small sofa in the far corner of the dark, wood-paneled room.

While he'd been out supporting the Dublin economy with what was left of his failed one, she'd changed into a sleek black skirt and a low-cut silk top of black that also seemed to shine dark red where the light from the brass chandelier overhead hit it. She also smelled wonderful, of exotic spices whose names he'd probably never know. Liam felt himself rising to the occasion. Ah, she was still his siren, and his alone.

"So your shopping trip went well?" Vi asked.

He focused on giving a lucid answer when reason was bolting for the door. "Well enough that all Meghan wants is room service and television."

"Grand," she said, then shook her hair, which she wore loose this evening, back over her shoulders.

She took a swallow of water, and Liam shifted uncomfortably. God, he was in desperate straits if the sight of her swallowing could make him ache even harder. He kept a smile in place and one leg crossed at the knee in a poor effort of camouflage as yet more admirers came to chat with Vi.

"I'm thinking we should move someplace more private," she said after the small group departed.

Liam downed his whiskey in one mad gulp and said, "Then let's go" over the fire in his empty stomach. He stood and offered his hand to Vi, who took it and rose.

"My room?" she suggested.

He wasn't fool enough to disagree.

They cut through the bar, hands clasped. While they waited for the lift to come down she said, "I talked to Nuala Manion again after you left the museum this morning."

Liam made what he hoped passed as a vague sound of semi-interest. He had no wish to talk of Ms. Manion or gold. In fact, all he wished was to be alone with Vi. Unfortunately, the floor number indicator was firmly parked at three. He was about to suggest the stairs when she spoke again.

"It's a sad thing, how much of our heritage ends up out of sight."

"True, but there's still ruins enough to keep the tourists hopping from town to town."

"That's hardly the point, now, is it?"

Again he thought of sailors and rocky shoals, for the seas were growing rough. "Have you something you wish to say, Vi?"

"I do. If any gold is found, we should give the museum the right of first refusal and sell to them at a reduced rate, of course."

Liam retreated into silence. It seemed to work well enough for Meghan.

Two... One... Finally, the lift arrived and a middle-aged couple emerged. They nodded a polite greeting, which Liam returned. He and Vi entered, and she tapped the button for the fourth floor.

"Have you nothing to say?" she asked as the door slid closed. "Not a 'you're so right' or an 'I'd have it no other way'?"

"I take it back," Liam said instead. "I take it all bloody back. I don't want women to say exactly what they're thinking, especially when it makes hell of my plans for the evening."

She raised her brows and tilted her head to an inquisitive angle. "Shall I take that as your vote against the museum?"

"There is no vote but mine."

Even after that pronouncement, she still held fast to his hand. Were this his ex-wife Beth and one of their disagreements, she'd be pinned to the lift's opposite wall about now, looking to get even farther away from him. But Vi gave him a slow smile, one so sensual in nature that his fingers tightened reflexively over hers.

"One vote only?" she said. "Really, now?"

He glanced at the elevator's display. Two... Three... Could this damned thing move no faster? "Yes, really."

She laughed. "You can keep thinking that, if it makes you feel better, but when the moment comes, Liam, I'll not let go of my rights. Sue me, fight me, do what you must, and be sure I'll do the same."

He blinked. "Am I right in thinking you just declared war?"

"I believe I did."

Finally, the fourth floor. The door opened, and Vi led him out. "Now, the way I'm seeing it, we have two choices. You can storm off to your room, and I to mine, or we can meet in mine and I can see how the rest of you looks naked."

There was something shocking about this talk of sex when a line had just been drawn. "I, ah..."

Vi released his hand and trailed her fingers warm and sure along the line of his jaw. "Go check on your daughter, Liam. Then come to room four-twelve."

She walked down the hall, slipping her key from a pocket in her skirt. He was still staring and likely slack-jawed when she unlocked her door.

"And don't be wasting time," she said before disappearing.

Liam shook his head. His siren was leading him, no doubt about it. And there was also no doubt that in this, he'd be well pleased to be dashed upon the rocks.

CHAPTER EIGHT

'I've seen you before,' as the cat said to the hot milk.
—IRISH PROVERB

"You've never exactly been a slip of a girl," Vi reminded herself as she stood sideways and regarded her naked reflection in the bathroom mirror. "And you'll not get there in the next five minutes, either."

She turned and gave herself a front-on view, which she found more satisfactory than the side one, despite the flaws there, too. Her months of frozen inactivity—both mental and physical—seemed to have expanded her bottom. Some might find it lush, but she was finding the thought of Liam seeing it bare just a wee bit daunting. Ah well, if a broader behind was the worst that resulted from her days of grayness, she was a lucky woman, indeed.

Tidy, teeth brushed and anxious to get the event rolling so that the self-analysis would end, she slipped on her crimson silk robe and then settled into a curved armchair by the window to wait for Liam. She had no doubt that he would arrive. She felt his need as strongly as she did her own, and hers already had her trembling. She stilled one shaking hand with the other, not ruing the way she felt, but marveling at it. It wasn't as though she'd not had a lover since Liam. There had been a decent number of them, always carefully chosen so that she might guard her heart, and surely never more than one at a time. Not once, though, had she felt this kind of hunger, as though she had to have him or cry to the moon.

Vi closed her eyes and pictured Liam striding down the quiet, carpeted hallway from his suite, giving the imagining enough depth and detail to will it into reality.

"Soon, now," she murmured.

She'd silently counted to *caoga* and then back down to *a haon* again when a knock finally sounded at the door. She rose and padded barefoot across the flowery carpet. A glimpse through the peephole confirmed that it was him, looking as on edge as she. Heart pounding, Vi opened the door. She'd no sooner closed the door behind Liam and perched herself on the edge of the bed than he began talking more quickly than a car salesman trying to sell poor goods.

"Meghan's still fixed in front of the television and room service has arrived, though I can't imagine how she'd be hungry again, with all the fried junk she's eaten. I've told her that we're going to the Italian place I saw round the corner, and should be back before nine. And I've brought these." He reached into his trouser pocket and dumped a fat handful of condoms on the nightstand.

Vi laughed. "A bit overambitious, I'm thinking," she said with a nod to the stash.

He prowled closer. "And if I arrived with one, I'd have been understating my goal."

"Which is?"

"You," he said. "All of you."

She shivered with pleasure. "Now you're sure about this?" she teased. "It's a risk, you know. One wrong move and you'll have destroyed a legend forever."

Surprise chased his brows upward. "A legend? I was twenty, for God's sake."

She scooted forward on the edge of the bed until she could unbuckle the fine leather belt he wore. Always the best for Liam. "So you're saying that now I've reached my prime, you've passed yours?"

He laughed. "No, for my ego wouldn't have it. I'm saying it was more about frequency of performance than quality back then. Now do I get all of you, or do we talk our stolen time away?"

Vi stood and wrapped her arms about his neck. "You get me."

Dark eyes intent, Liam worked his hands beneath the Chinese-embroidered lapels of her robe, spread his fingers wide and wrapped them over her shoulders. He trailed his thumbs back and forth over the ridge of her collarbone a few times before easing the robe loose so that it slipped with silken ease to drape low on her arms. She would have shrugged the rest of the way out of it, but he stopped her.

"Not yet. We'd best take this part slowly. The way I'm feeling, the rest will go fast," he said, then added, "...the first time, at least."

Slowly? He asked for the impossible when already she burned. But for Liam, she would try.

He brushed his fingertips over her breasts, then around to the undersides, lifting them slightly. "They're fuller than when you were seventeen."

"Unless you like fuller, don't be looking at my rear," she said and immediately wished the nervous words back.

Liam laughed. "God, I'd forgotten what a mouth you have."

Vi hadn't forgotten his, especially the way it felt when he drew hot and wet on her nipples. And she wanted that perfectly marvelous mouth on her now.

"I need your kisses," she said.

"Where?"

"Here," she replied, raising her left hand and touching the very corner of her jaw.

He used his fingers to sweep her hair—which she'd worn down the way he'd always liked—round her ear, then he obliged her with a slow and tender kiss. Smart man, he knew to tease her well.

"And here," she said when he was done, settling her fingers against her throat.

Even better this time, he kissed her open-mouthed, his tongue pressing against the pulse strongly beating just beneath her skin. Then he suckled there, ever so briefly, earning a gasp from her and a chuckle from him.

"I'll not mark you," he said. "That is, unless you want me to."

The summer she'd been seventeen, she'd worn the marks of his kisses on her throat as though they'd been jewels. She'd been young and foolish and quite sure they were the only two in the world who so understood grand passion.

"No marks," she ordered.

"More kisses, though?"

She smiled. "Always more kisses. *Always,*" she repeated, guiding his head to her with one hand, and holding her breast for him with the other.

He was also an obliging man, Liam Rafferty. He replaced her hand beneath her breast with his, then flicked her nipple with the tip of his tongue. A small thrill shimmered straight to her toes, and gooseflesh began to ripple across her skin. He tasted her in earnest then, his mouth closing over her as wet and hot and perfect as she recalled. Her breath left her in a gasp.

As he kissed first one breast, then the other, she sifted her fingertips through his thick hair, remembering well these conflicted feelings of control over the moment, yet total abandonment. It had always been this way with Liam, life a confusing, heady mix, defying logic. When she was ready to beg him for even more, he instead let his mouth leave her. He still touched her though, fingertips tracing the contours of her shoulders.

"I've always missed you, Vi. Even when you were out of my thoughts." He shook his head. "I don't know.... It's as though you're in my bones."

Vi's heart—always too bloody easy—began beating faster. It was in that easy heart of hers to tell him that she felt the same, but for once, caution guided her words.

"I've missed you, too," she said.

When Liam reached for her robe's sash, she was ready, broad bottom be damned. She let the garment go to the floor and stood willing beneath his gaze. He walked a close circle around her, and she had to admit to a moment of nerves when he was catching the full backside, but when their eyes met again, she had no doubt that he'd liked what he'd seen.

He touched a lock of her hair where it lay against the upper slope of her breast. "You're a woman for the ages, Vi Kilbride. And I'm one lucky bastard, having you naked before sundown."

"Ah, but barely before," she said, as the sunlight chasing through the part in the draperies was weakening. "And there's some unfairness afoot, here. Barefoot, actually," she said with a glance to her toes. "You're able to gawk at me all you please, while I'm getting a businessman, still all buttons and starch."

"You're meaning these?" he asked, gesturing at what were

doubtless expensively tailored shirt and trousers, when she was more interested in what lay beneath.

"I am."

He grinned. "What'll you give me if I take off the shirt?"

Vi's smile grew. Another game, and it had been so very long since she'd had a chance to play like this.

"Arrogant man. The question you should be asking is what you'll give me." She reached out and unfastened his shirt's top two buttons.

"But we already know what I want to give you," he said with a mock leer and a waggle of the brows that would have done any over-actor proud.

Vi laughed. "And you've not heard me complaining, which should be gift enough."

She worked free the rest of the buttons, including those on his cuffs when he presented them one by one. Instead of tugging the shirt off, she strolled behind him and slid her hands underneath the fabric and onto his bare skin. At the feel of his muscles beneath her palms, she drew in a sharp little breath of pleasure. He was broad shouldered, a man who had done his share of physical labor. She moved her hands round to the front, tracing the lines of his ribs.

Rising on tiptoe, she said softly into his ear, "You know, I'm thinking we can leave your clothes on, and maybe even forego the main event. I'm sure I can find plenty to do with my hands as it is."

That grand lie busied him.

"Not a damn chance," he said.

He had toed out of his shoes even before she could come around front to watch the show. Shirt joined her robe on the floor and trousers soon did the same, which left him doing a mad jig to rid himself of socks and then boxers. When he was finally as bare as she, Vi took her time admiring him. Liam had filled out to be most impressive, and the more she looked, the less inclined she was to remain standing.

She walked the few steps to the bed and pulled the thick feather down duvet to the footboard. Liam quickly walked to the other side and did the same. They each climbed onto the bed and lay on their sides facing one another. Vi propped her head on her hand so she could have a fine view.

It wasn't as though she hadn't looked at him when he was twenty. She'd been relentless, treating him as her own private plaything, touching and tasting and learning what aroused him...and her. She knew the coarse feel of his pubic hair, the taste of his mouth, the scent of his skin as they made love. She smiled, recalling all of that.

Liam drew closer to her, or perhaps she to him. However it happened, their mouths met and then met again. Hungry nips, slower kisses, their hearts sped. As he caressed her breasts and kissed her yet more, she draped her leg over his hip, bringing them nearer still. She was a strong woman, and more or less fit, too. Yet he rolled her onto her back with an ease that impressed her, though it would never do at all to admit that to him.

He moved between her open thighs, kneeling above her. She wanted to reach for his erection and run her hand up and down it until he'd be done with this playing about, but he touched her between her legs first. The feel of his fingers, of the way he knew to stroke her, was familiar, yet not. She closed her eyes for a moment and focused on the sensations, the tightening of inner muscles as he worked one, then two fingers inside her. He found a rhythm with his thumb she was certain he hadn't known last time they'd done this, but she didn't want to think of him with other women. Not now, in this intimate moment. Surrendering herself to his sure touch, she rested her hands, palms up, on the pillows above her head. As her passion built, Vi could feel an utterly abandoned smile work its way across her mouth.

Liam's answering smile was slow and a wee bit smug. "Herself is pleased?"

"Working my way to it," she said.

"It seems to me I'm doing all the work, just now," Liam teased, then moved his hand away long enough to resettle next to her.

She did reach for him, then. He was a large man in all ways and the feel of him hot and thick beneath her sensitive fingers sent a tremor of pure passion through her and then into him. She ran her thumb over his erection's head, where moisture had begun to bead. She wanted to taste him, but knew they were both too close to the edge, and told him as much, too.

He groaned.

She gave him an arch smile. "Then you're through being slow?"

"I am." His gaze was vague, somehow, as though if he looked directly at her, he'd turn to cinders.

Without otherwise moving, she reached out her right hand and felt her way across the nightstand to his mound of condom packets. When she had one between her fingers, she waved it in his face with a quick twist of her wrist, as one would a flag at a parade.

"Get busy," she instructed her man.

He took the packet from her, opened it, and withdrew the goods. Vi watched as he rolled the condom into place. He braced his weight over her. She guided him until he was poised to enter, then smoothed her hands over his hips to the firm muscles of his bum. Lucky man, he'd experienced little of the expansion she had. She supposed she'd forgive him that flaw.

Then his gaze met hers, deep and serious. "I would never have thought..." he murmured.

Vi didn't need him to finish his words, for she had never thought this would happen again, either. Then the sheer miracle introduced an uninvited guest: worry.

"What if it's not the same?" she asked. She'd been teasing earlier, but not now. Admittedly, her timing had gone lackwit, as he was already partway inside her, and her body was easing to permit him the rest of the way.

His smile was brash. "Ah, but what if it's better?"

"Impossible."

He kissed her once, his tongue teasing hers, and he pushed his way home. "But I think, my fire, that I just might be finding my prime again."

My fire. He'd called her that all those years before, and until just now, she'd forgotten...or perhaps not permitted herself to remember. Time and earlier sorrows slipped away. In her heart if not her body she was seventeen again, burning for Liam. She tried to pull him even nearer, but he shook his head.

"Not yet," he said. "But soon."

He moved slowly at first, seeking an angle that would please them both. His questions of "like this?" and "deeper yet?" were nearly unanswerable, for she loved it all. Vi gave him the one word she could: *more.*

And more he gave her until she was twined about him, holding fast as their urgency grew. She couldn't get close enough, couldn't hear enough of his words, ones of praise, desperation, and need. She returned the same in a scattered, gasping mix of her dual languages of *Bearla* and *Gaeilge,* two halves of the whole that she'd become.

This was what Vi had recalled—pleasure almost too much to be borne. She was so close to peaking that nothing seemed to be left of her will. She closed her eyes, focusing on that retreating sense of self. Then Liam wrapped one hand behind her head, clasping her skull.

"No. Look at me," he said. "At *us.* "

She knew his demand for what it was. He wanted an acknowledgment that this moment was more than just hers. It was a ceding of power to give him this, but it was what honor demanded. She opened her eyes. Bracing his weight fully above her, Liam withdrew until they were scarcely joined. He lifted her head until she could see where his body entered hers, then he pushed forward. She gasped at both the intimacy and the utter eroticism of what she saw. Twice more he entered and withdrew, until all Vi could say was the truth.

"We're beautiful, aren't we?" she whispered.

Liam eased her head back to the pillow. "We are." He surged fully into her, picking up and maintaining a harder rhythm.

"Come for me," he demanded. His words were rough, on the very edge of control, but she had already passed that point. Her orgasm claimed her, making her muscles go stiff as she cried his name. She shuddered as the shock of pleasure rolled outward. Liam joined her in the moment, going rigid. He gasped her name, then held himself fixed above her, his expression one of fierce pleasure. She'd thought herself spent, but crested on another wave of emotion that nearly knocked the breath from her.

Liam folded to the pillows, leaving them still intimately joined, but much of the bulk and weight of his body just beside her. Vi's peak passed. Eventually, the wildness ebbed, leaving her with one exhausted man and two troubling thoughts for company. First, how had she lived without these feelings for so long? And very worst, how was she to soon live that way again?

* * *

Liam sat still naked on the edge of the mattress, drinking the rest of the glass of bottled water he'd poured for Vi after he'd recovered enough to leave the bed and take care of matters. She'd thirstily swallowed half the water, then fallen back on the pillows, claiming strength to do no more.

Changes and none, he thought. He was older, world-weary, and in many ways a chastened man. And yet when he was with Vi—*in* her—he felt twenty again, with the hunger to own the world and the balls to take it.

Aye, changes and none. Vi was no longer a slender, coltish seventeen. She had a ripeness to her curves and a bite to her words. If possible, he liked this Vi better than her youthful iteration, and then she had been the center of his world.

He set the empty glass on the nightstand and shifted to look at her. She was as unselfconscious as always, sprawled across the bed with no need for covers. He couldn't say for sure that she was sleeping, but because her eyes were closed he stole the luxury of watching her unobserved. The world had marked her, as it had him. A scar shone silvery across her belly. He hadn't fully noticed it earlier. Then again, he'd been driven in his intent. He followed the line with his index finger, then leaned down and settled a kiss directly center.

"This is new," he said when she stirred.

She hesitated less than a heartbeat, then stretched and sighed. "Old, actually, and quite all better, but I'll thank you for the kiss before reminding you that it's not kind to point out a woman's flaws."

Liam smiled at her nip of a reprimand. He could lose himself in this woman. It was a romantic's thought, that. And the same thought had once been a threat to his existence. But he was older now, and sometimes wiser, too, than he'd been at twenty.

For two and a half wild months, he had indeed lost himself in Vi Kilbride. He'd let her goals become his own, her dreams consume his. In fact, he'd very nearly fallen in with Da's plan that he stay in Duncarraig and work at the pub until he had money enough for university. Vi had been all for it, talking of how they'd backpack through Europe when he was on his school breaks. She would sing on the street corner for money, and they would make love in every ruined castle they could find. Fine dreams, at least for an ambitionless man.

So what had hauled him back to reality? In a word, condescension. Two American college girls had come to visit his cousin Brian. They were blond and pouty-breasted as a pair of overendowed laying hens. Liam had taken a nearly instantaneous dislike to them, but that was because they'd treated him as though he were the dumbest Rafferty yet, good enough to tease but not made for talk. Not that he'd ever been inclined to take them up on their half-veiled invitations for a random ride. All of which made learning what Vi had believed of him the greatest insult of all.

It was a lifetime ago, he reminded himself, and he'd be doing no good by letting it cast its shadow this long.

"Roll over and I'll rub your back," he said to Vi, thinking it would be a pleasurable distraction.

She moved onto her stomach, and Liam looked down at her feeling like a starving man finally at the banquet table. Vi had always been white-skinned, but never pale. No, she was milky-rich with whiteness, except for the small strawberry colored mark she'd always had just above the curve of her right cheek. He intended to work his way there and taste it...in his own time. For now, though, he would touch and recall and learn anew.

He moved to the end of the bed and grasped her long and slender feet in his hands.

"Those aren't my back," she murmured.

"They're not," he agreed.

He massaged her feet until she had relaxed to near bonelessness. Then he permitted his attention to wander north, along finely muscled calves, and slowly up the backs of her thighs. She *was* in his bones, so much a part of his memories, of what he deemed appealing.

Liam knew that he'd landed in Beth's bed because she'd had a way about her rather like Vi. It had been illusory, though. He'd mistaken American assertiveness for the same certainty of spirit that Vi possessed. By the time he could discern that essential difference, it had been too late. Beth had been pregnant with Meghan, and after much persuasion, she'd agreed to marry him. Proper choice, bad results—at least with respect to the adults involved. Meghan, he'd never regret. Misunderstand, become furious with, and otherwise act like a parent toward, yes. Regret, no.

Liam ran his hands across Vi's bottom and to the small of her back, where he circled his thumbs to either side of her spine. Once, all those years ago, they'd spent hours touching each other like this. Until she'd closed him from her world.

"Paradise," she said, sounding nearly drunk with pleasure.

He worked his way up, kneading his fingers over her already lax muscles. When he reached her shoulders, he detoured back to her hip to kiss that bit of strawberry that had tempted him. He kissed once and nipped once, in subtle retaliation of having been deprived this particular spot for so long. Then he straightened and went to work on her shoulders, earning him more words of praise. At least he assumed it was praise, as most was given in an unintelligible Irish slurred with sleepiness.

Done with her neck, Liam took the return route down her body, then spread her legs enough that he could kneel between them and pay special attention one final time to her lower back. At least that was the noble thought he ascribed to himself. Less noble and far more human was how hard he'd grown again. He slipped his fingers between her legs and lingered at the slick flesh where she'd held him so well. She jumped slightly at his touch.

"And that's neither my back nor my legs," she said, raising herself up on her arms and looking over her shoulder.

"Do you want me to stop?" he asked, hoping she'd answer no, and feeling his fierce hunger double when she did. She settled back into the pillows and he touched her as he wished.

Soon he felt like that near-man of twenty again, desperate to come inside her. She'd been as necessary as air to him, and he'd never been so angry and alone as when they'd parted. Starved for her, Liam was breathing as though he'd just run the Dublin marathon. Bracing his weight on one hand, he reached for the nightstand, snagged a condom, and dealt with it. Since Meghan's unplanned creation, he'd been scrupulous about such things.

"I need to be inside you," he said to Vi. "Now."

"Insatiable." She rose to her hands and knees. "Remember what this was like?"

Liam shook with the memory. If she was willing to try it again, he surely was. He entered her in one stroke, then held fast to her hips as he moved. Liam looked at her, so exposed, vulnerable, and faceless to him. She wanted him to remember. God knew he did. Love given heedlessly, recklessly given, then ripped away. They'd made such a mess of matters.

Liam stilled. This was wrong. He needed her eyes, the assurance that it was truly Vi he made love to. Though it nearly killed him, he withdrew.

"Liam?" Vi asked immediately.

"I need to see your face," he said.

They untangled and she lay back against the pillows, open to him, eyes, soul, and emotion. This time when they joined, he moved hard and fast. This time he would make it right. This time there would be no hiding from each other, from the truth. It would be different, for he'd not lose her again. Gritting his teeth so he'd not cry out, Liam arched and came, then collapsed over the woman who'd stolen a boy's heart so that he could fight to reclaim it as a man.

Vi had reached an important decision. She would never leave this bed again...especially if she could persuade Liam to bring her some food. Sadly, he seemed disinclined to move. Could she not see his back rising and falling as he lay face down in the fluffy pillows, she might think that he'd suffocated.

"Hungry?" she asked, for a woman could always hope.

"Wouldn't make it as far as the lift," he said. "Room service, maybe?"

"Too slow." It was a good thing that she was accustomed to assuring her own survival. She slipped from the bed and went to the desk, where she'd left a small bag of biscuits she'd bought while off on her own that afternoon. Food in hand, she returned to the bed. At the crinkle of the biscuits' plastic covering, he turned his head her way.

"For me, too?"

They were chocolate covered, which meant it was an especially difficult sacrifice. In the end, though, Liam was chocolate-worthy.

"One, I think," she said.

He sat up, pulling the covers over his hips. "How hard does a man have to work for two?"

Smiling, she handed him an additional biscuit. "Tit for tat, I suppose."

"Kind of you." After he'd finished eating, he said, "Vi, we have to talk."

Damn, but how she hated that phrase. "We do?"

"About what happens after today." He smiled. "Other than more biscuits, that is."

"Ah, the gold...should it be found."

He nodded. "I'm trying to be forthright with you, not make the same mistakes I did fifteen years ago."

Which was all well and good, but Vi knew they had a great, fat lot more mistakes they could make. If she could save them at least the one she sensed coming, she'd be pleased.

"Before you tell me your plans, I need to give you a bit of a story," she said.

Liam's mouth curved into a brief smile. "I've heard your bits. I'd best make myself comfortable, then." He plumped his pillow and settled in.

"Several miles out Slea Head Road from Ballymuir is an ancient stone ring fort called Dun Mor. It overlooks the Blasket Islands, and is a favorite spot of mine to go and think. Two summers ago, someone—likely a local farmer looking for more land to work, free of tourists and the like—took an excavator to the earthworks that surround the fort and removed an ogham stone at the entry."

"Lamentable, unless you're the land-starved farmer, I suppose."

Vi's frustration heated. "Whoever did it has no excuse to destroy history," she snapped before schooling herself to a calmer tone. "I admit maybe I felt the loss too deeply, but we've had so much taken from us, Liam. Fast-food trash has blown from Tralee to Dingle and even here and there in Ballymuir. Scarcely anyone speaks Irish daily, even in the Gaeltachts, and our punts have been replaced by those wear-out-in-a-week euros. This isn't the land it was when you left fifteen years ago, and I'm beginning to feel as though if we trade more of our past away, we won't be the same people."

He remained silent, not hostile, but not precisely the willing audience she'd hoped for, either. Vi went for the grand sum-up. "All of which is a roundabout way of telling you why I feel as I said in the lift earlier. If we find the gold pieces and sell any part of them, our buyer should be the State."

He sat upright. "Vi, I've told you, there will be no 'we' about this."

She didn't want to battle when persuasion might work better. "Pity, then, for with that attitude, when I uncover the gold, it will be an *I,* as in Vi."

She'd thought her comment would eke at least the shadow of a smile, but she got nothing.

"Look, I'm in trouble," Liam said. "I need money, and a great deal of it."

She hesitated, sorting though the possible meanings. "This is a need and not a want?"

"It is."

Vi lay silent thinking of Liam the youth. He'd been made of wants. Wanting wealth. Wanting endless things from the finest car to the grandest home. Wanting to lead and never follow.

"Why?" she asked.

He shifted so that he stared up at the ceiling, and took so long before he spoke that she had begun to doubt that he planned to at all. "I've not said a word of this to my family, but I'm near to losing my business. My partner has screwed me royally, using our assets to steal from others. What he's done cannot be easily undone. When all's been repaid, I'm going to be starting anew. That is, assuming anyone will hire me for more than my deep-diving skills, and I'm getting too damn old to be doing that day in and out."

"I'm sorry," she said. "Have you many employees to be affected?"

"I do, though I've managed to refer some to competitors, which was another nail in my coffin. News of what Alex has done isn't yet public, but word is already out that we're going down and no new work is coming in."

"Honor can be a bit of a bitch, can't she?" Vi said.

He returned to his side and drew her close. "The worst. I spent my whole youth being 'one of those Raffertys.' Half my teachers couldn't tell me from my cousins or even from Cullen, who's three years younger. All I ever wanted was to be my own man, to be something apart from them."

"I always knew who you were," she said, then curved her hand against the side of his jaw. He turned his face to kiss her palm, and she closed her eyes, savoring the warm intimacy of the moment. Aye, she'd known who he was and had loved him from the start.

He took her hand and laced his fingers between hers. "I'm going to tell you something as a point of courtesy, Vi, and I'd be grateful if you'd not take my head off in repayment."

She looked at their hands and reminded herself that she yet had one free to swing if it were as bad as he had her thinking.

"About the gold," he said, "I've already put out a quiet word for collectors—"

"You are the optimistic one, aren't you?"

"I can afford to be little else. Reparations must be made for Alex's thefts, and I need cash beyond that to survive." He held tighter to her hand, and his squeeze of warning translated to tension in her. "In any case, I've heard back from an acquaintance in Boston. The man made great money in the computer industry and collects virtually anything Irish. Including his most current wife."

"Am I to laugh at that?"

His expression bore a mix of hope and resignation. "Well, smile, at least."

Vi seemed to have misplaced her sense of humor. "And what he owns already, does he at least lend to museums?"

"No, not that I'm knowing, at least. He has rooms next to his wine cellar that house the collection."

She tugged her hand loose and moved toward the mattress's edge. "I don't like this, Liam. I understand that you're needing money, but to even think of selling the gold to someone who would take it from home and store it in their—what?—cellar?"

"And you think it would fare much better in Dublin? Vi, it could as easily be stored in one of those boxes we saw."

She stood. "It doesn't matter. You're not serving honor."

Again he sat upright. "As you pointed out, she's a bit of a bitch, and too costly in this case, too."

"D'anam don diabhal," she said, thinking of a phrase Nan had

used when talking of those who had betrayed self and others. "Your soul to the devil."

Liam looked shocked. "You wish that on me?"

"No, that's what you're doing for yourself." She walked the room, noting her nakedness only when a chill rippled over her skin. She plucked her robe from the floor and pulled it on. "You'd bargain away your heritage to feed your pride."

"This isn't about pride. It's about who I am and what I've made of myself."

"Perhaps your soul is there already if you can't separate who you are from what you do as work," she said as she yanked her sash tight.

"Do you make that separation? Now, answer me honestly. Are you 'Vi Kilbride, the artist' when you think of yourself?"

It was a hard question, especially given her current lack of self, but also a fair one. Vi took her time in answering.

"I'm Vi, the artist, but I'm also Vi the sister, the neighbor, the vegetarian, and—"

"Well, I'm Liam Rafferty, marine salvor, king of the bloody high seas, and if I'm not that, I don't know who I am anymore."

She'd struck a nerve, indeed. If she couldn't sense his pain, she'd be smiling a bit at his sheer truculence. "And do you think some extra money will buy you this knowledge?"

The set of his jaw was stubborn. "Money will put me back even, at least. I need it, Vi."

That ran a grand "so bloody what?" on her importance scale. "We all need money. Do you think I'm selling Nan's house because I want to? I'm doing it because I have no choice."

"Why?" He sounded startled.

"Danny wants to go to university, but can't."

"And?"

"What do you mean...*and?*"

"I'm failing to see how your brother's plans have much anything to do with you."

Vi was coming to understand that his family might be too much for him, but hers had fully ceased to act as one years before and she was starved for connection. His attitude was a slight of what little she had.

"Because he's mine," she said. "Because I've damn well raised him for the past two years. And because I won't let him go through what I did."

"What did you go through, Vi?" he asked, his voice soft and low.

The concern she heard drew her from her anger. She realized that she'd said more than she'd meant to and could offer no more. "It doesn't matter. All that does is that Danny knows he has family who cares."

"Fine, then. With Danny to think of, if a young buyer came for your nan's house...someone with your tastes...would you take less than you might otherwise get?"

"That's not a fair question."

"And neither is yours a fair demand." Liam glanced at the bedside clock and muttered a quiet "damn."

"We need to finish this, but I can't now," he said. "Meghan will be expecting me and a shower's in order, first."

And Vi needed time to think. She waved him on, gesturing to the bathroom. "I know. Go ahead."

He left the bed and came to her, settling his hands on her waist. "Don't be angry."

He leaned forward to kiss her, and at the last moment she moved her face so that his lips brushed impersonally against her cheek.

"Take your shower," she said, forcing a note of cheer into her voice, but it sang false.

He picked up his underclothes, giving her a last view of strong shoulders and muscled haunches, and then closed himself in the bathroom. Soon the sound of running water came from the small room. Alone, Vi straightened the bed and looked at the condom packets still left on the nightstand. She gathered them into her hand and tucked them back into his trouser pocket. She didn't regret what they had done, but also knew she was in no hurry to do it again. Too much remained unsettled, most especially her mind.

Readjusting her robe, Vi walked to the window. She pushed aside the curtain. Rain had come in, spotting the glass. The yellowish glow of the streetlight was mirrored in the drops, obscuring the view. After a bit, the shower stopped, and minutes later the high whine of the hair dryer fixed to the bathroom wall began. She turned her back to it, thinking of taking and needing, and how miserably confusing it could all be. Gold, lovers, family...the frustrating lot.

Liam emerged and dressed.

"Do I look as I did when I arrived?" he asked, checking his reflection in the dresser mirror as he buttoned his shirt just so.

"You do," she said, and it was true as far as surfaces went.

He kissed her once, not with passion but more as a goodbye.

After Liam was gone, Vi showered, the water hot and needle-sharp against her skin. When she came out of the bathroom, she glanced into the same mirror that Liam had used. She shook her head at the woman looking back at her. "No marks," she'd said when they'd begun their lovemaking, but she'd forgotten about those that ran deeper than the skin.

CHAPTER NINE

If you want to know me, come and live with me.
—IRISH PROVERB

Dublin on Sunday morning turned out to be exactly as peaceful as Liam deserved. Meghan had been hell to wake from her adolescent comatose sleep, and then Vi had forcefully persuaded the lot of them into Mass at St. Patrick's, saying that a bit of reflection would do them all good.

At church, Meghan had fussed and sighed, Vi had gone someplace deep inside herself, and Liam had tried to locate that elusive sense of comfort that almost never came to him in a crowd. After that, it was breakfast and a tour of Christchurch Cathedral, where he caught Vi eyeing his daughter and then the ancient and well-used stocks in the church's cellar exhibition with a most speculative expression. He couldn't say he blamed her.

Now that they were in the car heading to Kilkenny, Meghan had found a new pastime, honing her accusing glare. Every time he checked the rearview mirror, she was sharply sending it his way. He supposed that his daughter was sophisticated enough to suspect that something more than friendship ran between the two adults in the front of the car. As far as Liam was concerned, it was none of her business. He'd returned to the hotel room before the appointed time, and without a hint of sex about him. Perhaps he might have eaten an order of garlic bread to attain that full Italian meal aura, but subterfuge failed to appeal.

No, he would settle for restraint. He would not hold Vi's hand or touch her leg just now, even though he craved the contact. He needed to know that despite their differences, they could carry on. Liam's mouth quirked at the thought of that phrase—"carry on." He wished to do it in a most literal sense, but they'd not parted well last night, and Vi was a woman of strong opinions. He glanced over at her, the remarkably clear November sunlight streaming through the side window and dancing off the lighter red in the countless hues that made her hair. She was still the most beautiful woman he'd ever known, if not the easiest.

Last night, he'd shocked himself by admitting weakness to her. It was a fool's move to hand ammunition to a redhead. He'd like to say that it had been a stratagem on his part, to bring her close and lull her into a sense of security as they searched for the gold, but it would not be true. He'd done it because with Vi, intimacy came to him easily. Perhaps too easily.

Soon Kilkenny loomed, then consumed them. In less time than he would have wished, they were parked in front of Vi's parents' home.

"I'll be quick," he said to his daughter before popping open the boot and exiting to help Vi gather her belongings. Shielded from Meghan, he took Vi's hand.

"I'll come see you at Nan's tomorrow," he said.

Vi glanced toward her parents' front window, where Liam could see the rigid figure of her mam peering out from a part in the lace curtains.

"I think I'll be needing a day alone," Vi replied, taking her hand from his.

He'd been able to sense her withdrawing from him all morning and he would not have it. "No running this time."

"I'm not running," she said, now gripping her overnight bag with both hands. "I have work to be done, you know?"

"As do I," he said.

She sighed. "Sorry. I'm being moody, and it's as though I can't help myself." She looked back to the house. "I'm not very good at being away from home for any length...and by home, I'm not meaning this place."

He kissed the warm skin of her cheek, savoring her exotically spicy scent. "I'll stay out from underfoot tomorrow, and even walk your wee dog for you, how's that?"

She gave him a fleeting smile. "It's more likely that Rog will be walking you, but thank you for the offer." She paused, then added in a low voice, "And thank you for Dublin, too."

As she neared the front door, he called one last time, "Tomorrow, then?" and smiled like a fool when she nodded her head in agreement. When he returned to the car, Meghan strayed from her usual silence.

"I don't like her," she said as they turned onto the Duncarraig road.

No point in pretending that he didn't grasp the subject of the comment.

"And that's something which you've not been too shy to share," he said. "I'd expected better of you."

"She made me go to church."

"Brutal of her," he agreed, tongue-in-cheek. "It's a blessing you survived."

"Forget it."

Liam pulled together his mantle of authority. "Meghan, I don't mean to make light of your feelings. At least, not too much. I'm sorry you don't like Vi, and hope you'll change your mind."

"Whatever," his daughter replied in a near-yawn.

"But—and this is the important part, love—you have to show respect. I'm not asking for anything more than good behavior out of you. If you can't be polite, you'll find yourself—" He'd been about to say that she'd find herself banished to her room, but that was her preferred state and no punishment at all. "Well, you'll find yourself having privileges revoked. No more Internet and messages to your friends in America. Understood?"

She nodded while shooting more daggers his way.

"Aloud, if you please," he said. "Do you understand?"

"Yes."

The word had been barely audible, but Liam was content.

"Good enough," he said, then let her lapse into a silent sulk.

Half an hour later, they were home and Liam's stomach was growling. He knew for certain that he'd left sliced ham in the refrigerator on Friday night. That and some of his mother's brown bread—which had an odd way of arriving on his doorstep—would make a fine meal. Mouth watering, he went to the fridge and opened it.

"Great stinking mountain of boiled tripe," he said to the empty white plate some ham-thief had left behind. "It takes balls bigger than the Brown Bull of Culaigne's to steal my meat."

Liam shut the fridge door and stalked to the dining room. His siblings' open-door policy was really beginning to grate. It wasn't as though he'd amble over to Catherine's and empty the larder.

"Meghan," he called to his daughter, who'd planted herself in her customary spot in front of a television. "I'm running to the market."

She looked over. "I'll come, too."

A surprising answer, but then again, after this weekend, any words from her surprised Liam. Together they walked through the town—a slow-moving place on Sunday—and to Nora's market.

As with all operations that were Rafferty-owned, the market was staffed mostly by Raffertys. Today's selection was a bit confusing to Liam, though. Da, who seldom worked anywhere other than the pub, was at the head of an aisle stocking shelves, for it seemed that the stockboy was ill. Cullen lazed about behind the register, talking on his cell phone. Liam would lay odds that a woman was on the other end, for Cullen was using his continental voice of charm.

Liam joined his father at the cart stacked with tinned fruit and vegetables, and began replenishing the shelves. Meghan wandered over to the news rack and riffled through the glossy magazines.

"So how was Dublin?" Da asked. "See anything grand?"

Liam had seen someone grand, to be sure, but that was not news shared with one's da. He opted for a better clothed answer.

"When Meghan wasn't busy buying all she could, we went to the National Museum," Liam said. "She'd heard me chatting with Vi about Rafferty's gold, and I thought a bit of education was in order."

"It surely never hurt a soul," his da agreed.

"It never necessarily helped, either," Liam said with a nod toward Cullen who was now preening before his reflection in the front window. And still talking on the phone, of course.

"You're right, there," Da said, then moved on to shelve the peas.

So long as he had Da available, Liam asked a question that had been niggling at him since before the museum trip. "About the gold tale, did Grandda always tell it the same way? I keep thinking I might have heard it differently once or twice."

Da laughed. "Likely more than that. It depended how much my da might have drunk. If it was too much, I tried to keep you children away, for the tales got mad."

"How so?"

"Well, putting aside the ones of your grandmother being a fairy he'd captured, you know the bit about Eoin Rafferty having found the gold and hidden it well away?"

Liam nodded.

"Past four whiskeys, your grandda would claim that Eoin saw to having half the treasure built into Castle Duneen."

"Built into the castle, how? It was already standing."

"Only parts, son," Da said as he grabbed a few more tins of food. "Along with the road, Dunhill was worried about having a chamber fit for Ormond when he came to fe—"

Da glanced over at Meghan, who was pretending to be enthralled by the pop star magazine she paged through. "I'm supposing you know well enough what himself wanted with Dunhill's wife. Anyway, the castle's New Tower was being built with all the modern conveniences...boxy oubliettes for feckless workers to be walled in forever, and the like." With that, Da shot a glare Cullen's way, who had failed to notice that a customer was nearing the register.

Liam was sure his father was longing for a return to the oubliette days. "So Grandda would say that at least part of the gold was in the castle?"

"He would, claiming that Eoin snuck in and walled it away in the New Tower. But it made no sense on two counts. First, why would Eoin put gold where he'd have to risk death to reclaim it? And beyond that, after the Republicans' bonfire ate the castle's roof and innards, it was a ruin for eighty years and more. I know you boys had run of it, as did I and half the town, in my day. If gold were there, we'd have learned so long ago."

But on the other side of the issue, where would the gold be best guarded, especially if it hadn't been Eoin's intention to sell it? Perhaps

Eoin had been as prudent as he was lucky. In any case, the castle seemed to Liam a far more manageable starting place than turning over Nan Kilbride's land a teaspoon at a time. Except for the complication of the American owners and a full crew of construction workers underfoot, he reminded himself.

"Tadgh was saying they're near completion, right?" he asked his da.

"He was, though you'd do better by asking the O'Gormans."

"The owners?"

"Aye, an American with a wife likely half his age. They're to the pub most Monday nights for our *sessiun*. Soaking up the local color and all that."

Liam could be colorful enough when the occasion arose. And it was rising fast. He smiled, pleased to have at least the seed of a plan.

"Would you look at that?" Da said, nodding toward Meghan.

She was ringing up the customer's goods as coolly as if she'd done it a thousand times before. Liam was quite sure she'd never touched a cash register, and that this ease in commerce was genetic...though it seemed to have skipped him as of late.

Liam smiled at his daughter. "She's a Rafferty, through and through."

"Have you thought of going into business, child?" Da called to her after the customer had left.

"I should probably go to high school first, don't you think, Grandda?"

"But after that?"

Meghan frowned as she considered her options. "I don't know..." Her face lit up. "Maybe a tattoo artist."

"Grand," Liam's father said. "We'll build you the first tattoo parlor in Duncarraig."

And Liam would have new skin art of his own—bite marks on his arse once Beth got wind of this conversation. "Thanks, Da. You've been at least half a help."

James Rafferty chuckled. "Any time, son. Any time at all."

Of that, Liam had no doubt.

* * *

Vi had always hated Sunday supper. When she was still in school, it had seemed as though Mam had been determined to take the weekend's fun and wring it from the family, so that Monday would be deadly tense. This supper was looking to be no different. The dining table was precision-set with the good china, the house cleaned to sterile perfection, and Rog had been banished to the front entry, where he moaned pitifully from behind the closed door. As Mam had Vi carry out cuts of roasted beef, the scent of which turned her stomach, Vi felt ready to launch a few howls of her own.

Da already sat at the table, wearing his "I'm thinking of finer places while I suffer the here and now" expression. Vi took her traditional seat opposite Mam. Grace was said, food was passed, and Vi received the standard maternal questioning regarding her refusal to eat meat.

They had scarcely made it to the midpoint of the meal when Mam began issuing her marching orders for the next day, commencing with the command that Da was to take her dresses to the dry cleaners, as she had no time with meetings scheduled for the garden club and her weekly tea group.

Da set down his fork and shook his head. "It will have to wait until Tuesday. I've meetings myself in Duncarraig."

"Meetings? Whatever could you have to meet about?"

"I'm considering a position there."

Vi smiled at the pride she heard in her father's words. "That's grand, Da."

"Don't interrupt," her mother said, voice icy as a winter wind. "A position, Michael? As what?"

"I'd be assisting a developer who's put together a new housing scheme. His right hand man, so to speak."

"In *Duncarraig?*"

Vi's da nodded. "In Duncarraig. If all goes well, we should think of selling this place and moving that way. Costs will be less, and with money from this house freed up, we could be of more help to the children."

"What help have they ever been to us?" Mam snapped. "And don't think I'll let you sell my house from under me, Michael

Kilbride. It's more mine than yours, and you'll not do it! If you're moving to Duncarraig, you'll be doing it alone."

"Tempting," Da said, then pushed away from the table and walked through the archway into the front room. He took his jacket from the back of his armchair and put it on, then was nearly to the entry before Vi could even speak.

"Da, don't—"

"Oh, let him go," Mam said with an angry wave of her hand. "He's spoiling my meal."

Damn you, Vi thought. *How can you be so without feelings?* But then she saw a brief hint of something startling in her mam's eyes. Were she to name that something, Vi would call it fear. She tried to let go of her anger toward her mother. Life would be so much easier if it were made of absolutes.

Freed from his prison when Da left, Roger trotted to his usual spot at Vi's feet. She wanted to hold him and find some comfort, but knew a dog at the table would send Mam the rest of the way round the bend. Her mam went to the sideboard, where she picked up a cut crystal goblet and filled it with liquid from a matching decanter.

"Sherry?" her mam asked, sounding as though they were at a cocktail party and not at another fine supper Kilbride.

"No, thank you," Vi replied with equal politeness.

Mam returned to the table, had a deep swallow of her drink and then said, "Ridiculous man. I don't know why he'd think I'd ever move to Duncarraig."

"It's not ridiculous. He was born there, after all, and if he can find work, would it not make sense?"

"Duncarraig." Again, her mother had said the word as though it was a form of plague. "What has it ever gotten me but ill?"

"You've scarcely been there."

"Not that it's mattered, with his mother there and you wandering off all the time." She swallowed the rest of her sherry and then stood to fill her glass again. "So, was this Liam the one?" she asked while her back was to Vi.

Vi's heart skipped a beat. "The one?"

Her mother turned about. "You know," she said impatiently. "Is he the one who got you pregnant?"

They had never spoken of it, not once since she'd been forced to call her home from the hospital in Kilkenny. She'd been underage, terrified, and in pain from what had turned out to be an ectopic pregnancy. It was Nan she'd wanted to call, but had slipped up in being too honest and admitting that her parents were her legal guardians. Da had been at work, and Mam had answered, which had been the beginning of the end between them.

"It was fifteen years ago," Vi said. "Why bring it up now?"

"I saw the two of you out by his car. I'm no fool."

"And I'm nearly thirty-three years old. Leave it alone."

Her mother took another swallow of drink, and Vi began to regret not having one of her own.

"I've left it alone for fifteen years," her mother said. "I didn't tell your father, just as you begged, and bore it on my own. It has hurt, Violet, all of it. Have you no idea what it's been like, a son in prison and a daughter turned up pregnant?"

"I've a very good idea, as a matter of fact." Vi pushed back from the table. "I apologized for letting you down when I was seventeen and apologized time and again after the fact, too. And I've done my best to forgive you for the hurt you've left me with." She bent down, scooped up Rog, and held him close. "All the time you spend at church, you'd think you'd have picked up a word or two about forgiveness, as well."

Her mother said nothing, just held tighter to her sherry glass and stared out into the front room. Again Vi saw it—that closed off fear in her mam's eyes—but she couldn't begin to find the desire to deal with it.

"I can't do this anymore. I've tried to hold us together even when no one else would, but I'm tired and out of the energy it takes to deal with you," she said, waving her free arm at the organized-unto-death house. "If Da asks, tell him I've gone to Duncarraig."

Vi took her dog, climbed the stairs, packed her bag, and got the hell out. It was, she was sure, what her mother wanted of her, too.

Sunday night, Liam sat at the dining room table, pen in hand, marking spots on the results graphs from his stroll with the ground-penetrating radar. To say that it was Greek to him would be an understatement, as he could find his way round Athens better than he could these jagged scribbles and dips. He rubbed his forehead and blinked dry eyes.

He knew that sneaking about in Castle Duneen appealed because it was adventure, not half-understood science. But he was the disciplined sort, or at least he used to be, before the business fiasco. Liam cut a bargain with himself: he would persuade his way into the castle once he'd at least investigated this portion of Nan's field.

A knock sounded at the kitchen door. Liam took off his reading glasses, set them on the table, then rose. He knew damn well no family member was out there, for they'd not bother with the formality of knocking. At the kitchen entry, he flipped on the porch light and felt his pulse jump, for Vi stood in the rain, not even bothering to shield her head. He opened the door and found that he was admitting both wet woman and dog.

"Couldn't sleep?" he asked.

His teasing question went unanswered. Head tipped down, Vi worked the buttons on her waxed jacket, then shed the garment, settling it over a chair at the table.

When she finally looked at him, his worry grew. "Vi, what's wrong?"

"Nothing," she said, but her expression hardly matched her words.

He tipped up her chin and looked at her in the light from the fixture over the kitchen table. "Have you been crying?"

"Have you ever seen me cry?" she asked, and he knew the question for the evasion it was.

"I know we've been at odds since last night, but you can talk to me. We're friends, Vi," he said.

Liam nearly winced after speaking. *Friends.* What a tepid word, worse than watered-down whiskey. Vi looked equally unimpressed.

She ran her hands through her rain-wet hair, then said, "You'd offered me your carriage house the other day. Might I use it?"

"Of course you can," he replied, for he would give her anything but control of the gold. "And for as long as you need it, too."

She shrugged, a flat, diffident, un-Vi-like gesture that amplified his worry. "A week, no more, then I have to be back to Ballymuir."

Words of leaving weren't what Liam wished to hear. Turning from her, he walked to the stove. "Tea?"

"Yes, thank you," she said, "And maybe some water for Rog?"

"Of course." Liam busied himself switching on the gas beneath the kettle and rattling about in the cupboard for a clean mug and bowl. "I'll ask again, do you want to tell me what happened?"

Vi took the bowl he'd retrieved and filled it at the sink. As she set it on the floor for her dog, she said, "The standard row, is all." She stood and met his eyes. "Mam and I have never done too well beneath the same roof."

"Ah." He wasn't sure where he wanted to go with her answer, if anywhere at all.

Roger finished lapping his water and issued a wet, satisfied belch.

"Wee pig," Vi said to her dog.

"They do have a resemblance about the belly," Liam offered.

Something near to a smile briefly appeared on her face. "Meghan will have no problem with me using her tower?" Vi asked.

"None that will be permitted to stand. I'm sorry for the way she acted this weekend," he said.

"She's a child yet. I wasn't expecting gracious when I was stealing her da from her, even for a moment."

"Life was easier when we were young," he said.

She fully smiled then. "You're mad."

"And glad for it," he said as he reached for the kettle, which had begun to whistle. He had no desire to wake his young bodyguard sleeping upstairs.

Vi settled in at the kitchen table while he made her tea. He handed her the mug, along with a sugar and a spoon. Then he sat opposite her, thinking how domestic this felt, and how he—the lifelong nomad—was actually enjoying it. Pretty bloody amazing stuff.

They sat in silence for a time, except for the sound of Roger snoring at his mistress's feet. Liam thought about the vagaries of his mind, how he could look at Vi and still see the seventeen-year-old just beneath the skin. At the same time, neither did he miss the fine lines of stress playing about the outer corners of her eyes.

This was not the woman he'd dropped off earlier in the day.

Something very specific and very painful must have brought her, damp of spirit, into his kitchen on this wet night. He wasn't a man for prodding emotions loose, or handling it well when others did it to him—a product of too many siblings nosing about in his life. But for the first time ever, he was sorely tempted to do the same. Twice he'd offered to talk, and twice she'd turned him down. If he were one of his brothers, he'd be threatening to kidnap her dog until she spoke.

Still, he wasn't yet like his brothers. He could afford at least one night of patience.

"Have you bags in your car?" he asked Vi.

She nodded. "The one on the front seat I need tonight, and the rest can wait."

"Finish your tea, and I'll bring your bag round to the carriage house."

"Thank you," she said.

A quick check upstairs on Meghan found her sound asleep, no doubt worn from the weekend's excursion. If Liam could have found a clear pathway through the clutter to the bed, he would have pulled the duvet over her. As it was, she'd have to continue to sleep face-down and still in the clothes she'd been wearing all day.

Then Liam was off to Vi's car, where he retrieved an overstuffed blue-and-green silken patchwork bag from her front seat and brought it into the larger of the carriage house's two bedrooms. He hesitated a moment, as this was the room with Meghan's favorite lookout, but surely she wouldn't be so adolescent as to object to Vi using it?

Decision made, he switched on the bedside lamp and dropped Vi's bag on the bed. He was downstairs fiddling with the little house's thermostat when Vi came in, water dish in hand and her dog trotting behind her.

"Your bag's upstairs," Liam said. "You'll find towels in the cupboard in the bath, and I'd like you to let me stay until I'm sure you're settled." He'd slipped in the last bit quickly, hoping she'd not object, for Vi had always been the sort to go off alone when hurting. He'd seen it enough before and could not live with himself if he were to let it happen tonight.

He watched as she sorted through his words, a frown settled

between her brows.

"I'm going to be fine, Liam. I'm just a bit tired is all," she finally said.

As he'd expected. "I'm being selfish. Do this for me, please, if not for you. I'll rest better knowing that you're comfortable."

She sighed. "I'm going upstairs to ready for bed. If you'll feel better seeing me tucked in, then grand."

"I will."

One corner of her mouth curved grudgingly upward. "Sometimes I understand you even less than others." With that, she started upstairs. Roger, naturally, trailed after her.

Liam settled in to wait in one of the two flowery armchairs in the small sitting room. From above, he heard the sounds of water running, doors closing, and then, finally, Vi calling his name. He toed out of his shoes and padded upstairs.

She was abed already. Liam paused in the doorway, a sense of something akin to deja vu slowing him. Vi leaned against the headboard, two pillows plumped behind her. Her hair was down, a tumble of deep red against the milky-white skin of her shoulders. She wore a deep blue nightgown of some sort, whether it was long or not he couldn't tell, as she had the sheets pulled up to her waist. He knew he hadn't seen her like this before, but he had wanted to. God, how he had wanted to.

"Do I look comfortable enough?" she asked, a measure of her usual tartness back in her voice.

"I'll need to come closer to be sure." Without waiting for her consent, he moved to the other side of the bed, turned back the sheet, and climbed in beside her. "Now, my fire, you're looking much closer to comfortable...but you're not yet there."

She obligingly moved into his open arms, resting on her side so that her head was pillowed against his chest and one of her legs was draped over his.

"And now?" she asked.

Liam closed his eyes, letting the feel of her against him fully register.

"Perfect." He was rousing to her, of course, for he'd have to be six months dead before having Vi Kilbride in his arms would have no effect. Still, much as his body hungered, he wished to give her intimacy of a different sort. It was time for a confession, one that he'd been far too arrogant to make fifteen years ago. He smoothed his hand over her hair, then traced the soft curve of her shoulder, all the while wondering what marvelous thing he'd done right in life to be given this quiet moment.

"That summer we had," he said, "I used to dream of this...of being in a real bed with you, of holding you close and watching you sleep."

"You did?"

He smiled at the surprise in her voice. "Hard to believe, considering the way I couldn't keep my hands off you, but yes."

"Let's stay this way for a while, then."

He nodded. "Let's."

The room was hushed, and the night was still. Vi sighed once, deeply, and he held her closer. In time he felt the tension leave her and true restfulness set in.

"Should always be this way," she murmured, words soft and slurred as sleep took hold.

An uncharacteristic tightness seized Liam's throat. "It should," he managed to say, then kissed the top of her head.

Long after Vi slept, Liam lingered, trying to understand why this one woman, tart and wise, stubborn and so shielding of her own pain, should again matter so much to him. In the end, he smiled at his folly, for a philosopher he wasn't, and answering the "why?" of Vi Kilbride would take experts, indeed.

Liam would just savor this moment, for he knew that life would never be this easy again.

CHAPTER TEN

Time brings the sweetest memories.
—IRISH PROVERB

Vi woke with a canine standing foursquare on her chest and stomach, and no man beside her.

"Doggie breath spray for you," she advised Rog while picking him up and depositing him to her left. "And a shower for me."

She rolled from bed and stretched, feeling very rested considering she'd had company at least part of the night. She'd never been much for sleeping with a man in her bed, as she was far too active a dreamer. Even wee Rog had learned from hard tumbles to the floor that low beneath her feet was the sole nighttime safe haven. Her final memories of last night, though, were of Liam's arms about her and his heartbeat marching with hers, both of which had brought a sense of comfort she had long lacked.

With Roger at her side, Vi ventured out of the larger of the carriage house's two miniscule second-floor bedrooms and toward the bath. Last night, she'd hardly noticed the details of her new surroundings. Both the night and her mood had been dark. In the light of day, though, she saw a place much like Liam's house. It had lofty ceilings with skylights, soft white stuccoed walls, and thick buff-colored carpet underfoot. Also like his house, it cried out for a splash of color. Pausing at the landing, Vi envisioned a Mediterranean blue on the sitting room wall, and three large abstracts, simply framed.

"Aye," she murmured, wishing for canvas and paints.

Beside her, Roger whined, reminding her that there were more immediate needs to be addressed.

"Walkies, eh?" she said to her terrier, then swung open the door to let him out. He immediately trotted to the far side of the courtyard, where a well-tended patch of green awaited his attention. Vi smiled, noting that Liam's car was still parked next to hers. She was beyond ready to see him again.

Once Rog was back inside, Vi showered, brushed her teeth, and dressed for the day. A quick trip to her car yielded more of her possessions, including the bagsful of yellowed notes and frayed journals she'd culled from Nan's collection the prior week. She dumped the lot in the carriage house's small sitting room, promising herself that she'd sort it all tonight. She hadn't even brought the bags into Mam's house, knowing that if she did, Mam would have pitched a fit over the additional mess.

Fairly starving for both food and Liam's company, Vi herded Rog to Liam's back door. She rapped twice, which she considered fair warning. Then she swung the door open and yelped in startled alarm, for two women were just the other side of it.

"Ah, we were just on our way out to find you," said Nora, giving Vi a friendly smile. "Liam popped over to see Cullen at the dry cleaner's. He should be back straightaway. Did you sleep well?"

"Are you hungry?" Catherine asked almost simultaneously. "I'm at that point where I could eat all day long, except my boyos, here," she said, patting her large tummy, "seem to have shifted my stomach to my throat. No matter, though. You can eat for me. Toast and marmalade, at least?"

Vi couldn't figure out how to float a word in the river of chat streaming at her. Even Pat and Danny, twins and thus not subject to the normal rules of human communication, didn't talk over each other quite this much.

"Toast is good," she managed to get in before Nora took control.

"Then come inside," she said, ushering Vi into Liam's house. "You're most welcome. And your dog, too," she added with a nod to Roger.

"Marmalade or strawberry preserves? Liam seems to have both," Catherine offered over her shoulder, already poking about in the refrigerator.

"Strawberry, please," Vi said absently. "So Liam will be back soon?"

Nora began pouring out tea for Vi. "We're thinking he will. We saw him with Cullen, but it's not as though we actually talked to him. He's of a foul mood most mornings, you know? You still take it with sugar and no milk?"

"I do." She tried to start some toast for herself, but Catherine shooed her away, saying she'd do it. Vi retreated to the kitchen table and watched the show.

"Do you still sing?" Nora asked.

"Whenever and wherever," she said, just then realizing that Saturday night had actually been the first time she'd sung in public since Jenna and Dev's wedding, all those months ago.

"Grand, then," Nora said. "Da and Jamie have a *sessiun* down to the pub each Monday night. Tonight, you can come with me and share a song. What do you say?"

Vi's answer was immediate. "I'd love to." She'd had little chance for female companionship as of late.

Nora put a mug of tea in front of Vi, then sat opposite her, a speculative expression lighting those eyes so much like her brother's.

"So," she said, "all these years gone and within days you and Liam are back to where you last left off."

Vi tipped a fat spoonful of sugar into her tea and began to stir. "I wouldn't say that." At least not aloud.

"But you're living in his house," Catherine pointed out.

"More nearby since she came in from the carriage house," Nora corrected. "Still, the point's the same. He had you to dinner, and he's not done that before."

"Except with Beth," Catherine said.

"True," agreed Nora, "but they were married and he could hardly have left her on the curb."

"What's she like?" Vi asked, then wished back the question. Beth should be none of her concern.

"Nervous and kind of sharp-like," Catherine said. "But Mam adores her."

Nora nodded. "I think she'd trade the whole lot of us for Beth."

"Well," Vi said, "you're safe enough from trade when I'm about."

"And will you be...about, that is?" Nora asked.

Vi sipped her tea. "A few more days, at least."

"So you have no plans with Liam?"

"Plans? Such as what?"

"Finally marrying him?" Nora suggested.

Vi nearly choked on her tea. "Marriage? We've been fifteen years apart and six days back in each other's company."

"Six days is time enough. I knew I'd marry Tadgh the day I met him," Catherine said, setting toast and preserves in front of Vi.

Nora laughed. "And it didn't hurt that you turned up pregnant ten weeks later."

"Now don't be sharing with Vi just how easy I was for the man."

Vi nibbled at her toast thinking this was how family should be—adversities conquered seen as positives, not creating anger simmered to a bitter brew.

"So has Liam improved with age?" Nora asked, a bold smile lighting her face.

It was Vi's turn to laugh. "Improved? Are you suggesting that I might have means of comparison?"

"All, well, there was the night years ago I went to borrow Liam's car. Coming closer, I noted that it was otherwise occupied. It didn't look very comfortable, the two of you being so tall."

"You *watched?*"

"Only for moment, and then only out of an interest in space-planning."

"Grand," Vi said, then finished off a triangle of toast.

"And as for now," Nora said, "I saw the two of you at dinner the other night."

Catherine nodded in agreement. "I was surprised Mam didn't try to cover Annie's virgin eyes, the way Liam was looking at you. And if he hadn't had you by now, he'd be up in flames."

And Vi, who scarcely ever blushed, wondered if her face wasn't much the same.

Liam came through his front door, distracted with thoughts of telephones and time zones—it was three hours later than Duncarraig where Beth was, and five hours earlier at his attorney's Boston office.

He pulled up short at the sound of a female voice coming from his kitchen.

"Aren't you overstating things?"

Liam smiled. That, he knew was Vi.

"Not at all. Vi, did you ever think about why there are so many Raffertys?"

He gave a resigned sigh, for those had been Catherine's dry tones. Extraneous Raffertys were in residence.

"Catherine's belly being case in point," Nora said. "We're all flat-out wild for sex."

Vi's laughter rang out, and Liam lost all thoughts of clocks.

"You're telling me it's genetic, then?" she asked.

"Our fatal flaw...or best aspect, depending on how one views it," Catherine said.

"So don't be trying to tell us that you two haven't found a private corner," Nora added, laughter in her voice.

Liam pushed through the kitchen door and came to stand behind Vi. "A private corner? Impossible. I can't seem to get one even in my own house."

"Or car," Vi said.

"What?"

"I'll tell you later." She smiled up at him so gloriously that he had to drop a kiss on her cheek, despite his prying sisters.

"I'm understanding it now," Liam said to Nora after she reached over and took a piece of toast from a plate sitting in front of Vi. "You raid my food so that I'm forced to go buy more at your store, is that it?"

She snorted. "Right. I'll conquer the town one empty kitchen at a time. We came to see Vi, you fool. Mam told us she'd seen her car out back."

Liam preferred not to consider why his mother might have been lurking behind his house. "Right, then. Now you've seen Vi and shared the family's dark and awful secret...such as it is," he said with a shake of his head. "How about being on your way and giving us that private moment?"

Catherine held a hand to her heart. "You'd not put a pregnant woman on the street, would you?"

"Not most," he replied. "But you for certain."

Nora filched another piece of toast for the road, leaving Vi with an empty plate and a hungry look about her.

"You don't have a bit of Rafferty hospitality about you," Nora said to him. "Come, Catherine, we'll stop to see Jamie at the pub. He's always been the nicest brother."

Liam waited until his sister had cleared the door to draw Vi to her feet and kiss her properly. Her lips were sweet with a hint of strawberry, and her feel was wonderfully solid in his arms.

"Better this morning?" he asked.

She nodded her head. "Much, though both Rog and I could use a full meal."

"I've some eggs if my sisters didn't steal them."

She smiled at him. "That would be perfect. And I've got Rog's kibble yet out in my car."

"You feed the beast and I'll get your eggs cooking. Is fried all right? You should be warned that I can't poach or do anything else too grand."

"You have your hereditary compensating talents," she said, then kissed him quickly before dancing out of his grip when he would have held her longer. "Fried is fine, and I'll be right back."

Liam pulled a pan from the cabinet next to the stove, then butter and two eggs from the fridge. He had the pan on and the butter was beginning to melt when the telephone rang.

"Don't burn," he ordered the butter, then strode to the front room and the phone. He grabbed the handset and headed back to his butter.

"Hello?" he said as he entered the kitchen.

"Liam? It's Beth."

If nothing else, this saved him the call he'd planned to make later. Along with daily e-mail, he'd also been trying to check in with Beth by phone at least once a week.

"How are you doing?" he asked. "I'd just been planning to ring you up."

Silence reigned, and it wasn't the comfortable sort, either.

"Meghan e-mailed me," Beth finally said. "And I don't know how to approach this, except just to say it. Do you have some woman living with the two of you?"

Quick at the keyboard, his daughter was. She must have gotten off a message just after breakfast, when she'd quizzed him about Vi's car and the voices she'd heard the prior evening, no doubt at approximately the same time she'd feigned sleep for his benefit. Liam turned down the heat beneath the pan and rocked it to spread the melted butter.

"A friend staying in the carriage house is all."

"A female friend, though?"

He answered with as much patience as he could find. "Yes, Beth, a female friend."

"Meghan's at a sensitive age, Liam," Beth was saying as he propped the phone between shoulder and ear and began to crack two eggs. "You can't have a stream of women—"

"It's one woman, for god's sake. One old friend. No orgies in the living room or...or—" Flaming dog's bollocks but he led a dull life. He couldn't even think of an image lurid enough to set off his ex-wife. "One woman, Beth. Have you not dated since our divorce?"

"Only when Meghan is at a friend's for the night, and I'd appreciate it if you'd do the same," she said primly.

Just then, Vi came in the back door. When she spotted him on the phone, she pointed outdoors and pantomimed the question, should she leave? Liam shook his head an emphatic no.

"So what you're saying is having her parents sneak about is healthier for Meghan than having her see respect and admiration between a man and woman?" he asked Beth.

"I'm saying she's upset. She wouldn't have told me about this if she weren't."

Liam dug through the utensil drawer for a spatula. "Of course she's upset. Her whole life has gone arse over elbows in the past month, and it has nothing to do with my guest. She's just an easier target for blame than we are."

Beth sighed. "This whole situation is so hard. I knew it would be bad, being away from her, but I can't stop worrying. I know you're right about this dating thing, but—"

"Then keep doing your work, and trust me to do right by Meghan. Everything is going as well as it can, given the circumstances."

"You're not lying to me, are you?"

"Careful with my ego, if you please. I wasn't the best of husbands, but I was an honest one, right?"

He smiled at the sound of her soft laugh.

"It was your sole saving grace, Liam," she said.

He felt a lucky man to have had at least one. "Will you be by your phone later today?"

"Yes."

"Then I'll have herself call you when she's home from school and tell you that the house has been tidy and orgy-free."

Vi looked up from the bag of dog kibble at that. He sent a smile her way.

"That would be nice." Beth was silent for a moment, then added, "So this woman friend... is it serious?"

Liam didn't know how to answer that. It was joyful, hot, confusing, and impermanent. He would return to America and salvage his life, and Vi would no sooner leave Ireland than become a nun.

"Complex," he said. "It's complex."

"I see," Beth replied, and he thought it an amusing thing that someone could voice understanding when he had none.

He glanced over at Vi, who had fixed her attention on Roger snuffling about in his kibble. Roses of color blossomed on her cheeks, markers of understanding that she was the conversation's topic.

Liam said goodbye to Beth, then set the phone aside and worked the edge of the spatula beneath Vi's eggs.

"More bad reviews for me on the kiddie front?" she asked when she'd joined him at the stove.

"I wouldn't be taking it personally."

"Oh, I'm not," she said with a serenity that raised her even higher in his estimation. "Now what's this bit about orgies?"

He scooped her eggs one by one onto a plate. "Nothing. Just trying to get a rise from Beth."

Vi brushed a kiss against his mouth, then took the plate from him. "Pity," she said. "And I'd had such hopes for the Rafferty profound appreciation of sex. Could be that you're past your prime, all right."

Liam laughed, digging out a fork from a drawer for Vi's eggs.

"We'll see if you're singing the same song tonight, once I've gotten Nora to keep an eye on Meghan."

She took the fork. "Oh, I'll be singing, but not quite the notes you're thinking. It's *sessiun* night at the pub, and I'm Nora's date."

Sessiun night, complete with the O'Gormans, and he'd nearly forgotten! The woman at his table eating eggs as though she'd best do it before they ate her was proving a distraction from a distraction. Liam smiled. Aye, she was complex, indeed.

At nearly two-thirty that afternoon, Vi hit her "I can clean Nan's no more" limit. After three-and-a-half hours of nonstop toil, the house was nearly presentable, and Vi was a dirt-smudged mess. All that could be dumped in the rubbish tip was there, and the rest of the house was orderly, if not precisely the perfection she craved.

After cleaning her hands and face with the bottle of non-rusty water and bit of soap she'd brought from Liam's house, Vi looked out the back bedroom window to see what man and hound were about. Liam was still trekking over the field, GPR rig in place, as he'd been since soon after they'd arrived this morning. Rog strolled behind him, likely glad to have finally found a human whose pace matched his stumpy legs. Vi shook her head at the sight—odd and even more oddly poignant.

Since it seemed that she'd be at the house a while longer, Vi sought reading materials. Three boxes remained next to Nan's little desk. In them were more journals and some ancient art supplies that Vi couldn't bring herself to pitch. She sorted through the journals and chose one simply because she liked the sketch of a wee bird on its cover. Vi was more abstract in style than Nan had been, but still she could see whispers of her grandmother in her own work. When she did any, that was.

Vi took the bird-journal to Nan's painted desk, then sat. With her eyes closed, she thought of Nan. She didn't picture her as she'd been near the end of her life, but as she'd been when Vi was small. Nan had never sat still, moving from one task to the next, and Vi had trailed after her...watching, learning, and in time, helping.

Vi let her hand hover over the journal for a moment, then chose a spot at which to open it, and began to read.

07 September 1964

Mam's got it in her head to die soon. There's no talking her back and I'd be doing her no service in any case. Her pain grows daily. I've promised to take her to Castle Duneen for one last look. This, at least, has calmed her.

Throat tight with emotion, Vi paged forward.

10 September 1964

It was Duneen today, and lucky for us the weather cooperated. Mam could see what had been there before, while I could see only what is now. She told me of dancing parties, women in fine French dresses, the food, the laughter, and the sweet smell of beeswax from the polished wood. It's a damp place now, stone mostly, with a few charred timbers above ... blackened bones, they looked to me.

I remember the night of the burning, its orange glow lighting the sky. How excited the men were, frenzied almost, laughing and drinking to their grand success. Mam sent me to bed, telling me that there were things on earth best not seen. Our whole world changed that night. The Dunhills left and never came back.

I would have worked at Duneen as a maid, too, had it still stood. Mam, both of my nans, they did, and seem to have mostly liked it, too. I don't suppose I would have spat on the money, but I've been content to have my time with my herbs and my cures.

Riveted by what she was reading, Vi paged on. There was chat of what Michael, Vi's da, was doing, and even a few words about young James Rafferty taking over the town's pub.

And on Vi read:

23 November 1964

I will miss Mam always. Some will say that it's wrong to be so relieved for her, that I should be tearing my clothes and weeping, but the hell with them. She lived well, Mam did, and every day I will do the same. That is how she wanted to be honored, and one day I shall ask the same.

Vi turned the page looking for more, but Nan's words had come to an end. The last third of the book was nothing but blank yellowed paper. She closed the thick cardboard cover and said, "So it was time for a new book, was it?"

After a glance out the window to see if Liam and her hound were closer to the house, Vi let her hand hover over the stack of journals and clipped papers in front of her, then plucked out the one that most drew her.

This one's cover was of faded yet thick green felt like material with a detailed concentric circular design worked in orange and yellow thread. After running her fingertip gently around the outermost circle, and feeling nearly a hum vibrate up her arm, Vi opened the book. The pages were so worn that a bit of one crumbled between her fingers, drawing a gasp of dismay from her.

"Careful, now," she warned herself, then began reading Nan's notes.

Teas—willow for fever, mint for stomach ill, and oak leaf and juniper berry when a man won't rise.

Vi smiled at the last, knowing it was the woman and not the man who would have approached outspoken Nan for the cure. She turned the page and stilled. Or perhaps they weren't after Nan at all, but Nan's mother, instead, for the page held a note dated 1905. That this book could have survived one hundred years of damp, dust, and chill was nearly a miracle.

Vi gingerly turned the pages, reading bits about births, deaths, and illnesses in the village. Matters as simple as the number of chickens brought to market or how much Nan's mother had saved from her wages at the castle took up most of the text, but to Vi it was a link to an era she was sure would have far better suited her...well, except for the washing of the Dunhills' linens and the toting of their fuel. She expected that she'd have been far too uppity for that, even if born in a more female-subservient time.

"What have you there?" asked a male voice from directly behind her.

When she'd recovered from nearly leaping from her chair, Vi said, "Most who've snuck up on me haven't lived to tell the tale."

Liam kissed the top of her head. "Then I'll count myself lucky."

Vi's answering smile was involuntary yet most heartfelt.

"So what are you reading?" he asked.

"Bits of life, really. Notes from my nan and her mother. I can tell you the price of a chicken at market and the silver pattern at Castle

Duneen."

"The silver pattern?"

Vi nodded. "Nan's mother worked as a maid there, and her mother's mother before that."

He settled his hands on her shoulders, his fingers softly massaging. "Perhaps I could have a read?"

Seducer, Vi thought, and hid her smile. He had that smooth tone at work, the same one in which he'd say "Aren't you warm with all those clothes on?" that long-ago summer.

"Here you go," she said, handing the journal up to him. "But have a care, for it's fragile."

He took it, and Vi began the countdown to what she knew she'd hear next.

Three... Two... One...

"But this is all in Irish," Liam said, sounding most surprised.

"That it is."

"I can't follow this."

She did smile. "It's almost enough to make you wish you'd paid better attention in school, isn't it?"

He handed the book to her. "I'd tell you that smugness isn't becoming, except that on you, it is."

"And flattery won't get me translating for you."

"How about this?" He swept her hair aside and kissed her neck.

Vi smiled as pleasure danced though her like fairy dust on a summer breeze. "Now, there you stand a chance, Rafferty."

His hands closed over her shoulders again, this time with a grip of pure possession.

"I shouldn't have kissed you," he said, "for now I want you naked. I've been thinking of little else all day while I walked that bloody field."

Vi drew a sharp breath as her own hunger shot through her. She closed her great-grandmother's book, starting as her fingers brushed the cover design and that sense of recognition again nipped at her.

Patterns...

She looked more closely, doing her best to push away more lustful thoughts.

This pattern was identical to the wax cast of the gorget's round pieces that she'd seen in the National Museum. Vi was certain of it. She subtly moved a piece of paper over the stitching. Aye, she'd translate for him, but this book very last. And sooner yet, she'd take the hot distraction he offered.

Vi stood and wrapped her arms around his neck. "How long do we have?" she whispered, her lips nearly touching his.

She knew his answer before he spoke, for he moved marginally away.

"Not long enough," he said.

She glanced toward the books she'd just covered. No, they would never have long enough.

CHAPTER ELEVEN

Speed and accuracy do not agree.
—IRISH PROVERB

Liam knew that life was filled with grand mysteries. It had simply never occurred to him that knowing for certain whether his daughter had completed her schoolwork would be one of them. Meghan said she had. Then again, Meghan had also said she'd cleaned her room, and any rational man could see that she had not.

It was hardly seven o'clock in the evening, and already he and Meghan had survived a burned supper (entirely his fault), a minefield of a conversation regarding Vi, a call to Meghan's mother, and a battle over the bedroom. They weren't quite done yet, either. For the first time since they'd arrived in Duncarraig, she was expressing an interest in meeting up with her cousins at tonight's *sessiun*. Studies, though, had to come first.

"So how do I tell if you've done all your work?" Liam asked his daughter, who was sitting cross-legged on her bedroom floor with books and most of her wardrobe strewn about her.

She gave a drama-girl sigh. "I've told you this before. I write all of the assignments in this notebook and I check them off when they're done," she said, holding up a black wire-bound book decorated with a pink skull-and-crossbones.

"This is where your system fails me. How am I to know that you've written everything down in the first place?"

She shrugged. "I dunno. I guess you have to trust me."

And therein lay the rub. They had no mutual trust and hadn't been permitted to begin building it in the normal way.

Liam scrubbed his hands over his face. "How about if you just clean the fire hazard you're living in, and then you can come to the pub for the *sessiun*?"

"I knew you'd come to see it my way," she said in a voice that was deadpan and yet somehow flip at the same time. A very scary talent, indeed, for a female just twelve years old. He knew he should give her a word or two about respecting one's elders, but he couldn't take another trading of barbs.

"We'll be leaving after I make a phone call. Be sure you're ready," he said and then headed downstairs.

Once there, Liam took the phone from its base, pulled a notebook and a pen from his canvas briefcase, and settled in at the dining room table—his designated office. Thus prepared, he dialed Stuart, his attorney in Boston. The haste with which he was put through by Stuart's assistant was unsettling.

"Liam, good timing," Stuart said by way of a greeting.

"Why's that?"

"Alex has gone missing."

Liam found little solace in knowing his instincts were good. He leaned back as far as the stiff dining room chair would permit and tried to relax. "You're sure of this?"

"Positive. I've been trying to work through the rest of the termination details with his attorney, who finally admitted that he hasn't heard from Alex in a week and a half. It gets worse, though. Your offices were raided by the FBI about two hours ago—"

"This makes no sense. We were cooperating with them."

"We were. Alex wasn't. His house was their first stop."

Liam's pulse quickened, and not in a pleasant way. "How about my town house? Any visits there?"

"Yes."

You're innocent, Liam reminded himself. Innocent yet so implicated—and violated—that he felt sick. He focused on what he could fix.

"Could you perhaps send someone over to clean before I return? I expect they weren't too worried about putting things back where they found them." It then struck him that he'd heard nothing about the office raid from Cami, his secretary. She had to have been there.

"Have you talked to Cami?" he asked Stuart. Cami knew that since Alex was *persona non grata,* Stuart had been designated to handle all crises while Liam was in Ireland.

"She's pretty shaken," Stuart said. "She asked me what was going on, but I thought you should handle that with her. I also told her to go home for the day."

It would be an interesting conversation when Liam did reach her. Cami had taken the job because she wanted something quiet in order to concentrate on her evening college classes. "Quiet" had clearly gone straight out the window.

"So what now?" he asked Stuart.

"Things with the government are going to roll faster than I first thought."

Liam would have responded with a good obscenity, but the well had run dry at a very poor time. He was teetering between survival and utter failure, and had hoped to thoroughly clean the company's image of Alex before news of his thefts became public. It appeared that the opportunity had passed. If the small bit of work still coming Liam's way dried up, he was finished.

A few weeks before gathering up Meghan and leaving for Ireland, he'd met with his banker to see if there was any way to extend the company's line of credit a bit farther. Their answer was no, and Liam and his accountant had then worked their way down the banking food chain until they were lodged with a lender of last resort. In addition to pledging all of the company's assets, he'd been required to provide a personal guarantee and a mortgage on the Boston town house. The only reason the Duncarraig property had escaped was that the bank didn't feel like spending the money to get its claws properly sunk in. Ironic, the one thing he'd be left with was what mattered to him least.

"So what happens next?" Liam asked.

"Probably the subpoena I'd warned you about."

"Should I return to Boston?"

"Not yet, but I want to get another of my partners involved. She usually handles our criminal cases."

The headache that had been forming when he was dealing with Meghan was an all-out killer now. "I'm no criminal."

"*We* know that, but it's going to take the government a while to reach that conclusion. The faster we can help them down that road, the better for you."

"I understand."

"So hang tight for now, and make sure we always have a phone number for you. The last thing you're going to want to appear is uncooperative."

"Agreed."

"And Liam, we've got one more thing to discuss."

"And that would be?"

"Bankruptcy," Stuart said as bluntly as only a business lawyer could. "I want you to be thinking about it before it's shoved down your throat."

"Grand," Liam said. "I'm thinking my first drink at the pub this evening should be arsenic."

"It's just business. Don't forget that."

"Right. I'll be talking to you soon," Liam said, then hung up.

Just business?

It was his life, and moment by moment he was losing control of it.

He looked at the notepad to see what he'd been scribbling while he talked to Stuart. It was nothing he'd want Meghan to see, that much was sure. Liam had had no idea that his subconscious could spew out so many variations on one key theme: *you're utterly screwed.*

It was a good thing that Vi was in Rafferty's Pub, for she needed a pint...or three. Of course, being there was precisely what had precipitated the need for drink. In agreeing to come sing at the *sessiun* with Nora, she'd overlooked one wee, well-dressed nit, and that was Una Rafferty.

Liam's mam wasn't being rude, exactly. In fact she had said nothing at all to Vi and was studiously not even looking Vi's way from her perch behind the bar. It had to be exhausting for Liam's mam, managing to be that oblivious to a soul's presence. Surely one brief hello would be much less painful.

Vi and Nora had already pulled two stools into the circle of musicians forming in front of the fireplace, where three bricks of peat flickered and smoked. While Nora turned away from the group and began tuning her fiddle, Vi glanced over at Una, determined to be done with the tension.

Vi briefly touched a hand to Nora's back. "Can I get you anything from the bar? I'm wanting a pint before we start."

"Raspberry vodka on ice," Nora replied, head tilted and bow drawn.

"Raspberry it is," Vi said, then went to face down the maternal presence behind the bar.

"Hello, having a fine night?" she first asked Jamie, who immediately stood taller, not that as the shortest male Rafferty, he'd manage to outstrip her in height.

"Now I am, and it's time you got up to the bar. I was about to risk the wrath of Mam for slipping away to see you," he said with a tip of his head toward his mother. In what Vi considered a sadly evasive tactic, Una was having an animated though one-sided discussion with an elderly man napping at the end of the bar.

"Brave, indeed," Vi said, then ordered her drinks. Jamie started the pint and while it half settled, poured the vodka and turned his attention to other customers.

Vi worked her way down toward Liam's mam. "Good evening, Mrs. Rafferty," she said once Una had given up on chat with the sleeper.

"Violet," Mrs. Rafferty said in answer.

Vi could nearly hear her nan counseling her that patience would eventually bring its own reward. "I much prefer being called Vi."

Liam's mam made a noncommittal sound in response.

"You'll be playing tonight, I hope?" Vi asked. Mrs. Rafferty had taught Nora the fiddle.

The older woman's expression softened marginally "I might. And you'll be singing, I suppose."

Vi smiled. "It's true I can't help myself," she said.

Mrs. Rafferty's firm nod was as close to cordiality as Vi could expect. It was also short-lived. A hand settled on the small of Vi's back at precisely the same moment that Una's expression grew more guarded.

"Mam," Liam said. "You're looking glorious indeed in that pink jumper."

"Don't be wasting your flattery on me," his mam replied, but Vi could see that she'd been pleased with the compliment.

Liam brushed a kiss against Vi's cheek. "I've brought a date of my own since you've taken up with Nora," he said, then cast a smile to Meghan, who was on his other side.

Vi stepped away from the bar just far enough to get a clear view of the girl. "Is that one of your Dublin purchases?" she asked.

Meghan glanced down at her hooded sweatshirt bearing the caricature of a wee monkey on a large green tractor.

"It's Paul Frank," Meghan said. "Cool, huh?"

Vi decided the best course of action was to nod knowingly, even though she had no idea if Paul might be the stern faced monkey or perhaps the garment's designer.

"Grand," she said. "Very imaginative."

The girl looked to be about to say something else when her grandmother cut in. "Meghan, your cousins are in the back office playing on the computer. Come round and join them."

Without so much as a look in her father's direction, Meghan scooted around the bar and then down a short hallway to a closed door beyond.

Liam laughed. "Fickle female."

Jamie returned with Vi's drinks. She dug into her patchwork bag, seeking the cash to pay him, but Liam retrieved his money faster.

Vi shook her head, having caught a brief downturn in Una Rafferty's mouth. "I'd rather pay."

"And I'd rather you didn't." He slid the money across the bar to Jamie. "Are the O'Gormans here yet?" he asked his brother.

"I've not seen them," Jamie replied, and Liam muttered a quiet curse.

Vi gathered her drinks and headed back toward Nora. "Who are the O'Gormans?" she asked Liam, who'd fallen in step beside her.

"They own Castle Duneen, and Da says they come to most *sessiuns.*"

Vi's heart beat faster. She'd brought her great-grandmother's cloth covered journal to the carriage house and finished paging through it in the quiet of the early evening. What she'd found had made a visit to the castle more than desirable. It had become necessary.

"The O'Gormans..." Vi rolled their name over in her mind, imagining how she might wheedle a tour where she could slip away unsupervised. Unfortunately, the only ideas that quickly occurred were drugs and handcuffs, neither of which suited her pacifist's soul.

Liam hooked his hand into the crook of her elbow, slowing her pace. Vi moved her pint away from her body so that if it was to slosh over the glass's edge, it wouldn't be onto her.

"Have you something you want to say?" she asked Liam.

"I was about to ask the same of you. I've seen that look on your face before, Vi, and it's always meant that trouble's afoot."

"No trouble," she said. "Just a wish to see the inside of the castle now that it's done."

"That's all?"

She wiggled her elbow a bit, hoping to loose him and move forward. "Of course that's all."

They were back to the circle of musicians. Vi handed Nora her drink, then sat on the tall stool beside her. Liam was still giving her a speculative look, and she needed him gone. "Unless you're going to favor us with a song, I'd suggest you join the spectators."

Liam left, as she'd expected. There had never been enough persuasion in the world to wring a song from that man.

The circle of musicians was nearly filled now, and Nora introduced Vi to everyone. Concertinas were elbow-to-elbow with bodrhans, guitars, and even a pair of spoons held by an elderly woman named Lizzie who could be sister to Breege Flaherty, Ballymuir's own silver-haired spoon player. Vi smiled at the sight, happy to have an image of home so close to her.

Before the first song began, she leaned closer to Nora. "Do you know the O'Gormans from Castle Duneen?" she asked.

Nora nodded. "Hank and Astrid."

"Astrid? Exotic."

"As befits a second wife...and retired lingerie model. I keep her in tofu."

Vi smiled at the image. "So might you introduce me?"

"Of course I will." Nora gave her a shrewd look. "Suddenly feeling social, or have you a particular interest?"

"Why do you ask?"

Nora hesitated, looking round the circle of musicians. It seemed she was satisfied that they were too involved in their own conversations to listen to what she might be saying, for she gave a quick nod of her head, then spoke. "We've a woman in town named Brenda Teevey who makes it her career to know everything about everybody. It seems she was by your nan's today, and as she passed, she saw Liam in the field with some equipment of the non-farming kind."

"Ah."

"Now, I'm not normally the snooping type," Nora said, and Vi managed to keep a straight face as her friend clearly believed this to be true.

"But..." Nora said, "I read the shipping receipt when Liam had equipment dropped at the market, and I've been asking myself what he'd be doing with radar of any sort out here. Brenda decided the answer for me and no doubt the rest of town, by now. Liam's after the gold, isn't he?"

Vi worked up her best incredulous expression. "Gold? Of course not. He's—" What possible alternative explanation could she give?

Nora laughed. "You're the poorest liar I've ever seen."

"There are harder fates," Vi replied. Just when she was ready to say more, the middle-aged man who seemed to be the unofficial leader of the *sessiun* called out "'Miss McLeod's Reel'" and with a few taps of the toe, the music picked up. As it was a song with no lyrics, Vi was at loose ends. Happy for both the reprieve from Nora's questions and the chance to look around, she sipped her pint.

The tune was halfway done when the pub door swung open and a pair of older men walked in. One she knew well, for she'd left him in Kilkenny last night. Vi edged her stool outward until she could escape from the circle without disturbing the other musicians. She met up with her da at the bar and gave him a hug. Una Rafferty pointedly looked the other way.

"Da, what are you doing here?"

"I stayed late after work to drop your mother's clothes at the dry cleaner's."

Vi gave an answer as tongue-in-cheek as her father's explanation. "I'm fairly certain she was meaning to have them done in Kilkenny."

He smiled. "See, now? That's the trick with delegation. You have to let go of the details."

"Won't she be looking for you? It's well after supper." A meal was a strictly scheduled event in Maeve Kilbride's life.

"Some time alone will do her good...and me better," Vi's da said, then smiled at her. "So, James says you're staying with Liam."

Una rattled the glassware she was stowing away, earning an "Easy, Mam" from Jamie.

"I'm staying in his guesthouse," Vi replied. "And I want you to know I'm sorry for any trouble I might have caused you last night."

Her da patted her shoulder. "You made no trouble at all. What troubles we had, we've been having."

Vi hadn't grown up with blinders in place. She knew that her parents' marriage had never been idyllic. Still, there was a reason they'd been together over thirty-five years, and she could only hope it wasn't inertia. The unhappiness in her da's green eyes hurt, though. She glanced away to see Nora waving at her. The reel had reached its end.

"Get yourself back," Nora called. "We're wanting *'Nil Se Ina La'* from you, and Jamie, another raspberry vodka for me."

"Time to sing," Vi said to her da. Jamie slid another small glass across the counter. Vi took it, sniffed its contents, and wrinkled her nose at the sweet yet strong scent. "And a drinking song, at that."

Da laughed, then his smile faded. "One thing, love," he said, leaning closer. "Don't let your mam and me put you off marriage."

Vi automatically glanced over at Liam, who was in conversation with his brother Cullen at the other end of the bar, with Cullen smirking and Liam looking annoyed. "Don't be worried. I've been off marriage much longer than just this."

Da kissed her cheek. "My Vi, more often thorn than flower. Get back to your music."

At that moment, she could think of no finer place to be.

* * *

Liam scowled at his brother Cullen. This was proving to be the sort of day to knock shite out of a man's optimism.

"I'm not after the gold," he repeated even though he knew it would do no good. Cullen had his teeth sunk into the idea and wasn't about to let go.

"Then why would Brenda Teevey see you out to the Kilbride property today? She says you looked a right fool, walking the field with equipment sticking out from you like a—"

"Enough," Liam said.

"Then you have an explanation? This ought to be brilliant."

"Vi was thinking a new well might be in order before she sold the place," he replied as smoothly as he could given the absurdity of his words.

His brother snorted. "Aye, and I'll be playing for Kilkenny Hurling in the All-Ireland matches next year."

Liam took a quick swallow of his whiskey and melted ice and tried not to look at the men gathering around Vi as she finished her third song of the night. Proverbial moths to the flame, they were. His damn flame.

"Don't be an arse, Cullen," he said.

"Come on. Admit it and be done with it."

"And if I am searching?"

His brother shrugged. "Good luck to you. The treasure's yours, after all."

Liam opted for a tacit admission. "I don't want word spreading."

Cullen laughed. "You'd be better off asking for a housebroken sheep. Brenda knows you're up to something, and the whole town will by closing time tonight." He inclined his head toward a table where a group of women were all looking their way. "She's started already."

As if to confirm the truth, Brenda waggled her fingers at Liam, who managed a half civil nod in return.

"You'd best find the gold fast, if it's to be found," Cullen said, then pushed away from the bar. "Now if you don't mind, I'm going to go charm a redhead."

Not if Liam got there first. When Cullen's progress was slowed for a moment by sour old Paddy MacGuire making for the door to have a smoke, Liam seized the advantage.

"I should have run him down," Cullen muttered, hard on Liam's heels. "Ninety-some years spent being mean is more than enough."

Liam arrived behind Vi just when she was taking her bows for her song. He settled a hand on her waist and said close to her ear, "I need to talk to you."

"After the next song?" she asked, looking over her shoulder at him.

"Now would be better."

She turned on her stool so she was facing him. "All right, then."

"Outside, I'm thinking," he said while subtly planting an elbow in Cullen, who seemed to be exploring what it might have been like to be a Siamese twin.

Vi frowned, and Liam prepared to apply stronger persuasion. She relented, though.

Once outside, they edged past Paddy MacGuire, who spat at Liam's feet, whether out of habit or in retribution for Liam's past sins, he'd never know.

"Down here," Liam said, taking Vi's hand and drawing her in front of the optician's shop next door.

"Why the secrecy?"

Why, indeed, except out of some futile hope that gossip could be stopped? "Just needing some fresh air, is all."

"You might have noted that we're now nationally smoke-free in pubs."

"Right. Of course." He took a second to assemble his thoughts. "Here's the thing, Vi. Word is out that I'm after the gold, which means I'll not be taking a step without someone behind me."

"Aren't you overstating matters? Duncarraig's a large town and with plenty else for entertainment."

"Something better than the promise of wealth? Not possible."

She shook her head. "That's a sad thing to be saying. I can think of dozens of things better than money."

He couldn't begin to see how his comment was sad and he needed to be pushing on in any case.

"Stay with me, here," he said. "Among my plans for tonight was to meet the O'Gormans and find my way into the castle, and your denials to the contrary, I expect you had much the same in mind."

"And if I did?"

"Time's not in our favor now that others will be watching us. We need to be working together now, Vi...not just in the same place." He hesitated as a couple walked by, the woman far taller than the man.

"Good evening," Vi offered.

"Good evening" came the reply in an American accent.

"The O'Gormans," Vi murmured, then moved to step in behind the couple as they neared the pub. Liam stayed her. He needed her word, and he would work out the consequences of getting it, later. "Together, Vi?"

She looked at the door that had just closed behind the couple, then back to Liam. "All right. Together, I suppose."

Her concession had been grudging at best. Liam took her hand and kissed it, then kept her fingers meshed with his. They walked toward the pub.

"It's for the best," he said. "Now let me handle getting us into Castle Duneen."

Vi halted. "You? And there's some reason you think you'll do a better job?"

"Desperation. Walking the edge of it makes a man sharp, and that's all I have left."

"Don't be forgetting massive ego. You've still plenty of that," she said, then swept inside before him.

"You should have known better than to have crossed her, boy," Paddy MacGuire opined and then threw a smoldering cigarette butt at Liam's feet.

Aye, optimism had died tonight, and Liam would drink another whiskey to mourn it.

Arrogant man, thinking he could charm his way into a castle better than she. She had charm—perhaps of an opinionated sort, but it was charm nonetheless. Vi looked about the bar and spotted the O'Gormans, drinks in hand, settling in at a corner table. Finding them was no difficult task as Astrid was even taller than Vi, and everything one would anticipate of a young and well-married former lingerie model.

Hank O'Gorman, on the other hand, looked much like what Vi expected Roger might, were a spell cast and he to shed his canine skin and take human form. She smiled at the thought of a wee male dog-selkie. It was an unkindness to the Irish legend, but accurate to be sure.

Closer to the fire, the musicians were just ending a harried version of "Malloy's Jig." Vi and Nora made eye contact, and Nora motioned toward the O'Gormans as she set her fiddle to rest.

As Vi walked toward the American couple, out of the corner of her eye she spied Liam and Cullen heading from the bar with equal intent. She picked up her pace, and she and Nora arrived at the O'Gormans' table simultaneously, with Liam and Cullen trapped behind them like the next couple in a wedding receiving line.

Hank and Astrid stood. Nora offered up introductions, playing hard on the note that Vi was an artist. Astrid perked up in a most gratifying way and offered Vi and Nora the two remaining seats at the table. Vi gave her a *"go raibh maith agat"* before sitting, figuring that a thank you in Irish was sure to earn her points with a couple enough in love with the land to sink unimaginable sums into renovating a castle. Liam's low scoff let her know that her ploy had not gone unnoticed.

She gave a glance toward the bar, where it seemed that James and her da had taken over tending duties. "Liam, would you mind too much bringing me a glass of water?" she asked him. "So long as you're standing, that is."

"My pleasure," Liam replied so sweetly that Vi knew he'd be sending some vinegar her way later.

"So, Vi, tell us about your work," Hank O'Gorman said.

"I paint, mostly, though I've been known to wander off in other directions."

"I've a painting Vi did of Castle Duneen above my fireplace," Nora said. "It's brilliant."

Slender and quite too beautiful, Astrid spoke. "You've painted Duneen? Wonderful! Is your studio in the area?"

"I'm afraid not. I live in County Kerry."

"Too bad. I'd love to see your work."

"There's always Vi's website," Cullen offered from his spot

watching over the table.

Vi looked up at him. "You've seen my website?"

"And beautiful you are in your green dress." To the O'Gormans he said, "Would you like to pop into the office and see Vi's work?"

They agreed, and the whole lot of them were trooping to the computer just as Liam was heading back in their direction.

"Have a rest, man," Vi said, hitching her thumb toward the empty table. "I've handled the castle for you."

"Not likely," he said, handing her the requested glass of water.

Once the younger generation of Raffertys were evicted from the office computer, Cullen settled in. Vi's website appeared on the screen nearly immediately. Hank and Astrid watched with rapt attention as Cullen brought up images of Vi's larger paintings on silk.

When he was done, Astrid took Vi aside. "Do you ever take on commissions? We're looking for an artist to do something like tapestries for the walls."

It was a question most artists hungered to hear, but not Vi, and for two reasons. Aye, she'd had some meager creative stirrings, but she'd hardly reclaimed the zeal that once had driven her to paint hours on end. And beyond that, even when the fires burned strong, she did best when answering to no one's expectations. Still she knew an opportunity when one was waved in her face.

If she answered yes to Astrid, she would be trading on the one tenuous gift she held above all others. But if she answered no, she might well be spoiling her chance to get inside the castle, and she was beginning to suspect that Liam might have found a drawing much like she'd seen in her great-grandmother's journal.

Liam was nudging her in the small of her back, and Vi was readying to speak when Hank O'Gorman stepped into the breach.

"At least come to the castle and have a look around," he said. "Then you can decide whether you'd like the job."

"Come to the castle? I suppose I could have a peek, right?" she asked, as though consulting with Liam.

"I have the perfect night coming up," Astrid said. "I've decided I want to try running a spa during the busy months, and we have an evening planned Wednesday for tour operators and magazine writers. It's an overnight stay with a full meal and spa treatments."

"Overnight?" Vi echoed. Liam nudged her harder, and Vi fought back a wee yelp.

Astrid nodded, her sleek blond hair shimmering in a way that Vi had only seen in television commercials. "Yes, if you're free."

"I'd love to," Vi said. "And if it wouldn't be too much trouble, might I bring a friend?"

"Then you, too, Nora," Astrid invited, sending her a smile.

Cullen cleared his throat in a way that nearly covered his laughter. Nora began stammering something, and Vi looked to the carpet in order to hide her smile.

She'd have to be doing good acts for the next decade in order to balance out the glee she now felt at Liam's roiling temper. She knew, though, that she could not leave him behind, not when he'd done it to her so often in life.

"If you don't mind, Astrid, I was meaning Liam," Vi said.

Astrid looked him up and down as though deciding whether the man might clash with her decor.

"You're a Rafferty, too, aren't you?" she asked.

"I am."

"There's an awful lot of you guys around here." After giving him one last considering look she added, "It's no big deal, but I don't suppose you sing or something?"

Vi shook her head. "He doesn't, but I do."

Cullen laughed full-out at that, and Liam made a low sound that Vi could only interpret as a growl.

"Wednesday, then?" Vi said.

"Four o'clock," Astrid agreed, offering her hand for a shake.

As Vi left the office with Liam all she could think was that some days it was a fine, fine thing to be queen.

CHAPTER TWELVE

Don't ever be in court or castle without a woman to make your excuse.
—IRISH PROVERB

Castles were interesting things, but on this Wednesday afternoon, Castle Duneen was sorely wasted on Liam. Actually, most anything have would been. Tuesday had been a day of relentless digging in the rain, with spectators dropping by fence-side at Nan's field. Wet to the bone and in a foul mood, he'd listened to them trading wry wagers on what he might find and how long it would take to do so. He'd found nothing other than a few rusted horseshoes and spent the whole bloody day doing it. Vi had visited from time to time, offering him hot coffee and amused commentary, one of which was appreciated, the other, not. Still he supposed he might have received worse from her, considering her attitude toward him on Monday night.

Since Liam's role for the balance of this day was clearly bag-handler for Vi, he was doing just that as Astrid O'Gorman led them down a posh hallway to their quarters. He stayed a step or two behind the women, half listening to their chat about the dozen other guests and Astrid's spa plans. More though, he mentally focused on the map that last night he'd had his brother-in-law Tadgh draw of the renovated castle. Tadgh had said that the New Tower—which they were now in—was fairly shot through with hidden passageways.

As a youth, Liam hadn't gotten much beyond one exterior room in this area of the castle. The New Tower was taller than the older parts of the structure, and less safe, also. Too many floors had been burned out, and even for a boy fond of risk, it had seemed potentially suicidal to climb high just to plunge through water-rotted wood. The one time he'd considered a look, ten-year-old Vi had been tagging along, and had threatened to run home and tell his mam. Liam patted the map in his jacket pocket, content that at least tonight's explorations would be rain and threat free. At that, Vi briefly turned to shoot an arch "really now?" look his way. Startled, Liam slowed. He'd forgotten that eerie knack of hers to occasionally catch his stray bad thoughts.

Astrid interrupted the odd moment, asking Vi, "I can understand why you might think a mud bath is a little much before dinner, but won't you at least try a hot stone treatment?"

"A what?" Vi asked.

"It's a form of massage," Astrid explained. "The masseuse places heated stones on your acupressure points. It's very relaxing."

Vi's shudder was subtle and likely discerned only by Liam.

"I've never been very fond of stones or burning," she said.

Liam grinned. Her type had never been.

They climbed another flight of stairs and soon stopped at a richly varnished door labeled "Sarah's Suite."

He didn't suppose that Astrid O'Gorman knew the full tale of Lady Sarah and how she'd met her end at the bottom of a stairway. Legend had it that her husband had become displeased when she'd refused to occupy his bed once she'd been given over to the earl of Ormond. One slight stumble and it had been nothing but darkness for Sarah.

"Brave woman," Astrid said to Vi, tapping once on the door's sign. "But not too practical about her position in life."

Then again, perhaps Astrid was quite sharp indeed, for those had been nasty times.

"I think you'll find this suite to your liking," their hostess said as she swung open the door.

"No doubt," Liam murmured, for the place looked to be as luxe as the expensive hotels he'd always treated himself to while on the road.

A small fire burned in the sitting-room fireplace, and on a low table in front of an antique sofa, a bottle of white wine sat chilling in an ice bucket with two glasses nearby.

"Cocktails are at six-thirty and dinner's at seven," Astrid said. "And I've scheduled you both for facials at five. I hope that you'll at least try those."

"We will," Vi answered, and Liam shot her a glare for the use of "we." His concept of luxury did not include pampering his pores or getting his nails all shiny.

"Perfect!" Astrid replied. "When you're ready, you'll find the spa rooms in the castle's old quarters. Just head down a floor and follow the west corridor. Vi, maybe when you're finished, we could take some time to talk about the tapestries?"

Vi nodded. "Of course. I'm looking forward to it."

Astrid moved toward the hallway. "Well, I'll leave you two to get settled. Is there anything else you think you might need?"

"Not a thing," Vi assured her.

The door had scarcely clicked shut before Liam let loose. "I'm to get *a facial?* What sort of Kilkennyman gets a facial?"

Vi laughed. "Your sort, I'd be saying. And I won't tell your brothers your dark secret...for a price, that is."

"And a high one, I'm sure," Liam said, pulling the wine from its ice bucket. If he was to survive the indignity of a facial, anesthesia would be required.

"Not so very high," the local witch replied from the bedroom. Liam watched through the curved archway as she slipped off her shoes, then fell backward, arms spread wide, upon the high four-poster bed. Vi gave a sigh that sounded of sheer comfort. "This will do quite grandly for the night."

He removed the bottle's foil with a deft cut of the corkscrew, then set to work on the cork. Liam poured a glass for Vi and one for himself, and then joined her in the bedroom.

"Wine?" he asked.

She sat upright and held out her hand.

Liam shook his head. "First, about this not so very high price you'll be charging?"

Her warm smile was the sort of enticement that had lured men to their dooms. "A full night in a bed with you, of course."

Doing his best to summon a put-upon expression, Liam handed

her the glass. "I suppose I'll suffer through."

"I'm sure you will," she said tartly. After taking a sip of wine, she placed the glass on the nightstand to her left, then patted the mattress. "Join me?"

He knew that if he did, they'd never arrive for their facial appointments, which was no sacrifice at all. However, neither would they get straight their plans.

"I think we need to talk about tonight, first."

She laughed. "And here I thought we just had."

Liam put his wine glass on the nightstand by Vi's, pulled out his map, and then sat on the edge of the bed.

"I had Tadgh draw this," he said, showing it to her. "While working, he and his mates used to explore the passageways in this part of the castle. I want us to walk them tonight, as according to my late grandda, at least some of the gold might be hidden there."

She arched a fine red brow at him. "You've been talking to your grandda from the beyond? Keep that up and you'll be making me redundant."

He smiled. "It's a job I'll leave for you. Actually, Da was telling me about it the night we returned from Dublin."

Vi nodded. "I think your da's got the right of it, too. At least a hundred years ago, the gold was there."

Now there was news to savor. "You know this for certain?"

"Be right back," she said, then slipped past him and walked to her bag, which Liam had left in the sitting room.

As she departed, Liam enjoyed the view. Vi walked like a warrior, straight and bold. To him, that gait was more arousing than the hip-wiggling shimmies favored by a few women he'd dated. They'd worked too bloody hard at being sexy. Vi simply was.

She returned and dropped her bag on the end of the bed, then began digging though it. Finally she settled next to him, offering a scrap of paper that had obviously been torn from a notepad.

"And this is?" he asked.

"Hand me your map," she said.

He did so, and she scanned it.

"Ah! Just as I'd hoped." She held both pieces of paper so they could look together. "See? That odd turn in the passageway Tadgh drew matches my sketch. And I copied this from something I saw in my great-grandmother's journal...you know, the one who worked here as a servant?"

"A fine coincidence," he agreed, feeling his interest begin to wake.

"The drawing was titled 'The Guardian,' which struck me as strange, considering it's nothing more than lines and sharp angles."

"Even better," he said.

"And the design stitched on the journal's cover exactly matched the wax cast we saw in Dublin."

"Sold," Liam announced.

"As was I." She handed him the sketches and returned to her bag. While she searched though it, Liam turned the papers about, confirming that the drawings did indeed match. It seemed that the passageway exited from a ground floor room that his brother-in-law had marked as a library.

"I've brought these," Vi said, pulling out two battery-powered lights.

He stood and gathered his bag, then pulled out the two lights he'd packed. "Great minds," he said to Vi, "frequently think alike."

At half-one in the morning, Vi had put aside any consideration of how great her mind might be. And as for Liam's mind, the way he was now wandering the O'Gormans' library, she was growing convinced that he'd misplaced it.

They had both been here before. In fact she'd happily lost her virginity here. It was a far finer room now than it had been then, complete with a locking door. True, the view to the King's River was presently obscured by drapes and nighttime, but the interior walls were uncharred and thick with books.

"The floor looks more comfortable," Vi said softly, so as not to disturb anyone else who might be skulking about, though she had her doubts that anyone would be. The group had eaten endlessly, drunk even more, then finally wandered to their rooms.

Liam, who was feeling his way along the paneling, glanced her way. "More comfortable than what?"

Had he not made the connection? It took a moment for Vi to get past that unsettling thought. "Why, the last time you had me here."

"Had you? How?"

She caught his smile as he gave up his search and came her way. It was then she realized that he was playing her as finely as his sister did the fiddle.

"Shame on you, Violet," Liam said, now beside her. "Did you truly think I'd forget?"

She punched him on the arm as much for the Violet as for scaring her so.

A kind man, he feigned pain. "Let's leave me both arms working, at least until we're through searching," he said.

Then Liam pulled Tadgh's map from the pocket of his denims and frowned at it for an instant. With a decisive nod, he walked to a bookshelf adjacent to the room's fireplace. "If Tadgh drew true, the hidden door should be right...about...here."

He worked his fingers into an indentation between the built-in bookcase and what looked to be solid paneling. A latch clicked and a narrow door sprung open.

"It looks nasty in here. You can wait," he said. "I'll be back in a heartbeat."

Vi peered into the darkness. Compared to some of the places she'd lived in her day, this was none too bad.

"You're not leaving me behind," she said.

"Just trying to be chivalrous," he replied.

"Castle or not, in this case chivalry is dead."

Liam gave a resigned sigh. He pulled out one of the two flashlights he'd tucked into the waist of his denims and handed it to her. Vi switched it on before tugging shut the small door to the outside world. Now they were stooped over in a dark, stone-walled corridor built for souls half her size and she was beginning to wonder if she might have a touch of claustrophobia. Not that it would matter, for she was determined to see this through.

"We'll head right," Liam said, and so they did with their flashlights trained downward. Vi spotted a small pile of empty wine bottles coated thick with dust. She wondered if it had been one of her ancestors in here, drinking filched Dunhill wine. She surely hoped so.

The further along they headed, the more the ground grew thick with rubble. Some seemed to be leftover bits of stone, whether from this renovation or an earlier one, she'd never know. Dirt was dirt and it all looked old to her. She shone her light upward. Cobwebs hung thick, and her nose began to itch at the sight of them. She rubbed at it, hoping to ward off the sneeze that was beginning to make itself known.

Twice they passed what were obviously other entries into the passageway. Liam paused at a third, then looked back her way. Even without light, Vi knew he was grinning, for the sounds coming from the other side of the doorway were unmistakably those of passion.

"More, Hank!" Astrid cried.

"Love match," Liam murmured and then walked on.

Soon they came to a T in the corridor. Liam paused and shone his light on the map, then turned left.

Vi hesitated. "I'm sure it's right we want to head."

"No, if we're to follow the map, it's left."

"Wait," she said, then heard the rustling of paper as Liam again pulled the map.

Vi peeked around him and bit back a groan. A well-fed woman with pampered skin shouldn't be in a position such as this. She reached forward with one hand and took the map. While shining her light on it, she whispered, "You've got it upside-down," then handed it back to him.

He peered at it a moment and then gave a subdued "Oh, right, then."

"And you're the grand adventurer, eh?"

"In the water," he replied. "Where I've little need for maps. Or redheads."

Vi ignored his complaint, for she knew they were both impatient and tired. It seemed they wouldn't have much longer to wait, though, for they had reached the sharply angled passageway depicted on her great-grandmother's drawing. And unless she'd been toying with her progeny, there should be a small chamber at the end of it.

"It's looking right to me," Liam whispered. "Though tight."

Vi moved until she was pressed against his back and aimed her flashlight the way he was looking. A small part of her—likely the same part that had experienced a brief and poorly timed thrill upon hearing the O'Gormans—relished this contact. Wrong time and place, but he still felt like a corner of paradise. Vi refocused, something she admittedly had little practice in doing.

The corridor they would next take was taller than the one they were in, but little more than a cut in the wall in width. Judging by the thick curtains of dust and cobwebs hanging from the entry, it hadn't been traveled in years. Liam moved sideways, back against the wall, and Vi did the same, thankful he was to take out the worst of the webbings.

The going was slow as the space grew narrower and narrower. Vi found herself holding her breath even when she knew that slight difference wouldn't ease her way.

"Stop," Liam said, then handed her his light. She angled it along with the one she already had to cover the greatest amount of wall possible. To Vi, it looked an unrelieved grey, with even the lines between the individual blocks of stone nearly indistinguishable.

"I'm not seeing anything," he said. "Hand me the lights and you try."

She did as he asked, then lay her palms against the wall, inching them across the stones' cool surface. Slowly, deeply she breathed, opening herself to whatever might be wanting to reach her...besides more dust motes.

"Are you feeling anything?" Liam asked in a hushed tone.

"Cross," she replied. "And tired and dirty."

"I meant anything from the wall."

He must have caught the look she sent him, for he added, "You know what I mean. I watched the game you played with the gold in Dublin. You were feeling something then and it will do you no good to deny it."

"I'm not denying it. This sense I get isn't something I can turn on like water from a tap," she said. "Even in the best of times—and this is not one of them—it comes when I don't want it and hides when I do."

"Try the other wall," Liam said, apparently undeterred by her ill attitude.

The two of them performed an odd dance, inching their way in a half-circle till they were facing the opposite wall. Again, Vi quelled the pleasure of his touch as he brushed against her in the tight confines.

Just inches in front of her, Liam swept the flashlight the length of the wall. Vi drew a sharp breath when the yellowish glow passed over a shadowed spot nearly mid-shin down the wall.

"You won't be needing my brand of sight," she said to Liam. "Look down."

"Damn me," he said, sounding awed. "It's real."

"Real as the dirt down my shirt," she said, earning a chuckle from Liam.

"This is it, my fire," he said to her. "Ready?"

She aimed one of the lights into his face. "Don't bloody tease. Just do it."

He grinned. "I've heard that before."

It was grand that his good nature was returning, but he needed the same reminder regarding setting and physical impossibility that she was giving herself. No matter, though. Excitement over both intimacy and discovery had her breathing enough dust that her nose was beginning to grow stuffy.

"Now, Liam."

"Right."

Reaching down that low in their narrow confines was no easy task. Vi finally backed up and Liam lay out flat on the grimy floor.

"Lower," he directed as she tried to aim her light for the niche in the wall. "Perfect."

Vi's heartbeat slammed in her ears as Liam sent his hand venturing forth. She closed her eyes, praying that they would find the gold, even though she knew the finding would bring consequences of its own.

"Hand down a flashlight."

Vi did, and seconds later Liam muttered an obscenity followed by one bleak word: "Empty."

God, how she was growing to hate that word.

Hope was quite possibly the most dangerous emotion a man could have. Furious that he'd let himself believe that tonight, treasure would be his, and he could grab back his life, Liam followed Vi through the passageway and back into the O'Gormans' library.

"That was a bloody waste," he said to Vi once he'd closed the door on his failure.

"At least we know where the gold is not," she replied while dusting off her clothing.

"Right. Not in the passageway and not in my pockets." Liam brushed ancient grime and grit from his shoulders. He hated feeling this way, filled with a frustration so brutally sharp that he burned to lash out and release it. It felt as though the gold had been stolen from him as neatly as Alex had thieved his livelihood.

Vi came closer. "You've cobwebs in your hair."

She raised a hand to free them. He flinched when she touched him, then muttered a "sorry." His anger—though God knew not at her—demanded settling. Liam glanced around the room in search of a cut crystal decanter of drink. Surely a library this well appointed would have one? It did not, and he was ready to explode.

"I wish it had turned out better," Vi said in a voice so kind that he felt a worse bastard for being in such a foul mood. Yet everything in life he'd worked to achieve was escaping and he was helpless to stop it.

She moved closer, and of its own volition his hand rose to rub a dirt smudge from the soft skin of her cheek. He'd never thought himself an especially tender man, but with Vi, it was hard not to be, even when dismally bitter. He kissed her and found it a balm better than whiskey. At least the anger was receding, even if frustration seemed a permanent guest.

"What a hell of a night," Liam said, drawing Vi into his arms. He closed his eyes and focused on the one person who could know how he felt.

Vi must have been doing the same for in a matter of moments she had brought her mouth to his and then nipped at his lower lip until he opened to her. Her tongue swept in. In just a few pounding heartbeats, hunger owned him.

They kissed until nearly breathless, then she drew back. "That helps matters," she said, her mouth still close to his.

Liam glanced around the room, seeking something—anything—

to focus on until he could get his need back under control, but his gaze kept settling on one tempting place.

"So do you think it was around there?" he asked, pointing to a spot now between two fat armchairs.

He could tell by the heat shining in her green eyes that she knew what he was speaking of—the first place they'd made love. He'd teased her earlier, but he'd never forgotten. And on nights like this one was proving to be—when luck was faithless—he would remember her passion, her laughter, and the way she'd given herself to him. She had been his most perfect gift ever.

Vi gave a considering look, as though measuring from the window to the place between the armchairs. "That seems about the spot."

Liam took her by the hand and brought her there, then nudged the chairs farther apart. They fit so neatly, standing there. Almost as if what he was considering next had been fated to happen.

"I'm feeling nearly sentimental. Would you kiss me again, Vi?"

One kiss was not an unreasonable request, and she consented. What *was* unreasonable was his body's response to hers. The need to possess, to have something good to take forward from this night, was too strong to deny.

He slipped his hand beneath the fabric of her top, seeking the warmth of her skin. Ah, this was what he needed. She was real—his to touch, his to kiss, and he planned to do it all. Vi's smart hands were equally busy, working the buttons down the front of his shirt. He voiced his pleasure in a low moan as she caressed him, too.

Soon, it wasn't enough. Liam stopped kissing just long enough to tug her top over her head and then unhook her pretty black bra and slip it from her, too. Whether it was the location they'd chosen— with both its aura of nostalgia and the danger of discovery—or the fact that frustration had transmuted to fire, Liam felt randy and ready as a twenty-year-old.

He kissed Vi's throat and grew impossibly harder at the feel of her pulse pounding beneath his mouth. His tasted her breasts, suckled her nipples, told her how exquisite she was.

She stripped his shirt from his jeans and worked open his fly. He took her face between his palms and kissed her deeply and with the fire she deserved. Dusty, disheveled, half-dressed, she was irresistible. He tugged at the waist of her khaki trousers, wishing to have all of her available for his touch.

"If only you were wearing the skirt you had on at dinner," he said.

Her laugh was low and incredibly sexy. "It was hardly snoop-about clothes."

He kissed his way across the top of one white shoulder and to her ear. "But then I'd be able to slip my hand under it and ready you, then rid myself of these," he said, taking her hand and settling it below the waistband of his open blue jeans, where nothing but some fine American boxers stood between Vi and his hard-enough-to-kill-a-man erection.

When she moved her hand beneath the boxers and circled her fingers about him, Liam was sure he was going to come then and there.

"And would you do something like this?" she asked before beginning to move her hand up and down the length of him. Liam moaned. Though it was the most difficult thing he'd ever done, he took her hand away, but only to tug her to the floor.

He pulled her khaki trousers and panties to her ankles, then was hampered from ridding her of them by some very substantial black lace-boots. No matter, for he could still touch her. Their eyes met and held. He drew her legs upward until her knees were bent and her footwear flat on the floor. Then he briefly slipped his fingers between her legs, and she gasped with pleasure. This was insanity, but he could no more stop himself than he ever could with Vi.

He kissed his way down her body, then brushed his fingers across the wonderfully red curls that covered her mound. Vi brought her hips upward, nearly begging for more, when she needn't have begged. Liam slid his fingers into her, and his erection jerked as he stroked her. He was mindless now, wanting only one thing...to surge inside her. It had been this way that night fifteen years before. This time as last, he shook as he knelt above her, pushing his clothing down his hips in one impatient move.

"Hurry." She bent her knees farther, fully opening herself to him.

Liam could scarcely draw enough breath to form words. "God,

Vi," he gasped as he settled against her, teasing but not really entering.

Vi could take no more. If she couldn't be filled by him now, she would perish.

"Please," she said, the word sounding loudly over the beating of her heart. She grasped the shirt still hanging loosely from him and tugged hard. "Now."

Liam looked down at her with such dark hunger that for a tiny instant, she wondered if she could survive her demand. He pushed his way inside her hard and fast, and she started to peak even before her body had adjusted to his entry.

Vi began to cry out, but he covered her mouth with a kiss and then moved harder and faster and her orgasm rocketed out of control. Unable to wrap her legs around him and hold on, she clutched at him with her arms as sensations continued to surge.

How well she recalled this—feelings of love and passion so huge that she couldn't hold them. She drew in a breath even sharper that her others at the thought of that word: *love*. Then Liam stiffened above her. Emotions shattered, she could feel him pulse as his seed filled her.

Seed that would never bear fruit.

The thought had never before struck her in quite this way. Now she was sure it was the reason for the tears slipping from her eyes. She let her arms slide from him and rest at her sides.

Liam lay over her, vulnerable in the aftermath of his release. She could only hope he wouldn't notice her tears. When a few moments later he moved to withdraw, she quickly wiped her eyes and turned her face to the side, eyes closed. She needed to gather herself.

"I'm sorry," he said once his breathing had slowed.

Those were not words she wished to hear.

He lifted himself up on his elbows and looked down at her, concern etching his features. "It's only the second time in my life I've let things get this far, unprotected. Once with Beth, and now this."

Vi's heart lurched. She felt as though the floor had dropped from beneath her.

"Three times," she said. "It would have been three times, then."

His expression fell blank. "What?"

"Three times. Remember the night by the river?"

She saw in his eyes the instant the memory registered.

"You're right," he said. "I can't believe I'd forgotten."

She couldn't, either, and the hurt, though irrational, was searing. That night had marked her forever.

"It was a long time ago," she said.

He nodded. "I hate to be asking this, but are you using birth control?"

Vi grasped for neutral words. "It's well controlled."

"Well, that's one less matter to be worrying over, at least," he said.

"True." As far as it went.

He brushed a kiss on her cheek, then rolled away from her. Vi began to wriggle her clothing back in place, anxious to be gone from the library. She glanced over to see Liam tucking in his shirt, and it suddenly occurred to her that he would be returning to the same room as she. The thought led to panic.

"I think I'm going to take a walk around the grounds," she blurted.

Liam paused in his dressing. "In the middle of the night and with no coat?"

Her fingers fumbled on her trousers' button when she realized how mad she'd sounded. "It was just a thought."

She continued dressing and was quickly as together as she could get.

He came to her and tipped her face up with the backs of his fingers. "Vi, are you all right?"

"Fine." The word had scarcely come out at all, so she cleared her throat and tried again. "Just fine, though I could use a moment to myself. Would you mind—" She waved her hand about the room. "Would you mind waiting here just a bit so I can settle?"

Without waiting to hear his answer, Vi unlocked the library door, stepped into the broad hallway, and closed the door behind herself. Her memories, gray wisps that clung to her more tenaciously than cobwebs, wouldn't be so easily escaped.

CHAPTER THIRTEEN

Man to the hills, woman to the shore.
—IRISH PROVERB

Liam didn't pretend to understand women. Not only were they softer and far more fragrant than he, they thought differently, too. He'd call the process byzantine, though never to a woman's face—especially Vi's, as he valued his life. Being no fool, he was well aware that their lovemaking in the library had shaken both of them. Even he, a man cursed with linear thinking, knew that something more than regret over poorly governed impulse had kept Vi sleepless once they were both back in their room. When he'd offered his comfort, she had moved to the edge of the mattress. Her rejection had hurt him, and deeply, too.

Waking and showering had occurred in silence, a state with which he was generally comfortable. Not so today. At breakfast, Vi had seized Astrid's suggestion that she stay about Castle Duneen for the day and soak up the atmosphere she'd need to complete the commission she'd officially accepted. There was a chance he suffered from paranoia, but Liam believed that Vi's enthusiasm had had nothing to do with an artist's desire to get to work and everything to do with escaping him. And the way that made him feel, he might as well have a fist squeezing the blood from his heart.

So here he was, alone on the road home, as tired as though he'd drunk a half bottle of whiskey last night, when he'd had none at all. The bugger of it was that even if he wanted to, the night's events weren't the sort of thing he could rehash with one of his sisters in order to get a female's perspective. He was on his own to untangle this knot and knew he was doing an idiot's job of it.

Liam pulled near the front of his house, then braked. A woman he'd never before seen was standing at the door. She was middle-aged and had the look of a businesswoman about her, with neat tweed slacks, a dark jacket, and a small briefcase. He knew on a rational basis that she could have nothing to do with Alex and the ugly mess in America. Still, tension made his hands grip the steering wheel tighter. She waved as he pulled round to the courtyard behind the house. By the time he'd retrieved his overnight bag from the car's boot—and ignored Vi's, for she could get it herself—the woman had joined him.

"Mary O'Sullivan from the *Kilkenny Courier*," she said, one hand extended.

Her grip was strong, and he knew she'd not be the sort to be left long on anyone's stoop.

"The newspaper?" he asked, then locked his car.

She nodded. "Aye, and a friend told me the town's gone wild with news of buried treasure."

"Wild might be overstating the case," Liam said. At least he was hoping so.

She shifted her briefcase from her left hand to her right. "Whatever the degree, it will be a fine local interest story. I've already heard from your father about the family legend and from others about your recent activities. So now I was wondering if you might consider being interviewed?"

"Not a chance."

"A few quotes, then," she said. "Just a bit to spice up the piece before I turn it in?"

"You won't be getting any," Liam said again, wondering exactly why his da would have been inclined to talk to the woman. That, though, was a matter to be addressed after he was rid of the reporter.

"Wouldn't you prefer to have your fate in your own hands?"

He laughed. "I've no illusions on that front, thank you. You write your story as you see fit, and without cooperation from me. I've greater matters I need to pry free from fate."

"If that's the way it's to be," she said, then gave a small shrug of her shoulders. "Have a grand day, Mr. Rafferty."

Odds were declining. Liam waited till the reporter was gone from sight, the tapping of her heels against the sidewalk the only evidence she'd been there. That, and his sure knowledge that what small peace he'd had in Duncarraig was about to end. He made his way into the house, dropped his bag in the kitchen, and considered what to do with himself for the day. Barring the door seemed a fair idea, as his siblings might visit. Meghan had gone straight to school from Catherine's, where she had spent the night, so he was otherwise free till three-thirty.

Solitude, though, remained elusive. At not quite eleven, his phone began ringing. The first call was from a local radio presenter nearly panting for an interview about Liam's fabled missing fortune. As far as Liam was concerned, the man could pant himself dry. The second call was from a purported "old mate" whom Liam could not recall, seeking treasure hints. The third was the most ominous of all—a request for an immediate appearance at Meghan's school.

Liam arrived at St. Brigid's minutes later, where he was ushered into the principal's office. Meghan sat opposite the principal, her face a pale mask of repressed anger. He knew the look well, for he'd worn it often as a youth, when taking the slagging of his larger and older cousins.

Mrs. McCormack, the school's principal, looked none too smooth around the edges. She rose as Liam came in, and then fussed with her watch as they exchanged greetings. He took the seat offered next to Meghan and waited to be told the reason for his summons.

"As you're aware, Mr. Rafferty, we've had a number of incidents with Meghan over the past weeks." She looked over the tops of her glasses at a file on the desk in front of her. "Multiple events of truancy...disrespect to teachers, failure to complete required work...." Apparently done with the shopping list, she cleared her throat, then pressed on. "I'm afraid we've reached the point where we must expel your daughter."

Liam was sure he'd misheard. "Expel?"

"Ask her to leave," the principal provided in helpful tones.

Right, then. "I know what the word means, Mrs. McCormack.

What are the grounds?"

"Fighting."

He glanced at Meghan and saw no physical evidence. "With whom?"

"A classmate in the library," the principal replied.

He looked more carefully at his child, who still wore that preternaturally composed expression. "Any reason?" he asked her.

She didn't respond, and merely kept staring at some fixed point on the wall behind the principal's desk.

"Meghan?" he prompted in a voice that generally scared the shite out of diving crews. She was made of sterner stuff than those work-and-life-hardened souls. She didn't even blink.

"Meghan claims she was verbally provoked," Mrs. McCormack said. "We've discussed the matter, and I believe she now understands there's no excuse for flinging a classmate from her chair and bloodying her nose."

Liam thought he might have seen the corner of his daughter's mouth curve upward for a ghost of an instant.

"I agree," he said to the principal while keeping an eye on his child. He also fully intended to get Meghan's side of this nose-bloodying tale.

Mrs. McCormack pulled a sheet of paper from her desk and offered it to Liam. "I don't wish to see Meghan fall behind in school. These are the names of instructors who might be willing to help her keep abreast of her studies on an individual basis."

"Thank you," he said, pocketing the names. He knew he could fight this, and might well do it, if he was convinced that staying at St. Brigid's was in Meghan's best interests. At the moment, though, he had doubts.

"One thing, Mrs. McCormack, the girl who provoked Meghan, will she, too, be expelled?"

The principal puffed up, reminding him of a certain fish he'd encountered in tropical waters. "Her situation is a confidential matter."

"I'd expect the same courtesy for my child," he said.

"We'd do nothing less."

"I'm pleased to hear that," Liam replied. The principal had said the right words, but he doubted the substance behind them. He knew too well how the gossip apparatus worked in Duncarraig.

"Do you have your belongings?" he asked Meghan.

"No."

"She can go round them up now," Mrs. McCormack said.

"After school," Liam replied, then motioned for Meghan and walked to the door. "Confidentiality, you know?"

And with that, he had a school-less daughter and not a clue what to do next. In what he considered one of his greater triumphs of parental responsibility over rashness, Liam waited until they were home and seated in the kitchen to begin to question Meghan.

"Care to tell me what happened?" he asked.

Her gaze skittered somewhere over his left shoulder. "Nothing."

"You hit someone. I'd consider that a very large something."

She shrugged. "She's a bitch."

"Language, please." The comment got him a full eye roll in return. "Meghan, you've been on the planet long enough to know that hitting someone is wrong. And you've also been around me long enough to know that I'm not so very skilled at this being a da thing. But that doesn't mean that I don't care, or that I'm not wanting to find some way to help you."

"Help me what?" she asked in a voice disquieting for its flat lack of tone.

"To talk about this and then to let go, lesson learned. I've seen that look you're wearing, and can tell you that bottling it all up will do you no good."

"I'm not bottling anything."

Maybe if he gave a bit of himself. It wasn't natural or comfortable to do so, but he was without other ideas. "Did you ever ask yourself why your mother and I found each other in America?"

He took her diffident shrug as reason to go on.

"It's because I couldn't live here. I always wanted more or bigger or different and I never could get anyone in Duncarraig to understand that about me. I'd grow angrier and angrier until—"

"Until you hit someone?" She'd asked the question with such obvious hope that he hated to deflate her.

"No, except for eejit Cullen when he was doing his best to

provoke me. Most often, I'd let the anger go by climbing something like the side of Castle Duneen."

"Heights suck. They make my knees all rubbery."

Well, that was a start on sharing, though not an especially helpful one. "I expect you've a great many things you're hating right now, like me for bringing you to Duncarriag."

A glint shone in her eyes. "I hate Kathleen Moriarty, for sure."

"Who?"

Meghan sat straighter, hands pressed hard on the table. "Kathleen-stupid-snotty-Moriarty. She runs that school. Mrs. McCormack and the teachers are her total tools. I hope I broke her nose. I hope she never gets all the blood out of her shirt. I hope—"

Liam raised his hand. "I'm getting the picture. What did this Kathleen do?"

"We were in the library for history class. I found the book I needed for my paper on Charles Parnell, and when I wanted to sit down, the only open chair was next to her. She's always been a bi—"

Liam loudly cleared his throat, and Meghan had the good grace to cut the word short before continuing.

"Anyway, she said I couldn't sit there. I was like, 'You don't own the library,' and she asked me why I'd want to sit where I wasn't wanted."

Meghan's mouth compressed into a small rosebud, reminding Liam so much of her as an infant that his throat grew tight.

"I expect there's more?" he asked.

She nodded and her mouth worked for an instant before more words escaped in a torrent. "She said that none of them wanted me and then her friends started whispering and snickering. And then she said that even my own mother hadn't wanted me since she'd left me with you. And— And—"

Her shoulders began to shake, and that hard mask of anger she'd been wearing started to erode.

"And what?" he quietly prompted.

"And I tackled her and hit her," she finished.

"Good for you" was what he wanted to say, but settled for "A bold move, to be sure."

A choked sound escaped her, the sort that Liam recognized as a warning.

"I hate it here," she said, her voice tight to breaking. "I've tried to be good. I've tried so hard for you."

She crossed her arms on the table, rested her forehead on them, and then the tears began in earnest. It was the sort of weeping that seemed to come from the very bottom of her soul, then work its way out, wrenching and awful.

"We'll make this work, Meggie," he said, using the nickname he'd given her as a baby, and then put away as his life grew distant from her. "We will."

"How?" Her voice was muffled, but Liam could still catch it. "You don't want me, either."

God, now there was a blow to bring a man to his knees. He was ready to cry with her. "Not want you? I've always wanted you, from the moment I knew you were growing inside your mother."

This in so many ways was his fault. He'd not thought long enough about all the departures from his daughter's life, beginning with his, four years earlier. Beth had told him that he'd hardly be missed, and he'd chosen to believe her because it had salved his conscience. Fat, hideous mistake that had been.

He stood and rounded to Meghan's side of the table, then awkwardly settled a palm between her heaving shoulders. He'd wanted communication, and he'd bloody well gotten it.

"It will be all right," he said, leaning closer and smoothing his other hand through her hair.

She no longer smelled like a little girl, all baby shampoo and filched cookies, his Meggie. No, now she smelled of too liberally applied perfume and pockets full of mint candies. He'd missed the transformation from child to this awkward in-between adolescent state, and knew there was no reclaiming the lost time. But he had made her a promise. He would make it all right. It was the very least he could do.

"Let's say we call your mother," he said.

Meghan's head shook from side to side. "Can't. She's working now."

"We can and will. Go wash those tears, and I'll scare her up."

Meghan sat up, another bit of progress. "She said I wasn't

supposed to call during work hours unless it was an emergency."

He smiled. "It's safe to say that your day qualifies."

She sniffled and then wiped her hand beneath her eyes. "I 'spose."

"Meet me in the dining room," he said, then went to his briefcase to find the emergency cell number that Beth had given him.

It took a few minutes to get the international dialing code straight, but by the time the phone was ringing, he could also hear the water running upstairs where Meghan was pulling herself together.

"Hello?" his ex-wife said over a great deal of background noise.

"Beth?" Liam asked, just to be certain.

"Liam, is that you?"

"It's me, and Meghan's needing a word with you."

"What?"

"I said that Meghan's—"

"Sorry. I can't hear too well. I'm in the field."

It sounded to Liam more as though she were inside a giant diesel engine.

"Look," she shouted, "can I call you back when I'm home in a few hours?"

Just then, Meghan came pounding down the stairs, face washed and an expectant light in her eyes. He walked to the kitchen, leaving his daughter in his wake.

"Can't you move away from whatever you're near and do this now? It's important, Beth."

"An hour, then."

"Fine. An hour." He hung up and rejoined Meghan in the front room.

"Where's Mom?" she asked, gesturing at the phone Liam held slackly.

"The reception was terrible, love. She'll be someplace better in an hour."

"And she's going to call back?"

He didn't like the doubt that made her voice waver. "She will."

"Okay," she said.

Meghan picked up a remote, settled on the sofa and switched on the flat panel television that hung above the mantel in lieu of artwork. Liam sat next to her and voiced not a complaint as she switched through channels too quickly for him to grasp even the images on the screen.

"How long has it been?" she asked three minutes later.

"Too soon to be asking."

"Right." She flipped through the channels again, then settled on an older American movie about angry teenagers serving detention in their school library. As it was apropos of her situation, Liam decided to gut out the film. Besides, the redheaded heroine put him vaguely in mind of Vi at that age. Of course, any female with red hair set him to thinking of Vi.

A quarter hour later, Meghan voiced her earlier question, then again on the half-hour. When they were three-quarters through the hour Beth had allotted, Meghan grew restless.

"Yeah, like you wouldn't fall through," she said to the boy on television, who was crawling across the top of a drop-ceiling. To Liam, she added, "It shouldn't be much longer, right?"

"Not at all," he assured her.

The appointed time passed, but the phone remained silent.

"I hope she's okay," Meghan said. "They've got terrorists and where she's working."

"There's security for the site. I'm sure she's safe, Meggie," Liam said.

"Then why didn't she let me come along?"

Sharp question from an all too perceptive child. "It would have been too disruptive," he said. And never safe enough. "Now, let's give your mother fifteen minutes, then call her."

When the time arrived, Liam called Beth and found only her voice mail.

"She's likely in a meeting," he said to Meghan, who had given up any pretense of watching the movie and instead was nibbling at her thumbnail. He knew better than to stop her. Fifteen more minutes had passed when Liam succumbed to impatience.

"I'll be right back," he said, taking the phone and heading to the privacy of the kitchen. Once there, he tapped redial and this time had Beth in moments. Her "hello" was distracted, but at least she was audible over the noise of her surroundings.

"You said you were going to call back," he said. "Meghan's grown worried."

Beth's sigh sounded to be more of impatience than regret. "I told you the timing's bad. My supervisor's here, and I can hardly tell him to go away. Really, tonight would be better."

It was a small thing his daughter needed, and he refused to fail at something this basic. Liam made his way to Meghan while saying in an undertone to his ex-wife, "Thirty seconds, Beth. She's had a bloody feck-all of a day, and I promised her this."

Meghan still sat on the sofa, feet tucked under her. "Is it Mom?" She held out her hand. "Let me talk to her."

Liam handed her the phone, hoping that Beth hadn't hung up.

"Mom?" she asked. Her face crumpled with relief when she heard her mother's voice.

"Should I go?" Liam mouthed while hitching a thumb toward the stairway, thinking she might want her privacy.

"It's okay if you stay, Dad," she said, then launched into conversation with her mother.

Dad. For the first time since they'd been together in Duncarraig, Meghan had accorded him the honor of that title.

It was a simple word, but apparently one he'd been longing to hear, for Liam felt ridiculously pleased. He walked to the front window, where he could look out and grin like a fool. Three letters—one American-sounding syllable—and his day had turned around.

Vi stood outside Rafferty's Pub, waiting for her da to join her while she took Roger for a late evening walk. Cullen had been kind enough to watch the wee hound while she and Liam had gone to Castle Duneen and pushed themselves to the brink of...

Vi frowned, sufficiently self-aware that that she could sense matters slipping from beneath her, but imperfect in her knowledge of what waited beyond.

"C'mon, Da" she murmured as Rog danced impatiently at the end of his lead. She knew it would be a few minutes yet, as Da had found more words in his couple of days spent in Duncarraig than she'd heard him use in the last decade. At a place such as Rafferty's there was always one more soul to talk with.

Not for Vi, though. Astrid had worn her thin with questions

and chat about matters such as fashion, which were of no import to her. Seeking a belated peace, Vi looked at the night sky, which was startling in its lack of clouds. The November full moon shone pale crimson, hovering over Duncarriag nearly as bright as a warning beacon. A dour thought, there, she chided herself. Best to embrace change and move on.

And move on she would, before the chill that had come across her soul last night could fully take hold. To accomplish that, today had been filled with necessary acts, all in one way or another related to a Rafferty. She'd signed a contract with a real estate agent recommended by Nora. Hired a local man lauded by James to pack the last of Nan's belongings and remove them to Ballymuir. Retained Cullen to keep an eye on Nan's property, as fools with shovels and metal detectors seemed to be flocking there this afternoon.

All was under control, with the notable exception of matters pertaining to Liam. It wasn't like her to flee. At least, that was what she'd believed of herself. And this, she knew, was flight—precipitous, rushed, and unguarded. It was a necessary act, too.

The pub door squeaked, heralding her da.

"Ready, now?" Vi asked once he'd joined her.

"Friendly-like place, isn't it?" Da asked, hitching his thumb back to the pub as they strolled down the walk and toward the main shopping district.

"Quite," Vi replied, then broached a tender subject. "You might consider bringing Mam for a visit one day soon, don't you think?"

When he kept silent, Vi glanced over him. He'd always been a handsome man and relatively youthful in appearance for his age. But whether it was a trick of the moon or of the harsh streetlights, his face looked drawn long and lined with worry.

Da walked slower, and Vi heeled Rog to the new pace.

"It's good you asked me to join you," Da said. "I've something I need to be telling you."

"And that would be?"

"Before you hear it from your mam or someone here in town, you should know that I've decided to stay above the pub in young Jamie's spare room for a while."

"You've left Mam?"

"Not left her, exactly. I'm just giving her some time to sort out her wishes. She might wish to appreciate me a little more, or she might not."

This was not the night to be discussing such matters. Once the moon had begun to wane and its pull on emotions had diminished, it would be far simpler. But then, she would be gone. Vi gathered her thoughts the best she could. "Da, shouldn't you be trying some counseling? I'm sure there's someone at your church who—"

"I'm sure all will be well, Violet."

Ah, *Violet.* The word remained a warning even now. When she'd been a child, she and Da had had a contract of sorts. If she was near to the edge of behavior he disapproved of, he'd call her by her full name. Gently, mind you, for that was Da's way. And she would call retreat, for she had pushed too far. Duly cautioned, Vi moved on to her own news.

"If Nan were here, she'd be simmering me a pot of carrageen soup," she said.

Her da was silent for a moment, and she wondered if he was going to catch her message. Her grandmother had always made carrageen soup prior to a special visitor's leaving. According to Nan, the seaweed would protect the traveler while journeying.

Vi was a believer in the theory for two reasons. First, her nan's ways made as good sense to her as those of praying to a designated saint, who must be spread quite thin, what with all the comings and goings in the world. Second, it had been a damn fine soup.

"You're leaving?" Da finally asked.

"It's time."

"Now you're sure this is what you want to be doing? You've been here just days."

Just days? The thought set Vi on her heels, as in some ways it seemed so much longer. She counted back and realized that it had indeed been only ten days since she'd first seen Liam again.

"I've finished my work," she said. "The truck will be here on Monday to pick up the things I'm keeping, and I'd best be in Ballymuir waiting for it."

"But—" Da hesitated and worked his jaw as though chewing something unpalatable. "I hate to be prying since you're a woman grown, but what about Liam? I had thought.... We *all* had thought...."

Vi chose her words with care. "Liam is a fine man, but I can't set aside the rest of my life as though it doesn't exist."

"And have you told Liam your plans?"

"Matters are complicated."

They walked on in silence for a few minutes before Da stopped altogether.

"Is it time to turn back?" Vi asked.

"I've kept my mouth shut through a lot, you know," her da said. "Mostly, it was easier that way, and sometimes I hadn't any idea what to say to the lot of you. This I do know. If you love him, it would be a sin to turn away now, after all you've been through with this man."

Vi's heart stumbled, then began to beat all too quickly. "Been through?"

Da sighed. "I'm not as thick as you'd think. I knew you fell in love fifteen years ago, and I knew you fell ill, too. Your nan might have kept the boy's name from me, but she wouldn't have kept it all. Your mother, though...." He shook his head. "I expect she's been holding it like a knife at your back all these years."

Vi held limply to Roger's lead, feeling somehow that the mundane task of walking him was her sole anchor to reality. "You knew. I can't believe you knew."

"And it hurt me to think you didn't want me to."

Tears started, and she'd been sure she'd cried her last before joining Liam in the cold bed they'd shared in Castle Duneen. "I didn't want to disappoint you. I didn't want you to think less of me."

"You're my child...then, now, and forever. I'd have been disappointed, aye, but I'd have held you and forgiven you all the same. But why I'm telling you this now is because you must love the man still, to be having him back in your life."

The need to confess was late in coming, but as Father Cready back in Ballymuir would say, it was better now than never. "Liam doesn't know about the pregnancy, and I don't know that I'll ever find the right words to tell him. And until then..."

Da shook his head and then looked to the skies as though seeking the patience to deal with her. "And so you're leaving instead? That makes my heart ache for you. Truly. I'm thinking that a sin against love is perhaps the saddest of all." He patted her cheek. "I'll be heading back to my new bachelor's quarters. You take your dog home, and while you're walking think long and hard whether this is what you want."

With that, her da turned away.

Past the shops and to the houses, Vi walked, Roger stopping to sniff at the base of nearly every lamppost. Last night she'd thought long and painfully about Liam. It had been an ugly moment, realizing that she had somehow come to blame him for her infertility. When he'd been nothing more than a memory, he'd been a convenient dropping point for those emotions. But now he was real, and she was finding herself near to in love with him all over again.

Love couldn't flourish in resentment. Vi feared having anger mar her words when she told him what had happened to her all those years ago. He deserved better from her, and she could not yet find the resources in herself to give it.

Vi walked past the front of Liam's house, where lights still shone. Utterly unprepared to say goodbye, she hurried into the carriage house. There, Rog was content to lounge on the sofa, an affair squat to the ground, much as he. Vi briefly smiled at his paws-aloft sleep position and gave thought to the escape of doing the same, herself. It was early yet—not even ten—but she'd fit two days worth of activities into one, and she planned to leave at first light.

"Coward," she muttered to herself. Tonight Nan would be seasoning her carrageen soup with a bit of thyme, to build some spine back into Vi. Even if she yet found her anger unconquerable and her personal peace a distant goal, she owed Liam a decent parting this time.

Fifteen years ago it had been disastrous. On a sweet summer night with the moon high in the sky, she had thought he was going to ask her to spend the rest of her life with him. Instead, he'd told her that in a week, he'd be off to America to attend a small college that had offered him a full scholarship. He promised he'd be back for her in four years and asked if she'd wait for him. Stricken and betrayed to the bone, she had stormed off, proving his claim: that he'd kept silent all summer because he'd known she'd take the news like a child instead of a woman.

Late that night, she'd seen him move into the shadows of a party being held at the riverside with an American tourist girl. Despite her grandmother's advice that she see with her heart, a far more perfect organ than her eyes, Vi had pushed Liam from her life. Her last words to him: that she would hate him forever.

How wrong she had been.

Before her courage could again flee, Vi crossed the courtyard. The moon had risen enough that it no longer seemed ominous to her. Indeed, it was more the guardian of contemplation that Nan had always called it.

Lights were still on within the house. She rapped at the back door. When no one arrived, she took the liberty of entering.

"Liam?" she called softly, then closed the door behind her.

She could hear the sounds of the television in the front room and walked toward it, hoping to find him alone there.

What she found made her already bruised heart ache even more. Liam and Meghan were both asleep on the sofa, with Liam sitting upright and his daughter curled up next to him. The low table in front of them bore evidence of a night's indulgence. Savaged bags of potato crisps competed for space with shredded packets of biscuits. Half empty bottles of Club Orange soda crowned the feast's remnants.

God in heaven, how she wanted this. She wanted her own child, not just Roger, love him though she did. To yearn this much and know what could have been was a pain she wished on no one. She could wake Liam, she knew, but she could taste that wholly unacceptable yet wholly human bitterness on her tongue. Vi would keep her words tonight, and share them only with the moon.

CHAPTER FOURTEEN

What the eye doesn't see will cause no sorrow to the heart.
—IRISH PROVERB

Liam woke slowly, with his joints locked and muscles knotted. The cause soon became apparent, for he was in no bed, but still in front of the television. The morning light glowing through the slats of the window blinds sent a jolt through him.

"Meggie, wake up," he said, reaching out and shaking his daughter's shoulder. "It's time for school."

He'd no sooner sounded the alarm than he recalled that there would be no school for her today or any day soon.

Meghan sat up and ran a hand through her hair, which was flattened to the side of her face that also bore the imprint of the sofa's unforgiving fabric. She looked even more muddled than he. "Gimme a second."

Liam stayed her when she was ready to rise. "Sorry, love. I should have let you sleep. You've no school, remember?"

"Holiday?" she asked blankly.

He watched as actual recollection returned.

"Oh, yeah. Expelled," she said, then scrubbed at her face with her hand. "Can I go upstairs and go back to sleep?"

He knew he'd be setting a poor precedent, but if she felt anywhere near as unrested as he, the day would be a wreck in any case.

"Go on," he said. "But I'll be waking you in a few hours."

"Okay." She stood, then took a nearly eaten bag of potato crisps from the table. Liam winced as she dug in a hand and began to munch while heading toward the stairs. A fine breakfast, there.

After Meghan was gone, Liam stretched his aching bones, stood, and cleared the table. He dumped the night's remains in the kitchen bin and then looked out the back window. Vi's car was already gone. She was off to her nan's, no doubt, and had likely been in a rush to be there before he could annoy her with direct conversation.

Hungry, he dug about in the fridge until he came up with a couple of eggs and a package of rashers. After he had some food in his stomach, he'd head to Nan's himself, and not just to corner the local ill-tempered redhead.

Vi had been right. He could at least finish confirming where the gold was not. And if that meant digging additional holes in likely spots, it was a more productive activity than contemplating his business and personal woes. Aye, he thought while pulling a frying pan and getting the rashers set, a move in any direction was more positive than standing still.

The rashers had begun to sizzle and his mouth to water. Their taste and scent were something he'd not been able to replicate in America. He'd tried Canadian bacon, Kentucky salt ham, and Danish bacon, but all to no avail. Irish rashers were just that, and while not reason enough to move back home, they came close.

Liam was getting some much needed coffee going when the phone began to ring. A hunt through the front room found it jammed behind a sofa cushion.

"Hello?" he said, pulling a biscuit packet's wrappings from the phone's resting spot.

"So, did you have another row?" his brother Jamie asked.

Since his brother had dispensed with politeness, Liam did the same. "What are you talking about now?" he asked as he returned to the kitchen.

"Vi, of course, you great eejit. She dropped in this morning to say goodbye to her da."

"Dropped in at your place? You're making no sense." Jamie lived in the flat above the pub—an unlikely place for Vi's da.

"I'm making fine sense. Vi's da is staying in the spare bedroom just now, and Vi was here along with her dog."

This was unthinkable. Impossible. Except he knew in his gut that it was all too possible.

"And is he there now?" he asked.

"The dog? No, Roger's gone with Vi."

Poorly-timed elbows to the ribs had always been Jamie's forte. He'd apparently branched out to the verbal equivalent.

"Her father, as you damn well know I was meaning," Liam said with what little patience he could find.

"No humor at all about you, is there? He's off to Brian's office for work. So did you have a row? If you did, I'm giving you fair warning, Liam. If you don't want her, I do."

"One thought in that direction and you'll be finding your teeth with your tonsils, understood?"

Jamie laughed. "Threats work only if you've ever once carried through."

"Try me on this one," Liam said. "And you won't be doubting me again. Now, stay safe behind your bar, Jamie, and let me deal with Vi."

He hung up before his brother could prod him again over words that were more easily spoken than lived.

In need of proof that Vi was indeed gone, Liam switched off the stove, crossed the courtyard in long strides, and entered the carriage house. He was up the stairs in two beats of his heart, and then into a bedroom empty of any evidence of Vi Kilbride.

"Damn you," he said once, then repeated it again, louder, angrier and still not enough to vent his frustration.

He was downstairs again and nearly to the door when on the kitchen counter he spied a folded piece of paper bearing his name. He opened it and read.

Liam,

It's poorly done of me to be leaving without saying goodbye and I have no decent excuse to offer, except you and Meghan were resting so well last night that it seemed wrong to wake you.

I've finished my work here and need to return to Ballymuir. I wish you luck in finding the gold and in all else that you do.

Fondly,

Vi

Her name was signed with a flourish, the only evidence he could find of the woman he knew and had made love to so thoroughly. Christ, she might as well have written "enclosed please find my apathetic disregard." He'd jotted warmer missives to total strangers. And as for luck finding the gold, ha! He crumpled the note into a tight ball and jammed it low in his pocket.

Appetite in its grave, Liam returned to the house, shoveled the rashers onto a plate, then stuck it along with the eggs back in the refrigerator. He showered and dressed in record time and then checked on Meghan, who was tunneled under her covers and sound asleep. He left her a note on the kitchen table, telling her he'd be visiting with Brian, then off to the countryside for a bit of digging. He signed his words, "Love, Da," feeling somehow superior to chilly Vi for having done it.

Was the truth so bloody difficult to put on paper?

Would a simple "call me" have been so painful?

He'd deal with her, all right, but first he'd let his temper cool, for he liked to think he'd learned something in the fifteen years since she'd last rubbed his nose in the dirt. Still, as he gathered the equipment he'd need to work at Nan's and set it behind his car, Liam couldn't escape his growing fury.

He knew this for a dire sign. He was gripped by feelings he'd not had in years: never in his failed marriage, and for that matter, with no other woman than Violet Kilbride. He damn well refused to call this "love," for the fire inside burned too hot for a word diluted by poets and syrupy songwriters. He needed the cant of incendiary rebels... the dead opposite of Miss Violet's sudden case of politeness.

Muttering a brief and blunt curse, Liam opened his car's boot, then stilled. What sat in front of him performed alchemy on his anger. Vi might be gone, but her fat patchwork bag rested just where she'd left it yesterday morning.

"'Fondly,' was it?" he asked, mocking the words of her note.

He knew better now. It took incalculable emotion for a woman to leave behind her perfumes and potions. Whether it was love or hate gripping Vi, its hold was fierce. And because he was a man who believed in hope, Liam could only believe that her emotions fell closer to love. Filled with a sense of victory, he laughed aloud. Vi Kilbride was running from him, and this time he would not let her go.

* * *

"Home again," Vi said to Rog, who hours before had given up tail-wagging at the car window for a glum slump on the seat, chin resting on paws. Were she not driving, she'd strike much the same pose.

It wasn't the return to Ballymuir affecting her mood. This village was home to her in a way that the place she'd been born had never been. The heathery sweep of rocky mountains to the shore, the sea-scented air, the richness of color even now when autumn had stripped bare the few stands of trees hardy enough to hold fast to the soil...all were usually pleasing to her soul.

Today, though, tension tampered with her nerves. Unfinished business was a poisonous brew, and in leaving matters so thoroughly incomplete with Liam, she knew she'd taken in a vile amount. There was no turning back. The cure would be even more lethal than the illness.

Vi drove past the arts village perched on a steep hillside overlooking the harbor. The small enclave of traditional-looking white cottages had been built years before by the government to lure artists. She had been well snagged, as her studio sat in the cluster. She would not go there today, though. The abandoned projects waiting within suffocated her, and already she could not breathe quite right. Panic crept upward, closing her throat, and she held tighter to the car's wheel. This would pass even before the moon had fully waned. She was sure of it.

On the seat beside her, Roger shifted and moaned. She glanced over at him, sorry that she'd let her turmoil unsettle even her dog. They both needed constancy and comfort.

"Shall we visit Michael?" she asked him. His ears swiveled at the familiar name.

"Grand, then," she said, as Roger sat upright.

Vi drove past her own house on the very edge of the village and then up the winding road that traced the terrain's change from hill to nearly mountain. The closer she got to her brother's house, the more quickly she drove. As she neared, the promise of peace teased her.

Michael's ways were the old ones—not quite as Nan had lived, but still with a distance from the rush and noise that was creeping into even the Kerry countryside. He built furniture and supervised his brothers in general carpentry tasks out of a stone barn behind the farmhouse that he and Kylie had bought from an elderly friend some time before. It was a peaceful place, and one of family. Unless he was with the twins at a job site, Vi stood a grand chance of catching all three brothers at once.

As she turned off the main road onto the smaller track that led to Michael's home, Roger stood and began snuffling at the air vent in front of him.

"Hold fast," she said as the car rocked from side to side on the rutted road. A veteran of such travels, he dug his nails tighter. Vi's tension-knotted muscles began to ease.

Then she caught sight of not only Michael's car, but also Kylie's parked in front of the large white farmhouse. At this hour Kylie should still be at Gaelscoil Pearse with her students. Vi pulled in next to Kylie's car, then let Roger have a go at his business before heading toward the door. She wasn't yet to the stoop when her brother came outside.

Vi doubted she'd ever take the sight of him for granted, not after the way they'd been separated for the fourteen years he'd spent imprisoned in the north, a victim of his own youthful gullibility. Today, though, more than other times, Michael Kilbride was exactly who she needed.

"Grand of you to drop by," he said in the calm and steady voice she loved so, "especially without having called me these past ten days."

"Keeping count, were you?" she asked as she approached.

"No, just listening to Pat and Danny moan about having no one to boss them about. As if I'm not enough," he added before folding her into a hug that was a balm to her uneasy spirit.

"Where are the boys?" And boys they would always be to her, though they were both now a head taller than she and grown so independent that she knew they'd be gone from her home before she could prepare herself to let them go.

"Danny's at Muir House, framing the folly Jenna's having built in her garden. Pat's working on Lorcan O'Connor's new wine bar."

Vi hid her disappointment. "Well, I suppose I'll see them tonight."

"You've no way of missing them, once I call and tell them the prodigal sister has returned," Michael said. "For now, though, come inside and watch Kylie with me."

"Watch her do what?"

"Just come along. You, too, Rog," he added, then ushered them inside.

"Love," he called into the kitchen, "can you hold up a few minutes? Vi's returned."

"Tell her I'll be just a sec," returned a muffled voice.

Michael gave a woeful shake of his head. "Right, you will."

"What's going on?" Vi asked.

Her brother tilted his head toward the kitchen. "Go have a look."

Vi peeked in the doorway, then glared over her shoulder at her brother. "Get in there and help her," she ordered.

Kylie—who in less than a fortnight had somehow expanded exponentially—was on her hands and knees scrubbing the baseboards. The sight pained Vi for reasons both charitable and not. First, Kylie was usually a slender woman and small of bone. Vi had no idea how, when so large with child, Kylie could get that low to the ground, let alone how she'd regain her feet. And then on the greedy, selfish, and appallingly self-centered front, Vi was jealous to the bone.

Seeing Liam with Meghan last night had made the lie she'd based her life on impossible to sustain. God, how she hungered to be pregnant, and how she would starve. It wasn't as though she begrudged Kylie, but that failed to ease her pain.

"Do you think I haven't already cleaned?" Michael said in an undertone, cutting into Vi's thoughts. He'd spoken quietly, but not enough so, for Kylie looked up and smiled at Vi, who couldn't seem to look away from her sister-in-law. Green with jealousy? No, the fitting shade was ash gray—dry, empty, and without hope of being transformed into anything finer.

Was it just her anger at Liam over her barrenness cutting her from all that was vital? No, for if that were true, recognizing it as she had last night would have made her whole. By Brid and the spirits, why was it easier to look into others than herself? Why must she always fight so bloody hard? Could she just not surrender?

"Just this last bit and then I'll come out and greet you properly," Kylie said to Vi, who managed a vague yet cheery response, likely insufficient to mask her turmoil.

Michael put his hand under Vi's elbow and led her to the sitting room.

"Are you all right?" he asked. "You're not looking yourself."

Whomever that might be. "I'm fine," she replied, then directed the conversation to a topic she knew would distract her brother. "How long has Kylie been cleaning?"

"Long enough," he said. "She called in ill at school this morning as her back was aching and she was having what she thought might be contractions, yet I've not been able to stop her all day. I scrubbed the damned kitchen floor till it was clean enough to have the village council dine from it, and she told me I've no eye for detail, then did it again."

"No eye for detail? She truly said that?" Vi asked. Now there was a thought to distract even her. No one had a better eye for detail than her brother. Already his beautifully sinuous furniture had been featured in lifestyle magazines and bought by celebrities, and he'd not yet been in business two years.

He nodded, his mouth shaped into an unwilling smile. "She's got sharp ways about her for a woman currently so round, eh?"

Vi smiled at the image. "So why the mad affair with cleanliness?"

"She's nesting, or so the books tell me," he said, pointing to the teetering stack on an end table next to the sofa.

"You've read all of those?"

"Parts. At least enough to know that childbearing is left to women for a good number of reasons. And in any case, the real expert will soon be moving on to the refrigerator hinges," he said, hitching his thumb toward the kitchen. "They've not been wiped down in at least a day."

"Amazing."

"Tiring," her brother added. "She's not due for another three weeks and I'm afraid by the time labor starts, she'll be exhausted."

"Three weeks? She'll be having the baby before then."

Michael's gaze was speculative. "Are you seeing something, then?"

The normalcy of the question—one she'd been asked countless times in life—soothed her. "Just that it's physically impossible for

Kylie to get any larger without exploding."

"I heard that," admonished her sister-in-law from where she'd appeared in the doorway. "And I fear you've got the right of it, too. I've decided to start my maternity leave on Monday. It's getting too difficult to keep up with the children. My back aches, and my temper's growing short."

Michael's relief was obvious. "Finally," he said, and then kissed his wife. "As my begging hadn't been working, I'd been hoping that reason would arrive."

"It's here and telling me that you need to get the furniture done and nursery painted...once we can settle on a color." She turned to Vi. "You're the family artist. Do you have any thoughts?"

Vi tried to look at her sister-in-law, yet not actually look at her, too. Since she hadn't the aptitude for the feat, she fussed with her shirt cuff instead. Thus occupied, she unwillingly considered the question. "Well..."

She meant to slough it off and avoid added pain, but she couldn't seem to gather her thoughts. Something was coming over her. Suddenly light-headed, she moved to an armchair facing the sofa and sat.

"Are you all right?" she heard Michael asking from a great distance away.

"Forgot to eat again," she said as awareness of her surroundings receded. Bright shooting stars gave way to a pattern of crimson circles, one inside the other, all shimmering like glowing embers. Instead of the anticipated fainting feeling swallowing her, a low buzzing sounded in her ears.

Could it be?

Damned horror of a gift, never coming when needed and smacking her upside the psyche when unwanted. Vi let her eyes fall shut. The fiery circular pattern remained, reminding her of her great-grandmother's notebook. The image faded, then slowly and none too clearly an impression of a baby girl with her father's green eyes and her mother's full mouth came to Vi.

"Pale lavender," she said to her brother, who she knew was hovering nearby, his worried thoughts so loud in her head that he might as well speak. "Paint the nursery pale lavender with a morning sky on the ceiling."

There, she'd done it. Now would this sensation leave her bloody well alone? She tried to rouse, but couldn't. Her vision of the babe was replaced by one of the same dark-haired girl years hence leading a flock of younger children in mischief. Not a single one among them could she call hers, either.

Her envy seemed to have one productive aspect, for the moment of seeing passed. Vi opened her eyes, drew in a deep breath, then raised a brow at Michael and Kylie, who were now standing in front of her. "And you'd best make sure that you've locked away the breakables and hidden the ladders."

Michael laughed. "That's unassailable advice. And don't think I failed to note that you chose neither boyish nor girlish colors for the baby's room. Some seer you've turned out to be."

"Really, and would you be wanting to know the baby's sex?"

Michael's *yes* clashed with his wife's alarmed *no*.

"No?" he asked Kylie. "If we don't let her tell us, once the baby's born, she'll just say that's what she saw."

Vi tried for some of their usual banter. "I'd never do that. At least to no one but you."

"None of your games, you two," Kylie decreed. To her husband she said, "I didn't ask my doctor and I'm not asking your sister, even though I expect she's more accurate. I've no intention of knowing what this baby is till I'm holding him—or her—in my arms. I need something to focus on during labor."

Chastened, Michael kissed his wife again. "We'll have it your way, then."

Kylie pinned Vi with a teacherly frown. "And no telling others, either."

"Of course not."

"The baby's healthy, though?"

"Quite," Vi assured her.

"Grand."

Michael gave Vi an appraising look. "You're still too pale. I'm thinking you need at least some soup before I have to do the unthinkable and carry you to your car, wee sweet Violet."

Only could Michael, broad of shoulder and soft of heart, get away with teasing her so. "For that, I should make you do it."

She glanced at her watch. It was already nearly three-thirty and much as she'd like to, avoiding her studio was no longer an option. With her waking dream had come a germ of an idea for the Castle Duneen commission. She wasn't so rich with inspiration that she could afford to ignore it

"And thank you for the offer of food," she said, "but it's to work for me—" She meant to say more but those circles had returned, dancing in fire. She wasn't sure how long she fell silent, except it was long enough for Michael to now be giving her a most exasperated look.

"You're getting fed before you float away altogether," he said before turning heel and heading to the kitchen.

Kylie walked to the sofa. She somehow managed to lower herself onto it and still look graceful. Another pang of jealousy stuck Vi, followed by the obligatory bite of guilt. Ah, yes, this was why travel to Duncarraig had sounded so appealing. She gave fate a grudging nod. It was a dark irony that she should have run to more sharply personal woes than those she'd fled. She kept her gaze on her sister-in-law's face while they chatted about village events over the days Vi had been gone.

Soon, Michael reappeared with a paper sack in hand. "I won't be standing between you and your work, but I won't be having you starve, either. There's bread, fruit, and cheese to tide you over till supper."

Vi rose, hastily telling Kylie to please sit back and relax when it looked as though she intended to move. Michael walked Vi outside and stood by as she and Rog got settled in her car.

"So now that Kylie's out of range, is it a boy or girl?"

Vi laughed. "I value my life, thank you, so I'll not be telling you."

"But I'm your very own brother," he wheedled. "I promise I won't tell her."

"No matter. You're mad in love with Kylie, and she with you. She knows you too well, Michael. One look at you and she'll be sure I told."

"Impossible. I'm not obvious at all."

Vi could only laugh at her brother's protest. "When it comes to Kylie, you've always been."

She briefly considered giving him family news of a sootier feather than the stork's—that of Mam and Da's battle—but discarded the notion. If Mam was hard on her, she was merciless with Michael. A prison stay, even one not quite wholly deserved, was a sin never to be forgiven according to Mam's commandments. Michael and Mam had worked a tenuous truce, but Vi doubted it would ever grow warmer between them.

Instead of cause for more upset, she manufactured her very best seer's smile and said, "Here's my gift to you, brother. I promise I'll tell you boy or girl before the babe is born...*thirty seconds* before."

With that, she rolled up the window, gave him a wave, and drove off.

"Ready for a marathon at the studio, *ma chiste?*" she asked her hound.

Roger whimpered, as would have Vi, except she knew it would change nothing. The fire was in her, and burn she would.

On a cold Sunday mid-morning, Liam looked out his window at another dozen or so reasons to be gone from Duncarraig. Yesterday, his family's tale of lost wealth had appeared in the *Kilkenny Courier.* The newspaper must have a rabid readership, for earlier he had awakened to a small gathering of the terminally optimistic standing out front of his house, in search of a leader.

In telling them to leave, he'd made the critical mistake of acknowledging them. It had been rather like letting a hungry stray dog look one in the eye. Bonding was instantaneous and irrevocable. They'd stood on the curb, bandying about theories, each less likely than the last. Disgusted, Liam had retreated to breakfast and the telephone. A call to the *Gardaí* asking for help had yielded little, as no actual trespass was taking place.

Liam walked away from the window before his entourage could take his regard as a sign of welcome. If it were just him, he'd have been gone yesterday and missed this scene. He had Meggie to consider, and God knew he loved her, but she had a way of making matters involved.

His mother had invoked saints he was sure didn't exist when he'd announced his intention to leave. According to Mam, there was Meghan's washing to be done, firm arrangements regarding lodging to be made, and Beth to be consulted. And though his mam had never directly mentioned Vi, she'd denounced Ballymuir as a wild and heathen place, and surely unsuitable for a child.

Liam had had no patience for Mam's subtext. He'd told her that he'd always favored exotic places and had no intention of changing. That had earned him Mam's silence, though he was sure his da was getting an earful on the topic. Liam planned to be well on the road before Mam could gather her resources for another attack.

"Hey Dad, if I threw a bucket of water from the window, I bet I could hit at least ten of 'em," Meggie called from upstairs.

That would nearly be a sight worth suffering for. "Then we'd have the *Gardaí* after me instead of them," he called back. "Just come downstairs, love. It's time for us to be off."

Without a glance in his followers' direction, he shuttled Meghan to the relative sanity of his mam's care, and took what subtle barbs Mam could send his way before escaping. After that, he was off to Nan Kilbride's for one last look about, his procession trailing behind him. Cullen, who was to be watching the place for Vi, let the lot of them enter. Liam watched as his shadows climbed out of their cars and began to band together.

"Could you not have stopped them?" he called to Cullen, who was lazing about near Nan's painted boulder, his smug expression looking very much like another reason for Liam to be gone.

"They'd just create a distraction on the roadside" Cullen replied as Liam neared. "What do you think of charging them three euros each as a car park fee?"

"And you'd be giving the money to Vi?" Liam asked, knowing far better. Even lazy Cullen had enough Rafferty opportunist in him to turn a money-making opportunity to his own benefit.

"I...ah...hadn't thought that far ahead."

"You just hadn't thought beyond your own pocket," Liam replied, then started a bit when the cell phone in his own began to ring. He extracted it, turned away from his brother and his followers, and then answered.

It was Beth again, the third time she'd called today, still in a state of high alarm. He had done his best to reassure her that all was under control—no mean feat, considering he'd also had to tell her of Meggie's expulsion. Even his promise to call their daughter's school in Atlanta first thing Monday and arrange for books and lesson plans to be sent by express courier hadn't calmed her.

"One last question," Beth said this time. "That woman who's staying in your carriage house, she's not going to Ballymuir, is she?"

"Vi's already there," Liam replied, wishing he were.

"I knew she was involved!"

His ex-wife didn't sound at all herself. Their divorce had been emotionally difficult, but even in those moments of stress, she'd not been vindictive. Liam attempted to calm matters.

"Beth, Meggie and I are staying in a hotel of sorts, not with Vi. She doesn't even know we're coming." Though she damn well should expect it, he could have added.

"I don't like this," Beth said. "I'm going to call my parents. Maybe they can—"

"Don't," he said with more force than he'd intended, but his pulse had jumped at her words— ones that sounded a threat to him, when a few weeks ago they would have sounded like nirvana. "Meggie's fine with me, and here she'll stay. I haven't had nearly enough time with her."

Out of the corner of his eye, he spotted a few of his followers making a break from the pack. "Hang on a sec," he said to Beth. "Cullen, get them away from the house, and then while you're at it, off the property."

"But my car park fees!"

Liam tallied the vehicles while he listened to his ex-wife threaten to hang up on him since she wasn't worth his full attention.

"I owe you twenty-one euros, then," he said to his brother.

It seemed bribe enough, for Cullen was on the move.

"Beth, about Meggie," Liam said into his cell phone, but it was too late, for Beth had been as good as her word. He redialed, got her voice mail, and left an apology even though he knew it would do little good. He'd spent his apology quota on Beth years before.

Cullen had the property cleared and a hand extended for cash with such efficiency that Liam was forced to feel some respect for the sluggard, if not the need to be around him very much longer.

And so Liam began a task surprisingly solitary in nature considering the number of onlookers lining the low stone wall that marked the border of Nan's property. An empty task it was, too. The sun had started to slip low in the western sky when Liam was forced to admit that Rafferty's gold wouldn't be saving his arse today. Or likely any other.

"I'll be heading home," he called to the remaining intrepid observers who were sharing both joking comments and what appeared to be a flask of whiskey. "And don't be expecting an invitation to supper."

Liam returned to town, noting that most of his entourage had stopped near the family pub. Now, at least, he grasped why his da had been so open with the reporter. Like Cullen, his father had been thinking with his wallet.

Glad to be rid of his tail, Liam moved on to his mam's house. When he entered, the first thing that struck him was the quiet. Usually she had the television going whether in front of it or not. He stuck his head in the small television room, but it was empty, as was her fussy front room.

"Mam?" he called.

Just then, Meghan came skidding into the hallway from the dining room. "You're back early, Dad."

Liam took in the over-brightness of her tone and the way her brown eyes shone with a contrived innocence. He might be a novice at parenting but he was no fool.

"I'm exactly on time. Where's your grandmother?" he asked as he strolled into the dining room. Meggie's blue daypack lay on the table with a scattering of girl-things around it, and an open bottle of Club Orange sat on the polished mahogany without a coaster beneath it. Clearly, Mam wasn't in residence, for she'd be having a seizure at the sight.

Meghan positioned herself between him and the door to the kitchen, which was ajar. "Aunt Catherine's barfing, so Grandma went to watch everyone. I'm staying here since I'd rather die than puke. I mean, what if Aunt Catherine has the flu or something? The last time I had it, I even barfed the water Mom tried to give me. It was totally gross."

Liam had begun to see a pattern in his daughter's habits. Sharing of random personal details meant she was hiding something else. He looked at her more closely. Her white long-sleeved shirt was splotched a brownish color here and there, and its cuffs looked to be both wet and stained with the same color.

"What happened to your shirt?" he asked.

"I don't see anything," she replied without even looking. Liam tried to glance around her, toward the kitchen, but she repositioned herself in his way.

"Odd. You see nothing at all, eh?" He took her by the elbow. "Let's go in the kitchen and—"

Meghan dug in her heels. "Wait! Grandma has this awesome soap bar by the washing machine. I'll get it. You wait here."

"So what is it you're not wanting me to see?" Liam asked as he released her, then managed to skirt past her and into the room she guarded.

The astringent scent of brewed tea filled the kitchen. Wet sheets of paper, all tinged an ugly light brownish color, lay across dishes lining the counter-tops. More were clipped to hangers suspended from every available cupboard knob or hook. And Jamie sat at the kitchen table, a mug of what else but tea in his hands.

"Jamie" Liam said, giving his brother an appraising nod.

"Liam."

"Do I want to ask what you're about?"

"Just having a cuppa," his brother replied with great calm.

"Right." Like Meghan, Jamie was more the Club Orange sort. "And the paper?"

"We're aging it," Meghan said as she came to stand behind her uncle.

"You're what?"

"Aging it. Uncle Jamie showed me how."

"I'm trying very hard not to sound an idiot, here, but why might you need paper soaked in tea?" Liam asked Jamie.

"He's going to make treasure maps for the people coming to town," Meghan said before Jamie could answer. "You know, like in the movies."

And there was the final hand in the middle of the back pushing Liam to the town limits. "Jesus, Jamie—"

"Mind your words," his brother said in a fine imitation of a parish nun. "There's a child present."

"One you're involving in a fraud scheme."

"Ah, come now, Liam. You've got to learn to go where the wind takes you. How do you think our ancestors managed to survive?"

"Through thievery and corruption, according to you," Liam replied. He flicked at an almost dry piece of paper on the kitchen table. "And this, I'd say, falls into the corruption end of the enterprise."

"Thievery, too, I suppose, as it's Mam's tea we're using," Jamie cheerfully pointed out.

"Grand," Liam replied while Meggie giggled.

"Just meeting a need," Jamie said. "I knew as soon as that reporter lady came to visit Da that there'd be treasure seekers arriving. And as long as they're seeking, why shouldn't we recoup some of the Rafferty gold with a map or two?"

"It looks more like a few dozen to me," Liam said. "And you don't sense a moral issue afoot in all of this?"

"I'm having some fun, is all," Jamie replied.

"Jeez, Dad, don't act like this is some big deal."

Liam didn't much like his daughter's comment, for this was a "big deal," indeed. If Beth got wind of Meghan's involvement in even this small scam, it would be yet one more reason to pull her from him.

"Meghan, why don't you go pack up your things?" he asked. "I believe I saw your bag in the dining room."

"But—"

"Now. And close the door, too."

Meghan did as told, but none too willingly.

"I'll give you a questionable sort of credit for initiative," he said in a low voice to his brother, as he knew his daughter would have an ear to the door. "But involving Meggie? I'd be better off letting Da open the tattoo parlor for her, as he's promised. At least that would be legal."

"Tattoo parlor? Hadn't thought of that one," Jamie said. "Do you suppose it could turn a profit in a town this size?"

"Forget the parlor," Liam said, regretting he'd even raised the topic. "Meggie and I are here until tomorrow morning. If you could keep your damn maps to yourself until then, I stand a far better chance of convincing her you meant these as overpriced souvenirs and not wholesale fraud." He glanced about the kitchen. "Oh, and good bloody luck in getting this room clean and all the stains out of Mam's rug by the sink. If you don't, she'll be chewing your arse till Easter."

Liam was sure that Jamie's response of "feckhead" was meant with the utmost of respect and affection.

"Come, Meggie," he said, pushing open the dining room door slowly enough that his eavesdropping daughter might dodge it. "Uncle Jamie says goodbye."

CHAPTER FIFTEEN

Desire makes hunting.
—IRISH PROVERB

"Rubbish and more rubbish," Vi decreed. Of course she had no one with whom to share the critique of the two canvases she'd created, as Pat and Danny had rescued Roger from the studio the day before. At least she thought it had been the day before, but she wouldn't wager much on it. Time had a way of fleeing while she worked.

Vi tried to tame her hair into a knot, then sniffed the air suspiciously. Something smelled a bit ripe. It might have been herself or it might have been an item among the food moldering away atop her glass display case by the cash register. She'd meant to tuck the offerings her brothers had delivered into the small fridge hidden in the back room, but had gotten sidetracked. She'd also stopped answering the phone and had in fact unplugged it, as she could bear no interruptions when consumed by an idea.

Unfortunately, it seemed that in this instance she had done the idea-consuming, then spat it out as two rather frantic and disjointed paintings. Hands on hips, she glared at her works. She planned to create four seasonal pieces—souls celebrating round bonfires burning on the riverbank near Castle Duneen. These first two, with Beltaine's watery springtime lushness and Samhain's crisp autumn shades, should have been the easiest to capture. It seemed, though, that putting the idea on canvas was the first step toward disappointment. Milky Imbolc and wild Lughnasa bonfires were still forming—or was it festering?—in her imagination.

She remained enamored of the concept, if not the execution. What better than community blazes of rebirth for a castle once burned? But her theme hadn't carried through clearly, for matters of personal passion wouldn't let her be. She was haunted by a man very much alive.

Physically, she might have left Liam in County Kilkenny, but someone had forgotten to inform her subconscious. The seductive heat of his kisses, the deep sound of his laughter when she would toss a comment his way, and the way he had of making her feel alive to her core—all had followed her to Ballymuir. And now she wanted him to be here, too.

If she closed her eyes, she could envision Liam down to his cuticles. And she could paint him to perfection, too—just nothing bloody else, it seemed.

"You're mad," she said to herself. "Not that it's any great news."

Deciding that a quick wash-up might change her outlook, Vi went to the small bathroom located in the back corner of the studio. She did the best she could with a toothbrush, a bar of lavender-and-thyme soap, and a sink too small to be of practical use. At least she could now bear her own scent. She left the shirt and brassiere she'd been wearing on the studio floor and pulled a well-spotted painting shirt over bare skin.

Buttoning as she walked, Vi passed a half-dozen other efforts on silk and canvas that in the past weeks she'd abandoned like changeling infants in the forest of her cluttered studio. She would not look at them, would not acknowledge the power they held over her with their failed faces.

She switched on the radio and listened for a bit of chat that might give her the day. Then, she returned to her Samhain canvas, which was still not quite spoiled, and looked again.

"All over too orange," she said. "Yet fixable."

Vi had just gone to her palette when a jingle of the bells tied to her front door signaled an intruder.

"Did I not tell you to let me be?" she called over her shoulder to whichever of her brothers had developed the desire to be flayed alive. "I'll call you when I'm ready to be brought home."

They knew her well, her brothers. Along with Roger's company, they had also deprived her of her car. Experience had taught them that she'd be a hazard on the roads when she was finally exhausted enough to stop work.

"I was under the impression that you'd not be calling me at all," Liam Rafferty said.

In that moment, words failed Vi even more dismally than her art. She spun to face him.

Ah, but the sight of him made her knees grow soft and her heart softer. If she were the least arrogant about her envisioning abilities, she might believe that she'd wished him here. She wasn't, though. He was here of his own accord and appeared none too pleased to have it so.

"You didn't read the sign on the door?" she finally managed to work from muddled mind to mouth.

"It was in Irish," he said, "which was never my language of choice."

"Still, I'm sure you recall that *dunta* means closed."

He strode closer, all clean and fresh and bloody well reeking of confidence.

"You forgot this," he said, dropping her patchwork bag at her feet. "And you forgot this, too."

He kissed her, thoroughly, deeply, and with an utter boldness that angered her as surely as it aroused.

"You owed me that for goodbye," he said when he'd finished.

She needed to regain her balance or her heart would be forever lost.

"I owed you that?" she asked. "And what might you deserve in the way of a welcome? Me on my knees before those fine shoes of yours?"

Liam laughed. "Reading my mind again, are you? Or maybe it's just an insight regarding men in general. No matter," he said, then began to stroll a loop around her studio. He touched a soft weaving adorned with seashells that she'd collected and gave a nod of approval.

"How long have you been here?" he asked when he reached her rather pungent food remains.

An easy enough question, most of the time. "What day is it?"

"Monday," he replied, a measure of surprise registering on his distinctive features.

"Really?" Another day had indeed slipped past her.

"It's not the sort of thing worth lying about, now is it? So how long?"

"Since Friday afternoon."

"And you slept here?" he asked, then with the tip of one shoe, nudged the tattered green futon she'd earlier spread on the floor.

Their gazes locked, and if emotion were a visible thing, Vi would find their sexual awareness a brighter crimson than the flames she'd painted.

"I've slept now and again," she replied.

"You must be wanting your bed."

Before she could frame an answer, he'd gone to stand in front of her two new canvases.

"Don't look at them," she said, alarm making her voice ring sharply in her ears.

"Why not?"

"They're not fit." And if he looked closely, he'd find himself in both paintings, along with the impossible bit of wishcraft of her at his side. In all, running naked through Ballymuir would create less exposure than what her brushes had produced.

"The paintings look fit enough to me." In spite of his words, he turned away, leaving Vi to gather her dignity.

"Did you think you could just leave Duncarraig?" he asked an instant later.

The jump in conversation brought her fully alert. Though he'd said Duncarraig, he'd meant himself. The fewer words, the better, in response.

"I couldn't stay anymore. I've a life that needs tending."

"As do we all. My complaint, Violet, is with the way you left."

Violet. He used the word to incite, but she would not be so easily played. "I apologized in my note. Quite nicely, too, I thought."

"You did," he said, prowling closer. "In a bland sort of way. Very tellingly unlike you."

"Tellingly? What do you mean by that?"

"Later," he said. "First, I want that welcome kiss, and then I want you in your bed...on the floor...against those unfit paintings. It doesn't matter, so long as I'm inside you."

She shivered when he touched her face and then the curve of her lower lip.

"Here, then?" he asked, flicking open the buttons of her shirt

Vi fumbled to cover what he exposed. "I haven't showered in days."

"I don't care."

She laughed. "But I do. I can scarcely bear myself."

He kissed her once, then again, quick persuasive nips. "Let me take you home. Now."

This would solve nothing. She would leave his arms as incapable of addressing their problems as she was at this moment. And yet she gave the answer that her easy heart dictated.

"Yes," she said.

Liam had been put out with the dog. Of the two of them, Roger seemed far more content with the situation. Liam had angled to be in Vi's shower, but had been told in blunt terms that as she actually planned to get clean, she would be doing it alone, thank you. He could tend to the royal hound.

While herself's dog sniffed about the back fence line, Liam turned up his jacket's collar and did his best to ignore the chill wind sweeping up the hillside from Dingle Bay. Roger, who wore a warmer coat, circled a low shrub once and then again in reverse, as though the act were part of a ritual.

Thinking he might as well put his time banished to good use, Liam pulled his cell phone from his pocket and readied to put through a call to Muir House, where he and Meggie were staying. The elegant manor house and restaurant, owned by an expatriate American chef named Jenna Gilvane, was hardly what he'd expected to find in this quiet part of County Kerry. It seemed, though, that others had found it, for even now, in the tail end of November, it was booked nearly to capacity.

After some persuasion and name-dropping of the Kilbride variety, he and Meggie had taken up residence in a two-bedroom suite on the top floor. Meggie had immediately embarked on a reconnaissance mission, certain she'd spotted some movie star named Sam walking the grounds.

Liam dialed Muir House and was quickly connected to his rooms. Meggie picked up after two rings.

"Have you called your mother as promised, love?" he asked after greeting her.

"Yeah, but I couldn't find her, so I left a message. And you'll never believe it, but I *did* see Sam Olivera, just like I told you. His girlfriend is the owner's sister, and they're so nice. He even gave me his autograph when I asked, and then they invited me to go with them for a bike ride to the village in a little while. Can I go? There's bikes for the guests and I promise I'll even wear one of those geeky helmets. Say yes, or I swear I'll die right here."

It was a near miracle, how she'd managed to fit all those words in one breath. "Mind the traffic, such as it is, and be sure you're back before dusk. We'll be eating in the restaurant tonight. The owner's invited us to a special dinner."

"So you mean I can go to the village?"

"Yes."

"You are the coolest dad ever! Hey, I gotta go find my camera." She hung up before Liam could say anything more, which was fine as his ability to concentrate was fading. He again pocketed his phone and settled one hand on the back door's knob.

"Ready yet?" he asked Roger, who seemed to be exhibiting a certain amount of canine glee in taking his time. Just as Liam was ready to go chase down the beast, he trotted up the steps.

"Glad to see you could work me into your schedule," Liam said to the dog, then closed them both inside.

Vi's modern house was an unremarkable white stucco on the outside. The interior, however, was as exotic as its owner. The walls were rich jewel-toned hues, and some had quotes painted upon them. The words were in Irish, naturally, and Liam's skills weren't up to accurate translations. He could catch a few bits, such as *tine,* which, as he recalled, meant fire, and *farraige,* which was the seaside.

The air carried a fragrant scent, too, of cloves, perhaps, and some flower he couldn't identify, except that it brought to mind wild pleasure on silken sheets. Of course, the scent of Roger's kibble might well trigger the same thoughts at this moment.

Seeking distraction, Liam returned to the canvases he'd noticed leaning three-deep against the walls of the back hallway, all unframed and clearly unattended. He flipped through the stacks and marveled at Vi's talent.

Some works were detailed, reminding him of the fire paintings he'd looked at in her studio until she'd chased him off. Others were more abstract, like that of Castle Duneen above Nora's mantel. But all were stamped with Vi's perspective and singularity of vision. Liam had no idea why she would be treating art this arresting as though it was queued up to be put out with the rubbish.

He was about to go through the canvases again, but a new, muted sound distracted him—that of Vi singing. Her voice lured him inward. Through the front room he walked, where Roger had settled on a small sofa in front of the fireplace. Liam ventured down a hallway until he came to a closed door, which he knew had to be the bathroom. There was no sound of water running, just that of her bright song.

"Vi?" He rapped on the door, hoping now, at least, for an invitation to enter.

"Don't even think of coming in," he received in answer. "My bedroom's the next room down. Go on in, but do keep Roger out. He's a bit of a voyeur."

Liam glanced toward the front room where he'd last seen the dog, but he needn't have looked so far, as Roger was at his heels.

"Think again, boyo. It's the sofa for you," he said when the dog tried to slink in the bedroom door. When working up a profession of love, the last thing a man needed was a wee beast laughing at him. Just then, Vi's clear tones of amusement came his way. Though of course, he mentally added, a woman's laughter would be a thousand times worse.

Vi stood in front of the bathroom mirror, trying to quell her smile and manufacture an acceptable pucker. She knew she was being ridiculous, trying to apply lip color that would be gone minutes from now, and doing a clown-poor job of it, too. But after the days locked in the studio, she looked like the dead. Even a vigorous scrubbing in the shower had done little to get her blood moving.

For the first time in her life she wished for wildly extravagant silken lingerie. Hand-stitched, French, and deep green in color would be quite grand. Naturally she had none, so the white of her skin would have to be adornment enough. She took one last glance at her face in the minuscule mirror and then gave a shake of her head so that her curls would tumble wilder yet over her shoulders.

"Fine enough for a dead woman," she said, then left the steamy warmth of the bathroom. At the bedroom door, she gave Rog a quick pat on his head, then slipped inside, leaving her hound in the hall.

Liam had turned back her bedcovers and lay there, as naked as she. The pleasure Vi got from looking at him made even her feet tingle. Liam's pleasure was far more obvious. He was hard for her, and she longed to take him in her hands.

"Grand, isn't it," she said as she prowled toward him, "us being past the age where we need to be coy?"

Never one to deprive herself pleasure offered, she settled on the mattress's edge and touched him. He didn't move his hands from behind his head where he had them casually cushioned, but she wasn't for a moment fooled. She knew what it cost him to hold back, as she was spending the same in not simply flinging herself on him.

"I don't recall you ever bothering with artifice," he said.

She smiled as she noted the slight hitch to his voice. "Aye, you're right. All that nonsense was too much work to manufacture, and only took away from the time we had to be doing this."

She crawled over him, knees to either side of his hips, then leaned down and settled her lips on his. Liam's reaction was immediate and breath-stealing. He rolled her beneath him, shielding her with his arms so that his weight stayed off her. Then he kissed her hard, as though it were a brand of possession.

Possession. Lord, how she'd always hated that word. She had chafed under the proprietary behavior of other lovers. Not with Liam, though. He might claim to own, but she in equal measure owned him. As she returned his kiss, she reached for him, hoping to urge his body into closer contact, but he would have none of it. He took her hands, locked her fingers between his, and pinned them to either side of her head.

"But is it all about this, Vi?" he asked. "Do you see us as the sum total of our body parts?"

These were the emotions she was ill-prepared to face, and if she could dance by them, dance she would. She let her gaze move leisurely down his body. "It's not such a horrible fate, Rafferty. Yours are some very fine parts."

He briefly squeezed her hands tighter. "Not this time," he said. "You won't be distracting me. I'm about to give you words that I threw about with far too little respect fifteen years ago. I love you, Violet Kilbride. Did always and will always. You can make light of this if you wish, but I came here because I love you, and when I'm moving inside you, it's more than fine body parts at work. I love you, and I'm awed to have the chance to say it again."

Vi hadn't realized that she'd begun to cry until the first tear rolled out of the corner of her eye and then was quickly joined by more.

Did she love this man? Aye, but to say the words and then lose him again would be more than she could bear. She tugged at her hands, trying to free herself, but he wouldn't let go, and instead kissed her again, then spoke.

"You're the other half of me...the one who has the bluntness to speak the truths I've been conditioned to only think," he said. "You're the one who never once laughed at my adventures, not even one as totally mad as looking for that gold. And you're also the one I've never forgotten. Not in one empty night of my life."

"I've never forgotten you, either," she said, her voice thick with what tears she'd managed to withhold. "I know we're more than this, I promise I do. But I'm not ready to give words, Liam. I'm just not," she finished, for words of love weren't the only ones difficult to summon.

"I've misjudged matters, then?" he asked.

She fumbled for something to say. "I truly appreciate your—"

"Appreciate?" He laughed, but it was a sound made more of frustration than humor. And she knew it was well deserved, too, for next she'd be spouting greeting card verse.

"Christ, after I praise your blunt ways, you mean to kill me with politeness?" he asked. "Tell me this. Right now, should I leave this bed, leave you and let you tend to the life you've got here?"

"No! Of course not!"

Tension left Liam's face. He closed his eyes for an instant and exhaled a slow, almost cautious, breath.

"Good, then," he said.

Vi smiled, though she knew it was a wobbly affair. "You might think of letting go of my hands, though. I won't hit you or run, I promise. I just need to wipe my tears."

"Ah, but that I can do for you." He dipped down and kissed her forehead, then either side of her face, at the wet and salty sensitive skin beneath her temples. Then he set her hands free. "I love you, Vi, and now I'll make love to you. Do you want me to use protection, or are we safe?"

"Just you inside me," she said, knowing that all but her heart was safe.

He kissed her breasts and belly, and stroked her between her legs as she caressed him. The afternoon sun spilled onto the bed from the open curtains, and she took pleasure in making Liam move just so, where she could watch the play of light and shadow fall across him.

Together, they were art and subtle miracles. They were the sort of beauty that always stayed just beyond her fingertips. She might not be able to capture it and have it serve her whims, but she could live it. In time, the sheets were a rumpled ridge at the foot of the bed, and Vi and Liam were angled across the mattress.

He entered her slowly, whispering, "My Violet." It sounded a sweet poem to her, and she considered that her name might sometimes actually suit.

They were totally skin to skin, and it was paradise. She ran her palms up his arms, feeling the strength of muscle and sinew. She drew his head down to hers and kissed him, letting her tongue slide against his.

When Liam began to move, it was such a slight action that at first she thought it might have been her imagination, or perhaps the instinctual rocking of her own hips, which she could no sooner stop than she could will her blood to move more slowly through her veins.

She asked him for more, but he shook his head. "Not yet. Move your legs up around me." When Vi did as he asked, he said, "Now close your eyes and just feel."

Vi felt the rising and falling of his abdomen pressing into hers as he breathed. She felt the tiny sting of flesh still relaxing to accommodate him, the pounding of her heart as her passion grew, and the fullness of Liam inside her. The tangy, almost primal scent of their lovemaking surrounded them, and the combined heat of their bodies rippled across her skin, making her feel as though she'd been dancing too close to a bonfire's flames.

She fixed all these impressions in her mind, for the artist in her was greedy, taking and keeping what was needed to fill creativity's wellspring. This wasn't using. It was simply who she was.

Vi opened her eyes and caught Liam looking at her with a tenderness that was enough to break her heart.

"Do you have it now?" he asked.

Her heart jumped, for he knew. In a way that defied reason and experience, he knew her down to her soul.

"This, Vi, is love," Liam said, then withdrew and returned into her, making her back arch and her breath hitch.

And he did indeed make love to her as he'd vowed, slowly and with a caring that diminished her defenses in a way that a show of breathless acrobatics never could. His words were simple and all bearing the same message—that she was loved. She'd never been so aroused.

Vi came to a shuddering climax and lay trying to regroup her resources before he'd even peaked. Liam withdrew from her, and she clutched his upper arms, trying to stay him.

"Where are you going?"

"Exploring," he said, then gave her a bold smile before heading south.

Cool air replaced the cover of Liam's warm skin. She lay replete and pliable as he slid her closer to the mattress's edge, until her lower legs were dangling. He nudged her thighs wider and kneeling on the floor, settled between them, contemplating her as though he'd never before seen a woman's body, when Vi knew for certain he'd seen plenty.

"Are we to be here a while?" she asked, earning the chuckle she'd hoped for with her casual tone.

"It all depends," Liam said.

"All, well, if it's depending on me..." She reached upward for the pillow she'd left behind, drew it forward, plumped it a bit, and then rucked it beneath her head. Even with the added cushion, she had to work up the energy to lift her head and watch as he brushed his fingertips back and forth across the hair at the joining of her thighs.

"My fire, for certain," he said, his attention fixed on what he was touching.

"Embers at best," she said. "You've done me in."

"A challenge, then."

Vi lay back and smiled, for she knew there was nothing Liam liked better than a challenge. He nudged her legs the smallest measure wider, and she swallowed convulsively as she felt him expose damp and tender bits not accustomed to the cool November air. It might be time to run the furnace and not just occasionally the fireplace, she thought.

And that proved to be the last wander her mind would take, for Liam's tongue gently flicked against what he'd exposed. As he dallied, pure pleasure worked its way up to her heart, which sped its beat. There was a possibility that she wasn't beyond rousing.

One particularly wonderful caress had her fully awakened, her toes flexing, then pulling tighter with a pleasurable anticipation that she hadn't expected to feel. When she begged him to come back and be inside her, he smiled up at her.

"Embers?" he asked.

"Arrogance," she answered, softening the word with a smile.

Liam crawled onto the bed, moving her upward enough that he could slide home.

"I love you, Vi," he said, then began to move with determination. "Did always. Will always."

This time when she came, Liam was there with her, and Vi knew that her world was forever and frighteningly changed.

There was no sound like a dog noisily sniffing at the bottom of a closed door. Liam smiled up at the ceiling as he listened to Roger, who was quite obviously curious about whatever might have taken place on the humans' side of the door. The dog could remain curious, too.

Liam swung his legs from the bed, then reached for his watch, which he'd left on the small table at the bedside.

"Damn." He'd slept longer than he'd thought, for it was nearly four-thirty. Soon he'd have to return to Muir House, but he'd hoped for a few more words with Vi before then, as he recalled that he was supposed to pass along an invitation from Jenna Gilvane for Vi to also have dinner at Muir House this evening. She was face-down, though, and closer to comatose than asleep.

Liam rose, gathered his clothing, and made his way to the bathroom he'd earlier been barred from. Once he'd showered and dressed, he checked on Vi again. Other than one finger twitching, she hadn't moved at all. Roger, though, had apparently made the great leap to the foot of the bed.

"Should she wake, tell her I'll be in the kitchen," he said to the hound.

Liam returned to the front room, then paused, thinking perhaps he heard someone upstairs. The noise didn't return, so he retraced his earlier steps to the back hallway, off which the kitchen sat. Feeling oddly at home, he opened the fridge and was thankful to find three bottles of German lager in the back corner. One could be taken without too much guilt.

He'd opened the bottle, sat at the kitchen table, and was taking a first long drink when a tall, broadly muscled, and very redheaded young man with a bandaged left hand came in. Liam suddenly wished for dry hair and a shirt buttoned to the top instead of three buttons still open.

"You must be either Dan or Pat," he said once he'd swallowed.

"Pat," the younger man replied, then reached into the fridge and pulled out a large bottle of still water. He began to uncap it, wincing as he gripped the bottle with his bandaged hand.

"Need some help?" Liam offered.

"It's just a few stitches. I can fend for myself." The youth succeeded, then tipped back his head and drank. When he was done, he gave Liam a level, appraising look.

"Who are you?" he asked.

"Liam Rafferty. A friend of your sister's."

"And of her shower, from the sound of things when I got home.

Where's Vi?"

"Asleep."

"Then you might as well be on your way. She sleeps for days after one of her runs in the studio."

"I'll wait a while, thanks."

Pat shrugged.

"This your beer?" Liam asked, raising the bottle.

"No, it's Danny's. Which is why I think I'll be drinking one later and blaming its disappearance on you, as well."

"Glad to oblige," Liam said, then had a swig of his beer.

Pat pulled out a chair and sat opposite Liam. "Have you known my sister long?"

"Since she was ten."

"She's never mentioned you."

"I knew her in Duncarraig, and neither of us has been there in a number of years."

"Ah."

Liam watched as the younger man drank more water and apparently waged some great internal war, based on the expressions passing over his face. Liam was willing to be patient. He didn't plan to walk from Vi's life, and having the trust of her brothers was crucial.

"You probably should know that I'm the smallest of Vi's brothers," Pat eventually said, stretching the fingers of his good hand as though readying to make a fist.

Liam nodded. "A burden for you, I'm sure," he replied, thinking the near-boy reminded him of his youngest brother, Stephen, off in Australia. Both still had a rawness about them, and strength both physical and mental yet to be tapped.

Pat frowned, clearly concerned his message hadn't been delivered. "Here's what I'm saying, Rafferty...that is your name?"

"My surname. All things considered, you might think of calling me Liam."

Pat scowled, and Liam decided to pass up any more attempts at humor.

"I just want you to know, *Rafferty,* that though Vi's my elder sister and would likely have me by the neck for saying anything at all to you, should you ever make her cry or hurt her in any way, I'll be hunting you down and bringing my larger brothers with me."

Liam nodded. "Fair enough. And I want you to know, Pat, that I love your sister and will do my best never to hurt her. But if she should cry—and women do that over programs on the television, you know—ask why she's crying before you come hunt me down." He reached his hand across the table, offering a shake. "Agreed?"

Pat mulled the matter a moment. "Agreed."

Of course he still had enough boy in him that he tried to crush Liam's knuckles together in a vise of a handshake. Liam masked his wince, for he still had a measure of boy in himself, too.

Once he'd freed his hand, he stood. "It's been grand meeting you, Pat. Now if you don't mind, I'll go say goodbye to your sister."

With that, Liam took his half-finished beer in his aching hand and left the kitchen, thinking that if Vi had handled his mam, surely he could take on three Kilbride siblings. Or lose a hand in trying.

CHAPTER SIXTEEN

Many a sudden change takes place on an unlikely day.
—IRISH PROVERB

Dawn and dusk could look one bloody lot alike to a woman who neither wore a watch nor got enough sleep. Uncertain of the hour, Vi hurried from bed and began a search for her well-worn robe. She found only several unmatched socks beneath her bed. From her small closet, she pulled one of her many work shirts and a long skirt she'd fashioned from soft jersey years before. Once she was semi-dressed, she ventured forth. Behind her, she could hear Roger's grunt as he launched himself from the bed and landed solidly on the floor, followed by the click-clack of his nails as he tailed her.

Liam must be in the kitchen, for he'd hardly leave without saying goodbye. Vi straightened the shirt's collar where it was turned awkwardly at the back of her neck. As she did, she experienced a half-recalled memory—or maybe a dream—of a man's kisses on her nape and a whispered invitation to dine.

In the kitchen, she found Pat at the table, one empty beer bottle before him and a nearly finished one in his hand, which meant it was likely evening. Her brother knew he'd not live to tell the tale of drinking beer for breakfast while residing in his sister's house. Still, Pat had a smug look about him, as though he'd gone one up in his quest for dominance chez Kilbride. Vi, however, knew how to squash her not-so-little brother.

"I'm quite sure that was Danny's beer," she said in her keeper-of-the-fridge voice.

"Rafferty drank 'em both. Damn thief," he said, then drained the bottle in his hand.

"Right, then," Vi said, figuring that Liam had suffered worse fates than being falsely accused a beer thief. "So where is he?" she asked, looking about as though he might be hiding in her worn cupboard.

"Gone a half-hour and more," Pat replied.

Grand. She was about to grill Pat for more information when the telephone rang. She hadn't heard one in so many days that she started at the sound. She walked to the front room, where the phone waited on its small table, shrilly demanding attention.

"Hello?" Vi said, thinking how much she hated this particular modern inconvenience.

"So you live."

Vi smiled, forgiving the phone its intrusion, for her beloved Jenna, best friend and veritable prodigy in the kitchen, was on the other end. "I do, though barely."

"I'd seen some evidence, but it's nice to be sure."

"Evidence?"

"About six-foot-four or five, dark brown hair and eyes to die for."

"Dev would be quite displeased if you died, I'm thinking," Vi said, referring to newlywed Jenna's businessman husband, who hadn't gone lacking in the looks department, himself.

"I'm married, not blind, and don't try to lure me off topic. Liam Rafferty said he was in Ballymuir to see you. Was he conning me?"

"No," Vi admitted.

"Good, because I'd hate to think that I had given my very best new suite to a con man."

"Liam's staying with you?" Vi said, feeling somehow as though her property were being poached on.

"Liam and his daughter," Jenna affirmed. "We had a really interesting talk this morning."

"About?"

Jenna laughed. "You, of course."

Aye, Rafferty was poaching. It might be unwitting on his part, but best friends were sacrosanct, damn it all. Vi began to pace her small front room.

"So is he your new boyfriend?" Jenna asked. "You've always kept them conveniently out of town."

And for good reason, too. "I wouldn't be calling him a boyfriend," she said aloud.

"What, then?"

"A grand entanglement," Vi replied.

Jenna laughed again, but at least this time Vi knew it was with her, and not potentially at her.

"With the two of you there, this will be the best victims' dinner I've had in a while," Jenna said.

So she hadn't imagined the dinner invitation. Victims' dinners were Jenna's term for meals made of new recipes she tested on friends before serving to the public.

"You're coming, right?" Jenna asked.

"I could hardly miss, as someone has to defend my reputation. Are you serving anything without eyeballs?"

"You're safe. My parents have threatened to show up for Christmas, and my mother has apparently gone vegan. That rules out anything I'd normally serve over the holidays, and if I ship in a box of tofurkey, my reputation will be shot."

"Tofurkey?"

"Never mind. You'd probably like it. Of course, by the time my mother gets here—if she actually shows up at all—she'll be on to eating only sushi or whatever the fad of the week is."

Vi was pleased that Mrs. Fahey had timed her vegan phase well, for the very thought of sushi made Vi mourn those fish. "What time, then?"

"Six-thirty, which gives you a whole hour to get ready and be here. And come straight to the kitchen, okay? I want the scoop on Rafferty."

No doubt she did.

Vi pulled on a jacket and went to her car to collect her belongings, which had been languishing there since her Friday return. It was then she discovered that her patchwork bag still waited at her studio. By the time she'd retrieved it, showered, and dressed, six-thirty had passed. It was a blessing that Jenna knew Vi was none too handy with time.

She was about to leave when Danny, now home from work, stopped her. "Vi, the removal company you hired called from Kilkenny early this morning. You can expect your load first thing tomorrow."

"Damn!" Yet another thing she'd forgotten. "Could you see if you can get the panel van from Michael? We've some furniture removing to do at dawn."

"Furniture removing?"

"Yes," Vi said as she mentally inventoried what would have to go. "Most everything on the ground floor, I'm thinking."

Wrapping her scarf about her neck, Vi rushed out the door, leaving behind her brother's protests. All the more reason to stay out late tonight, for he might just cool by morning.

Vi reached Muir House fifteen minutes tardy, which was very nearly early for her. On the short drive there, a nasty mix of rain and icy sleet had begun to fall. Up in the mountains it might be lovely snow, but not so close to the shore as Muir House. Vi pulled into the car park and readied herself to leave the shelter of her car. Remembering Jenna's request, she jogged round the grand manor house to the kitchen door.

Aidan, Jenna's second-in-command, was in back at the broiler. Brushing icy pellets from her hair and shoulders, Vi called a greeting to him. After leaving her jacket and scarf on a hook at the door, she located her friend in the front half of the kitchen. Jenna was fussing around with some wee vegetables, more toy than food.

"I take it you think vegan is code for miniature?" Vi asked.

"No, it's code for I damn well better make it look nice because here on the edge of civilization, it's hell to come up with the right flavors this time of year."

Vi laughed at Jenna's out-of-sorts comment. For a woman so overtly feminine in appearance, she had some sharp teeth to her.

"Don't worry," Vi said. "We'll all lie and say everything's wonderful."

"Thanks," she replied as she whisked some stuff in a bowl.

"That's all that's bothering you?"

"The vegetables, and Sam and Reenie. They're having one of their fights. It's like living in the middle of a stage production when they visit."

Reenie was Jenna's younger sister, lover to a movie star, and before that, already quite well spoilt by her jet-setter parents.

"And there's more," Jenna said, pouring the bowl's contents into a larger bowl filled with frilly lettuces. She began tossing it. "I had an unexpected visitor a while ago."

"Who?"

"Your mother," Jenna answered, but only after widening the gap between Vi and herself. "She got here just after we talked."

"My mother? You're sure?"

Jenna started to mound the lettuce onto white salad plates. "Of course I am," she said as she worked at a lightning-fast pace. "She looks the same as she did at Michael and Kylie's wedding."

Which meant royally peeved.

"Put four roasted beets at the edge of each of these," Jenna directed Vi, who was glad for the distraction.

"I don't suppose you told her you're booked?" Vi asked as she fumbled with the tiny vegetables.

"Right. Then she'd be at your door."

At that miserable thought, Vi abandoned the beets and pulled the bottle of white wine that Jenna must have been cooking with. She poured some into a water glass from the tray by the hall entry, then shoved the bottle back to her friend.

"I could have offered you better," Jenna said.

"This will do." Vi took two large swallows and winced as they hit her empty stomach.

"Hope so, because I've invited her to dinner."

"Bloody damn hell! Why'd you do that?"

"It's Monday, which means the restaurant is closed, and when I suggested a few places in the village, she pulled a helpless act."

"Aye, she's helpless as a shark." Vi sighed. "And how long is she staying?"

"She asked for the reservation to be open-ended. Since we close for Christmas holidays, that gives you a little less than a month, at the outside."

Vi finished her wine and tried to reach for a refill, but Jenna moved the bottle out of range. "Go to the lounge. Dev will pour you a glass of something you'd better not swill."

"You're sure you need no help in serving?" Vi asked, as always unwilling to face her mam.

"You're out of luck. I have a server arriving any second. Go on out there and face your fate."

"Fate with a wee shove from you."

"Could be worse. At least you've got Liam Rafferty waiting for you."

That sped Vi's steps, for the thought of Liam with her mother was enough to put her hair on end.

Vi entered the lounge, where the group was having cocktails. It appeared a quiet gathering, and Vi supposed she could always count herself thankful that no one in the room was pregnant or apt to yatter on about babies and nappies and such. However, ensconced on the sofa was indeed Maeve Kilbride of Sixteen Curlew Court, Kilkenny, where Vi heartily wished her mam had stayed.

Next to Mam sat Meghan, who had pulled up her sleeve and was showing off what appeared to be a new tattoo on her forearm. "It's henna," she was saying to Mam. "Grandda gave me a kit before we left Duncarraig."

Mam limited her comment to one disapproving arch of her brows.

Liam came up and settled a hand on Vi's waist, then gave her a brief kiss. "You look beautiful," he said in a low voice. "Almost as much so as earlier, on your bed."

"I'd have been a bit underdressed had I arrived like that," Vi said, then looped her fingers through Liam's, intending to drag him with her for this mam-greeting.

On the way, she said quick hellos to Sam and Reenie, who appeared to have survived their latest tempest, and to Kate, who was Dev's mother, and her lover, Brendan Mulqueen, a sculptor famous enough to also be a tourist attraction. Dev was behind the small bar set up in the corner of the room, too far off to be used as an additional evasion.

Vi leaned down and gave her mother a quick kiss on the cheek. "Hello, Mam, it's a surprise to see you."

"Of course I'm here. I've a grandchild on the way." She held out an empty martini glass. "Freshen my drink, would you, Violet?"

Taking it was a rote action, as Vi's mind was too busy filtering its way to the truth of her mam's statement to actually direct her hand.

"Be right back," she said to Mam, thankful for Liam's palm beneath her elbow as she made her way to the bar.

Of course Maeve had a grandchild on the way, and had known so since early summer. Until now, the news hadn't been enough to make her pick up the telephone or write a letter inquiring after Kylie's health. No, this had to do with Mam, not babies, and not her own children, whom she spoke to as infrequently as possible.

"Holding up all right?" Dev asked once Vi had rather firmly deposited the martini glass on the bar's small ledge.

"Better with wine, I'm thinking," Vi answered. "And don't be wasting your fine Chateau Frou-frou wine on me. I'm drinking for effect, not flavor." She glanced over at Liam. "What are you drinking?" she asked, thinking she'd just go for the same.

"Chateau Frou-frou," he said, then tucked his arm around her waist, drawing her closer. As Dev laughed and then poured Vi her very own flighty French wine, Liam said to Dev, "And make Maeve's martini a double-shot." He squeezed Vi momentarily tighter and said, "You have my word we'll lull her into complacency."

As Vi had no better plan, she went with what was offered. She and Liam returned to the sofa, and Liam sent Meghan off for another Club Orange. Vi settled in at her mam's right hand and Liam at her left.

"So truly, Mam, why Ballymuir just now?" Vi asked.

Mam took a quick sip of her martini and then said, "If your father can have a holiday I can, too."

"I wouldn't call it a holiday that Da's having."

"I would," she said with clamp-jawed finality.

And on second thought, so might Vi. Bachelor days in Duncarraig had likely sounded too tempting to pass up.

"Shall I take you to visit with Kylie tomorrow?" Vi asked Mam, who had dredged the stuffed olive from her drink and was giving its contents a suspicious, squinty-eyed look.

"Visit Kylie?" she echoed, as though Vi had suggested a day at the dog track.

"Aye. She's home now, just waiting for the baby."

"I can get there well enough, myself," Mam said. "But do tell the boys I expect supper with them tomorrow."

Which would no doubt take place at Vi's home. She sipped her wine and prayed for some form of divine intercession. Mam rendered suddenly mute had a fine appeal.

Just then, Jenna came into the lounge. She had changed from her chef's jacket into a soft blue woolen jumper. Her husband arrived at her side with such speed that Vi had to hide a smile at their obviously love-sotted state.

"If you'll all follow me into the dining room and prepare to suffer," Jenna said. "The victims' dinner has begun."

Liam was hard-put to decide which had been the greatest woe of his evening: eating a meal that he could have as easily cropped from a field, or having to do so under Maeve Kilbride's disapproving glare.

He'd thought the copious Russian vodka she'd been plied with would have calmed her mood. Instead, she had grown more cross with every passing moment. Luckily, she had gone upstairs as soon as the meal was finished, claiming a headache. If she had lasted much longer, he feared that Vi would have ended the evening tongueless. He'd never seen her hold back so many comments.

And as for Jenna's meal, Liam knew it was a fine example of what it was meant to be. It had had flavor and color, just not a damned bit of meat, which had him nearly as out of sorts as Maeve. Vi, on the other hand, had reveled in the food, even stealing from his plate. It was just as well, for in the future when they dined out, he could eat their entrees and she could graze on the garnish.

For the past hour and more they had sat in Jenna and Dev's library, enjoying coffee rich with liqueur and a chat. Upon hearing that Liam was a diver and worked in marine salvage, Dev had immediately led him to a series of books on treasure and shipwreck off the Dingle peninsula's coasts. It seemed that in the era of Auld Queen Bess, this area had been quite the hotbed of smuggling and sedition. Liam had immediately culled one book on Spanish gold and planned to read it later tonight, as he knew sleep would be slow in coming. Vi's tension seemed to have funneled itself into him.

As conversation meandered from local characters to politics and

Ireland's economy, Liam relaxed. He savored the smoky scent of the peat smoldering in the fireplace, the camaraderie, and the incredible sensation of Vi tucked at his side. He'd never really stayed in one place long enough to experience this. Definitely not with Beth, who'd developed a set of friends and social life that had nothing to do with him. True, he had his mates always up for a drink when he arrived again in a port, but he had nothing this steady...this right.

A distant buzzing sound drew Liam's attention from the conversation.

"Is that the front bell at this hour?" Dev asked Jenna.

Liam glanced at his watch and was surprised to see that it was nearly eleven.

"I'll be right back. It's probably just a guest who forgot their key," Jenna said while rising.

"All the same, I'm going with you," her husband replied. "Carry on," he added to Liam and Vi.

Feeling unsettled, Liam rose and after nudging aside the drape a bit, looked out the side window. Floodlights set to accent the house's gardens exposed a heavy drift of white in the air.

"It's snowing, and in no small amount," he said to Vi. "I'd feel better if you'd let me give you a lift home."

She laughed. "I've been driving these roads nearly twelve years. If you weren't staying here tonight, I'd be making the same offer to you."

He smiled as he returned to her. "And now that you've put it that way, I'd be taking you up on it. Still, I'd like to coddle you a wee bit. It's part of being in love." He again sat next to her on the broad sofa and put his arm around her shoulders. "Should I feed you peeled grapes, or paint your toenails, or better yet, Roger's?"

Laughing, she swatted his chest. "You could always shut up and kiss me, you eejit."

"Best idea of all," he said, then let action follow word. God, how he loved this woman, and how he dreaded making a misstep large enough to lose her. She always seemed poised to flee. With that thought in mind, he cupped her face and tried to draw out the kiss to eternity.

Liam came up short, though, for someone cleared their throat, signaling a return to the room. Vi broke their embrace and scooted a bit away from him. He was about to tug her back and tell her that Jenna and Dev surely knew that lovers liked to sit closely together, but something in her expression stopped him.

He looked to the door, and Dev, who had someone standing behind him, wore an even odder expression.

"Sorry to interrupt, but Liam, I have someone here for you," he said, and then moved aside, bringing a tall, blond, and familiar woman into view.

Liam felt as though his world had been put into a giant shaker and tossed around.

He stood. "Jesus, Beth, what are you doing here?"

"Hello's a pretty standard greeting as opposed to 'Jesus, Beth,'" she said as she entered the room. "And I'm here to get Meghan."

Liam had already guessed the reason for her arrival, but hearing the words was like having his heart stop beating. He'd just started to learn Meghan's quirks and talents, her charms and the ways she had yet to grow. He wasn't ready to hand her back like so much excess baggage.

"I'll leave you now," Dev said. "And Jenna will be here with a warm drink for you shortly, Beth."

She thanked Dev, but Liam saw that her attention had shifted to Vi. He gave a names-only introduction between the two women, as more words would only mire the situation.

Beth, who looked as weary and rumpled as he'd ever seen her, sat in an armchair at a right angle from the sofa. While she was settling in, Vi nodded her head toward the door, obviously asking if she should leave. Liam gave a negative shake of the head in answer. And though he knew it was a politically dicey move, he returned to his seat next to Vi. He needed her presence too much to care if Beth was somehow offended.

"Where's Meghan?" his ex-wife asked.

"Upstairs asleep these past few hours."

She nodded. "Good. She'll need her rest. I won't bother waking her until it's time to leave."

"And where is it you're thinking of taking her? Not back to your job site?" He fully hoped she'd say yes, so he'd have firm grounds to fight her.

"No. I quit my job on Saturday and have been working toward getting here ever since. I've flown stand-by and with everything but cargo, but here I am."

"So you are. And do you have plans?"

"We're going back to Atlanta. I have enough savings to make it a few months unemployed. In that time I should be able to come up with a job that's suited to raising my daughter."

"Our daughter," he corrected.

Beth tilted her head and looked at him. After a moment she gave him a half-smile.

"What?" he asked.

"I never would have believed it. You're late to the party, but welcome to parenthood."

Liam seized the opening offered. "That being the case, would you give me at least a few more weeks with her?"

Vi rose from next to him and walked to the door. Liam watched as she took a mug of something from Jenna and delivered it to Beth. After giving Vi a curt nod of thanks, his ex-wife took a sip and at least made a show of considering his question.

"She's supposed to be in school, Liam," she finally said. "From what you've described, she's missed a month of any real studies already."

"But I called her school this morning. Her books are being shipped and she'll do most of her assignments via e-mail. This is no great risk, Beth."

"I'm the custodial parent," she said. "And I don't want her running wild out here."

The way she'd said that, then eyed Vi, was an annoying echo of Liam's mam. "She'd not be running wild. We're just here for a visit, and—"

"How long of a visit?"

"Two days, two weeks...what does it matter? I'll take her to archeological sites and have her write a bloody paper. How wild is that?"

"That's not the point."

"Then what is?"

"She needs to be in her school, with her teachers. We can make arrangements for a few weeks with you this summer. How's that?"

"Not bloody good enough."

Beth sighed, then glanced at her watch. "Meghan and I are booked on a flight out of Shannon Airport tomorrow morning at ten, which means I'll need to be back on the road by...what?" She pinned Vi with a demanding look.

"With the weather, no later than five," Vi said. "But this is all a bit sudden, don't you think? Perhaps if you stayed here at Muir House just a few more days?"

"I think this doesn't concern you," Beth said in a far less genial tone than she'd been using on him.

"She's right," Vi said to Liam, then began to rise.

He settled his hand on her knee, halting her. "If it involves me, it involves you. Stay...please."

This time, his asking did no good. "No," she said. "This is between you and Beth. I'll be waiting for you in your suite."

"The one where Meghan's sleeping?" Beth asked.

"Bloody hell. I wasn't planning a mad shag on the sofa," Vi snapped.

Beth glared back at her.

Vi took a deep breath, exhaled it slowly, then spoke again. "Fine, then. Come find me in the kitchen when you can, Liam."

As Liam took in Beth's angry gaze, he knew two things: he would not win any more days with Meghan, and he could not get to Vi soon enough.

CHAPTER SEVENTEEN

When things get tough for the witch, she has to run.
—IRISH PROVERB

It was the sort of Tuesday morning where one was best served by hiding indefinitely under the duvet. Despite Liam's insistence that she go home and not worry about him, Vi had spent the night at Muir House. There had been only one bedroom left, which she'd quickly ceded to Beth. The library sofa was less diplomatically perilous territory.

Liam had come downstairs long before it was time to ready Meghan to leave. Vi had awakened to find him sitting in an armchair nearby, nearly a specter of a man. She had cocooned with him on the sofa and let the warmth of her body give him peace, or at least a passing illusion of it.

At four-thirty, Liam returned to his suite. Vi stayed in the library until the very last, then came to the front hallway to say her goodbyes to Meghan. The girl was muzzy with sleep and gave her father a muffled one-word farewell, which Vi knew hadn't been intended to sting, but clearly did. After mother and daughter had departed, Vi brought Liam back to his rooms.

"What a goddamn awful start to a morning," were his last words before she made quiet love to him, then let him drift off to sleep so his spirit could mend.

Having him close worked a spell of sorts on her, too. Soon she was dreaming of long-gone days of perfect youth. Nan's cottage was as it had been when Vi was younger, and the well-tended maze of wild roses and herbs smelled like heaven on her dream's soft, rain-kissed day. Vi saw herself and Liam walking down the lane toward Nan's painted stone. Liam was saying something to her that she sensed was important, but a shrill ringing drowned him out.

And woke Vi, too. She sent one hand venturing for the telephone, which seemed to be near her right ear.

"'Lo," she croaked once she'd retrieved it, her throat dry as a crone's.

"That you, Vi?"

"Tis."

"You'd best come home," Danny said. "I've got all but one of Nan's pieces inside, and none where you wanted them, I'll wager. The last is sitting out front, and I'm thinking it's going to freeze over before we can make proper room for it."

Vi shot upright, sending the duvet off Liam in the process. "God in heaven, Danny! What time is it? Why did you not wake me earlier?" Without waiting for an answer, she dropped the phone back into its receiver and scrambled from the bed.

"Troubles?" Liam asked, his voice also rough with sleep and no doubt the excess of the past twelve hours' emotions.

"Nan's furniture is at my house and I'm not," Vi said.

Liam swung his long legs from the bed and stood. "Then let's be quick."

All Vi had was the dress she'd worn the prior evening, so she pulled it back on, wishing for time for a shower and a change of clothes. They were downstairs in a matter of minutes, then nearly out the door when Dev stopped them.

"This arrived for you earlier," he said, handing Liam a fat courier's envelope.

Liam thanked Dev, and on they rushed.

Vi was traveling the coast road to the village and feeling thankful that the rain had stopped when she glanced over and saw Liam frowning at the package.

"Who is it from?" she asked.

"My attorney."

"Aren't you going to open it?"

He turned it face-down. "Later. I've got enough troubles to digest at the moment."

"It could be good news."

Liam snorted. "If it were, Stuart would have called, just for the bloody novelty of it."

And to that, she could say nothing. Vi returned her attention to the road, and soon they were at her small home. Vi parked, and she and Liam exited. On the short walkway in front of Vi's house stood a brightly painted kitchen cupboard and two elderly women.

Vi called a good day to Breege Flaherty and her flatmate, Edna McCafferty. With their children long-grown and gone from small Ballymuir, the elderly women had thrown in their lots together and taken a flat in the middle of the village.

"That's a grand piece," Breege said to Vi as she and Liam grew near. "Did you paint it yourself?"

"My Nan did, actually," Vi said.

"Would you look at all the bits and pieces attached to it?" Breege said to Edna, who was using an already damp handkerchief to dab at the raindrops also decorating it. To Vi, she added, "Are you thinking of selling it? Young Danny hiding inside wouldn't bargain, and Pat left the property altogether."

Vi glanced at the front window where she saw Danny skulking about.

"We'd never get it up the stairs," Edna pointed out to Breege.

"Which is well enough, since I'm afraid it's not for sale," Vi said firmly. If she showed any inclination to bargain, Breege and Edna would have her occupied until nightfall. The two older women were sharp indeed, hiding their skills at their favorite avocation behind kindly faces. Danny had been wise to retreat, and Pat wiser yet to flee.

"Ah, well," Breege said, her attention now wandering to Liam, "it seems as though you have more than one new thing in your life."

"All quite old, actually," Vi said, earning a wry quirk of the mouth from Liam. She introduced him to the two women, then left him to fend for himself under their questioning while she slipped inside and got Danny to help him muscle the cupboard in.

An hour later, Vi had showered and dressed in fresh clothing for the day. Nan's cupboard had replaced Vi's prior one in the kitchen, which now blocked the entry to the back hall, waiting to be moved elsewhere. While Vi resettled her belongings in the painted cupboard, she smiled, imagining her mother's reaction once she saw this.

The first time Mam had been in Vi's kitchen, she'd been appalled to see that Vi had ripped out the modern fitted cabinets and replaced them with a large, free-standing oak cupboard. This new iteration, with its vivid primary colors, would send Mam around the bend. *Mam.....* Something niggled at Vi's memory.

"Damn!" Vi dropped a handful of forks onto the cupboard's wide top and hurried to the front room, where Liam was reading his packet and Danny was lounging.

"Danny, where do you want Mam to dine tonight?" she asked while riffling about on a shelf for the phone book.

"Argentina?" he suggested.

"With you," she clarified. "Hadn't I mentioned that?"

Danny pushed himself from his armchair and stood, hands clenched, as though readying for battle. "Holy shit, Vi! You've set me up."

"You and Pat, both, but I prefer to view it more as sparing myself," she replied as she thumbed through listings in Dingle, the closest town of size. "And on this, you'd best not cross me." She glanced up at him. "Have you had a visit with her?"

"She arrived this morning before I'd had time to choke down my coffee, and thanks for the warning, too."

"Sorry. I'd meant to give word, but last night wasn't quite as planned." She gave a nod of her head toward Liam, whose attention was focused elsewhere.

Danny eased off a bit. "Pat's with her now. She wanted to see Michael's workshop. Fine timing, too, as he's off to Kenmare, delivering a table."

"Smart man," Vi murmured, then lifted the phone and dialed a small bistro across from Dingle Harbor where the food was good and the final bill within Pat and Danny's means.

"You sure you don't want to come along tonight?" Danny asked.

Vi didn't bother to comment.

He muttered in the background while she confirmed they were

open in the off-season and made a reservation for three Kilbrides.

"All set," she said to Danny. He stomped upstairs like an overgrown infant. Liam kept riffling through the papers he'd been sent, seemingly oblivious to the game of pass-the-parent occurring in front of him.

Vi settled on the sofa next to him. "And the news?"

He returned the papers to their packet. "An offer on my company's assets."

"Is this wanted?"

"No, it's the carrion birds gathering." He glanced at his watch. "Nearly eleven. I'll be needing to make some calls. I suppose I should get to Muir House," he said most hesitantly. "Would you mind giving me a lift?"

"You can call from here, or if you like, come to the studio with Rog and me." The words had been automatic, and once they registered in her mind, their full import shocked her. She detested having people in her studio and survived the comings and goings of tourist season only because the tourist's euros patched her moth-eaten pockets.

"I'll stay with you," Liam said. "I keep feeling at loose ends, as though I've misplaced something. And then I realize it's Meghan."

Vi had much the same feeling when Rog wasn't about, but decided she'd best not share that. She didn't mean to make light of Liam's situation, but she still had this wee *crosdiabhal* sitting on her shoulder and muttering angry words, much as Danny had just done. She wanted rid of it—to be fully accepting of fate—but wanting and knowing how to lose the demon were separate acts.

"Well, come along to the studio," she said, "though I'm sure once I start painting, you'll find Roger better company than I."

He leaned over and kissed her, stopping only when Danny and his sizeable shoes came clomping back down the stairs from the gabled room he shared with Pat.

"Watch her," Danny said to Liam. "She only seems nice." With that, he exited.

Vi and Liam soon did too, driving to her studio where she got about her business, first hiding the Beltaine and Samhain paintings with Liam in them while he was occupied on the telephone. She tried to keep her ears to herself as he talked with his mam about Beth's arrival and the details of getting the balance of Meghan's belongings back to her.

Even with Vi's half-listening and Roger's distracting snuffling about her feet, she was struck by a pang of yearning for some sort of normalcy with her mam. It was that hope, futile as it was mad, that sent her back into Mam's orbit when her other siblings were pleased to stay in the fringes of her universe.

Liam finished his call and dialed another. Vi continued to stare at her empty canvas seeking wild Lughnasa inspiration and getting only fun-obliterating Mam-vibes. Finally, she moved to a less intimidating pad of paper and pencil. Liam's call, briefer than the first, ended. He came to stand behind her, wrapping his arms about her waist.

"I'll be hearing back from my attorney soon. I hope you don't mind that I gave him this number."

"I can ignore his call as well as any other," she said, then tilted her head back for his kiss, which he granted.

"That I'm sure you can."

Vi set aside her pencil and turned in his embrace. "Are you wanting to sell your business?"

"Christ, no! What I'm wanting is for my partner to be dealt with, business to resume, and my life to go on as it was."

Seventeen-year-old Vi would have cried, *"But what about me?"* Adult Vi kept silent the hurt of the cut to her heart.

"Of course," Liam said, "I'm also wanting to climb Mount Everest without oxygen tanks, and I've got a far better chance of that."

"So what will happen?" she asked.

"I've a feeling it's either sell it myself or wait for the banks financing me to do it on worse terms. I've plenty of assets...crane-barges, diving equipment, and even the fast boats that my partner used for a bit of pirating, but no cash to tide me over."

She wanted to give him something, to return at least a measure of optimism to his mood, for she could bear no more. "You know, you might still—"

His glare was fierce. "Don't say 'find the gold.' Just. Don't. It will be bloody weeks until Duncarraig calms enough for me to go about my search without a parade of fools behind me. And that will be too damn late."

"I'm just looking for some way to make this better for you and coddle you a little," she said, reminding him of just last night, when his mood had been lighter. "Shall I paint your toenails? Or better yet, Roger's?"

He chuckled at least, and for that she kissed him. When she was done, both of them were smiling like a pair of love-drunk fools.

"I don't suppose any of these paints of yours are water-soluble?" Liam asked while tracing a fingertip over the curve of her right breast.

"I've some fingerpaints I keep for school visits," she replied, much liking the course of his thoughts. Painting his body would be the best preparation for a Lughnasa celebration scene that she could imagine.

"And a lock to the door, too?" Liam murmured, kissing the side of her neck.

"Aye," she said, then sighed at the pleasure of his touch, impermanent as it was. She was about to suggest that he turn that very lock while she closed Roger in the back room, but wasn't quite quick enough, for her offer was interrupted by the chime of the front bells.

"It's messy in here, Violet," Maeve Kilbride said as soon as the door closed behind her. "How ever do you manage to sell a thing?"

Vi stepped from Liam's embrace. "I sell what I mean to," she replied.

"Hello, Liam," Mam said in a tone neither cordial nor hostile. She unbuttoned her coat and held it out as though waiting for a butler. Vi hurried to take it.

While she hung Mam's coat on a peg at the back of the studio, getting a "Mind the fabric!" from her, Vi listened to the ease Liam showed in talking to Mam. *Easy when she's not yours,* Vi thought. As she approached, her mother's frown deepened.

"Pat and Danny will be driving you to Dingle for supper," Vi said, scrambling to take hold of the conversation before Mam could trample her. "It's a lovely town, and I'm sure you'll enjoy having a look about."

"I suppose," her mam replied.

While she spoke, the phone began to ring.

"Shall I?" Liam asked, gesturing at the thing.

"As often as you choose," Vi said.

Liam took the call, then reached for his papers, where they sat atop a display case. While he spoke in stern tones to whomever was on the other end, Vi summoned some chat for her mam and even succeeded in keeping control for a minute or two. Then Mam launched one of her infamous announcements.

"They've started whispering about me already, you know," she said.

"Who?" Vi asked, unable to imagine Jenna or anyone at Muir House treating her mother poorly. But that was half the challenge of conversations with Mam, trying to make the leap from topic to topic. The only assured constant was a Mam-centric theme.

"The women in my tea group, of course."

"Surely you're imagining it," Vi said, then afforded herself a glance in Liam's direction, but he was deep in conversation. He looked nearly as ill-tempered as Vi was beginning to feel.

"Oh, I know that pitying look," Mam said. "I saw it often enough when the twins went to visit you."

Vi conquered the smile trying to fight its way out. Even after nearly a full year, Mam still referred to the boys' decision to move to Ballymuir after finishing school as a "visit."

"Next they'll layer on the false sympathy, too," Mam said. "I've seen them do it before. 'Whatever will you do now that Michael's moved out?'" she mimicked. "He's on holiday, I'll tell them, and it's the truth, too. He'll be back."

"Have you talked to Da?" Vi asked.

"Whatever for? He'll just give me more of the same, and I heard enough of that while he was packing his bags."

"Then you know why he's left?"

"He's not left," Mam repeated with enough vehemence that Liam sent a concerned glance their way. "It's a grand male holiday, chasing his lost youth through Duncarraig. He wants to be at the pub to all hours with his mates and forget he has a wife waiting for him."

Even Mam, who was well-versed in altering the truth, hadn't voiced that last bit too well. And Vi was finding words hard to get past the nearly-ill feeling tightening her throat. This was not her trial, not her burden to bear. Except no one else would give Mam the truth.

"He's looking to be needed. He's worked his whole life and isn't ready to stop."

Mam's sigh was thick with exasperation. "He's needed. He's needed at home."

"To take out your dry cleaning, or is it more than that? Do you even admire him anymore? When he comes through the door, is your heart lighter?"

"And you're some grand judge of love?"

Vi looked over at Liam, who had finished his call and was now feigning great interest in the canvases stacked about. Her heart sped.

"I'm no expert, but I'm beginning to learn. And I'm not the one worrying about whispering tea groups. Is it love making you wish Da back?"

"That's between myself and your father," her mam snapped, color riding high on her cheeks.

"Then you'd best share it with Da," Vi said. "I'd wager he hasn't a clue how you feel about him."

"You always were one for overstepping. Rules, respect, it doesn't matter to you, does it?"

"It does matter. Very much." It was simply that her rules differed from her mother's. "And though you don't always make it easy, I love you."

Mam could have looked no more shocked if Vi had struck her.

"I'm going back to Muir House for a rest," she said, turning heel and walking to the peg holding her coat. "Tell Pat and Danny to be at the door no later than five."

After she was gone, Vi picked up her sketchbook and gathered her thoughts. She was beginning to believe that, like Rafferty's gold, her mother's good graces could not be found.

After Vi's mam finished her grand exit, Liam eyed Vi carefully, deciding if she was fit to approach. While on the phone, he'd had the displeasure of listening to Stuart, his attorney, account how quickly matters had gone south. Liam's four remaining field engineers had faxed their resignations just this morning. Naturally, all would soon turn up working for Midmarine Salvage, the competitor offering to buy his hard assets.

Liam had a week to consider the offer's terms. Though he didn't need seven days, he planned to burn every last one. He owed his pride at least that much, especially since Stuart had been told by a friend on the inside that Liam's subpoena was forthcoming.

In a matter of days he would have to return to the States and recite chapter and verse of his stupidity regarding Alex to a room of strangers. At least, though, he could finish the trip on an upswing with a visit to Meghan. He was sure Beth wouldn't begrudge him that.

She did, however, begrudge him Vi. That much had been clear last night. He wondered if Beth would feel the same just now, or would figure he was getting the woes he deserved. Vi's brows were knit and she was angrily drawing on a pad of paper, her motions better suited to slashing than sketching.

"So you and your mam are through torturing each other?" he asked.

"We don't—"

She broke off with what she was saying and a reluctant smile came to her face. "We do, I guess, and always have. Smart man," she said, then continued sketching.

He strolled closer, wanting a look at her drawing. "Not smart, just one who's done a fair bit of torturing, too."

"Don't look," she said, shielding the sketch pad with her left hand. "That's not what this is meant for."

Good enough. God knew he had plenty more to look at in this chaotic place. He could see, though, where order had once rested. It was as though papers and paintings and small piles of seashells and stones had drifted down like dust, settling over what this studio had once been.

"What are these?" Liam asked, placing a hand on the papers atop an old many-drawered piece of furniture.

Vi glanced over at the pile. "Letters and such. Now be quiet or I'll send you home with Rog."

Silence came, but it wasn't the creative sort. It was the silence he'd felt last night in the library as he'd watched Vi sleep and asked himself how long until she, too, was gone from his life.

To distract himself, he leafed through the stack he'd asked Vi about. It held e-mail print-outs and envelopes bearing postage not only from Ireland, but England and France, too. Before looking more, he glanced at Vi.

"Go ahead, nose about if it pleases you," she said.

It did, so Liam began to read in more detail. Requests for information mixed with headier notes, suggesting gallery showings and even a licensing opportunity.

"Have you answered any of these?" he asked.

"Not quite yet. My business manager forwarded them when we parted ways. Career-planning issues," she added at his "Why?"

Liam inventoried dates and postmarks. "Not quite yet" seemed to connote up to a six-month delay.

"And why have you not answered?"

"I've nothing to show."

He loved the very breath of her, but there were times he did not understand her at all.

"Jesus, Vi, you're stockpiled to the Second Coming." He walked to a large piece of silk stretched tight and painted in abstract with a scene of storm over roiling sea. "This? What's the matter with this?"

"The gray of the sky has too much green."

"Too much green for whom?"

She ignored his question, frowning and pointing a finger at the lower left corner of the picture. "And look down there, the silk snagged a bit when I accidentally knocked it against another piece. Can't you see the pull?"

"It's visible only to you."

"And to anyone else with eyes." She picked up her pencil and began to tap it against the side of her work table, the rhythm hard and fast.

"Only if you point it out," he said.

Liam took her hands in his, stilling the angry tapping. "What's this about? I've seen the paintings lined up at the back door of your house, and now this hostage-taking in your studio. This can't be the same woman with people begging for her work."

"It's not ready," she said to him. Liam recognized her tone of voice, for it very much matched what Vi's mam had used on her minutes earlier.

He knew this was a topic to be pushed no farther, yet he couldn't help himself. "Did it occur to you that your art is the better for its flaws?"

"The better? And one of your salvage jobs, is it the better if you make a sod-all mess of it?"

He grabbed the storm painting. "We're not talking about sod-all messes, Vi. We're talking about human imperfection."

"I can do better. I *have* to."

"Or what will happen?"

"I don't know." She paced the room, then swung back to face him. "I don't bloody know, but it will be bad."

"Telling the future, are you? I'm thinking you might be a bigger witch than your nan."

He'd meant it as a harmless joke, to lighten the moment, but if Vi could hurl lightning bolts, he would be dead. She reached into the pocket of her trousers.

"My car keys," she said, and then tossed them at him. "Go where you have to, and be gone by the time I'm back. Roger! Walk!"

The wee dog slunk from beneath Vi's work table, looking at Liam as though seeking intercession. Liam gave him a "sorry, old friend" shrug of the shoulders. Vi flung on her cape, snapped Roger's lead to his collar, then strode out the door.

Liam watched from the front window. On the downhill slope, Roger kept up admirably well with Vi's long legs. The uphill, Liam feared, would be another matter, for she was walking like a woman driven.

After she and her dog were gone from sight, Liam walked outside and turned over the sign on the studio door from *Dunta* to a welcoming *Oscaillte*. The act was symbolic, considering that art-shoppers looked to be rarer than placid redheads on this cold Ballymuir day, and likely temporary, too, since Vi would see the change on her return. But she would grasp his message and not his throat, for Liam planned to give her miles of space for the rest of the day. After all, he was a gambler, but never foolhardy. Except perhaps in love...

* * *

Men. Bloody awful, annoying, know-everything men. Liam was no artist. He had no idea the troubles in the process or the deathly lack of certainty. Vi couldn't walk quickly enough to escape her anger at Liam or the uncomfortable sense of foreboding that had set in just prior to Mam's arrival.

And Mam. Bloody awful, annoying, know-everything Mam, for that matter. What was to come next?

More walking, at least that was for certain.

Vi crisscrossed her village's small net of streets, returning greetings, but stopping for no talk. As she passed in front of O'Connor's pub, she recalled that tonight would be *sessiun* night, and for the first time in nearly forever, she had no desire to attend.

She walked to the edge of town and looked longingly to the hills. High above Ballymuir sat beehive huts—small stacked stone structures that had been there likely before the New Faith replaced the Old. Some said that holy people would use them as places of meditation and rest on their solitary pilgrimages. Vi needed both contemplation and quiet, but rather doubted that she or Rog were suited to lives of asceticism.

Realizing that in the end, she had nothing to do but go back the way she came, Vi turned toward town center... such as it was. Hungry, she paused to take a peek in the windows of Spillane's market. Seamus ran an account for her, so having been careless enough to bolt her studio without pocket money would not make her go hungry. She tethered Rog to the lamppost out front, assuring him that the indignity would be short-lived.

Vi stepped into the warmth of Spillane's, greeted Seamus, and then headed to the sweets section. She was not a chocolate-eater by nature, but today she felt deserving. There, in front of the sweets stood her sister-in-law Kylie, hands on hips, large belly jutting out of the dark blue coat that would clearly no longer button over her smock. Vi dragged her gaze back to Kylie's face, which seemed to bear marks of tension, much as Vi imagined hers did.

Kylie greeted Vi in Irish and they continued the conversation in that language solely, as they always did when it was just the two of them. Much as they tried to teach the others, they were the only fluent members of the family.

"I'm glad to have run into you," Kylie said. "I've had a bit of a surprise."

"It seems to be going around," Vi answered rather dryly. "You've seen Mam, right?"

"Seen but not spoken to. I saw Pat leading her out to the workshop this morning, but they made no stop at the house. I did call Michael and gave him the news. I expect he's taking the slow road home from Kenmare, just now."

"All the better," Vi said. "Mam's in a mood."

Kylie dropped an Aero bar into her basket, then said, "Which is sure to change one way or another. Your da's on his way here, too."

"He is? But I'd heard nothing."

"As I'd heard nothing about he and Mam. You might have told me they were having more troubles, Vi."

"I didn't want to upset you." Or have to look at you too much longer and know what I have not, she could have added.

"I'm pregnant, not ill," Kylie said before scooping up a CurlyWurly and a Dairy Milk and adding them to her stash. "I've offered him a room at our house. I know Michael will be glad for the help finishing the baby's room."

"You might not be ill, but aren't you a bit overextended for guests just now?"

"Not at all," Kylie said. "I've already tidied the spare bedroom and the second bath."

To microscopic cleanliness, no doubt. Vi selected a Dairy Milk of her own. It sounded somehow healthier than the other chocolates.

"And I'm planning a family luncheon for tomorrow," Kylie said. "I've a baby coming any day and I'm tired of watching Mam and Da bicker and the lot of you act like martyrs every time you're in the same town."

Vi had never experienced quite this level of bluntness from her sister-in-law. It wasn't that Kylie didn't have the matter by the throat, simply that she was usually a woman of softer words and a gentler approach. Vi put the change down to Kylie's altered body.

"If either of us does the cooking," Vi said, "Mam and Da will either be poisoned by poor skills or on the road in no time."

"That's why I've settled on a luncheon. I can't foul up a chilled platter and surely you can manage a green salad. And bring your man, too."

"My man?" Word traveled faster than sound in Ballymuir.

"Breege called to tell me about your Liam."

Of course, Breege. She'd always been a surrogate nan to Kylie, and had no doubt rushed home to share the news.

"Perhaps Mam will watch her words if he's there," Kylie suggested.

"Until he crosses her. Shall I bring anything else to this gathering of yours?"

Kylie smiled. "Fishes and loaves and perhaps a stray miracle or two."

Vi was beginning to feel as though it would take a raft of miracles to refloat her family.

CHAPTER EIGHTEEN

Each child as he is reared, and the duck on the water.
—IRISH PROVERB

If you don't wish to, you really needn't come to the luncheon," Vi said yet again to Liam as they started the drive into the hills where her brother lived.

"Too late now, my fire. And as I told you the last three times you said that, if I hadn't wanted to come, I would have said so."

The fact of it was, Liam could think of places he'd rather be, but none of them held Vi. They had negotiated a tenuous peace last night, and he planned to hold on to it as long as possible. This morning, while she had painted, he'd remained at Muir House, where Dev and Jenna had offered him use of the house's office. Liam had made reservations to return to Boston on Friday. He intended to tell Vi this...no later than Thursday night. He knew he was delaying the inevitable, but sometimes an inevitability was best delayed. The news he needed to give echoed too strongly of the last time he'd left. Even he, a generally blundering male, could grasp that.

Sooner than he expected, Vi pulled up to a solid-looking white farmhouse with several cars already out front.

"It looks as though we're the last ones here, so be prepared," she said after she'd turned off her car. She reached into the back seat and juggled forward a large plastic bowl, nearly losing its cover and spilling its contents into his lap.

She said something in Irish that Liam knew for a curse, then snapped on the bowl's lid.

"Nerves, I'm thinking," she said. I've had a case of them since yesterday. Would you mind carrying the salad?"

"Better carrying it than wearing it," he teased, easing the bowl from her tense grip.

They were climbing the steps when the front door opened. A man Liam knew had to be the younger Michael Kilbride greeted them.

Vi gave her brother a warm hug, affording Liam the time to look at the two of them together. Physically, they bore a resemblance, as both had the same shade of green eyes, but it seemed more than that. The way they had with each other spoke of a kinship of spirit that Liam couldn't say he possessed with any of his innumerable siblings.

"Liam, this is Michael."

They shook hands and Liam said, "It's been a long time."

Michael smiled. "Aye, it has."

"You two have met?" Vi asked. "When?"

"A lifetime ago," Michael said. "Nan had me to visit alone the summer you must have been eight or so."

"And your brother and I were caught swilling from whiskey glasses at Da's pub while your nan and the rest of them sang," Liam added.

Vi shook her head. "Bloody Philistines. Have you no appreciation for fine music?"

"Some, but more for whiskey," Michael replied. "And I'm ready for one now."

Vi swatted his arm, then said, "Let's get this done with."

As they were heading to the dining room with Vi, naturally, in the lead, Michael lagged back and said to Liam, "If you see me going to the kitchen, offer to come help. I've a bottle at the ready. And trust me, we'll be needing it."

It took not an hour in the combined company of the Kilbrides to see what Michael had meant. Pat and Danny sat at the far end of the table, one in competition with the other to see who could say the least. Vi's da tried to carry the conversation for a time, but became weary, joining his youngest children in silence. Michael devoted his energies to assuring that his wife lifted nothing heavier than a fork.

And Vi and Kylie kept slipping off to the kitchen, claiming some task or another to complete. But for Kylie's pregnant state, he'd think the women were at the same bottle that he'd earlier managed to sample with Michael

Liam toyed with his wedge of cold smoked salmon and brown bread, thinking what next to float out there as conversation. Just then, Kylie said something to Vi in Irish. Liam had no idea what, but Vi very quickly masked a look of concern. She responded to Kylie, and of course he stood no chance of catching those words, either.

"In English," Maeve Kilbride decreed. "It's not polite to cut the rest of us out."

Kylie and Vi rose simultaneously, though it took Kylie a bit longer.

"We'll be right back," Vi said to her mam in English, then shot Liam a look he interpreted as an order to follow, though her expression was none clearer to him than the Irish she'd been using.

He was about to make his excuses when Pat and Danny stood.

"Cigarette," Danny said, apparently speaking for both twins. The front door slammed behind them two heartbeats later.

"Michael, if you could give me hand," Kylie called from the kitchen.

"Sorry," Michael said. "I'll be right back, too."

And then there were three...

Liam cleared his throat and gave up playing with his food. He'd just taken a mouthful of water when Vi's father spoke.

"So, do you plan to marry our Violet this time round?"

When he'd managed to stop sounding like a drowning victim, Liam said, "We've not talked marriage. With Vi, considering our history, I feel lucky enough that she doesn't smother me in my sleep."

Maeve puffed up. "Is that meant to be humorous?"

It was, and harmless, too, though he supposed he might have better considered his audience. He pushed back his chair.

"I think I hear Vi calling me," he said. "Might I get you anything from the kitchen?"

"A few family members," Vi's da said, then smiled. "And some of the *fuisce* I know you and Michael junior had to be trying."

That, at least, redirected Mrs. Kilbride's ire to her spouse.

"Michael! You know how I feel"

After giving Michael the elder a smile in exchange for the man's broad wink, Liam escaped. A man could do miles worse than Mr. Kilbride as a father-in-law.

In the kitchen, Liam found Michael glaring at Vi, Kylie looking a bit pale, and Vi as though she wished herself someplace else.

"I'm thinking it's time we leave," she said to Liam.

"That would have been before I had your mam ready to see me dead."

"She's just treating you as part of the family," Vi said. "Now, Michael, tell me where you've put my cape and Liam's jacket, and—"

Kylie gasped. When she'd gotten her breath back she muttered something to Vi that sounded like "ten minutes" in Irish. Liam was pleased that his grasp of the language had stretched that far.

"Jackets, Michael?" Vi said again, sounding nearly alarmed.

"Ten minutes, and *what?*" Michael asked, ignoring his sister.

Kylie raised one finger, then walked to the other side of the kitchen. Back to them, she braced her hands against the sink. Liam watched, transfixed, as her slight shoulders rose and fell. He'd seen this before, when Beth was in labor. He looked to Vi, whose eyes were dark with something like panic.

Vi grabbed Liam's hand. "We'll just be going now."

Michael stayed his sister, one hand on her upper arm. "Violet, ten minutes, and *what?*" he repeated.

"Nearly made it, too," Vi said, glancing longingly toward the kitchen door. She let go of Liam's hand, but moved a step closer to him. "Michael, it seems Kylie's been in labor since early this morning."

Liam watched as all color drained from Michael Kilbride's face. He recalled that terrified feeling well, for no amount of classes or cheerful films prepared a man for the moment of truth.

Kylie returned, her hands bracing her lower back.

"And you didn't tell me?" Michael said to his wife, tipping up her face as though he could determine her progress by checking the whites of her eyes.

"I didn't mean *not* to tell you," Kylie said. "I was thinking it was more of those false contractions. I'm sure we have hours yet before anything happens."

"Anything, love? As in you having the baby and we're not even packed for the hospital? That *anything?*"

"If it helps you, we'll go upstairs and pack as soon as I've—"

An odd, almost whimsical expression crossed her face.

"What?" her husband asked. "Is it another pain? Shall I go—"

Kylie took Michael's hands. "Love, promise me you won't panic, but my waters have just broken."

She took a step back. All who could see Kylie's feet, which excluded Kylie, looked to the floor. Sure enough, the pale blue cloth rug where she'd stood displayed a darker blue splotch.

Vi grabbed a tea towel. "Slip out of your shoes," she told her sister-in-law.

The hell with Michael, Liam felt his knees grow weak. He couldn't believe this was making him squeamish, but the thought of a woman as slight as Kylie giving birth to what looked to be the world's largest babe was more than he could handle.

"I'll be in the dining room," he said to Vi, then walked off while he could still do it on his own. "Keep them occupied," he heard Vi command. Aye, when he went unconscious they'd be occupied enough.

Lord, she'd been so close to escaping that she could almost taste it, Vi thought. She and Kylie had had it well planned. Kylie would speak to Michael while Vi gave word to the rest of the family members and herded them to her house, blissful miles from the birth itself.

Instead, here she was wiping her sister-in-law's quite wet legs and feet. There would be no leaving anytime soon, she knew. And she could nearly hear Nan's hearty laugh from above, telling her this was just what she needed to face.

Bloody annoying know-everything spirits.

Vi had Kylie as cleaned up as she could get her. "Maybe you'll be wanting to go upstairs and settle in," she said.

Kylie shook her head. "After I say goodbye to my guests."

"I'll still make your excuses. Even Mam will forgive this one."

"Enough, already," Michael said. "There's no time to talk." He lifted a set of keys from a teacup hook on the cupboard. "Vi, would you pull up my car?"

"We won't be needing it," Kylie said.

"Not *needing it?*"

Vi had never before heard her brother's voice reach so high. Perhaps he had a future as a tenor once his preferences turned from whiskey to music.

"I've been seeing a midwife along with the doctors in Tralee," Kylie said. "I didn't tell you before because you've been fretting enough already, but I want to have our baby here."

Michael looked wildly around the kitchen. *"Here?"*

"Upstairs," she corrected. "In our house, with my husband, and now it seems even with your mam and da here."

Michael gently cupped his wife's face between his hands and kissed her forehead. "You know I love you more than life itself. You're the greatest miracle I've been given, though just now I'm also thinking you've lost your damn brain. We're going to the hospital, and that's the end of the discussion. I'll get your coat, and we'll have Vi follow later with a bag. You've that list on our bureau, right?"

Kylie said nothing, instead giving her husband a patient look.

"She's already called the midwife," Vi said.

Michael stepped away from Kylie and came looming close to Vi. "You knew and you let her?"

"What would you have me do? Tackle her and rip the phone from her hands? A fine sight that would have been. Kylie's young and in perfect health. There've been no difficulties with the pregnancy, from what she says. Why not here, Michael? There's no great risk."

Her brother's frown was quite ferocious. "And when did you become an expert on childbearing? I'm the one who read that stack of—"

"Stop!"

Vi and Michael turned to look at Kylie, who was now leaning against the cupboard, hands low on her belly. Her face had gone milky-white, and her scattering of freckles stood out in sharp relief.

"We're past the time to be discussing. You'd best be getting me upstairs now," she said to her husband. "I'm feeling a bit odd. I didn't think this was to happen so fast."

That, Vi thought, had to be a grand understatement, for Kylie had begun to pant again.

Michael, wise man that he was, didn't wrestle with the inevitable. "All right, upstairs, love, and no arguing, but I'm calling a doctor, too."

"Fine," Kylie said between shallow breaths.

"And you." Michael shot a glare Vi's way. "I'll be talking to you, later."

"One thing, first," she said to her brother, beckoning him closer. When he was near, she went up on tiptoe. "It's a girl," she whispered, "and she's going to run you mad."

In that moment, she was sure that Michael Kilbride was a true believer.

The midwife arrived, and the doctor, too. Trying to hold the most emotional part of herself distant from the events around her, Vi ushered them upstairs to Michael and Kylie's room. Next came Breege Flaherty and Edna McCafferty, for Kylie had asked Michael to call Breege. The women joined Vi, her mam, da, and Liam in the front room.

Da switched on the television and had it playing loudly to block the sounds from upstairs, Vi assumed. Little good it did. Though it was the last thing Vi wanted, she was so attuned to the events one floor up that she fancied she could hear each breath her sister-in-law drew. Pat and Danny ventured in and out of the house, hiding in the kitchen to avoid Mam's horrible childbirth stories, smoking cigarettes out front, and wandering out to the workshop.

Dusk slipped into nighttime, and Michael popped downstairs to say that all was well and they expected it wouldn't be too much longer. Her brother was a disheveled mess. Vi couldn't begin to imagine how Kylie looked. Feeling none too collected, herself, she moved on to the kitchen for a glass of water. Liam came along, and they sat opposite each other at the kitchen table, hands meeting and clasping midway across its surface. They talked of nothing of consequence, but for Vi, Liam's presence made the room an island of calm.

"Vi! Where are you? She's here! The baby's here!" came a cry from the front room some time later.

Vi pushed to her feet. "She's here. Thank God she's here." She rushed to join her family, Liam on her heels.

She wasn't quite sure what she'd been expecting to see—a babe in pink, cooing, perhaps. What she had was Mam hissing at Da to turn off the television, Pat and Danny looking bashful, and a midwife, tired but content.

"Mam and baby are well," the midwife said. "And the new da will be bringing baby down to meet you as soon as the doctor's finished looking her over." Just then a shrill squall drifted down to them. "As you can hear, her lungs are working just fine."

It was another thirty minutes before Michael joined them, a bundle in his arms.

"This is Margaret Mary Kilbride, named for Kylie's late mam." He gazed down at the babe, and Vi wondered if she'd ever before seen such love. "I think we'll be calling her Maggie."

"Named for Kylie's mother, you say?" Mam asked, sounding quite slighted.

"Well, Mam," Pat said, "at least you know what you'll have to do if you want the next one in your name."

Emotions too close to the surface and bubbling higher, Vi laughed, then quickly covered her mouth with her hand as Mam glared at her. Liam looped an arm about her waist, and she was thankful for his steady presence.

"Patrick Anthony," Mam said, "you'd best be watching your mouth or the next one will be named after *you.*"

Michael came to stand on the other side of Vi. Her heart swelled near to breaking as she looked at this new little life.

"You and Kylie did fine work," she said.

"Aye, we did, didn't we?" He smiled at Vi. "Would you like to hold her?"

Her palms grew immediately damp and her stomach knotted. "I—I..."

"Don't be worried," Michael said. "She's like her mother... not nearly as fragile as she looks."

Vi had held friends' babies countless times, but she couldn't seem to lift her arms, nod her head, or even make an excuse.

"Saints above, Violet," Mam said, moving in front of Michael. "One would think you'd never seen a baby. Let me hold the child."

Michael handed his daughter over to his mother, and it seemed to Vi that the room stilled. Mam fussed with Maggie's blanket a bit, then said, "Fine work, indeed. Pity, though, she wasn't twins. Now, Violet, hold out your arms like a good auntie."

"I'm . . . I'm needing some air," Vi said and bolted from the house, not even first looking for her cape.

The night air bit into her skin as up the hill she went, away from the warm light of the house, nearly stumbling in the darkness. When she reached Michael's workshop, she felt for the door and stepped inside, not even bothering to switch on the light. She wrapped her arms tightly around herself, hoping to hold at least some of the damn selfishness inside.

"If this was a test, Nan, I've failed," she said.

Nan gave no answer, though Vi soon heard human footsteps approaching.

"Vi, are you in there?" Liam called.

There was no dignity to be gained in hiding. "I am."

He came inside and turned on the lights. Vi focused on the toes of her shoes, telling herself that she was doing so only to let her eyes adjust and not out of a sense of shame.

Liam drew her into his arms. "Are you all right?" he asked.

"I was just needing a moment to collect myself." She hurt down to her bones with the worry she'd had for Kylie and with the knowledge that she was so much less than the woman she aspired to be.

"Understandable," Liam said. "It's been quite a day, hasn't it?"

"Overwhelming," she replied.

Vi inhaled deeply, both to calm her nerves and to catch the scent of the workshop. Tangy cedar overlaid other less distinct wood scents, making a perfume that she loved.

She and Liam stood silent for a while, and she began to believe that she might yet survive this night.

"I remember the day Meghan was born as if it were yesterday," Liam said, putting out that small flicker of hope she'd just admitted to.

He slid his arms lower on Vi's waist, but didn't let her go. "Hard to believe it was over twelve years ago."

"I'm sure," she said, wishing she could cry *"Any bloody topic but this!"*

"I haven't been the best of fathers."

"Nor the worst, either. Meghan knows she's loved," Vi said, easing from his embrace and eyeing the door. She'd best get home and feed Roger, and then—

"And I know what I've missed, too." He shook his head. "I never thought I'd be saying this, but seeing your brother's child and missing mine so..."

He was going to have her heart to dine on, wasn't he? It took none of Nan's vision to know what was coming next. Vi steeled herself for the blow.

"Have you thought of having children, Vi?"

She forced a smile into place. "What, and upset Roger? He's been an only child for far too long."

"I'm serious." He took her hands, and she wondered how he could miss the way she was trembling.

"Vi? Are you in there?" called Danny from just outside the half-closed workshop door.

Vi slipped her hands free. "Aye, Danny. Me and Liam, both."

Her gaze locked with Liam's and shame was hers again. She'd done a poor job of hiding her relief at the interruption, and hurt a man she loved.

"Breege and Edna need running back to the village," Danny announced, oblivious to the charged emotions around him. "Both don't like to drive after sundown, they say. And they won't have me or Pat take them, as they've seen the way we drive." He made a scoffing sound. "Heathens, Edna called us."

"I'll run them back," Liam said. "Would you like to come now, Vi?"

She forced her voice into cheerful tones, though she knew there was no fooling Liam, nor any need to fool Danny, who was more forthright than sensitive. "I'll stay on a bit, if you don't mind. Pat or Danny can run me home."

"I'll come back," Liam said.

"You really don't need to."

"I'm thinking I really do. And at least come back to the house for your cape. It's freezing out here."

So it was.

Vi escorted Liam and Danny to the house, took Liam's kiss on her cheek before he left, then went to the kitchen, switched off the light and sat at the kitchen table. This time, should someone come in, she'd run for those beehive huts as she should have yesterday. She'd never felt so utterly desolate. Or devastated.

She curved her arms into a semicircle on the cool wood of the table, then rested her head, too. The front room's television was set to some sporting event or another, and she supposed that her parents and the twins were in front of it. The ecstatic portion of the Kilbride family was no doubt bonding upstairs. She closed her eyes and tried to put herself someplace more personally peaceful, but remained anchored to Michael's kitchen. She didn't doze, but still had lost track of time when she was roused by the sound of her mother's voice in the dining room.

"Where do you suppose Violet's got herself off to?" Mam asked.

"She must be with Liam," her da replied.

"She could have at least said goodbye, don't you think?"

"I think the night's been a wild one. A lapse in manners can be forgiven."

Chairs scraped the floor, and china rattled a bit. She imagined her parents were taking seats.

"We're grandparents, now," she heard her da say to her mam, wonderment in his voice. "It's a fine thing, isn't it, Maeve?"

"I've always loved babies," her mother said. "They're so perfect... so unspoilt."

Vi had never thought she'd agree with her mother on anything, but she, too, had been stricken—aye, that was the word—*stricken* with the beauty of that little girl, messy, red and ready to squall as she was.

"It's only when they grow older, eh, love?" her father said. "That's when the road grows rocky."

"That's when I have to admit I failed."

"Failed?"

"Yes, failed," her mother said flatly.

"You and your affair with perfection! Have you looked at our children? All are either doing something they love or are on their way to it. We made our mistakes, and they thrived anyway."

"You're too easy on the lot of us. Others have doctors and accountants for children, and we've turned out former convicts and starving underachievers."

"We have content children," Da said, apparently unwilling to take a full dose of Mam's bitterness. God knew Vi was reeling from what she'd already heard.

"Our children might not be what you want, but they're not starving or criminals... no, not even Michael," Da said. "They are as they wish. Is that so damn bad? And have you listened deeper to those tea ladies with their children grown to be doctors and accountants? Christ knows I've had to, lately. It's not so bloody feck-all perfect with them, either."

"Michael, language!"

Vi half-smiled into the circle of her arms, imagining her mother's appalled expression.

"I'm right though, aren't I?"

"I suppose," her mother conceded. "But don't expect the tea ladies to be admitting it."

Da chuckled, and then the room fell into silence.

"You know," Da said after a bit, "Maggie coming into the world tonight has made me sure of one thing. We've got to seize our happiness now, and seek our forgiveness. We're getting no younger."

"And what is your happiness, Michael? Is it leaving me in Kilkenny?"

"No, it's being needed. It's having a purpose again, not wandering about our house, dreaming maybe I'll get the old job back, and wondering how many more days I can go on if I don't."

"I see. So I'm not a part of this at all."

"Of course you are! But I need you to bend far enough to see that our life's not going to be what it's been for all these years. I won't stay in that house, Maeve, and be useless. And if that means we move, I want it to be us, and not just me."

"But I don't want to have to."

"And I'd like my hair to stop thinning, but that doesn't change matters. We've had our good days, and plenty of them, too. We need to build new ones, and we need them with all our children. I know you feel the children's struggles reflect on you. But they're grown now, and what they do is their choice. They can call you or not, and see you or not. Can you try, Maeve, to let go of some of the anger? We won't be seeing much of them if you don't."

Mam's answer was slow in coming.

"I can try, not that they'll even notice." The words were laden with skepticism, but still more positive than what Vi had prepared herself to hear.

"And can we try to be kinder to each other, too?" Da asked. "Can we find those good days again?"

Silence stretched so long that Vi began to wonder if she'd dreamt what she'd heard thus far.

"I suppose we should," her mam said. "It's only right with a grandbaby to be thinking about."

"God love and protect Maggie, but I'm thinking of us right now. Do you want to try again for *me?*"

Her mother's answer was muffled. Vi lifted her head and listened more acutely.

"What did you say while sipping that tea?" her da asked.

A teacup rattled. "I said I do, Michael Kilbride, as you damn well knew."

Her da laughed. "Language, now, Maeve." There was the scrape of a chair against the wood floor, then a moment's silence. "And I do, too," said Da after what Vi wagered was a kiss, startling as the thought was.

Mam's laughter was a sound rarely heard, but it rang out now. "Look at us, practically marrying again in a dining room. It's mad."

"Aye," Da said. "But we've made our promises, and once we head home the real work begins."

Vi resettled her head against her arms and moved back into her world of one. She should be happier at this moment, for at least her parents were going to try again. Instead she felt nothing except exhaustion and emptiness.

After more china rattling and the sound of shoes against the floor, Vi heard the door between the dining room and the kitchen open. She didn't lift her head, and if the soul who peeked in—be it Mam or Da—saw her, they didn't say a word.

She was becoming more of a ghost than Nan Kilbride.

CHAPTER NINETEEN

Better a good run than a bad stand.
—IRISH PROVERB

Liam could sense Vi spooling out the rope by which he was to hang. Last night, when she'd dropped him at Muir House and then told him that she needed some time to herself, he'd not argued. Neither had he shown the foresight to negotiate detailed terms. "Some time" had already eaten into the waking hours he had left in Ballymuir.

After breakfast and a raft of business calls he'd had to make, Liam rang both Vi's house and her studio, but didn't raise her. Jenna assured him that phone-unplugging was standard Kilbride behavior. Just past noon, he set himself on Vi's trail. The studio was empty, and despite his insistent pounding, her house's door was going unanswered. He knew by the car out front and the dog peering through the window at him that she was there.

Frustrated, he pounded again. "Dammit, Vi, come let me in!"

"I'm thinking she doesn't want to see you," called a voice from across the street. Liam looked over to see an elderly man, eyeglasses perched low on his nose, standing on the opposite stoop.

"She just requires some persuading," Liam answered, then knocked up the door again and shouted even more loudly. All he got in response was Roger's gruff bark.

"Five euros says you can't convince her to let you in," the neighbor called, pulling a billfold from his back pocket.

"You're on," Liam yelled back, then rubbed his cold hands

together for at least a little warmth.

Despite what he'd said to Vi's neighbor, Liam knew that she wasn't the sort to succumb to persuasion once her mind was set. And he damn well couldn't reason his way to her though a locked door. His best hope was to raise her ire.

He knocked again, and inside Roger's barking grew more agitated. Liam smiled, for the dog's irritation was his inspiration. Drawing a deep breath, he tipped back his head and let loose a long, loud, mournful howl. It was convincing enough that on the other side of the window Roger joined in, and across the way, Vi's neighbor gave a hoot of laughter. Liam stretched the sound as far as he could. Wind exhausted, he paused, then started again.

Vi's front door flew open, and he stopped mid-howl.

"Are you mad?" She looked up and down the street at the tightly-set houses. "You've got everyone to their windows. What am I to do with you?"

"You could always let me inside," Liam suggested.

"I'm working."

He took in her clothing—a too-large men's shirt and a faded and tattered pair of paint-smeared denims—and then her face, the side of which was also smudged with green paint.

"So I see, but I'm afraid the isolated, suffering artist bit is going to have to wait. We need to talk, Vi."

"Tomorrow, then. I'm tired." She went to close her door, but he wedged his shoulder into the gap.

"No, you don't. I've got five euros on the line." And one hell of a lot more than that, but he'd made the mistake of trying to bare his heart to her last night, and he'd not do it again. At least not until he was back from the States and had the time to learn what was making her pull away. "Just let me in, Vi."

"Put away your money, Mr. Hanratty," Vi said to her neighbor, who now stood on the walk, five-euro note in hand.

"So you'll not be letting him in?" the man asked, hope in his voice.

"Sorry, but I will."

"Then it's his."

Liam accepted the five-note, for this was a matter of a man's honor. Vi pinched it from his fingers before he could pocket it, though.

"It's going to charity, for neither of you deserve it," she said.

Laughing, Mr. Hanratty crossed to his side of the street, and Liam worked his way into Vi's house before she changed her mind. The smell of paint was thick in the air, and the place wasn't much warmer than the outdoors.

Vi walked toward the kitchen, and Liam followed, wondering why the hell he hadn't spent at least part of the morning deciding how to broach matters. Ah, well, it was improvise now...or die.

"I've—" he began to say, but halted, trying to grasp what was taking place in her kitchen. The floor was littered with balled-up pieces of paper, but that was the least of it.

She'd just recently painted the chairs to her table a green that matched her nan's wild cupboard, which at least explained the paint fumes and the open kitchen window. Among the other items on her table sat a fat jar of strawberry preserves with a knife beside it. Judging by the plate with nibbled crusts nearby, some of the preserves must have made it onto toast. A fair amount more was spread like a lumpy single-hued rainbow across a white sheet of paper, too.

"Do I want to know what that's about?" he asked, pointing at the paper.

"Just considering the color."

He decided not to ask for what.

"I'm guessing you wanted to talk about something more than the mess in my kitchen," she said as she picked up a pencil and a sketchpad from the cluttered table.

"I do." Uncomfortable, he looked around for a place to sit, but that would be impossible unless he wished to be green-arsed. "I've mentioned Alex, my former business partner, haven't I?"

"You have," Vi said, her hand flying across the sketchpad.

"Well, it seems he's gotten the attention of some law enforcement types, and by extension, they're interested in me."

"But you've done nothing wrong...right?" She glanced away from her pad long enough to give him a guarded look.

"Only if fool complacency is criminal." He scrubbed his hand over his face, thinking that he was getting nowhere dancing around this. "The problem is, I have to go back to America. In fact, you might say that my presence has been compelled."

She set down the pad and pencil. "You've got a dangerous fondness for springing this sort of thing, don't you? When are you leaving?"

"Early tomorrow." He'd said the words quickly, rather like one extracted a sliver.

"Tomorrow," she repeated with at least a surface calm. "And how long have you known this was to happen?"

Liam hedged. "I know it doesn't look good, me waiting until now to tell you, but—"

"How long?"

"A while."

She signaled her dislike of his answer with a frown. "Care to be more specific?"

Actually, he didn't, but he saw no way out.

"That it would happen eventually, I've known for weeks, now. But I didn't have the details until a few days ago. And I want you to come along," he said, the last bit of inspiration just coming to him.

"Well then," she said, "at least I should be honored you've asked me...*this* time."

He'd known that she would allude to their last parting, and he'd also known that it would be a stab to both his heart and pride.

"See?" he said. "This is why I waited to tell you. I damn well knew you'd find some way to bring a summer fifteen years gone into this."

She might be carrying those memories like chains dragging behind her, but he was, too. He stalked closer, angry enough that he wanted his face in hers.

"You knew I was with no other girl that last night," he said. "You knew deep inside that it was Brian you'd seen leaving with the tourist, and yet you used it as one more reason to claim you'd been betrayed. If anyone did the betraying, it was you, Vi."

"I betrayed no one," she said flatly.

"You betrayed *us*. All I wanted was to get out of Duncarraig and make something of myself. It was no sin against you. Yet you turned your back on me so hard that even Nan couldn't get you to sway. I told you I'd be back for you when I was through with school, and still you acted like a damn child."

She took a step backward and gripped the edge of the table. "Of course I did. I was seventeen!"

"You were. But now you're in your thirties and too old to be feeling wronged over events that were as much your fault as mine. I forgave you. I'd think since you were hurt far less—"

"Hurt *less?*" Her hand wrapped around the jam jar on the table, and before he even knew what she was about, she hurled it at his head. He sidestepped the missile. It bounced off the front of the painted cupboard, making a hard sound, then shattered on the tile floor.

Adrenaline surged, yet shock kept him in his spot, trying to understand what had just happened.

"Jesus, Violet. And here you've been calling yourself a pacifist all these years. What the hell's the matter with you?"

Vi was whiter than he'd ever seen her, which was saying much. Her chest heaved, and she looked as though she might either cry or launch herself at his throat. Liam felt as though he faced a stranger. Perhaps he did.

She spun away from him. "Get out."

"Do you at least want to tell me why I deserved that?"

"I said, get *out!*"

Liam stood there a moment more, deciding what to do. Vi had wrapped her arms about her midsection, as though hugging herself. Despite his anger, he wanted to hold her. She clearly felt nothing the same about him.

"I'm leaving, if that's what you want," he said.

Fool optimist to the end, he waited for her reply, but none came. She didn't even turn back to look at him.

"I'll be at Muir House tonight," he said. "And I'll be sure to leave my Boston numbers with Jenna. I'm hoping to be gone less than a month. When I return...and don't be thinking I won't...we'll get to the bottom of whatever has you aiming for my head."

He stepped around the jammy mess on the floor. The sight started his anger simmering all over again.

"And Vi, I love you, but you throw like a girl."

As Liam walked to the front door, Roger trotted behind him.

"Keep an eye on her, my friend," Liam said, then left.

All things considered, it was a marginally better parting than the one fifteen years ago. Last time, she'd ripped out his heart. This time, at least he'd managed to keep his head.

Cleaning could be cathartic. At least that was what Vi attempted to persuade herself as she readied to attack her kitchen. Cleaning was also the nearest to wielding a brush as she'd come in the week since Liam had left. And even a scrub brush was a step closer to sanity.

She'd been mad, throwing that jar at him. She wouldn't eat meat, for it meant the harm of another creature, yet she'd aimed for his head with every intention of knocking him senseless. It had been as though her self-control had been obliterated when he'd claimed she'd been the less hurt of the two of them.

Lucky man he was, indeed, that she threw like a girl. And luckier woman she was that the sound of the jam jar shattering had startled her out of her rage. She'd managed to at least guard her tongue and not rashly blurt out what he needed to be told carefully and quietly.

He'd called in the past week, of course. While she'd quickly apologized for throwing the preserves at him, she'd avoided any discussion of why she'd done so, for that was best done face-to-face. Instead she'd told him that she'd already received an offer from a couple to purchase Nan's property, and how word had it that Duncarriag's treasure hunters were beginning to find more productive pastimes. He'd said little of his interviews with the authorities, but had mentioned that he'd agreed to sell what was left of his business. They were tiptoeing across the surface of matters, but it was a start.

Vi looked about the kitchen and decided that top down seemed a reasonable approach to cleaning. She wet a rag, wrung it out until it was just damp, and then carried it to Nan's cupboard.

"You're one grand dust-gatherer," she said to the piece.

She wasn't sure the statement Nan had been trying to make by attaching such an array of found items. No matter what their shapes, all were decorated with varying patterns of concentric rings and shields of knot-work. The end result of all the attachments was a surface so rife with nooks and crannies that even Kylie in nesting mode couldn't have cleaned it well.

Smiling at a passing thought of baby Maggie, who already ran her parents' house and had stolen the entire family's hearts, Vi reached up on tiptoe to wipe the cupboard's top rim. When she brought the rag back down to refold it to a clean surface, she winced. It carried small dollops of the strawberry preserves she'd flung. To be sure, Vi touched her fingertip to one bit, and it was sticky.

"Soap's in order," she said, as was a boost so that she could see what she was doing. Vi rinsed and readied the rag, then dragged her sturdiest chair to the cupboard. One thorough pass over the top of the cupboard's face wasn't enough. It seemed the jam had bonded with the paint's surface.

Vi scrubbed more vigorously. This had been Nan's, and Vi wanted it perfectly tended. Determined to have this right, she concentrated on the outer perimeter of one of five round pieces on the rail.

"Not there yet," she said to herself, then started as a small wave of numbness rippled through her hand, up her wrist, and nearly to her elbow. The sensation was the same as when her iron had once shorted out while she was ironing. She'd tossed the evil appliance and quit wearing clothing that had required its services. She could hardly do the same with Nan's piece.

Vi checked the rag to see if perhaps it was a sliver that had nipped her.

"Bloody hell."

There was no sliver, but she'd cleaned the finish right off Nan's work. Flecks of the cupboard's green base paint speckled the rag. She stepped off the chair and stood at the kitchen sink, water running as she rinsed the cloth and fought down a wave of remorse. Had she not thrown the jam in the first place and had she not been so concerned about having the cupboard perfect, it would be intact. Instead, she'd ruined it.

Danny came wandering into the kitchen, just home from work.

"What's the matter?" he asked. "You look as though someone's kidnapped Roger, but he's snoring on the sofa."

"Can you see anything wrong with the cupboard?"

Danny glanced over at it. "Other than it's green, which I hate, and one of the ugliest things Nan ever painted, no."

Vi hauled him closer and pointed. "Up top. Can't you see where the paint's flaked down to the wood?"

"No."

"It is, and I just did it while cleaning."

"So then you have a distressed finish. Michael's got customers who pay extra for those." Danny shook his head. "You scare me sometimes, Vi. If it weren't for the fact that you're still a bloody slob about the house, I'd be afraid you're turning into Mam, the way everything has to be just so."

"I'm nothing like Mam. I'm so not like Mam that I'm the anti-Mam."

He laughed. "You're more like her than you think. You're both crazed perfectionists."

"I'm not!"

Danny snorted. "Aye, and I'm not wanting a beer." He went to the fridge, pulled one out, and then said, "The cupboard looks fine. Find something else to obsess over."

He left the room before she could tell him to get stuffed. With nothing else to do, she glared toward the sound of his feet as he pounded upstairs. Bloody elephant.

"Obsess. Right," Vi muttered, trying to brush off the comment. It wouldn't leave, though, for he'd hit too close to her secret fear—that she'd be anything like her rigid, "all must be perfect or it might as well be trash" mam.

Vi pulled a chair away from the table and sat. She thought back to Liam pushing her to sell her work when she was sure it wasn't ready. And then she considered her behavior the night of Maggie's birth, which naturally then led to thoughts of her own physical flaws—damned imperfections—that made her unable to have a babe of her own. And when she reexamined her actions in each instance, what she saw was a woman so immobile that she might as well be encased in amber.

Could her raw, large-footed, and often emotionally oblivious brother be seeing things she'd missed? Was she so obsessed with having things right that she'd stopped moving forward altogether? A voice—not from Nan or the spirits, but from deep inside Vi—was whispering *yes*. She was harder on herself than Mam had ever been.

Vi's palms grew clammy and her stomach unsettled. She would think no more about the way her inadequacies circled in on themselves like the knot-work her nan had painted on the cupboard. It was too personal. Too painful.

Vi stood, then stepped back onto the chair she'd been using as a stepstool and ran her hand across the area she'd been scrubbing. Again that feeling zipped though her hand. She tried to pull away, but it was as though she couldn't. She slid her hand to the cupped and painted metal disc to her far left, the largest of the objects Nan had added. Immediately, her heart began to slam.

She was hearing that low, primal buzz of voices she'd last heard in Dublin.

At the museum.

While near ancient gold.

She pressed harder, and her hand was shaking now. The sound grew. She couldn't be imagining this.

Vi began to pick at disc's surface, seeking loose paint flakes. She didn't want to harm it, but she needed to know. Finally, she caught a poorly adhered spot, and the metal she exposed was gold.

She leapt from the chair with about the same grace that Danny and Pat showed in climbing stairs. Vi riffled through the cupboard's drawers. God, what she wished for was a well-stocked kitchen where she'd have countless tools from which to choose. At least she had a butter knife.

It was slow work, gently winnowing the knife's blade beneath the edge of the disc, but she was a determined woman. In time, the disc popped free. From behind it fell a small, folded wedge of paper. Rather than risk bumping the piece in her hand, Vi let the paper drop to the floor.

Holding her potential treasure in her right hand, she stepped more carefully from the chair this time, then sat before examining what she'd found. The nervous tremble in her hands became an excited shake.

"God in heaven."

The backside of the disc hadn't been painted and it was decidedly gold!

"Slow now," she counseled herself. Gold in color didn't necessarily mean gold in fact. Recalling the bit of paper that had dropped, she set the disc on the cupboard's broad base shelf, then bent down and retrieved it.

It had been neatly folded, reminding Vi of origami. Once she'd gotten it unfurled, she began to read Nan's familiar handwriting, which covered both front and back:

So you found this note, did you? You always were a smart girl, Violet. Nearly always, at least, though I suppose that from the grave isn't the finest location for me to be bringing up Liam Rafferty.

I trust you to do right by Rafferty's Gold, for neither you nor I, nor the women who held it before us—save one—could know the truth of why we hold it. And that one chose not to share what she knew.

I've left the gold's fate in two sets of hands. What pieces aren't on the cupboard, you'll find buried beneath my painted rock. I'm sure you knew that already, as the patterns on the boulder match these, and you're reading this.

Nan had given her too much credit, as that rock was hours away and, together with the land beneath it, about to be sold.

"Danny!" Vi shouted without looking up from the paper. She heard the rumble of his feet as he pounded downstairs.

He appeared in the kitchen almost instantaneously. "Are you hurt?" he asked.

"I'm fine," she said. "Though I'll need you to watch Roger for a day or two. I've a small trip I have to make."

For Vi was going back to Duncarraig....

CHAPTER TWENTY

Better a man of character than a man of means.
—IRISH PROVERB

Three weeks later...

Vi was rich. Perhaps not pop star rich or film celebrity rich, but safely bundled in a box at the very back of Nan's cupboard was enough wealth that if Vi were frugal, she could see Danny though university, Pat with seed money should he care to start a business of his own, and herself in oil paints and canvases and silks and Japanese rice paper. Or she could be silent rich like Nan and hide the treasure away, then live as she'd been. Aye, she was rich, and if she chose the last course, Liam never need know.

Between what the cupboard had yielded and what she had found in a metal strongbox beneath the rock in Duncarraig, she possessed a tidy stash, indeed. Once she'd gathered the pieces, she had discovered that she wasn't quite ready to take them to Nuala Manion at the National Museum, as she'd told Liam she would. It was far more difficult to be noble when holding gold than when dreaming of the promise of gold.

Instead, she had taken the smallest of the paint-covered pieces to Simon, her silversmith neighbor at the arts village, whom she'd known for years and trusted very much. His wife was a former museum conservator from Berlin. After much hand-wringing and warning that all manner of things could go wrong, Elke had agreed to try to remove the paint. It had taken a week of painstaking work with the mildest solutions possible for Elke to work her way down to the base, but true gold it was.

And thus the deliberations of what to do with the treasure had begun. Vi had not shared her find with anyone, nor told Simon and Elke that she had more than the one piece. She had asked them for their confidentiality, and given their kind natures, she estimated she had at least a few more weeks until they succumbed to the Ballymuir bent for gossip. And if they whispered, Vi would forgive them, as she had already forgiven herself her hopefully brief onset of greed.

In fact, forgiveness had become Vi's newest form of exercise. Just under three weeks ago, on the drive back from Duncarraig with her gold dug under the light of the moon, she'd had time to think about the expectations she'd set for herself. It wasn't wrong to strive for perfection, but it was poisonous not to forgive herself when she fell short. When weeks before she'd lectured Mam about forgiveness, it would have done her well to turn an ear to her own words. And with that in mind, she had since forgiven herself for having a body that would bear no children, and for having hands and a mind that would never work together quite well enough to create the shimmering perfection she could see.

Absolution granted, her first act had been to repair Nan's cupboard. Not everything on the cupboard had been gold, so the non-gold pieces Vi had carefully reattached, then supplemented with her own work, creating an imperfect collaboration that she adored.

Tonight, though, Vi would be working on her most treasured imperfect collaboration, for Liam was returning to Ballymuir. He'd called four hours ago from London's Gatwick Airport, where he awaited his connecting flight to Shannon Airport, still two hours off. The waiting seemed interminable, but he would be in her house—and her arms—soon enough.

Vi fully intended to take advantage of the event, too. She'd already told Danny and Pat to bunk elsewhere for the night—a mate's floor, above O'Connor's Pub, she didn't care where. Roger had been well fed, coddled, and firmly lectured on the meaning of closed bedroom doors. And Vi had showered, scented, and primped more in this afternoon than she ever had for a man. A check in the bathroom mirror confirmed that her hair, while still damp, had not yet coiled to its usual Medusa-inspired state.

"Grand of you to cooperate," she said, running her fingers through her hair one last time.

She was about to go to the bedroom and sort through her incredibly small collection of enticing garments when Roger began his madman's—or mad dog's—bark that signaled someone knocking up the door.

"Just a sec," Vi called, looking down at the lovely combination of painting shirt and bare skin that she currently wore.

Roger ratcheted his enthusiasm up a notch.

"Roger, stop!" Vi shouted as she flew from the bathroom to her bedroom seeking something to wear. "I'll be there!"

When Rog fell silent, she knew her hound well enough to sense it wasn't because he'd finally grasped the English language.

"Is someone out there?" she called as she tore through her wardrobe, seeking one item of clothing that might cover her better. It was a pity she'd let laundry fall by the wayside these past days.

"Pat, is that you?" she called at the sound of footsteps and Roger's happy-song. "Danny?"

She wrenched on a pair of pale green and coffee-stained yoga pants, then rushed into the front room.

"I found an open seat on an earlier flight," Liam said to Vi while taking off his jacket and hanging it near the front door on the hook that held Roger's lead.

"Easy, boy," he said to Roger, who clearly believed that there was a walk in the offing. Liam bent down and picked up a small decorated paper bag that sat next to his suitcase.

"I meant to have wine ready and a fire burning," Vi said while undoing a button or two on her oversized shirt in an effort to look more casual-sexy than casual-sloppy. "And I was going to be wearing something enticing."

"The hell with the wine," Liam replied as he came closer. "And the fire, too. I'm here, you're here, and the rest isn't needed. God, how I've missed you."

He kissed her deeply, and then while her mind was still in a hungry whirl, handed her the small gift bag.

"It's nothing grand," he said.

Curious, Vi pulled aside the red tissue that tufted out of the top of it, then reached in and removed a slope-shouldered soft plastic bottle filled with something reddish.

"What is it?" she asked as she flipped it label-side toward her.

"Squeeze strawberry preserves," he said, sounding a bit sheepish. "Well, actually it's squeeze strawberry spread as the bits of fruit in preserves would muck up the works. It's popular with children in the States, and I was in the market and saw it...and..."

She smiled, both at his gift and at the odd, uncomfortable expression on his face. "Fine joke, Rafferty."

"It's a joke, but it's more than that, too. What I mean it to say is this.... I won't be shaken this time, Vi. You can throw all you want at me, though I'd prefer you stick to plastic, if you do," he said with a nod to the bottle he'd gifted her with.

"About that," Vi said, knowing the time had come to see if they'd truly earned a life together. "I've some things I need to tell you. Will you come and sit with me?" she asked, motioning to the sofa.

Feeling as though his life were starting anew, Liam joined Vi on the sofa. He smiled as she fussed with her bottle of squeeze spread. Its purchase had been a mad impulse, but also evidence that she never left his thoughts. Not when he'd been untangling the mess that had consumed his company, not in his bed, which had been by far too empty without her, and not even while visiting Atlanta when he had walked the supermarket aisles with Meghan.

"These things you're needing to say?" he prompted Vi while gently removing the bottle from her grip and setting it on the floor for Roger to inspect.

He watched as she drew a deep breath and then settled one hand over the other in her lap.

"We'll start with the most important," she said. "I love you, Liam, and as you said to me, did always and will always."

Liam fixed his gaze on the fireplace, with its fire set, but not yet lit. Irishmen didn't cry, at least not without a great amount of whiskey and a stirringly morose song playing from the corner of the bar. In this, he was failing his fellow men, for the sharp feeling in his throat could presage nothing but tears.

"Thank God," he managed to reply without his voice doing anything as embarrassing as breaking.

"There's more, and it's not nearly as easy for me to say."

He took her hands and wove his fingers between hers. "Vi, I've always loved you and I can think of nothing you could tell me that would change that."

She closed her eyes, and the wave of pain that crossed her face seemed to ripple from her to him through their joined hands.

"I'm praying so," she said, "for here we go..." Her gaze met his and her green eyes seemed shadowed, nearly bruised. "That night at Castle Duneen, when we made love unprotected, it hurt me terribly that you'd not remembered doing the same fifteen years before. It wasn't till later that I accepted that the memory couldn't possibly hold the same weight for you as it does for me."

"How, Vi?" he asked, a sick feeling already brewing in the pit of his stomach.

"After we'd argued and parted, and you'd gone on to America, I fell ill." She looked down at their linked hands, and he held tighter to her, fearing that she was about to pull away. "It was an ectopic pregnancy. A fertilized egg had implanted in one of my fallopian tubes. I had surgery, and—"

"You didn't call me. I could have been there. Damn it, I *would* have been there." He'd been given shocks before—like that of Beth being pregnant with Meghan—but he couldn't recall this feeling of having the earth ripped from beneath him.

She nodded rapidly, almost frantically, and still clung to his hands. "Yes, I should have. I know that now, but I was seventeen and frightened I was going to die. I wasn't thinking clearly, if at all. Mam was contacted by the hospital, and after that it's all rather a blur, even now. I was young and rash and, well, a bit prone to drama. I blamed you for the longest time, and myself for even longer."

Words were inadequate, embarrassingly so, but they were all he had to offer. "God, I'm so, *so* sorry."

"And I thank you for that, but what you need to know...and to fully believe...is that it wasn't your fault or mine," she said. "It was just a random, very sad thing. As were the troubles I had with internal scarring after..."

Liam freed one hand to wipe away a tear tracking down her face, and she turned a bit to kiss his palm, then took his hand again.

"You'd asked me the night Margaret Mary was born if I had thought of having children," she said. "I tried to joke away the question, but the real answer is that I think of it often, and barring a miracle, it's likely never to happen. So if you want to step away now from what we've started, I'll understand. Truly, I will."

Now she'd push him away? After they'd gotten past the worst of it? Aye, he loved her, and she needed someone like him around to remind her she was still, as she'd said, "prone to drama."

"Jesus, Violet, are you trying to skip canonization and whatnot and move straight to sainthood? You'd *understand* if I walked away? Ha! That's the maddest thing I've ever heard you say, and God knows you've said some wild ones. I love *you,* and not so you can be some sort of breeder, though the act leading to it has its charms." Liam shook off that last thought, realizing he was straying. "If I came to you and told you I was sterile, what would you do?"

She hesitated. "Tell you that if we wanted children, there were other options?"

Her answer had sounded too much like a question for his taste. "You're bloody damn right you would. And to expect less from me? What must you think of me, Violet?" He was on a roll and had no intention of hearing her answer. "I do want other children, but if we can't have them ourselves, there's a world filled with others very much in need of a home. And you, Vi, would be an amazing mother, if you so chose. And don't you dare think—"

He had to stop and clear his throat, for now his voice was breaking as he considered a terrified seventeen-year-old in a hospital bed, so terribly alone. "Don't you dare think of taking a burden such as you did by yourself, ever again. We've the two of us now, and there's no turning back, you hear me?"

She nodded, smiling through the tears on her face.

"I'm no grand prize," he said. "I've no job, paltry assets, and an expensive and likely futile taste to look for the treasures off this coast that I read about in Dev Gilvane's books. But balancing all of that, I can promise you no man will ever, in all of time, treasure you more than I do, or know you better. We've traveled the long road here, but I want you to marry me, Violet, and I won't be taking no for an answer."

"You won't be getting no, either," his first and final love, his fire and treasure said. "Of course I'll marry you."

And then she was in his arms, and Liam Rafferty knew life could get no better.

Very, very late that night...

Her lover slept the sleep of the replete...and the exhausted. Vi tiptoed into the kitchen, shoveled some more kibble into Rog's dish, then knelt in front of Nan's cupboard.

"Where are you, love, in the kitchen?" Liam called from the bedroom.

Vi rolled her eyes. So much for the sleep of the replete.

"Yes, in the kitchen," she called back.

"Could you bring me some water...and maybe a bit to eat?"

She smiled at his wheedling tone. "I'll shake something loose," she called back.

And that she would. Vi stretched her arm past the cupboard's contents until she reached the box in the far left corner. Once she had it out, she set it on the kitchen table, opened it, and looked at the pieces within.

"The gorget, I'm thinking," she said to herself, for surely Rog, happily bolting his food, did not care.

Wrongly taken from a Rafferty or honestly given by one, it no longer mattered. Together, she and Liam would decide the gold's fate, and she knew that her trust could rest with him.

Vi picked up the hammered gold gorget and slipped the collar around her neck. The metal was cool against her bare skin, and a shiver rippled all the way down to her equally bare toes. Though not as fine as the wax cast she'd seen in Dublin, this piece, which had been beneath Nan's painted rock, was no small treasure. For added effect, Vi slipped on two thin armbands she'd also unearthed. All the pieces from the strongbox were in remarkable shape, the rich patina of their gold making them look like old silk.

"And some wine?" Liam called. "Have you some wine?"

"Wine, then," Vi absently replied, pulling a piece of notepaper from the box…something Nan had left, explaining how, at her own elderly mother's urging, she'd moved the gold from Castle Duneen.

Vi tucked the note into an empty wine glass, then gathered that, the wine, and a glass for herself before returning to Liam.

The bedroom light was dim, too much so for Vi's current needs.

"Could you switch on the lamp?" she asked Liam as she set the wine and glasses on the nightstand at her side of the bed.

"I can find you well enough in the dark, my fire," he replied.

Aye, she'd definitely stopped short of replete. "Humor me."

"Stubborn woman," Liam said, laughter in his voice.

The light came on. Vi held herself as tall, still, and proud as any woman wearing only three pieces of gold ever had. Her gaze locked with Liam's, who seemed to have frozen.

He cleared his throat. "I, ah…I don't suppose those are costume pieces."

She smiled as she moved across the bed to kneel above him, her knees to either side of his. "I don't suppose they are."

He reached one hand up to touch the gorget about her neck. "It's a good look on you, love."

"That's all you have to say? I bring you a treasure and—"

He smiled. "You'd brought me a treasure when you came back into my life. Now this is very grand," he said, "but not nearly as fine as the woman wearing it. Still, I'm thinking you'd best take it off."

"You're afraid I'll damage the pieces, then?"

"No, I'm afraid I will, as it's time to make love to you again."

"So you don't want to know how I found the gold on Nan's cupboard and under the painted rock on her property?"

He paused for a moment, and a broad grin lit his face. "Which would go far in explaining the watercolor of the rock that she left me."

"She left you a watercolor? How could I not know? But that makes the note I found a bit clearer. She said that she'd left the gold's fate in two sets of hands and I have only one."

"Later, love. All of that later," he said, putting his own hands to very good use. "Now slip free of that gold, if you please. The people at the National Museum won't take well to our playing in it."

"So you agree to sell it to the State?" she asked slipping the armbands off, then dipping down to kiss him.

"All but the necklace, which we'll hide again," he said. "We can't have a legend die, now can we?"

Vi slipped off the gorget and handed it to Liam, who turned it over once in his hands, then set it gently on the nightstand.

"Now come down where I can kiss you, Violet, my love."

Lord, but he was all smooth sex and persuasion.

"With pleasure," she replied.

And as he kissed her, Vi Kilbride not only fancied herself a fine collector of men, she was thrilled to have kept her very first and best one of all.

Thanks you so much for reading my book!
If you enjoyed your visit to Ballymuir,
please consider leaving a review!

About the Author:

Dorien Kelly is a *New York Times* and *USA Today* bestselling author of over fifteen novels. She lives a very exotic life (not!) in Michigan. Dorien loves hearing from readers.

Visit her website at **www.dorienkelly.com**. You can find her on Facebook at **www/facebook.com/authordorienkelly**.

53873115R00178

Made in the USA
San Bernardino, CA
30 September 2017